nnie O'Neil spent most of her childhood with her
g draped over the family rocking chair and a book
her hand. Novels, baking, and writing too much
nage angst poetry ate up most of her youth. Now
nie splits her time between corralling her husband
o helping her with their cows, baking, reading,
rel racing (not really!), and spending some very
py hours at her computer, writing.

n and raised on the Wirral Peninsula in England,
rlotte Hawkes is mum to two intrepid boys who
her to play building block games with them and
object loudly to the amount of time she spends
er computer. When she isn't writing—or building
blocks—she is company director for a small
lo/French construction firm. Charlotte loves to
h from readers, and you can contact her at her
w site: charlotte-hawkes.com.

Also by Annie O'Neil

A Family Made in Rome

The Island Clinic collection

How to Win the Surgeon's Heart by Tina Beckett
Caribbean Paradise, Miracle Family by Julie Danvers
The Princess and the Paediatrician
Reunited with His Long-Lost Nurse by Charlotte Hawkes

Available now

Also by Charlotte Hawkes

The Doctor's One Night to Remember

The Island Clinic collection

How to Win the Surgeon's Heart by Tina Beckett
Caribbean Paradise, Miracle Family by Julie Danvers
The Princess and the Paediatrician by Annie O'Neil
Reunited with His Long-Lost Nurse

Available now

THE PRINCESS AND THE PAEDIATRICIAN

ANNIE O'NEIL

REUNITED WITH HIS LONG-LOST NURSE

CHARLOTTE HAWKES

MILLS & BOON

Published in Great Britain 2021
by Mills & Boon, an imprint of HarperCollins*Publishers* Ltd,
1 London Bridge Street, London, SE1 9GF

www.harpercollins.co.uk

HarperCollins*Publishers*
1st Floor, Watermarque Building,
Ringsend Road, Dublin 4, Ireland

Special thanks and acknowledgement are given to
Annie O'Neil for her contribution to The Island Clinic miniseries.

Special thanks and acknowledgement are given to Charlotte Hawkes
for her contribution to The Island Clinic miniseries.

THE PRINCESS AND THE PAEDIATRICIAN

ANNIE O'NEIL

MILLS & BOON

For tropical islands that pare us down to our essence
and let love bloom. I know it sounds crazy,
but I was proposed to on a tropical island,
so I LOVE them and hope you do, too.

CHAPTER ONE

THOUGH LIA WOULD never admit it, there were some perks to being a princess.

'Champagne?' asked a passing waiter.

Flutes of fancy fizz when you were really, really nervous was one of them. If only it could make her feel as bubbly as it looked.

She scanned the room to see if she could catch a glimpse of her boss, Dr Nate Edwards, for a confidence-boost. She hadn't seen much of him around the clinic lately, so she'd thought perhaps they'd catch up tonight at the gala. She'd even shown up early, to check out all the donations from local businesses who seemed to have outdone themselves with their generosity of amazing-looking food, floral displays and just about everything in between for the silent auction.

She scanned the room again. Nope. No Nate. She was beginning to regret the effort she'd gone to with her 'princess' gear. Swishy dress. Actual make-up. Tiara.

Only her huge-hearted boss and a good cause like the St Victoria Foundation could get her to pull out her blow dryer and mascara wand, let alone the tiara. Otherwise she'd be parked in the corner of her extra-comfy cottage, wearing her softest cotton jim-jams and watching a box set.

But tonight the box set would have to wait. The Foundation was holding its annual charity gala, and guests hobnobbing with a princess helped boost the coffers. It didn't mean it made her any less socially awkward, though. Casual chit-chat was definitely not her forte.

She was about to accept a glass of fizz when she pictured the white-blonde, pinch-faced woman with a clipboard who attended official events with her back in Karolinska. She could practically see the woman wrinkling her nose, then hissing, 'Say *No, thank you*. And you've got lipstick on your teeth.'

The flipside of the perks.

The Princess Faux Pas Posse—or the PFPP as she called them—was a little tribe of helpers the palace back in Karolinska sent to babysit her on the rare occasions when she participated in an official event. They pointed out things like…oh, ketchup on her face, a bit of spinach in her teeth, or—the one the press hadn't let go of for ages—her hair blowing across her face so it looked as if she had a Victorian moustache.

This wasn't even her official event—it was Nate's. He was the founder of The Island Clinic here on St Victoria, her Caribbean home away from prison.

Home! She meant home away from *home*. *Obviously*. A palace was hardly a prison.

She sniggered. Try telling that to the Tower of London.

She gave her head a shake. She wasn't British, nor waiting to get her head chopped off by Henry VIII. And she'd left modern-day Karolinska, where royal traditions felt like medieval shackles, three years ago now. The warm nights and sea-salted air were regular reminders that she had changed her life to be precisely that. *Hers*. St Victoria spoke to her every bit as much as her homeland did.

Luckily, Karolinska had diplomatic ties with the government here and, unlike her homeland, St Victoria boasted a glorious tropical sprawl of warm beaches, an extraordinary medical clinic, and—more to the point—no PFPP.

Here, she felt able to breathe. She could work without worrying about being *'The Spinster Surgeon Princess'*, as she would no doubt be described in the headlines of the papers back home. She'd been every manner of princess—*single/alone/lonely/little*—since her parents had split. Now that she was in her early thirties she could add 'spinster' to the list.

Being labelled by the media was something she probably should've got over a million years ago, but…

It wasn't all bad, of course. Loath as she was to admit it, sometimes it was fun dressing up. And this was the one night of the year she went full-on glam. And who didn't like the swish of fabric against their legs when it had been… oh, about three years since they'd felt the touch of a man's hand?

She gave her head a short, sharp shake. Where had *that* come from? She was quite happy with her job and with being one hundred per cent in control of her life, thank you very much.

Well. Most of it. The palace was pretty good at tightening the noose when it wanted to.

She thanked the waiter but refused the drink. She was a representative of The Island Clinic tonight, and as such needed to keep her wits about her. She'd have a glass once the press had left and there was no danger of an 'incident' being reported back to the palace.

And by 'incident' she meant embarrassment. Members of the Karolinskan Royal Family did not embarrass The Crown. 'Twas ever thus.

Which, of course, brought out her mischievous side.

She pulled her mobile out of the delicately woven palm frond clutch one of her patients had given her and, after a surreptitious glance around, took a goofy selfie in front of an enormous floral display, which was designed to look like a tropical flower guide to the Caribbean Islands.

She tapped in her cousin's number. He had donated the special *grand cru* for this event. He was probably out on a peace-keeping mission with the rest of his squad. It was how Jonas spent most of his time these days—in well-worn army fatigues, keeping the peace in volatile hot spots in the world. Places she should be as well, providing medical care, but wasn't thanks to the King and Queen…aka Grandmama and Grandpapa.

Yes, thanks to them, and to her father's inability to stand up to them on her behalf, instead of following up the years of military medical training she'd poured her heart and soul into with an appropriate career, she 'kept the peace' in a different way. Patient by patient, case by case, at The Island Clinic.

She'd been drawn to the clinic after reading about its extensive charitable work. And events like tonight's ball would help ensure the clinic could carry on with the promise that no patient in need of their elite treatment would be turned away. She genuinely loved it. She was a neurosurgeon, and there were some incredibly interesting cases which she never would've seen if she hadn't wrangled her way round the palace's rules and found this job.

Another one of the catering staff swept by, miraculously managing to balance a tray filled with sparkling glasses of fizz even as her hips moved to the rhythm of the guitarist who was warming up on the small stage.

The woman did a quick double-take when she recognised Lia, and instantly swirled the tray round in front of her. 'Champagne?'

Lia flushed, as she usually did when she was recognised, and said, 'No, thank you.' Then, in a burst of spontaneity, she tapped the side of her nose and with a grin said, 'Not yet, anyway.'

The woman sashayed away with a knowing laugh.

Lia looked around the room and, as she was on her own, let herself have a sway to the music, too, crossing her arms so that one hand rested on each hip.

It really had been a long time since she'd been held by a man.

She pulled a face. Being horny was not usually her thing. Nor was it helping her align her focus to where it should be. On the guests about to arrive.

They were going to have such fun tonight. Beautiful music, amazing food—all supplied by talented and warm-hearted local businesses—and, thanks to the ballroom staff here at the Harbour Hotel, in an absolutely beautiful location. If ever there was a night to donate a million dollars to an excellent charity, or to…say…share a first kiss…this was it.

The event team had extended the sumptuous floral aesthetic of the loggia surrounding the sprawling hacienda-style building into the ballroom. All of the carved wooden sliding doors had been tucked away into invisible corners, so that the glittering harbour could be seen twinkling away. The arches soaring up to the double-height ceilings were hidden behind massive palms bearing swirls of fairy lights. The tables were dappled with beautifully perfumed flowers perched in cleverly crafted banana leaf 'vases'.

The overall effect was tropical chic at its finest. A true celebration of all that was beautiful on the island of St Victoria, and a reflection of the spirit of the community who lived on it. Generous, kind, gorgeous people Lia hoped she would never have to say goodbye to if—heaven forbid—duty ever called.

Speaking of which…

She tapped out a quick message to her cousin.

Hey, Jonas, what do you think of my island look? I'm sure our grandparents would love it! LOL. We're in the throes of the rainy season, but tonight it's dry and deliciously cool. For the Caribbean, anyway. Still not worn a jumper. Has the snow started back home? Ha-ha. Kidding/not kidding. Enjoy your summer if you're home. Catch-up video-call soon? Lia x

Her thumb hovered over the 'send' button as she took a moment to examine the photo she'd just snapped. Her long, very Scandinavian-looking blonde hair was in a thick, loose plait, woven together at the back of her head with a smattering of the beautiful tropical flowers that bloomed here year-round. The delicate purple of the blossoms was a nice accent to the eggshell-blue maxi dress she'd decided to wear tonight. It managed to both look elegant and be comfortable—one of her prerequisites now that she was choosing her own outfits.

After years of being handed photos by the disappointed palace press secretary, who loved to point out how awkward and uncomfortable Lia looked, she'd finally asked for 'classy, but with room to breathe' to be the guideline for all the clothes designers sent to her.

It hadn't made much of a difference.

Moving countries had.

Since she'd moved here to St Vic, well out of 'lens shot' of the paparazzi, the designer clothes had dried up and—surprise, surprise—she'd begun to look less awkward and uncomfortable in the rare photos she appeared in. Clothing, she realised, had had nothing to do with her discomfort.

Smiling and looking pretty as a princess simply wasn't her thing.

Doing something that made a genuine difference was.

She felt her smile falter as she thought back to the days when, as only sixth in line to the throne, she'd never taken centre stage on the palace balcony family portraits, but had always been required to *be* there, waving, smiling, looking out over the fairy tale main square of the capital city of Karolinska and, more importantly, at the people who revered the royal family and all they stood for.

Stoicism. Duty. Scandinavian pride.

In fairness, her country *was* beautiful. Nestled between Sweden and Denmark, it was almost entirely comprised of little islands dotted about the Baltic Sea—except for the capital city which stood proudly on the mainland coast. A beacon of Scandinavian beauty and civic pride.

As a nation, they were highly regarded for their strong moral compass on matters of global import and for their generosity when it came to the social well-being of their citizens. As her grandfather the King often said, 'We set the standard the rest of the world must follow.'

She had a few rebuttal points for that, but… Loyalty, loyalty, loyalty! That was how it worked in her family.

She shivered as she felt the claws of family obligation dig deep into her core. How was it that they still held so much power over her, three years after she'd left the snow-capped rooftops of Karolinska behind?

She squinted at the photo, trying to divine if something—*anything*—had changed in her in the time since she'd arrived on the pristine white sandy beaches of St Victoria.

She blinked in surprise.

Gosh…

Three years of island life *had* changed her.

She looked happy. Genuinely happy. And why not? She

was mostly free of the royal shackles that had weighed her down back home. The loneliness. The hunger for a so-called normal family. Well… Okay, so she was still lonely, and she was absolutely without a doubt single. And, judging by all her not entirely appropriate thoughts she was a little bit lusty… But at least her grandmother wasn't trying to set her up with 'suitables', as she called them.

Here, Lia was on the periphery of a different type of family: The Island Clinic. It was a mismatch of international and local doctors and health professionals, brought together by the clinic's American founder Nate Edwards.

To the staff, she wasn't Princess Amelia Margit Sigrid Embla Trelleburg of Karolinska, sixth in line to the throne, as she was back in Europe. Here she was free to be plain old Lia. Or Dr Li-Li, as some of the nurses and patients called her.

Not that it happened that frequently… Being comfortable in her own skin was still something she was working on. As was trusting people to be her friend for no other reason than that they liked her. But she'd get there one day. So long as everyone who was in line to the throne before her stayed healthy and well. She *never* wanted to take The Crown. Managing her own life was hard enough, thank you very much.

Soon enough the room began to fill, and introductions came in a long stream of names she'd never remember. It was overwhelming, but all for a good cause.

As she eventually wended her way through the tables towards her own seat she fought the lonely feeling that inevitably began to hollow her out at big events like this. The tables were filled with people dressed in all of their finery, chatting away, laughing, smiling, listening. Oh, she could put on a show and do the same, but her childhood hadn't prepared her to feel at ease in a crowd…

A mother who'd hated the limelight, a father who'd bowed and acquiesced to the throne, and a shocking divorce had meant the palace had taken over the 'finer points' of her upbringing and given short shrift to that. One-on-one interactions were more her style. And even then…

She smiled and nodded, shook the odd hand, gradually feeling more and more isolated as she approached the head table where she guessed Nate wanted her—*still no Nate!*—and stood behind her chair.

Why did being in a crowd always feel like the loneliest place in the world?

She held back the inevitable grimace, weighted with bad memories. There were a thousand reasons why and all of them had to do with growing up in her family. One that could've been happy if only—

She forced her thoughts to screech to a halt.

If only nothing. What was done was done. If she wanted to carry on being happy here on St Vic, she'd have to find a way to re-establish how she dealt with people. Just because her parents were divorced, and her mother had been ostracised, and Lia had been sent off to moulder away in a remarkably unpleasant convent school for the entirety of her childhood, didn't mean her adulthood had to be miserable. Just as she had the power to change someone's life in the operating theatre, she also had the power to change her own.

Having told herself off, she scanned the vast room and forced herself to think of all of these people as potential friends. Or… Her eyes skipped from one male face to another. Potential boyfriends? It was an area of her life she was particularly gun-shy about. The last few had wanted to live the life they'd thought royals led, only to discover it wasn't quite the way the society papers would have had them believe. Suffice it to say being dumped by text when you were a princess was a double blow.

There had been one name—well, a face, really—that had stood out from the crowd earlier. A paediatrician from the UK whose name she hadn't been able to catch, because before he'd got to her in the greeting queue he'd spotted a little boy who'd been treated at the clinic. He'd left the queue and shared a jolly greeting with the lad and his parents before the pair of them had completed a very intricate handshake only the two of them seemed to know.

She'd liked that. Honouring a child she presumed had been his patient over kowtowing to 'royalty'.

Well. Royalty. Without the quotes.

She was genuinely royal, whether she liked it or not.

Out of the corner of her eye she saw a rather lovely male hand take hold of the back of the chair next to hers. It looked strong, capable, and oddly callused for someone she presumed was a doctor.

'Is this seat taken?'

She was about to say yes, that they were all assigned seats, when she realised the very man she'd been thinking of was standing next to her. Tall. Athletically lean. Short caramel-blond hair. And piercing blue eyes that sparkled in the twilight hues of the ballroom lighting.

Unlike a lot of the guests who didn't seem able to look her directly in the eye—because of the princess thing—this man didn't seem the slightest bit intimidated. He had an aura of strength about him that spoke of a deep-seated kindness, an inner peace that didn't necessitate any shows of bravura or machismo.

She glanced down at the name card.

Oliver Bainbridge.

She surprised herself by fixing him with a cheeky grin. Something about him made her feel comfortable. And, even more surprisingly, sexy. An internal glittery sensation she hadn't felt in ages lit inside her, making her feel as effervescent as the champagne everyone was drinking.

'It is taken, but I suppose we could switch the name cards to make it yours. So long as you promise to be more entertaining than the real Oliver Bainbridge. He sounds a bit of a bore, don't you think?'

His eyebrows quirked at the challenge.

She pressed her lips forward in a *Go on, I'm waiting* moue. Was she flirting? *Crumbs.* She was flirting!

'Oliver's not exactly a name that soars up the sexy charts, is it? Would it help if I told you my middle name was Casanova?'

She hooted with laughter, and through a giggle managed to say, 'I think that would be worse.'

'Well, then...' He took her hand in his and raised it to his lips. 'Would you be satisfied if I were to stay plain old Oliver?'

He pressed the softest of kisses to the back of her hand, sending a spray of heat through her body, highlighting the more...*ahem*...erogenous zones.

This Oliver Bainbridge could be rather dangerous. Dangerous and yummy. The problem being, Princess Amelia Margit Sigrid Embla Trelleburg of Karolinska didn't find men 'yummy'. She found them *suitable.* Or *appropriate.* Or, in the case of her last boyfriend, *well-vetted.*

But Lia, for the very first time in her life, fancied a bit of *yummy.*

Her eyebrows arrowed up into what Jonas called her 'imperious Empress' expression. 'I suppose the name will have to do until we come up with a better one. Now, then, as we're seated next to one another, do you think you'll be able to keep me entertained all night? I have very high standards, you know.'

Who *was* she—and where had plain old Lia gone?

'I shall endeavour to do my very best.' His lips twitched as if they'd just shared a private joke of a much more carnal nature. 'If you'll allow a humble paediatrician the pleasure of trying?'

'Oh, the pleasure is all mine,' she said grandly, knowing as she did so that never before had truer words been spoken.

CHAPTER TWO

SO *THIS* WAS Princess Amelia of Karolinska—AKA Dr Trelleburg.

She was far more beautiful than the handful of staff photos he'd seen on his weekly visits to The Island Clinic. And...dared he say it?...she was funnier than he would've thought. If this had been a blind date, he'd have wanted another. And very likely another after that.

But it wasn't. It was a formal charity event. And, whilst their banter was fun and light-hearted, at times crackling with a few unexpected frissons, no doubt the haughty humour would turn out to have an edge...an icier hue...

He pulled out her chair, which she accepted with thanks and, if he wasn't mistaken, her cheeks pinkened with a hint of shyness.

Oliver dialled back his cynicism. It wasn't her fault she'd been born to a royal family and defaulted to haughty as a form of humour. Just as it wasn't his fault that he was—

'Champagne?'

He waved it away out of habit.

'On call?'

Princess Amelia nodded at his card which—yes—did say what he did and where he did it. Standard practice for events like this, so that guests of honour didn't have to be embarrassed by getting the details of would-be donors incorrect.

He shook his head and answered mostly truthfully. 'You're not drinking, so I thought decorum dictated that I do the same.'

The last thing he wanted to be around a woman whose presence was tugging at the more primitive parts of his body was drunk.

She pushed her lips into a thoughtful pout, then said, 'Hmmm… I would've thought an Oliver Bainbridge, no matter where he stands on the sexy name scale, would have a bit more backbone than that. A man who sets his own agenda, not someone who would kowtow to the outdated dictates of another country's aristocracy.'

To mask the vein of truth she'd unearthed, he grabbed his chest and feigned pulling a knife out. 'Oh, did you, now?'

Oliver laughed—more at himself than anything. She was right. He'd never expect anyone to treat him differently because of who he was. It was nice to see she didn't expect people to change their behaviour around her just because of her parentage. 'And here I was thinking I was just being polite. Tell me…' he met her clear-eyed gaze head-on '… what else do you think an Oliver Bainbridge would be like?'

She tipped her head to the side and gave him a scan that felt more physical than it should have.

She wouldn't know it, of course, but he'd grown up in a world remarkably similar to hers.

'I think he'd be kind,' she began, 'this Oliver Bainbridge character.'

He nodded. If kindness was a religion, he'd be kneeling at the altar.

She tapped her chin. 'Diligent in his line of work. It's a calling, not a job.'

He smiled at this. Yes. She'd got that right as well.

She smiled back, and another hit of connection flared between them.

'I think he likes reading stories to his patients when they're sad.'

He let out a low whistle. She was good. *Very* good.

'Sounds like a wish list,' he said, wondering if he could tap into her psyche the way she'd tapped into his.

'Hmmm…' she smiled, non-committal, as she took a sip of sparkling water.

'When do I get to turn the tables?' he asked. 'See what my inner crystal ball reveals about you?'

'You don't,' she quipped lightly.

His smile broadened. They really were similar. Happy to talk endlessly about work and other people, but when the observations turned personal…? Not so much.

'That's not exactly fair, is it?'

She gave an untroubled shrug, her shoulders shifting under the light blue fabric that somehow made her skin look like golden sugar.

He caught himself imagining what it would taste like if he were to drop kisses along it, then abruptly stopped the careless fantasy. A princess with a reputation like hers—private, private and even more private—would hardly be up for a bit of canoodling away from the crowd.

It was quite a feat to have kept herself to herself as much as she had on this small island. The Island Clinic was renowned for its ability to keep its clients' comings and goings out of the public eye as much as for its medical prowess, but she'd been here three years to his two, and they'd never once crossed paths. Granted, most of his time was spent at the St Victoria Hospital, rather than the clinic, but even so… There weren't that many places to grab a bite to eat.

Was she hiding something?

A twinge of the pot calling the kettle black bounced against his conscience. He met her gaze with a look he hoped said that he got it. He understood what a life weighted with expectations beyond your control was like. Suffocating. Lonely. Painful.

Something flared hot and bright between them as their eyes clicked and cinched.

Kindred spirit... That was the first thing he felt break through their magnetic connection.

Interested... That was the second.

Well, what do you know?

This evening was suddenly looking up in a very different and unexpected way. He'd anticipated a bit of dry chicken. Some uninspired speeches. The inevitable silent auction aimed at increasing donations beyond the breathtakingly high price of buying a table.

Not that raising money for a free medical clinic was a bad thing. Far from it. But an unexpected flirtation definitely improved the prospects of the evening.

He returned her appraising gaze, enjoying the way her hips shifted against the fabric of her dress as if he had actually run his fingertips along them.

She looked as if she could walk straight into one of those 'destination wedding' photo shoots that often populated the immaculate coves and beaches of St Victoria. Her skin was barely touched by make-up. A bit of mascara and little else. She had a golden tan that added a healthy glow to her pink cheeks. Her satiny white-blonde hair was all but begging him to run his fingers through it. And her light blue eyes were communicating exactly the same thing he was pretty sure his eyes were telling her.

I fancy you.

Oliver only just managed to restrain himself from leaning in to the soft cloud of scent she left in her wake as she turned away.

Three hours later he was properly captivated.

Lia wasn't a cardboard cut-out royal, as so many of them were at these events—shuttled in to make sure the money flowed, then shuttled back out through a private exit to a private car or a plane, back to their private residence.

She was cut from different cloth.

Funny. Beautiful. Charming. Passionate about her work and genuinely committed to the charitable work at The Island Clinic—which, if rumour was to be believed, had seen more film stars than some Hollywood studios had.

Yes, she was incredibly private, but she was as well-schooled as he was in the fine art of being born to shoulder the burden of your forebears and she knew how to hide it.

She'd managed to extract a bit of background from him. The fact that he'd been born and bred in the UK. A paediatrician by choice, not by family tradition. And the fact that, like her, he was very happy here on St Victoria, where if the sun wasn't shining the rain was falling, and all of it was beautiful, lush, tropical…and, like tonight, heated. Very heated.

He wanted her. More than he'd wanted a woman in a long time.

As if the heavens were assisting him the meal finished. After a whispered bit of news that the clinic's founder, Nate Edwards, wasn't able to kick things off, the dancing was set to begin. Oliver saw that the mayor, seated on Lia's left, was leaning across to ask for the first dance.

In a move he wouldn't have expected of himself, he decided to pip him to the post. Pushing his chair back, he held out his hand. Lia's eyes darted away and then back. Decorum dictated she should dance with the mayor, the more senior of the two in social profile, but as a doctor at St Victoria Hospital, which had a very close relationship with The Island Clinic, it wouldn't be too unseemly for her to dance with him instead.

As the conductor held the small orchestra in an expectant trill of flute and violin, he felt another flash of connection as she lightly put her palm on top of his. Moments later he was holding her in his arms. Her scent, the softness of her skin, the swish of her hair against his hand... He would be hard pressed to think of another moment in his life when he'd have been perfectly happy for the rest of the world to fade away.

His fingers lightly grazed her bare skin at the deep V in the back of her dress. She shivered.

'Cold?'

She shook her head, clearly unable—or unwilling—to put a name to what it was that had sent goosebumps skittering along her arms.

He knew what it was. Because he was feeling it, too.

Desire.

They didn't exchange another word for the duration of the song, but the space between them at the end was definitely much, much smaller than it had been when he'd first slipped his arm round her waist and pulled her to him for the slow, mesmeric dance.

When the music stopped she took a step back, her breath quicker than it should have been after a slow dance. He presumed she was going to excuse herself and accept a dance with the mayor, who was waiting rather expectantly at the side of the dance floor.

But she leant in close and, instead of saying *Thank you* or *That was nice*, she whispered in lightly accented English, 'Do you want to go for a walk on the beach?'

He did. Very much so. But that didn't mean it could happen.

'Don't you need to stay?'

'Yes,' she answered, with a smile an outsider might have

mistaken for meaning that she thought it was nice he was a children's doctor.

But everything about the electricity zinging between them was saying something else entirely. It was saying *I want you.*

A shared, unspoken understanding meant they knew they couldn't leave together. But that same understanding also made it clear that before the night was over they would be in one another's arms.

'Is an hour long enough?' he asked.

She nodded.

'Which beach?'

The one at the front of the hotel wouldn't do. Not with the crowds of tourists and locals flowing in and out of the bustling restaurants and hotel bars dotted along the main harbour.

His mind whirred with possibilities. 'Sugar Cove?'

She arched an eyebrow, then gave an infinitesimal nod.

For the crowds looking on, he gave a courtly bow of thanks. For Lia, he gave the inside of her palm a light press with his thumb. A touch he hoped indicated that he wouldn't let her down.

Then he walked away so she could meet some of the other guests.

After a tactical 'walking to be seen' stroll through the crowd, he paused in front of a large group of colleagues and pulled out his beeper. He gave his forehead a slightly dramatic run-in with the heel of his hand. He worked with kids. He was used to playing to a crowd.

'Ah, bad luck, Oli!' one of them called out, clearly rather jolly after the endlessly flowing champagne. 'Is that the hospital?'

He gave one of those *What can you do?* shrugs. 'Kids, eh?'

'We'll see you tomorrow, Ol!'

He gave them a wave and, because he believed in the cause, pulled out his chequebook and a pen. 'Better do this before I go…'

A chorus of 'Take cares!' and 'Hope everything's all right, Dr Bainbridge!' followed in his wake as he threw them a wave and then left the venue.

As he had an hour, he did actually swing by the hospital. His happy place.

He popped his head round the corner of a room that had a little girl in it he knew would far rather be anywhere else but in hospital. Yup. He was right. Élodie was wide awake and looking scared. His heart squeezed tight. He cared for all his patients, but there was something about Élodie that bored straight through to his heart.

'What are you doing up, love?'

The little girl looked across from her picture book and gave him a tearful smile. 'Dr Bainbridge!' Her smile faded. 'I'm *peeyops*!'

Oliver hid a smile. The creole word meant 'going crazy', and he could certainly relate. His fingertips were still tingling with the memory of holding Princess Amelia in his arms…alive with the anticipation of much more. *If*, he abruptly cautioned himself, that was why she wanted to meet.

Maybe he'd read it wrong. Perhaps she wanted to talk hospital logistics or… His stomach clenched at this thought. Or she knew who he really was.

Right. Distraction. That was why he was here. For both himself and Élodie. He scooped up a pile of fairy tales someone had donated a couple of weeks back and crossed to her.

'Why can't you sleep?'

She made a squishy face, then said, 'It hurts.' She tapped

her chest and flopped back, her sprawl of dark, curly hair haloing around her on the pillow.

'Why don't you have some oxygen?'

Her face crumpled. 'I just want to be normal!'

His heart ached for her. Élodie's health demanded that she acknowledge that she wasn't. She'd contracted malaria a few years back, in the wake of a devastating hurricane, and as she already had weak lungs from her asthma, was prone to recurrences.

'When can I go home?' she asked.

Oof. That was a weighted question. The hurricane that had compromised her health had also taken her mother and father. She lived with her aunt and uncle now, but they had several teenaged children of their own and, with low-paying jobs, found Élodie's health problem a burden they struggled to fund and, more often than not, didn't attend to. He knew they used her hospital visits as a form of the day care they couldn't afford, but the alternative—leaving her on her own—simply wasn't an option.

Before he could answer, Élodie gave him a narrow-eyed gaze, then beamed. 'You look like a prince. Have you been to a ball?' Her small shoulders lifted and dropped as she gave a huge, painful-sounding sigh. 'Will I ever get to go to a ball?

Oliver's heart constricted. She'd been asking about leaving for a week now, but the hospital was the safest place for her. He hated that reality on her behalf. He hadn't been an orphan, but he knew what it was like to feel like an outsider in your home. As such, he'd privately funded a few extra days for her to stay in hospital, to ease the strain on her aunt and uncle and also, in all honesty, to ensure he could keep a closer eye on her.

He worried about her, and he knew he'd hold himself

personally responsible if her health deteriorated outside of his watch.

'Soon, little one. You're doing amazingly well, considering how high your temperature was when you came in.'

'I suppose…' She frowned her displeasure that the malaria had come back at all.

He fanned out the books. 'So… Which one will it be?'

Élodie's eyes widened, her distress temporarily forgotten, as she pointed at one of the books. 'Can we read about a princess?'

Oliver gave a silent groan. Of all the nights to read about a princess! Why hadn't he checked the books before offering her a choice?

'Absolutely.'

He pulled a chair up beside her bed, and before he opened the book did a quick scan of her stats and gave a surreptitious glance at her chart, to check the last time she'd been given her pain meds. Then, with a smile, he opened the book.

'Once upon a time…' he began.

By the time Élodie had gifted him some thank-you sweeties—sour apple, her favourite—and he'd looked in on a couple of the other children, he was buzzing with adrenaline. He hopped into his Jeep and set off away from Williamtown, the story of *Sleeping Beauty* still swirling round his head.

The fictional Princess had proved fairly tricky to woo but, after hacking down a palace's worth of thorns, discovering an entire sleeping royal court, including the most beautiful slumbering princess in the world, it appeared all the Prince had needed to do to restore harmony was give the Princess one life-affirming kiss to wake her from her slumber so that joy reigned and they all lived happily ever after.

He snorted. If only real life were that easy. Not that he

was after wedding bells or anything—the drama that would ensue once his family got so much as a whiff of an heir to the family title would be off the charts—so he'd take the life-affirming kiss for now.

He tried to wipe his mother's inevitable disapproval of a late-night liaison from his mind, then laughed. He was meeting a princess for a moonlit walk by the sea. His mother would be the first one to approve.

The cove was only a five-minute drive away from the hospital. One he knew like the back of his hand, because his seaside home was just around the corner. Lia wouldn't have had a clue that it was his favourite place on the island, and yet like someone who knew him like the back of their own hand she'd chosen his 'go to' spot.

No matter what mood he was in after an inevitably long day at the hospital, or an even longer one at The Island Clinic, from the moment he first stepped out onto the beach it felt like he was in a different world. Secluded, and slightly tricky to get to unless you were a local, it was surrounded by tiny footpaths unlit by streetlights. They were the only way to get there.

When he arrived—tie off, shoes off, warm sand beneath his feet and the phosphorescence of the waves doubly bright with the addition of the night's nearly full moon—he thought it would be impossible to find anywhere more romantic.

He was just about to begin undoing the buttons on his dress shirt when a female voice said, 'I thought that might be my job.'

CHAPTER THREE

What?

Lia was beginning to feel as if an entirely different woman had poured herself into her body when she'd put on her gown tonight. Maybe it was just the dress, but... She didn't say sultry things like that. Or give naughty little smiles after she'd said them. Then again, she was hardly one to invite a man she'd met at a charity ball to a remote beach cove for a midnight walk either, so...

Was this a magic dress?

She looked at Oliver—still in his tux, minus the tie, which was hanging loosely round his neck. There was the tiniest hint of a five o'clock shadow. *Mercy.* She barely contained the urge to lick her lips. He was positively scrumptious. A little rumpled, perhaps. But who wanted perfect when history dictated that perfect was unsustainable?

This man... *Mmm*...this man was something else. A man who knew his own way. Someone who'd tapped into a part of her she hadn't even known existed. The sexy seductress who felt every bit as powerful and self-possessed as he seemed.

This wasn't at all her normal modus operandi. And what was more she liked it.

Only a few hours in his company and already she liked herself more with him than without him. Which was something she'd have to cap, because it was the same dangerous path to 'head over heels in love' her parents had followed and that hadn't exactly ended well.

And yet it was very tempting to throw caution to the wind.

Just for tonight.

Obviously.

Not only was Oliver intelligent, funny, and openly passionate about his work as a paediatrician, he was just about the most attractive man she'd ever laid eyes on. Or perhaps he was attractive *because* of those things. He might not be everyone's cup of tea—there was a little scar on his left eyebrow, a smattering of freckles that arced up and over his nose that hinted at the boy he'd once been, and when he smiled the crinkles around his eyes betrayed a slightly weather-beaten aesthetic—but Lia liked every single centimetre of him.

Like a woman possessed, she watched herself reach out and tease open the top button of his shirt.

He exhaled at its release.

She skidded her fingertip down his Adam's apple, along the short hollow between his collarbones to the next button.

The air between them crackled with invisible electricity.

'Your dress only has the one tie?' he asked, after she'd released another button.

She watched his eyes drop to the wraparound cloth belt that held her dress together. 'Looks like it.'

He reached out to touch it, but she took his hand in hers with a *No, you don't* click of her tongue. 'Good things come to those who wait.'

She moved his hand to her hip.

Who on earth *was* she tonight?

Someone strong. Someone who went for what she

wanted and didn't wait for the palace to give her its stamp of approval.

She'd never felt more alive.

She saw him clock the big straw tote she always brought whenever she went to the beach.

'Towels,' she explained as she released another button then met his eyes. 'And whatnot.'

She'd been given a bottle of the vintage *grand cru* champagne by the staff at the hotel after the event. She'd thought of saving it until her cousin came out in a couple of months, for his annual leave, but here and now might be the perfect place to drink it. If they were going to be sitting and chatting, that was…

'Whatnot?' Oliver's mouth twitched into a smile.

Medieval convent schools in Karolinska had never made much of a point of being 'down with the kids', so her vocabulary sometimes erred on the side of very old-fashioned. Tonight she was going to let that be an asset.

'Yes.' She undid another button, then met his eyes. 'Whatnot.'

There were plastic cups, a container filled with an array of sweet tropical fruit, and an opulently inviting box of chocolates. But she didn't want any of that now. She wanted him.

Instead of saying as much, she tipped her head towards the sea. 'We might fancy a midnight swim.'

'I didn't bring my bathers,' he said.

He didn't sound sad about that at all.

'Nor did I,' she countered.

He nodded, then tipped his head to the side so that the moonlight caught the fine cut of his jawline. He looked, just at that moment, as if he'd been sculpted.

He moved again, and before she could catch her breath she was in his arms and he was kissing her. Softly at first.

Inquisitively. He tasted of salty air, the tiny bit of white wine he'd had at the ball and, interestingly, of sweeties. Sour apple, if she wasn't mistaken. But mostly he tasted of that indefinable essence that made him irresistible to her.

Eau de Oliver Bainbridge.

Whatever it was, it consumed her.

Their breath became one as they touched and tasted each other. The soft rasp of his stubble against her lips made her draw in a quick breath. His hands gently cupped her face as he held her away from him to see if she was all right, then brought her in close for an even deeper kiss. One she never wanted to emerge from.

When they finally broke apart, he dropped one of his hands to her throat, his thumb lazily tracing her collarbone as his other hand slid down the entire exposed length of her back until it made contact with her dress. Their bodies organically arced towards each other. There was no mistaking his arousal.

'Should we take that swim?' Oliver tipped his forehead to hers. 'Cool down a bit?'

She knew what he was asking. Did she want to make love to him now, or cool things down so they had a chance to decide properly if they were making the right decision.

She did want to make love to him. And the pulse between her legs was doing its best to vote for immediate satiation of its desire. But she also didn't want this magical night to end. She'd never been skinny dipping before, and the thought of that warm tropical sea surrounding her naked body and his naked body, the two of them kissing with all that deliciously warm water around them…

She took one of his hands and moved it to the flimsy bow tied at her side. 'I think we should take a swim and then perhaps engage in a little…whatnot. If you're willing?' she tacked on, suddenly aware he might be the one trying to back out.

Having an HRH in your name tended either to pull in the wrong kind of suitor—the kind who was desperate for some sort of link to royalty—or, as had been her last experience, repel them because of the floodlights her family occasionally shone on her life. Even in a place as remote as The Island Clinic.

Oliver ran his fingers along the soft fabric of her dress's bow and then, as if he'd made a decision, moved his hand to her arm.

Her heart twisted with a tight ache of longing. She wanted this man. And she'd been certain up until about two seconds ago that he wanted her as well.

But he was right to step away. There was no future in this kind of physical attraction. Her parents' marriage was proof of that.

Besides, she tried to tell herself as her body screamed its protest, she liked her life the way it was. And Oliver had made it very clear he liked living a life under the radar. Dating a princess—even one five thousand miles away from home—simply didn't allow for that.

Oliver ran his fingers down her side, eliciting another rush of goosebumps, and then, sensing her change of mood, pulled back again. 'Are you looking for a commitment, or one night of whatnot?'

He didn't colour the question in any way and she admired its openness. They were adults, both in their thirties. They had professional lives they clearly loved. His question was telling her all she needed to know. Whatever happened between the pair of them—one night, a few dates, something more—was up to her. Not out of a lack of interest… being this close to him assured her he was *very* interested… it was more a matter of consent.

So. The ball was in her court.

She made her decision. 'One night to remember seems a perfect way to end the evening, doesn't it?'

His voice was rough when he answered. 'As long as you're sure.'

In one fluid move she tugged the bow of her dress loose, revelling in the sensation of its fabric slipping along her body and down to the sand as she ran towards the sea.

'I want a night of freedom!' She whooped. 'A night of whatnot.'

If he wanted to join her, she thought as she ran into the sea, that was up to him.

She dived into the water, astonished at how luxurious it felt. Warm, sensual, moving her body with the gentle rhythmic undulations of the sea… Though she'd hardly thought of swimsuits as cumbersome, swimming naked in a moonlit sea with Oliver watching was on another level. Her body was positively thrumming with desire.

When she came up for air a few metres along and looked back to the shore she didn't see him at all.

Her heart sank.

Ah, well. She'd given him a choice and he'd made the sensible decision. Never mind. At least she could tick skinny dipping off her—

She felt a tickling against her legs, and then a whoosh of movement as Oliver surfaced next to her and pulled her into his arms. His body, fully naked, pressed against hers. She could feel his arousal as he pulled her legs up and around his hips and began to kiss her as if his life depended on it.

She felt his touch everywhere. His fingers tangled in her hair. His hand pressing against the small of her back to draw her closer to him. Then both of his hands were sweeping along her thighs and her bum as if she were a goddess, sent this one moonlit night for the express purpose of being cherished.

Soon enough she was returning his touch, her hands unable to resist touching his hair, his athletic shoulders, his chest. She dipped her head to give his nipples soft, swift nips, then raised her head to give him a salty kiss.

The water supported much of her weight, and he lifted her up so that he could caress and gently swirl his tongue round the taut tips of her breasts. She barely contained a moan of desire. He walked the pair of them into deeper water, so that when he lowered her for another hungry kiss, her entire body felt as though it had been submerged in their shared desire.

She'd never experienced a more erotic moment in her life. The soft breeze played amongst the droplets on her shoulders as the warm water brought them even closer together than they already were. They swam and kissed and touched and explored. It was the most intimate Lia had ever been with someone, and yet she'd never felt more comfortable in her own skin than she did here and now, with this man she might likely never see again.

'Are you warm enough?' he asked, after another soul-quenching kiss.

With the heat they were sharing? Oh, definitely.

'Mmm…but…' This was the tricky part. She didn't want to have sex without the all-important protection. 'If things progress… I'm not prepared.'

'My cottage is a two-minute walk away.' His voice was a low rumble of desire. 'I've got some things that will make "whatnot" safer. Shall we grab those towels of yours?'

He didn't have to ask twice.

Wrapped in huge fluffy towels, they rounded the corner of the cove to another, smaller inlet. When Lia saw where Oliver lived, she laughed with sheer delight.

Though it was bathed only in moonlight, and the finer details weren't entirely clear, Oliver's home would have put a luxury Swiss Family Robinson treehouse to shame. What looked to be four or five rooms and open-walled seating areas dappled the treeline, hung like beautiful baubles above a small sky-blue wooden cottage with a gorgeous wraparound porch. It was, in short, a tropical tree house mansion.

She gave him a dry look—difficult to do when she was feeling exceedingly lusty and there were only a pair of towels between them. 'You call *this* a cottage?'

'It's got a picket fence, hasn't it?'

'Yes, but…' She dissolved into giggles. 'I still don't think this qualifies as a cottage.'

Oliver gave a self-effacing laugh. 'Well…it started that way.'

Lia shook her head in amazement. 'I can see why you chose paediatrics over geriatrics. You're a dreamer, aren't you?'

She thought of her own, largely undecorated living quarters that were part of the clinic's staff accommodation. The house itself was exactly the kind of thing people in Karolinska who wanted a luxury holiday in the Caribbean would daydream about during the long, snowy winters: a sky-blue cottage with a pristine white porch, dripping with flower baskets and other unexpected touches of luxury—an outdoor shower *and* bath, a 'widow's peak' balcony with a mosquito-netted daybed and, in her bedroom, a very, *very* large four-poster bed.

None of which she'd put her own mark on in the three years she'd lived there, as Oliver had with his own home. He was clearly a man who wanted to settle down, have a home. Whereas she… She was ever grateful for the tide that washed away her footprints, leaving not so much as a trace that she'd ever been there.

Oliver was grinning at her, obviously taking the back-handed compliment on the chin. 'I call it believing in possibility with a practical edge. I bought the cottage—all two rooms of it—when I moved to the island. It had been deserted after the hurricane and was barely habitable—which gave me an idea. Why not build up, rather than out? The tree canopy provides some protection from the winds, and… Well, who doesn't like a tree house?'

His enthusiasm was infectious. 'It really is amazing.' She held up her hands in awe. 'You've created a personalised paradise. Colour me impressed, Peter Pan.'

He grinned and gave a playful kick at the sand as if her praise had embarrassed him. When he looked up there was a very grown-up heat in his eyes that swept through her like wildfire.

'I guess that makes you my Tinker Bell.'

She gave an obliging laugh, only just catching a glimpse of something flashing across his face that unexpectedly tugged at her heart. It was sadness. Not a fresh grief. It was something that had become a part of him. She decided not to press. If his past was anything like hers, it was worth leaving precisely where it was.

'Well, if that means I can fly and get a magic wand I approve.'

He gave a self-conscious, *'Ha!'* and then explained as he led her towards the porch. 'It really did start out as just the cottage. Turns out I like to do a little DIY in my spare time.'

She shook her head, amazed. 'Your spare time sees a lot more action than my spare time.'

'I doubt that.' He ran the backs of his fingers along her cheek, then swept her wet hair into a loose knot at the nape of her neck as he dropped a kiss on her shoulder. 'You're a doctor. You know as well as I do that every day doesn't go as planned. We do what we need to do to regroup after work. I build things. I'm sure whatever you do is equally healing.'

The look he gave her was so honest, so complete in its belief that Lia's moral compass was as solidly grounded as his was, that a rush of emotion flooded her chest. There was absolutely no judgement in his tone. He believed in her.

She could fall for this man if she didn't watch herself.

'I sail,' she said, to fill the silence.

She'd grown up sailing, and whenever things had grown too lonely at boarding school, or too claustrophobic at the palace, she'd run down to the harbour, jumped onto her boat and relished the relief of feeling her mind slowly return to her body as she got further away from the shore.

Being alone was so much better than feeling lonely in the middle of a crowd. But these days she didn't sail so much to escape her life. It was more to give herself room to breathe between its more intense moments. Sailing a boat demanded her full attention—physical and mental—and, as such, was the best way to clear her mind after a long, difficult surgery.

She'd thought she had found the perfect balance. But this man… He'd built an actual dream house.

She tamped down the urge to ask him what sort of dreams he'd had for inside the house when it was built, just as she could see him biting back an urge to ask her about her sailing.

They'd said one night only.

He took her hand in his and led her into the house, the atmosphere between them shifting once again.

With each step she felt the flickering desire she'd felt in the sea build and gain purchase. They barely made it to the porch before she had to kiss him again.

It was a porch that demanded moonlight kisses. It featured a wooden couple's swing and a well-loved hammock. There was a stack of books beside each of them. And there was, of course, a door that led up into the magical maze where, somewhere amongst the trees, was Oliver's bedroom.

When he swung open the door she felt another, indefinable click of connection. The small sitting room was immaculate. Not institutionally so—it looked comfortable—but there was something very familiar about it.

'Boarding school?' she asked, before she could stop herself.

He gave her a quick look of surprise and then released a self-effacing laugh. 'That obvious?'

'Takes one to know one. The only thing that's out of control in my place are the piles of books.'

He pulled her to him and gave her a light kiss on the lips. 'I have a feeling there's going to be something other than book piles that are out of control tonight.'

Heat rayed out from below her belly button. Oh, he had that part right.

With nothing but towels between them, Oliver was finding it difficult to control his more primal instincts. As he guided Lia up the stairwell his fingers twitched with the urge to tug the thick cotton away from that gorgeous body of hers and have her here and now. But if they were only going to have one night he wanted to make sure each moment was more memorable than the next. One-night stands weren't really his thing, but something told him tonight had to be the exception to his unspoken solid rule.

When they arrived on the next level she suddenly stopped, her blue eyes alive with pleasure.

'What?' he asked.

'I feel like I'm walking through your imagination.'

Her smile was both intimate and delighted as she wandered through his living room—a largely open-air space, which was much more homely than the room downstairs. Cushiony sofas. Tumbles of tropical plants. More books. And,—one of his favourite elements, on full, proud display here—the thick trunk of the tree the house was balanced in, soaring right through the middle of the room, complete with a swirl of solar-powered fairy lights.

She smiled at him, and the warmth of it hit him right in the chest.

'Your house is like those Russian dolls.'

'How so?'

'But instead of getting smaller and smaller, the rooms become more and more like the real Oliver.'

When he didn't answer she took a step back, as if questioning her own judgement and checking herself for having got it wrong.

He thought of telling her she was spot on, but he closed the space between them, responding with a light kiss on the cheek instead. If this really was going to be a one-night thing, keeping his emotional distance was probably wise.

The real answer, of course, was much more complex than a simple *yes*. To his parents the 'real' Oliver Bainbridge had a title. A family seat back in England. A reputation to uphold. And there were a few other, darker edges to his past he'd rather forget. As a result, the Oliver she was meeting was the Oliver he'd been for the last two years, here on St Vic. He had taken some getting used to, but at long last he really liked the guy. He was anonymous. Loved his work. The only thing that was missing was—

He checked himself. Best not go there. Tonight was about enjoying Lia's company.

When they climbed one more level and reached his bedroom she let out a happy sigh and clapped her hands. 'You sleep here?'

She twirled round in disbelief, then grabbed hold of his hands for balance when the spinning got the better of her. She looked young and beautiful and more at ease than he'd seen her all night.

'I'm insanely jealous! It's beautiful, Oliver.'

He drew her close, then turned her round so he could wrap his arms round her waist and they could look at the room together. It was one of the highest rooms in the house, and his favourite.

At the centre was an enormous four-poster bed, featuring the towering tree trunk at the back. As was necessary in any tropical country, the bed was shrouded in diaphanous mosquito netting, billowing in the soft breeze. The hush-hush of the receding waves upon the beach were all the lullaby he'd ever needed here. But tonight wasn't about sleeping. Not yet anyway.

'Shower?' he murmured.

'Mmm...'

It was all the response he needed. He led her into the bathroom, which he'd managed to kit out with all the mod cons. Teak flooring stood in for tiles, and the water tanks hidden further up in the jungle canopy allowed for a nice hot shower out on the starlit balcony—or, on days that demanded a soak, for the filling of the claw-footed bathtub it had taken him and six other lads to pulley up the tree. The bath sat in pride of place at the open French windows.

He lit a couple of candles in the hurricane lamps he'd hung about the place, watching their light flicker against the windowpanes and the solitary floor-length mirror. Then he turned her to face it, untucked the fold of towel that hid that beautiful body of hers, and kissed her neck with a low, 'Now, then. Where were we, exactly?'

Warm water was soon cascading over the pair of them as they caressed one another's soapy bodies. It was enough to push them both to the edge of insanity.

Lia had barely dried herself before Oliver scooped her up and carried her to the bed. He had no idea how, but as virtual strangers they seemed to share the same sexual heartbeat. Intense and fast shifted to slow and luxurious, then moved back to desperate for one another. Time became elemental. The tickling of an eyelash against his cheek made him feel as though an hour had passed. A kiss lasted for ever and not long enough. The pounding of her heart against his fingertips stopped time.

'Please,' she finally begged, her fingernails scraping the length of his back. 'I want you inside me.'

He swiftly sheathed himself and then lifted her, so that she was kneeling above him. Slowly, achingly slowly, she began to lower herself on to his erection. Hot, profound surges of desire made maintaining his control next to impossible. She teased him and dipped herself lower and lower, so that he felt, just for a nanosecond, what it was like to be completely surrounded by her.

'I want you...'

Her lips brushed against his ear as she lowered herself completely on to him, her fingertips moving along his sides until her light touch drove him to a near frenzy. In one swift move he slid his hands over the soft curves of her bum and flipped her on to her back. It was his turn to set the pace.

His hips latched with hers, pushing and thrusting into her honeyed essence, their movements organically syncing with the cadenced undulations of her hips. The energy connecting them grew in intensity until it became all-consuming... fiercely passionate in a way he never known himself to be. He wanted her, too. Their individual desires combined into one mutual longing. Something more powerful than he had ever felt.

No words needed to be exchanged for him to know that something bigger than either of them—the universe, maybe—had set everything that had ever happened in their lives into motion in order to bring them together on this one perfect night. It would, he had no doubt, set the standard for any relationship he would ever have in the future.

The warmth of the night and the heat of their bodies seemed to increase their energy, not drain it. As one, their bodies began to rock in a sultry, delicious rhythm, a beat that swiftly increased and then, without any sort of warning, hit a speed that seemed out of their control until finally, as one, they climaxed.

They made love a second time. More slowly…almost sleepily…but with a familiarity that hinted at a long-term relationship—which, for the second time that night, struck Oliver as strange. Having Lia in his arms gave him a warm, comfortable feeling of déjà-vu. But he'd definitely never met her before. There would have been no forgetting someone who tugged at his more primal elements with such precision. And yet being with her felt…familiar. She'd got close in a way none of his girlfriends had. As if they were two people unable to resist the magnetic lure of an attraction that went far deeper than the physical.

When dawn came, she looked at her watch and started saying something about the forty-minute drive to the clinic and a long day on the surgical ward. Her reminder that this had been a one-off.

He made her a cup of coffee and didn't press to see her again. They sat on his porch, watching the sea birds dip and dive as a glittering shoal of fish shimmered past, the silence between them light and comfortable. Not a hint of expectation weighted these last moments they would spend together. If they met again…he would welcome it. If they didn't…he now knew being with someone just the once could mean much more than he'd ever believed possible.

She handed him the coffee mug and gave his lips a soft peck, after which she thumbed off some lipstick. 'Sorry,' she said.

He caught her wrist and dropped a kiss on it. 'Don't be.' He took her other wrist in his hand and gave it a kiss as well. 'For balance.'

The smile they shared was complicit and warm—and more than that it was kind. A smile between two people who understood that they had shared something both beautiful and rare. A perfect night.

'Thank you,' she said, shouldering her tote, which still held the champagne and chocolates. They'd not needed any help in the aphrodisiac department.

'Thank *you*.'

He got up with her and watched until she disappeared round the far edge of the cove without so much as a farewell wave.

That's how it is with princesses, he thought with a rueful smile as he began to get ready to head into the hospital. *One minute you're dancing together at a ball, with nothing between you but a shared heartbeat and stardust, and the next…*

He looked out to the sand where—ha!—a gold flip-flop had fallen from her bag. It was no glass slipper, but he'd remember her by it.

Who was he kidding? He'd remember her without it. From this moment on he'd always have a part of his heart bearing the imprint of Princess Amelia of Karolinska.

CHAPTER FOUR

One month later

'HE WAS LUCKY.' Lia lifted her hands away from the patient and, after peeling off her surgical gloves and popping them in the disposal bin, gave her lower back a much-needed knuckle-rub.

Thirty-two years old was a bit young to start feeling the aches and pains of standing at the surgical table, but… who knew? Her whole body was being weird lately. Stress, maybe. It had been crazy busy over the past month. So much so she'd only just managed to overcome the urge to drive to the other side of the island and accidentally-on-purpose run into a certain paediatrician at the St Victoria Hospital.

Realising her team were still looking at her, she held up a set of crossed fingers. 'Let's hope he gives up the motorcycle and finds a safer mode of transport.'

She wasn't one to be preachy, but on an island where 'open-air transport' was the preferred means of travel, she wished holidaymakers in particular would pay attention to the speed limit. It was there for a reason. St Victoria was a spider's web of curvy roads, and the more mountainous tracks, like the road the patient had been driving on, were made up of sharp-angled switchbacks.

He was lucky he'd crashed on the road, where their helicopter had been able to airlift him to the clinic, and not at the bottom of a cliff. As things stood, the blood clot she'd just removed from his brain had been milliseconds away from changing his life for ever. And not for the better.

A sudden wave of nausea swept through her.

Uh-oh. She'd thought she'd curbed her queasy stomach over the last couple of days with some healthy doses of chicken soup.

'Okay. We can close now.' She needed to get out of here. And fast.

'So he's clear? We can talk to the family?' asked Nate Edwards, her chief of staff.

Not an unfair question about such a high-profile patient, but she really had to get to the ladies' room.

'Lia?' He called after her, even though she was halfway to the door. 'What do I tell the family? Is he in the clear?'

She tried to sound bright as she fought yet another wave of nausea. 'You know how I feel about pronouncing someone in the clear.'

She headed for the door, simultaneously assigning closing procedures to her team and trying to visualise the fastest route to the closest private restroom.

Nate bounded ahead of her and held open the operating theatre door for her. 'I know. I know. "Saying a patient is in the clear puts them right back in the danger zone."'

'Close.' She gave him a playful elbow in the ribs as her dislike of being misquoted briefly overrode her queasiness. 'Saying a patient is in the clear makes them *behave* as if they haven't just had brain surgery—and *that* puts them right back in the danger zone.'

Nate tugged off his face mask so that she could see his smile. 'Thanks for jumping to the fore on this one,' he said.

'Pleasure.'

Late-night calls were something she'd been used to in her days of training with the military back in Karolinska. Back then a pre-dawn alarm had meant putting herself through brutal physical workouts or studying as if her life depended upon it—because out in the battlefields someone else's life eventually would.

Her family had put a sharp halt to her doing active duty, like her cousin, but she saw her work as a neurosurgeon as a similar call to service. She'd never leave a patient in the lurch. Especially one in critical care.

Her smile turned serious. 'Ryan was lucky he had the accident on St Vic and not on any of the other islands.'

Nate shook his head and gave a soft laugh. 'Spoken like a true neurosurgeon.' His expression sobered. 'His wife's probably thinking he would've been luckier if he hadn't had it at all.'

The comment landed with an unexpected barb. Up until now, Lia had never given a second thought to anyone worrying about *her* if she had an accident.

Her hands swept over her belly. 'I've got to dash. Sorry, Nate.'

Her boss gave her arm a quick squeeze, then excused himself. She knew he would give Ryan Van Der Hoff's family the good news. Lia preferred to stay out of that sort of thing—particularly when there was a celebrity involved. And Ryan had starred in an international spy series that just about everyone in the world seemed to have watched.

As far as medical centres went, this one was at the top of the list in maintaining privacy and offering service with a gilt edge. Not actual gold, of course, but the service here was off the charts. Nate was a great boss as well. As someone who hated the limelight as much as their patients did when it came to personal matters, Lia was always happy to leave the *Good news, the surgery went well* talks to Nate.

You never knew if the paparazzi had managed to weasel their way in, or if a patient's nanny had been paid to surreptitiously take snaps of the medical team that had just performed life-saving surgery on her employer. It was rare. But it happened.

All she wanted to do was her job. Something she couldn't do when she was fighting this extreme—suddenly the penny dropped—*nausea*!

Twenty minutes later, with a test stick in her hand, Lia could barely hear for the buzzing in her ears. Pregnant? There was only one man who could be the father, but… *Pregnant*?

Equal measures of hope, fear, panic and, most surprising of all, undiluted joy bounced around her chest as she tried to still her thoughts and wrap her brain around this new reality.

She was pregnant with Oliver Bainbridge's child.

Energy charged through her, almost physically escorting her out to her car so she could drive over to his side of the island, climb up that wild treehouse of his and into his bed, and pop the news. Open it up to fizz and delight like the champagne they'd never ended up drinking.

Then that energy crackled and crashed through her heart, surging up to her brain.

What was she thinking? No. She shouldn't tell him. She shouldn't tell anyone. Not until she'd figured out a bulletproof plan to keep the palace's controlling tendrils off her baby.

The palace.

An icy shudder swept down her spine.

She glanced at her watch.

The staff at her grandmother's office would just be getting into the office about now.

The temptation to bang her head repeatedly against a wall seized her.

She should have put together this puzzle on her own—without the aid of a pregnancy test. Her period was late. Her breasts were...well, rather buxom these days. Her lower back hurt when it never had before. And, of course, the nausea.

It was just...

A child.

She was going to have a child.

Someone she could love without rules and regulations—

Her hammering heart pulled up short, then froze in place.

Princesses from Karolinska didn't have children out of wedlock. They had very public weddings and magazine-friendly honeymoons, and did photo shoots a minimum of a year later with their grinning husbands by their side as they celebrated the birth of their children, had a few days off, then gave their lives over to supporting The Crown and snipping red ribbons at charity events—

Her heart launched back into action.

Husbands. She didn't have a husband. Oliver had been more than happy to have their night together be a one-off, so it was more than likely he wouldn't want to be a husband—let alone be *her* husband.

She could try asking him...

Her heart lodged in her throat, making even a practice run impossible.

Marrying a man she'd met a sum total of once was right up there in the Very Bad Ideas department. It might even be the actual worst idea ever.

Her parents had met and married in a matter of weeks, and look how well that had turned out. One wandered round the palace like a robot, dutifully carrying out his royal duties as assigned to him by his parents, the King and Queen. The other, a commoner had fallen so very much in love with a prince, and given him a baby daughter, but had been held in contempt by The Establishment, ultimately leading not only to her divorce, but to her walking away from her daughter as if she was too cruel a reminder of that chapter of her life.

So, no. Marrying the stranger paediatrician who had made her tummy do funny things was not a good idea.

Her heart, already battered from wrapping itself round the revelation, squeezed so tight she could hardly breathe.

The palace would want to take over her life the instant they knew. Their meddling had been at the heart of her parents' break-up and she didn't even have a relationship to break up. How would they deal with that? Give her one? Pre-vetted?

Too easily she pictured a dungeon down in the bowels of her grandparents' castle…dark, dingy, and filled to the brim with prospective husbands for wayward princesses.

Her heart slipped down her throat, then free fell to just above her baby, a sharp breath only catching it short of landing right on it.

Interesting…

She really wanted to protect it.

She pictured Oliver down in that imaginary dungeon, those lovely hands that had spent the night caressing and pleasuring her now strained as they wrapped around the thick iron bars, his beautiful, male, lightly stubbled cheeks pressed between them, calling her name again and again.

She scrunched her nose.

Pure poppycock.

She barely knew Oliver… Well… She knew that light kisses along his neckline tickled him. She knew that lowering herself onto him with the patience of a devotee made him groan with pleasure. She knew he smiled when he slept, that he smelt like the beach and pineapple and something else intangibly male.

Up until she'd met him, it had seemed as though she'd only ever had sex with past boyfriends. With Oliver, it had felt like making love.

Up until now, she'd thought of their night together as something precious. Unique. A rare moment held in a beautiful chrysalis of unspoken connection.

Because, her pragmatic side reminded her, they'd had absolutely no commitment to one another. A beautiful night of the best sex she'd ever had and then, before the sun had had a chance to rise, she'd been blowing him a farewell kiss from the doorway. *Sayonara*, sunshine.

Abruptly, painfully, as if an actual dagger was plunging into her heart, she felt the anguish of that day her mother had been escorted from the palace grounds lance through her.

That was what really happened when you married a royal.

Destruction.

She forced her breathing to steady. Giving herself a panic attack and passing out in a locked women's bathroom no one knew she was in wasn't going to help anything.

She splashed some cold water on her face, dragged a scratchy paper towel over the droplets, then stared herself in the eye.

This would be fine. All of it would be fine.

She dropped her gaze to her stomach and silently vowed to the teensy-tiny baby only just beginning its life in her belly that it would be fine, too. She'd do everything in her power to offer it the kind of childhood she'd never had. Be a mother who didn't bow to the power of their forebears.

Sure, people loved the tradition of the Karolinskan royal

family, but it wasn't as if it was a religion. Or law. They were figureheads. Little more than the icing on top of a very decorative democratic cake. They needed to look to the future, not bow to the restrictive measures of the past.

Yes. She would look to a future in which her son or daughter would know the one thing she'd never had: freedom.

Okay. Good.

She gave her reflection a solid nod, as if she'd just come up with the perfect way to perform a difficult surgery. So that was settled. All she had to do was call the palace, tell them she was pregnant, then ring Oliver and let him know he was going to be a father but that he definitely didn't have to worry about marrying her because she had it all in hand.

She picked up her phone and thumbed through her contacts until she found her father's number. Protocol dictated that the palace be informed before the father of her child. Hopefully her father would help buffer the much stronger reaction she knew King Frederik and Queen Margaretha would have.

She forced herself to press the little green button on her phone. After two rings her father picked up.

'Lia? What's wrong?'

She winced. Trust her father to think she'd only ring if she had bad news. A darker, more painful thought entered her heart. Perhaps hearing from her only made him think of all the bad things in his life. She, after all, was one of the main reasons his marriage had fallen apart.

'Papa.' The word felt as foreign upon her tongue as the two that were to follow. 'I'm pregnant.'

Two hours of explaining later, the call that now included her grandparents had reached a crossroads.

They wanted her to marry Oliver.

She did not.

'I don't think it's a good idea,' she persisted, not really wanting to go into detail about how little she knew him.

'We do,' her grandmother said, as if that put an end to the matter.

Lia rolled her eyes, thankful that this wasn't a video call. She'd offered them a thousand options apart from the one they wanted: love, marriage, baby carriage. There was one card left to play. She hadn't wanted things to go this far, but she didn't need their money, their status or, more to the point, their boa-constrictor-like rules.

'What if I give up my title?'

There was a deafening silence on the end of the line, followed by a very curt, 'I don't think going in that direction would be wise, Amelia.'

Grandmama. She always helmed the ship in moments like these.

Unfortunately for Lia, her grandmother had a point. The fall-out of such a move would be brutal. The one thing she'd ached for her entire life was to feel as if she was part of a big, happy family. She'd got the 'big' part. Just not the 'happy'.

And walking away would mean the tenuous threads of connection she had to her father would be severed for ever. Her grandparents would pretend she'd never existed. Her beloved cousin Jonas would be told communicating with her was forbidden. Finding her mother at this juncture would be a) impossible and b) really stupid, because all she'd be proving was that history really did repeat itself.

She broke the silence. 'I'll talk to Oliver.'

'Perhaps you should leave that to us,' her grandfather cut in.

'No.' She shook her head at the phone and involuntarily ground the word out a second time. 'No. This is my...*situation*. I'll talk to him.'

'And tell him what, exactly?' her grandmother asked, as if she'd just smelt something vile and was demanding to know its source.

'The truth,' Lia snapped back, fatigue fraying what little remained of her patience.

'Which is…?' her father asked. 'What is the truth?'

Lia stopped short. She'd been about to say that she was going to tell Oliver the palace was demanding they get married, and that if he was prepared for a life of being micromanaged he could go for it, but she wasn't all that keen, so if he was all right with it she'd be looking to move to another island. Alone. Maybe not this nanosecond, because she really liked her job and would definitely need an income as the palace would for sure be cutting off her allowance. And, no, she didn't want child support. She didn't know what, if anything, she wanted from him…

All of which reminded her that this was her father, asking her how she was going to treat the father of her child.

It was the first genuine curiosity she'd heard from him in years, and unexpectedly it softened the shard of unspent anger she'd held on to at the fact he'd sent her away to boarding school so young.

'I'm going to tell him I'm pregnant and that I want to keep the baby.'

'That's it?' her grandmother asked, in a tone that made it distinctly clear she was turning puce with anger right now.

'That's it.'

'And then what?'

'I'll listen to what he has to say, and we'll take it from there.'

Lia looked at her phone and ended the call. She turned it off, just to ensure it wouldn't ring again in five seconds, with her irate grandmother the Queen demanding she show more respect to The Crown.

This was about her, Oliver and their baby, and no one else. They would decide what they wanted to do and then they would tell the palace.

CHAPTER FIVE

'SHALL WE SHAKE on it?' Oliver knelt down so that he was at eye-level with the five-year-old who had quite an impressive bump on his forehead.

'But I like going on the slide with my friend,' came the plaintive reply.

Oliver laughed. 'I know. Going on the slide with a friend is fun. But what if their head accidentally hits yours when you've already got a bump? Probably best to slide solo for the next couple of weeks.'

The little boy shot a *Do I have to?* look at his mum, whose *Yes, you do* expression left little room for interpretation. He stuck out his hand and reluctantly shook Oliver's.

For a millisecond Oliver let himself wonder what it would feel like to hold his own child's hand in his.

If things had been different…

If things had been different he probably wouldn't be here, treating this lovely little chap.

He held his grip on the small hand in his, honouring the trust that came with the gesture, then let go, gave the lad a smile and closed the moment with a high five.

Wondering about things that hadn't come to pass or, more to the point, might never happen wasn't worth the airtime.

He opened the door for the pair of them, reminding the

boy's mother to bring him in if he began to be sleepy at unusual times or exhibited any of the other signs of concussion outlined on the cheat sheet he'd written out for her.

A glimpse of white-blonde hair caught his eye midsentence. His chest filled with a huge, hopeful inhalation, then froze in place when it disappeared. It couldn't have been Lia. Not in this wing of the hospital anyway. Unless… Would she be looking for him?

She'd not broken the 'one night only' decision they'd made, and he'd respected that. It hadn't stopped him hoping their paths might cross again, though. What they'd shared—the electricity—hadn't just been physical. It had run deeper. Their connection had been…visceral. As if they already knew one another. Two halves suddenly, finally, becoming whole. Which, of course, was insane. They were strangers. Strangers who had shared one extraordinary night.

'Dr Bainbridge?' the mum said, loudly enough to suggest she'd already said it once before.

'Yes…sorry?' He forced himself to refocus.

'Should he not stay the night?'

'No, honestly,' Oliver assured her warmly. 'I know a bump of that size can seem frightening—and, be warned, it will go some unusual colours—but he passed all the cognisance tests and seems right enough in himself. I think he's walked away with a bruised ego, more than anything.'

The mum laughed and said, 'Boys. You can't stop them from pushing things to the limit, can you?'

Oliver laughed along, feeling the sliver of his heart that ached for children of his own taking up a fraction more room in his chest than it normally did. Was it meeting Lia that had made his hunger for a child, a family of his own, inch to the fore over these past few weeks?

No, he thought, struggling to keep the anger at bay. It

was having the option taken from him before he knew it even was an option.

He shook his head, to clear it of thoughts of the defining moment that had played a role in bringing him here to St Victoria. Though it had been nearly six years ago now, it had left wounds that should've been healed by now— perhaps by a family of his own— but had somehow always festered. Staying single, focusing on his work—those things had kept the raw pain of his past at bay. But nothing yet had allowed him fully to heal.

He looked down at the little boy who was beaming up at him.

Moments like this helped.

He thanked them, then waved off the mum and her son, his last patients of the day, and went back into his office to finish up his paperwork.

'Oliver?'

He turned, so startled by the sight of the woman standing in his doorway that words logjammed in his throat until he finally managed to croak, 'Your Highness—'

'Lia,' she corrected him tightly. 'Can we talk? One of your colleagues…' she pointed vaguely down the corridor '…said you were finished for the day.' Her brows drew together. 'Maybe somewhere outside the hospital?'

For a nanosecond he thought she was going to suggest another swim, but she looked serious. Too serious.

'Of course. Is this—? This isn't about a patient, is it? A professional consult?'

She gave her head a solitary shake in the negative. 'It's personal.'

The way she bit out the word dropped a lead weight in his gut. This didn't sound good. Had someone taken pictures of them swimming in the moonlight? It was exactly the sort of photo that could win a paparazzo a healthy pay cheque. Unless, of course, they were trying to blackmail her with it.

This was just one of the reasons why he'd come here. To escape the prying eyes of the press. So far he'd been lucky. He'd never courted the society papers back in the day. Had only ever appeared in the Easter and Christmas photos his mother always insisted upon, trying to keep up with royalty. As if! They were in another league of aristocracy. One his parents kowtowed to every waking moment of their lives. More because it was ingrained in them than anything, but still…

His anonymity here was a freedom Lia had never known. He felt for her. From what he'd seen, she only ever used her title for good, and if it was now being turned against her… Well… The world was a crueller place than he'd given it credit for.

Stemming a few colourful words, he grabbed a light parka off the back of his chair, pulled his office door shut behind him and locked it. 'I know a place.'

Her features softened in gratitude. He fought the urge to pull her into his arms and comfort her. She seemed so vulnerable, so frightened…his heart ached for her. But if this *was* blackmail, or pictures destined for a gossip magazine, the last thing he wanted to do was add fuel to the flames.

St Victoria Hospital was open to all—unlike the exclusive clinic where she worked—so the fact that she'd ventured out to find him, where paparazzi might easily be lurking, meant that whatever this was, it was screaming *Important!*

With her silent agreement, he led her to the discreet exit towards the rear of the hospital where he was parked. He drove them to one of the higher outcrops overlooking Williamtown, that featured sprawling tropical gardens dappled with secret little nooks and crannies where, with any luck, they could have a private conversation.

Silently they walked along the paths, tension crackling between them, until Oliver pointed towards an area with a small brook running through it. He gestured to a bench, waiting for her to sit before he took his own seat.

'Your Highness—' he began.

'No.' She shook her head. 'Please. It's Amelia…or Lia. Or—' her voice shook slightly as she swallowed, then forced herself to continue '—or the mother of your child.'

The news hit him like a wrecking ball. Bashed into his heart and then lodged there, where, in the blink of an eye, it turned into a hot, brilliant ball of sunshine.

'Seriously?' He shook his head in disbelief. They'd used protection. Was this real? A chance to be a father? 'You're… you're pregnant?'

She nodded.

'You're going to keep it?' he asked, before he could stop himself.

She looked at him as if he were mad even to consider otherwise. He forced himself to regroup. This was Lia, not Sarah. Lia had chosen to tell him about the pregnancy, to include him. Surely she wanted this baby?

'So…if you're going to keep the baby, if it's what you want, why do you look so serious? So…' He sought a gentler word and couldn't find one. 'Unhappy?'

Lia dropped her head so he couldn't see her eyes, and mumbled something he couldn't quite make out.

He put his hand on her shoulder, then crooked his finger under her chin so they were looking at one another properly. Her light blue eyes glistened with tears.

'They want us to be married,' she bit out, as if the idea were detestable.

'Who?' He shook his head, confused.

'The palace,' she explained, just as he came to the same realisation. 'My grandparents and I spoke early this morning and they have spoken to the council—' She stopped herself, as if the life had been drained out of her, then met his gaze and said, 'The King and Queen of Karolinska will not have any heir to the throne born out of wedlock.'

'Fine.'

Lia's clear blue eyes blazed as if he'd just insulted her. 'What?'

'Fine. Good. Yes. I'll do it.'

Oliver clapped his hands together and gave them a rub, trying to channel the adrenaline coursing through him and failing. Whatever it took. He'd do it. There was no chance he was stepping away from another chance to raise a child. His child. Their child.

'Sooner the better.'

'You don't want to think about it?' she asked with a dry laugh.

'No.'

There was a side of him that was telling him to slow down. Think about it. But he wanted to lift her up and twirl her round. Shout, *I'm going to be a father!* so loud the entire island heard. He wanted to take care of her. Peel her grapes. Swaddle her in cotton. Rub her feet. Whatever it took.

But he could see she was anxious, weighing up the options—and why wouldn't she? Her life and her body were changing for ever, and it was all so unexpected. Understandable, then, that she might not seem excited. Even though for him—whether he wanted it to or not—an ancient, protective, paternal instinct was overriding everything else.

Lia's features were decidedly wary. 'You know what marrying me means, don't you?'

He shrugged and looked around, as if the answer was

obvious. 'Live our lives, raise our child—' He stopped himself as the penny dropped. 'The palace will want full coverage of the new royal baby.'

Lia nodded. '*And* the engagement *and* the wedding. If there is one,' she added gravely, her expression now completely guarded. 'It's not all glitz and glamour, you know.'

He nodded. He knew. First-hand, he knew.

'We won't be going to galas like the one where we met every night. I won't be prancing around in a tiara.'

'That's a shame,' he said, realising too late that she was in no mood to make light of the matter. And she was right. A child's future was at stake, and her life was about to change. Both their lives were about to change.

She gave a heavy sigh and dropped her head into her hands. 'They haven't had the council vote yet, so there's still a chance they won't make me do it.'

'Make *us* do it,' he corrected firmly. Whether or not she liked it, they were in this together.

She sat up straight, her expression morphing from helpless to defiant. 'We can't...we can't just let them play us.'

'It's not playing if we set the rules.'

'We don't have the power to set our own rules. Not with them.' Her laugh was utterly bereft of humour. 'Besides... You don't know me. You're not in love with me. You won't fight to the death for me.'

She held her hands apart and stared at him as if the last condition was the most crucial.

'I'd do *anything* for you—and for our child.'

There must have been something in his voice that reached her heart, because her next question sounded softer, as if he just might have cracked open the doors of possibility.

'Why?'

Everything in him stilled. This was a moment that could

change the rest of his life. It was up to him if it was for the better or, more worryingly, for the worse.

He took her hands in his and looked her straight in the eye. 'I want to be a *parent*.'

The word seemed to resonate. She nodded, sucked in her teeth, wrinkling her brow as she considered him. 'Let me guess… Boarding school as early as they would take you?'

He smiled at how easily she'd made the connection. 'Yup.'

'Snap.'

Their smiles broadened and held long enough for them to exchange a mix of relief and empathy at this shared understanding, but his was swiftly tinged with guilt.

He should tell her the story. The whole story.

He curled his hands into fists, trying and failing to tamp down the vein of pain he'd thought long since extinguished.

Lia wanted to keep the baby, but it was her body. Her life. He respected that. Yet he couldn't forget the fact that his ex-girlfriend had taken matters into her own hands when she'd found out she was pregnant.

They'd been finishing their internships at a hospital in Oxford, filling out application after application for the futures neither of them had been able to wait to begin, when, one day she had casually informed him that she'd fallen pregnant but had 'sorted it'.

He had understood that it was her body, and her choice to make—that she was on the verge of a new life that didn't include a baby and so was he. Yet he would have been happy to support her, make a life with her and their baby. It had hurt that she hadn't wanted to discuss it with him, or considered his feelings in any way just as his parents had done on countless occasions.

'You'll stay with Nanny.'

'You leave for boarding school on Monday.'

'You'll be home in time for six as your father needs you for a father-son photograph for the papers.'

It was why living here was about as close to heaven as it got. *His* life. *His* decisions. *His* future.

But now he was going to be a father.

'What kind of parent do you want to be?'

Lia's question was so quiet it was almost as if she had thought it rather than spoken it.

'A *present* one,' he answered, with enough darkness to make her raise her eyebrows.

She stared at him hard, then looked away—as if his answer had raised a thousand new questions, none of which she knew how to ask.

His had been a soulless upbringing, by parents whose only real interest in having a child had been producing an heir. Job done, they'd left his upbringing to staff—which, to be honest, had been perfectly fine. Perhaps wise beyond his years, he'd never been compelled to seek love where he knew it couldn't and, more to the point, *wouldn't* be returned. Which was why, when his relationship had gone south and his medical internship had been completed, he'd come here to St Victoria—to live an anonymous life as plain old Dr Oliver Bainbridge.

Lia shifted on the bench, then swept her hands across her belly. The reality that their child was growing in there hit him afresh.

He was going to be a father.

A husband, if—

Well, there were a lot of ifs.

If Lia would have him.

If the Karolinskan Crown was satisfied by him.

If he thought he'd be doing the best by his child by marrying her at all.

Because once she found out he came with his own set

of aristocratic baggage that symbiotic link he thought they shared might evaporate as quickly as the morning cloudbursts here did.

Some women—like his ex—simply weren't suited to marrying into a family like his. He closed his eyes at the memory of his parents meeting Sarah. Her lack of a title hadn't made for warm chitchat over the canapés. But, to be fair to his parents, Sarah hadn't exactly been all smiles and how-do-you-dos either. She'd talked about how outdated the aristocracy was, and how large estates like the one he'd grown up on and would one day inherit were shameful symbols of a past mired in inequality and the unfair bias of bloodlines rather than merit.

She'd been rude.

They'd been rude back.

None of it had ended well.

He blamed himself. He should have realised earlier that it would never work.

Moving here had seemed the best way to try and chisel away at a 'to-do' list that had seemed impossible back in England. He really did want to meet a girl and fall in love… have a family of his own. The trouble was, shaking off the darker edges of his past wasn't easily done. It wasn't how he was built, to turn his back on everything.

He'd thought of relinquishing his title, but the anguish he knew it would cause his parents wasn't the sort of pain he wanted to inflict on them. He didn't want to inflict *any* pain on them. He just… He wanted them to understand he was cut from a different cloth. A new cloth. One that didn't need to be edged in gilt or embroidered with his initials.

They weren't bad people—they were just of another generation in a so-called 'class above'. One that dotted its 'i's and crossed its 't's and had five-thousand-acre estates and stately homes that echoed with emptiness when they should be filled to the brim with life, laughter…grandchildren.

He pulled a couple of bottles of water out of the backpack he'd brought from his car—keeping some there was a habit he'd developed when he'd first moved to the hot, tropical island. He offered Lia one and then, after taking a swig of his own, felt an idea hit. The fact he was heir to a dukedom would probably help his stance in whatever the Karolinskan palace thought of him, but it probably wouldn't help with Lia. He had a limited amount of time before she found out who he was, and something told him there was no chance she would agree to marry him until she got to know him.

The *real* him.

He took another swig of water, then said, 'Before you call the palace…how about you and I go out on a date?'

She crinkled her nose and half smiled at him. 'What?'

'You know…' His own grin grew as he continued. 'One of those old-fashioned things. Dinner and a movie?'

She snorted. 'You want to go to the movies?'

He shrugged. 'Your call. Movies. Dinner. A walk on the beach.'

Now she outright laughed. 'Walking on the beach is what got us into this pickle!'

Flashes of their shared night returned to each of them. Their eyes met and the air between them crackled with electricity—a physical reminder of the sexual chemistry they shared.

'Good point.' He got down on one knee, then looked her in the eye, enjoying the return of that crackle of attraction. 'Lia?'

'Yes?' she replied, still wary, but also struggling to keep a smile off her face.

'Would you like to join me for dinner tonight?'

She burst into hysterics. 'Oh, thank God. I thought you

were going to push the marriage thing. I seriously would have to consider moving to a desert island if you were that quick to agree.'

He let the comment lie where it had landed. Between them. He wanted to get married. She didn't. But she'd pushed the door of possibility open just a little bit further.

Just enough space for him to stick his foot in it.

He rose and held out his hand. 'Have you ever been to Anton's Fish Shack?'

CHAPTER SIX

'IS THIS QUESTION eighteen or nineteen?'

Lia shrugged. She was losing count. 'Eighteen?'

Eighteen questions out of twenty and she still hadn't asked the important ones.

Namely, the *Do you really want to marry me?* question. There might be Crown Jewels and ermine capes involved, but there was also the proverbial shotgun.

How could someone marrying a woman under duress ever fall in love with her?

She parted her lips, felt the words surge up her throat and lodge there. She finally managed to squeak, 'Favourite colour?'

'Green.'

'Favourite fish?' Lia gave a pointed nod at the mouthful of fish Oliver was about to bite.

'The one in the film.' Oliver grinned.

'What? *Jaws?*' Lia joked.

'The stripy one that talks and makes jokes.' Oliver shook his head as if it were obvious.

Then he handed her a chip. An extra crispy one. Her favourite.

Lia couldn't help it. She sighed a little. 'You really were destined to be a paediatrician, weren't you?'

He grinned and looked down at the ketchup on his tray,

which he'd squirted in two circles and one arced stripe. In other words, a smiley face. He dunked a chip along the length of the smile, then gave her a cheeky grin. Her heart skipped a beat as she saw a dimple appear. She fought the urge to reach out and touch it with her fingertip.

His smile changed as their eyes met. Softened. Then he licked his lips.

Her heart slammed against her ribcage and her vision blurred everything around her apart from his mouth. Too easily she could imagine climbing over the table and demanding a thousand kisses. Something she never, ever in her life considered doing. Her tongue swept along her own lips. His was a mouth she could easily enjoy kissing for the rest of her life.

Was that enough?

Could lust keep a couple together?

A car horn sounded, jarring her back into reality. This wasn't about lust. It was about love, and whether or not it was something they might ever have. Even more importantly, it was about mutual respect.

She considered the last hour they'd spent down here on the harbour. She pretty much hadn't stopped talking. He drew information out of her like water out of a tap. Not deep, dark feelings, more the tiny little things that made up the woman she was. Loving sapphire-blue—the colour of his eyes—mac and cheese being her favourite comfort food, especially if it was combined with her favourite activity: curling up with a good book on a rainy day.

She'd talked a bit about boarding school, leaving out the part about how achingly lonely she'd found it, and how rejected she'd felt by her father, who'd kept himself holed up in the palace, and her mother, heartbroken after her failed marriage, who had not only left the country, but the hemisphere, and was now pouring herself into a life of charity work on a remote island in Southeast Asia, proactively blocking out the fact she'd ever had a daughter.

She'd admitted to wanting a dog one day, to dreams of starting a vegetable patch because she loved baby carrots. And she'd confessed, with a flush creeping along her cheeks, how much she would love, love, *love* the impossible chance to relive some of her childhood, so that she could experience, 'You know…a childhood.'

Oliver nodded now, as if he'd been taking down the symptoms of an illness, then said, 'You know what they used to call me at school?'

Lia hazarded a guess. 'Doc?'

'Mr Fix-It.'

Lia tried and failed to shove sexy images of the adult Oliver with nothing but a tool belt around his waist, addressing her life's problems. 'Did you have a fix-it kit?'

He shook his head. 'First-aid kit.'

'Seriously?' Wow. Medicine really was his calling.

'It was mostly filled with sweeties and plasters, but…' something dark shadowed his eyes. 'I don't like seeing people in pain. Especially children.'

She felt a depth of compassion in his voice, as if he'd pulled her into his arms and assured her he would do everything in his power never to let her feel pain ever again.

Her phone rang. They both looked at the screen.

Grandmama.

Also known as the Queen.

'Want me to give you some space?'

She picked up the phone but kept her eyes on him and shook her head. If Oliver and she actually agreed to this insane wedding, he'd need to see the vice-like grip the palace could put on a person if it wanted to. It had ended her own parents' marriage. It could easily prevent hers from ever happening.

She put the phone on speaker. 'Hello, Grandmama.'

'Amelia? We've got some notes for you to take down,' her grandmother said, in lieu of something normal, like *hello.*

She rolled her eyes. No need to ask who 'we' was, but for Oliver's sake she did it anyway.

Queen Margaretha rattled off the names of her own press officer, the King's, her father's, and the palace's private secretary.

Her father was on the call, too, but noticeably silent. Tears pricked at the back of Lia's eyes as she wondered what it would've been like if she'd grown up with a father who had actually wanted her around. Who, when she'd been hurting, would have defended her.

She glanced across at Oliver and easily imagined him with a little first-aid kit by his side. One filled with sweeties and plasters. Maybe he still had it. He had, after all, smelt of candy that one magic night that had changed everything.

'Ready?' she whispered, bracing herself for a command to fly home or, just as terrifying, prepare for the Princess Faux Pas Posse to arrive.

'What's that noise? Are we on speaker? Is *he* there?' the Queen asked in their shared native tongue, as if she was asking if a dog had just defiled her throne room.

'Yes. Oliver's here. He is fifty per cent of the equation,' Lia replied in English, with more bravura than she felt.

The Queen cleared her throat, then said in cut-glass English, 'We're ready to announce the wedding. End of the month.'

'But I haven't agreed to it yet!'

'I have,' Oliver said.

Everything in her stilled apart from her eyes, which locked with Oliver's. What was he doing? Undermining her?

'The announcement will come out today,' her grandmother said crisply. 'We've got to act fast to try and blur any confusion about your "premature honeymoon baby".'

Lia's hand flew to her stomach, as if shielding her child from her grandmother's autocratic dictates. 'You've even got the birth story ready?'

Her grandmother made a sound that most people would have thought unbecoming to a queen. 'That's what happens when a princess makes mistakes. The palace is here to fix them. Now. I've spoken with the Duke and Duchess of Banford, and they're quite willing to host any sort of engagement parties that might be required—'

Oliver coughed… Or was he choking? Whatever it was his face had gone much paler than it had been a moment ago.

'Who are the Duke and Duchess of Banford?' Lia asked.

There was the briefest of pauses—one that gave a microscopic hint that somewhere, lurking beneath all that brusque efficiency, her grandmother might actually be feeling some compassion for her. Or maybe she was smirking. Who knew? They weren't exactly the sort of family to sit around the kitchen table and play board games together.

'As you know, the Duke of Banford holds one of England's most honourable seats…' her grandmother began.

Lia made a face at Oliver that she hoped said *I have no idea what she's on about.*

'Amelia?' Her grandmother gave an impatient tut. 'You do know that the man you had your…*dalliance* with is to become the Duke of Banford one day, don't you?'

Oliver shifted uncomfortably.

Oliver was a member of England's aristocracy? What the hell was this? She felt as if she was being trapped in a vice.

Her eyes began blinking so fast that Oliver looked as if he were caught in the flares of a strobe light. She wasn't completely au fait with the British gentry, but even she knew that the Duke of Banford was a mainstay amongst the establishment…which meant Oliver was, too.

And the Duke was rich.

Very rich.

So this wasn't a 'marry rich to save the poor aristocratic family seat' thing.

What the hell was it, then?

Why hadn't he said anything?

As her grandmother continued to talk, she felt as if the words were impaling her. *Heir... Country seat... Impressive estate...*

The wedding would take place at the Harbour Hotel, as it would keep the 'awkward nature of the event' more low-key. The palace would see to the logistics.

'We've scheduled another talk with the Duke and Duchess to settle the matter in an hour.'

Oliver looked everywhere but at her as her grandmother prattled on about how many guests there would be, which socialite magazine would receive exclusive coverage, and on and on.

Lia's bloodstream turned icy cold. She'd known it. Whatever it was they'd shared had been far too good to go any deeper than the one-night stand they'd agreed on.

Weighted sheets of anger, hurt and confusion fell over her in enormous canopies, pressing the oxygen from her lungs as each one landed.

Shakily, she began to rise from the picnic seat.

Oliver took hold of her arm. 'Sit down, Lia. Please.'

'Amelia?' Her grandmother's voice broke through the increasingly thick tropical air that normally signalled a rain shower. 'Perhaps you should ask your…*friend* to step away? Or take the phone off speaker. I'd rather not have him listen in on our private conversation?'

'It's hardly private!' Lia snapped back. 'Seeing as he's going to be *family* in a month's time.'

Oliver winced as she ground out 'family' as if it were a bad word.

A low buzzing began in her ears as her grandmother handed the conversation over to one of the press secretaries, who rattled off a series of dates. Today for the engagement announcement, then a press statement detailing their 'love at first sight' meeting at the gala, where their shared passion for charitable events quickly blossomed into something deeper and, as such, led to their swift decision to marry.

When you knew, you knew—that was the long and short of it.

Lia forced herself to look at Oliver. Had she known the instant she met him that she wanted him?

Yes.

That she loved him?

Her insides crumpled. She didn't know. Her family was led by a king and queen more in love with their obligations to The Crown than one another. Her father had let the monarchy—his parents—destroy his marriage and bully his wife into a modern-day banishment which had culminated in a depression so deep he'd sent his five-year-old daughter off to boarding school, where she had spent years aching for something she had never really been able to name because she'd longed for something she had never known. A happy family. Love.

So, no. The one thing she definitely didn't know anything about was love at first sight. And yet here she was, toeing the same line. Fulfilling her royal duty not to embarrass The Crown on behalf of a nation whose moral compass could never be seen to waver.

She trained her eyes on Oliver's, willing them to tell her

something—anything to assure her that, whatever happened, they could weather the storm.

He looked every bit as rattled as she did.

And then, as if a switch had been flicked, his entire physique changed. He rolled his shoulders back, straightened his spine. He practically glowed with an aura of control. He looked taller, stronger. Capable. Able to surmount each and every hurdle that the palace might put in their way—which was when it hit her.

Oliver was rising to the challenge.

Rather than wanting to run away to another, even more remote island, like she did, he was squaring off with his past. Confronting a childhood of being forced into a box he'd never wanted to be in. He was doing exactly what she'd told him she wanted from a man. Becoming someone prepared to fight to the death for her.

And suddenly—desperately—she wanted this to work.

They clicked. The reason she'd felt safe with him that one wild night was because they knew exactly what the other was made of. Sugar and spice and everything royal. Well… That was what little princesses were made of. She wasn't entirely sure what prospective dukes were made of, but she had four weeks to find out before she married him. If, of course, they came up with an acceptable game plan.

Because that was what this would be. A game of wits. She and Oliver joining forces to fight The Karolinskan Crown for control of their child.

Lia clicked off the phone whilst the press secretary was still in full flow and fixed Oliver with a look that said, *This is what you're asking to be part of. And by 'this' I mean Crazyville.*

'We can do this,' he said. He took her hands in his and with a soft, kind smile. 'We can do this for our child. We can play their game and win.'

A flicker of belief lit in her chest. It was faint and wary, and a thousand shades of nervous, but he was right. This was bigger than either of them. She wasn't just carrying her child. She was carrying *their* child. And that child's future was worth fighting for as a team.

It was time to be brave.

She looked up into his eyes. 'Do you really want to do this?'

'I really want to do this.'

Oliver felt both shell-shocked and shot through with single-minded focus.

He was going to get married.

Correction. He was being told to get married, be stripped of his anonymity and likely have zero control over anything beyond his career over the next month.

He should be feeling as though he'd leapt out of the frying pan and into the fire. Lia was from a family like his. Worse, actually, if that phone call was anything to go by. And the fact that he was giving his father another heir meant the pressure would ramp up on him to return home. Assume some of his father's social duties and, while he was there, take care of the estate.

The bulk of the sprawling estate was tenanted out to farmers, but the manor house was every bit as big as any in those 'how the other half lives' series on television he could never quite get himself to watch.

On top of which, arranged marriages had a long and not very successful history in his family. Everyone stayed married because it was what titled people did, but there was no happiness in it. No joy.

But none of it mattered because he was going to be a father, a parent. And with the first woman to make him feel properly alive again in six years.

Lia was tracing her finger round a set of initials that had been carved into the picnic table. Her body language suggested she still wasn't entirely convinced that getting married was the best of ideas. Without looking up at him, she asked, 'Why didn't you tell me you were a duke?'

'I'm not a duke,' he replied. *'Yet,'* he added, more honestly.

He moved round to her side of the table so that she had to look at him. If he wanted transparency from her, he owed her the same. 'I'm sorry I didn't tell you about the duke thing.'

Lia huffed and rolled her eyes, murmuring something about honesty being a fairly useful policy. She was right.

'I don't like being judged by my title,' he said. 'I want people to judge me for who I am.'

'And just who is that, exactly?'

Oliver ached to pull her in. Soothe her defensiveness away. He was feeling as blindsided as she was, but the shock felt surmountable. Something the two of them could face head-on.

'I'm a paediatrician who loves his job, doesn't love the aristocracy, and is insanely happy that we're going to have a baby.'

There was more, of course. Other chapters in his life that had made him the man he was today.

'And what makes you think we'll work…as a couple?' She turned her hands towards herself. 'It's not like you really know me.'

He thought of their shared night of passion. His hands caressing that sweet dip between her ribcage and hip before he slipped his fingers between her legs. How she'd moaned in pleasure when he'd lowered himself into her. How their orgasms had come at the same time and they'd both laughed with disbelief and pleasure.

He knew elements of her. And once again, for the first time in a long time, he was very much looking forward to getting to know her better.

'That's why we're here, eating fish and chips,' he said instead.

She snorted, clearly not pleased. 'You think a meal out exchanging favourite colours and comfort foods makes us a match?'

'No,' he countered. 'I think whatever it is that made two people who don't do one-night stands have one does.'

She looked at him sharply, then covered her face with her hands. He didn't press. If her brain was whirring as fast as his was, she needed the thinking time.

Eventually, she peeked out at him between her fingers. 'What are we going to do?'

'We're going to get married,' he said.

They'd each managed to escape the grip of the past before. They would be able to do it again. And, as his favourite headmaster had told him on that first bewildering day at boarding school, *'You can do anything for ten seconds.'*

He'd done a lot of things for ten seconds, and then another ten, and another. It had taught him that he could withstand almost anything that was thrown at him. But he knew he wanted more than anything to be with the mother of his child, and be there to support them both, as a family. To be a father.

Lia was staring at him. 'How can you sound so certain?'

'Because I like you,' he said honestly. Then, more to the point, 'And I am not going to leave you stranded in this situation. You didn't get here on your own.' He swallowed against a surge of emotion. 'And I want to be there to raise our child.'

'Don't you want to—?' Again, she stopped herself short, swatting away what looked like her own rush of emotion.

Fall in love? Was that what she was going to ask?

Hell's teeth.

Of course he wanted to love the woman he married. And she was right. He barely knew her. But his hands twitched with a muscle memory that said otherwise. He'd known her body's secret desires well enough. Could he grow to know her heart's?

Time and circumstance were not luxuries they could play with. There was only one way to find out if they were a match. Pour their energies into getting to know one another.

He stood up and gave her a courtly bow, just as his parents had taught him when he'd first met the Queen.

'What do you say we go down to the beach? We can watch the sunset, play another round of Twenty Questions. Do it every hour of every day, if you like. Unless, of course, you have other plans for your evening?'

'Other than preparing my trousseau…not really,' she said with a self-effacing laugh.

'You didn't grow up embroidering your wedding veil for this very moment?' he joked, but instantly knew he'd overstepped the fragile weave of their new relationship as her smile slid into a frown.

Lia swept some strands of hair away from her face before she spoke. Her voice was deadly serious as she said, 'This isn't a fairy tale. You know that marrying me means an end to your quiet, anonymous life, don't you?'

'You're carrying our child. That takes precedence. *You* take precedence.'

A flash of something he couldn't identify flared in her eyes. 'What if I refuse to marry you?'

A blaze of alpha energy shot through him like lightning. There was no chance he would let this second, precious opportunity to become a father be snatched from him.

It took every ounce of self-control to keep his voice level

as he looked her in the eye and said, 'I will love our child with every fibre of my being. I will respect you and honour you. We have a connection. You know that. The only question is, are we brave enough to find out if we can make it into something that will last a lifetime?'

Lia's heart was pounding so hard she could barely register her own thoughts, let alone absorb what Oliver had just said.

He'd look after her. He'd love their child. He'd do his best to care for her.

It wasn't exactly the outpouring of love she'd one day hoped for...but perhaps this was better. Mutual respect and understanding.

Instinct was telling her she would instantly have rejected any declaration of love after so little time knowing one another. It would have rung false and given his every move a sheen of dishonesty. Of wanting something other than to accept his responsibility as a parent. The pain of her parents' rejection had never left her, and heartbreak was something she wasn't sure she could endure again.

She looked deep into Oliver's eyes, exploring the rich kaleidoscope of blues framed by pitch-black lashes, and saw something that moved her on a profound level. He already loved their child. In a handful of time—minutes, really—he'd received two huge life bombs. An unexpected pregnancy and decreed-from-above nuptials. Yet somehow he'd managed to absorb the far more pressing truth: they were going to be parents. And his gut response was love.

It shone a completely different light on the future the palace was trying to superimpose on them. If he was strong enough and brave enough to pull his heart out of his chest and put it on his sleeve in this way, he might have the strength to stand up to her family in a way her mother never could.

Did she have the strength to do the same thing?

She looked at him. Really looked at him. His blue eyes were alive with…what was it, exactly? *Presence.* He was here with her—body and soul—asking her if she would take the same risk he was willing to take in order to ensure their child grew up feeling loved.

She tipped her head to the side, feeling stupidly shy, and asked, 'How do you feel about a fiancée who can't cook?'

His eyes lit up. 'So long as you're happy with toasted cheese sandwiches and orange slices, I'm fine with that.'

It wasn't the most obvious way to say, *I'm in. Let's get married,* but in another one of those silent exchanges they both knew what had just happened.

They were going to get married.

They gave the moment some air, then Oliver reached his hand out to hers, his fingers weaving through hers as if they'd done it a thousand times before. The gesture spoke volumes. They were a team now. They were going to get married and have a child.

Was it terrifying?

Absolutely.

Was her gut telling her to run for the hills? Become a hermit living in a cave somewhere?

Not anymore.

She'd never met a man willing to confront what he knew would be a difficult future hand in hand with her.

'I've got an idea,' he said.

She raised her eyebrows and nodded for him to go ahead.

'Let's shelve all talk about weddings and babies for tonight. Carry on with our date.'

Her chest filled with warm gratitude. There was so much going on in her head right now she was almost too frightened to speak. And he was giving each of them space to digest this tectonic shift in their lives.

After the sun had dipped below the horizon they strolled along the beach, throwing one another the odd 'softball' question. Favourite sport. Least favourite food. Favourite spot on the island. But mostly they lapsed into thoughtful silence as each of them let their new reality settle deep into their bones.

Without having talked about it, they ended up at Oliver's house, with the faintest remains of the sunset still pinking up the sky. She let herself really absorb the place. Whilst from the beach the house appeared to be hanging in the trees, it was actually very firmly built into a sharp rising stone bluff dappled with old-growth trees.

'I like how you can see the sunset on this side of the island,' she said as they made their way up a flight of stairs to the kitchen.

'Tired of the sunrise over on your side of the island, are you?' He stopped mid-step. 'Unless, of course, princesses don't get up that early.' He dropped her a comedic wink to ensure she would know he was kidding.

She rolled her eyes, then said, 'I'll have you know I never sleep. It's all those pesky peas finding their way underneath my mattresses.'

'Mattresses, eh? I only have the one.'

'I remember,' she said airily, a few vivid memories of their night sending a flush to her cheeks.

Oliver's tongue swept along his lips—a clear sign that he remembered their shared night of passion with equal clarity. He ran his index finger along the curve of her cheek. Her breath hitched in her throat as his fingertip reached her lips.

They were halfway between the bedroom and the kitchen. It would be a matter of a few steps to change course and go to his bed.

Oliver abruptly led her into the kitchen. He was right. Tonight was for talking, not confirming what they both already knew. Their sexual chemistry was never going to be a problem.

The kitchen, like the other rooms, was fronted with a long row of floor-to-ceiling retractable glass doors. There was a small native hardwood kitchen table inside, and a much bigger one outside on the covered deck—which, Lia was delighted to see, had two large trees growing through the decking that soared up into the tropical canopy above. The back of the room was a long line of doors.

'I thought there was a cliff back there?'

'Cupboards,' Oliver explained, opening a couple to show her the contents, as if everyone had massive storage areas for food and kitchen implements in their luxury treehouse.

Her version of haute cuisine was pretty much limited to fruit. The staff restaurant at The Island Clinic was staffed by Michelin chefs, and even their casual 'snack food' was on another level.

Beneath three large filament bulbs in the centre of the room a gorgeous sprawl of marble topped a kitchen island, at the centre of which was a lovely fruit bowl. She closed her eyes, imagining what it would be like if she were the type of woman to sweep the bowl off the counter and to replace it with herself.

'Want something to eat?' he asked.

Her eyes flicked open to meet his.

No. She didn't. She wanted him.

He must have seen her hunger for him flare in her eyes and thrown his own reservations into the bonfire, because before she could draw a full breath he was kissing her. Urgently. Possessively. Tenderly.

Their shared energy was urgent and gentle. Generous and hungry. Though their words remained unspoken, they both knew these were precious moments—the ones before the palace descended. There would be staff. Rules. Endless instructions. But this…here and now, before anyone, anywhere, boarded a plane with so much as a solitary fabric swatch…this was their time. Time she wanted to put a glass cloche over and preserve, as if it was the most precious thing in the world.

Though they'd made love before, this time it felt entirely different. As if their bodies were making vows to each other. To care and protect. To adore. To love.

Lia feared drowning in it. Losing herself to the very thing she'd promised herself she'd never do: the Palace's bidding. But Oliver exuded a confidence about their shared future that charged her own faltering belief in herself. This was about *them*, not Karolinska, or his family's title. Just the two of them—and, of course, the child she was now carrying.

With each caress, every kiss he tenderly dropped on her belly, she felt as though she was absorbing his silent promises.

We'll be different. We won't let them change us. We won't let them take away the happiness we want for our child. For our family.

As the energy between them grew more charged, more intimate, she finally allowed herself to give in fully to her own body's longing to offer Oliver the same silent vows.

What the palace didn't know wouldn't hurt them. Would it?

CHAPTER SEVEN

'YOU READY?'

'Not *camera*-ready,' Oliver replied, giving his hair a ruffle that made him look even less so.

Nope. Not so much as a smile. *Okay...* So someone wasn't pleased about the palace photographer tagging along for this 'spontaneous' sailing trip.

'There she is.' Lia pointed to the end of the dock to her sailing boat.

The teak-decked *Island Dreamer* had two huge masts, a dozen rigging lines—at least that was what Oliver thought they were called—and, slightly disconcertingly, only one visible flotation device.

'You're not planning on drowning me at sea, are you?' Oliver joked as he looked at the impressive sailing boat, then back at his bride-to-be.

Bride-to-be.

He shook his head. What a difference one night of passion with a princess made. Well… One night, a month's break and then several more nights, during which both of their worlds had changed completely.

All the things that needed to happen on a practical level—like actually discussing their Harbour Hotel wedding—had yet to happen. It was as if discussing it would make it real, without time to take a breath and think about what they wanted, and they were both feeling bowled over by the Karolinskan palace-led reality.

They'd agreed to sit down and talk about it every night after work. And they had met. Only there hadn't been much talking. Without so much as a whisper of a decision about what type of flowers they'd like, or what flavour of cake they wanted, they'd end up in bed. Which, to be fair, was no bad thing. It was not entirely useful when it came to answering the palace's never-ending stream of emails… but it seemed to be the one thing they could cling to that was solely theirs.

Today, however, was different. Today was 'palace-sanctioned.' The family's official photographer had arrived. Tomorrow the wedding planning team would set up camp at the same hotel where they'd had the gala. It was where Oliver and Lia had met, and it had been deemed 'the most suitable' location.

Today was their first 'accidentally on purpose' photo shoot, and Lia was as skittish as a highly bred racehorse. As beautiful as ever, but…less accessible. And he was feeling the loss of their shared connection. If it was a sign of what was to come for them—a withdrawal of her affection whenever the palace was involved—he wasn't entirely sure their future would be as rosy as he'd hoped.

But he pushed his concerns about shared custody and having to move to Karolinska to ensure he'd have a relationship with his child to the side. They weren't there yet, and with any luck they never would be.

Lia laughed at his feeble quip, but her eyes remained on the sailing boat. 'Consider yourself lucky. I don't take just anyone out on her.'

'No? Why not?'

'It's my happy place. Once that tether's undone, it's just me, myself and I.'

Her expression remained the same, but the ghost of a shadow darkened those light blue eyes of hers—as if she were remembering countless other places that made her sad.

Oliver winced in sympathy as an instinctual tug of protectiveness leapt to the fore. Though they'd not spoken about it explicitly, he knew their childhoods, although hundreds of miles apart, had been remarkably similar. Hers had compelled her to choose the life of a loner, to keep the pain at bay, whereas he had thrown himself into the fray. He had always loved bringing joy and happiness to others.

A niggling thought surfaced. Had *all* his happiness been by proxy?

She caught him looking at her. His expression must have still been caught in the wince, because she added a mischievous, 'Don't worry. Only people I genuinely like are allowed aboard. There are more flotation vests down in the cabin.'

Her eyes left his and travelled to the two sails bound tight against the masts. One was a deep blue, the other brilliant white. The colours of the Karolinskan flag. So there was some national pride in her. But not any sense of freedom.

He wondered if there would ever be a day when the two could be combined. When she could do her royal duty, but also feel she was living the best version of herself. He stopped short of wondering the same thing for himself. The family seat had always felt like a mausoleum to him. He was dreading the inevitable question his brief chats with his parents were building towards.

When will you come home?

He scanned the length of the boat until his eyes hit the stern, and there it was, the royal family's crest emblazoned on a blue and white flag, fluttering in the light breeze, giving the odd snap to attention, as if it was aware Lia was about to board.

His own family's crest wasn't dissimilar. A lion, an axe and a dragon were all shared symbols. Things that ruled with might. Hers, however, beneath the golden crown, also bore the scales of justice.

She caught him examining the crest. 'Hope you like it. They'll be stitching it into your boxers before long. "Property of the Karolinskan Crown."'

His clipped laugh matched the dark humour of her comment. Just the reminder he needed that they weren't alone.

He swung his duffel bag onto the deck of the boat and said, 'I hope the clothes I've brought please The Crown.'

He'd been running late, so hadn't given much thought to the clothes he'd stuffed into it. His mother would have been horrified. She planned the look of their family portraits for months beforehand, so in fairness his boxers—at home, at least—really did symbolically bear the Banford crest sometimes. But the rest of the year he was plain old Oliver Bainbridge. And he liked it that way.

As if a knife had been abruptly shunted between his ribs, Oliver absorbed the reality that the minute he became Lia's husband all of that would change…

Too late, he realised that he was frowning, and that Lia had noticed.

She bit down on her lower lip and gave it a chew, as if debating whether or not to tell him something. Clearly something that had been weighing on her.

It had only been a few days since they'd learnt about her pregnancy, but so much had happened since then. Press releases had been written and lists of the things they had to do to make the 'party line' from the Karolinska press office bear weight had been issued. Which was why, after another full day in surgery for Lia and full office hours at the hospital for him, they were down here at the private yacht club for a photo shoot.

It was meant to look as if they were casual snaps of the couple caught by surprise, but Oliver was swiftly learning how pre-planned the rest of his life might be.

He reached out and touched Lia's arm, warm with the late-afternoon sun. 'Are you all right, Lia?'

'Absolutely.'

Her voice was light, but there was something behind it. Something she wasn't saying.

He took her hand in his and tipped his head towards the entrance of the small yacht club, where the photographer was already standing, multiple lenses slung round his neck. 'We don't have to do this.'

'Yes,' she replied with a *This is precisely what I warned you about* smile, 'we do.'

She gently tugged her hand free and made a move to board the boat.

She turned suddenly, her body language radiating defensiveness. 'Unless you're having second thoughts?'

Her tone was sharp, remonstrative in a way he wouldn't have expected from someone who was almost literally in the same boat as him.

'I'll never have second thoughts about being a father to my child.'

Her entire body grew taut with coiled energy. He'd clearly said the wrong thing. But with a photographer a handful of metres away, this wasn't the time to have it out, so he stuffed his hands in his pockets, his fingers catching on the small square box he hadn't told Lia about.

It wasn't a traditional engagement ring. It was an eternity ring. A symbol he hoped would remind her, every time she looked at it over the coming months, that the child she was carrying would link them together for ever.

She glanced at her watch. 'C'mon. Let's get this over with.'

An hour later the photographer had what he needed and they sailed out of the protected harbour area and beyond the island. Though the shoreline was still within view, the holidaymakers on the beach appeared as tiny figurines on a film set representing yet another perfect day on St Victoria. The only thing missing was the happy atmosphere that Lia had intimated would exist once they'd been 'caught' in an embrace as they prepared the boat for departure.

She'd changed clothes and poses three times in order to give the palace photographer plenty of material to work with. Shorts and a T-shirt. A sundress dotted with poppies. And now a pair of figure-hugging navy pedal-pushers with a blue and white scarf standing in as a belt and a white shirt, knotted at her belly button, sleeves rolled up to her elbows and, a bit disconcertingly, unbuttoned to that sweet spot just at the arc of her breasts.

It was teasing at the memories Oliver had of last night… giving her nipples hot, swift licks, then drawing them into his mouth for another swirl and a light rasp of his teeth as she groaned her approbation.

There was no such sensuality in the atmosphere today, let alone the primal hunger they'd shared. The past hour had felt impersonal in a way that had surprised him. Lia had directed him, *sotto voce*, to kiss her shoulder as she looked out into the middle distance, or to turn his face in a particular direction so the light was right when they looked into one another's eyes before untying the yacht from the dock.

Now, with the sails loosed from the masts and easily catching the breeze, the boat looked utterly resplendent. Free. He looked at Lia, standing at the steering wheel with the wind in the strands of white-blonde hair that hadn't been caught in the knot at the nape of her neck, and he saw the woman he'd originally met at the charity function. One too aware of all eyes being on her. Of judgement being cast without consideration for her feelings. She seemed trapped in a cage.

He looked over to the small speedboat that had followed them out of the harbour. It sounded its horn and then turned back to shore.

When he looked at Lia again, and their eyes met, he wasn't sure who he was looking at. Not the woman who had danced in his arms and kissed him on the beach. But nor was it the *Look that way*, media-savvy, aloof princess she'd been the past hour.

A part of him wanted to pull her into his arms and tell her that as long as they did things together—as a team—they'd be fine. But this photo shoot had unleashed an uncertainty in him that he was finding hard to shake. He felt as though he'd been pushed a cool arm's length away from Princess Amelia and he didn't like it.

He wanted Lia, who had walked with him in the rain last night, talking about her surgeries. The woman who'd made love to him in the outdoor shower before seductively slipping under the bedcovers and beckoning him with impossible-to-resist bedroom eyes.

Not this picture-perfect bride-to-be. Laughing on cue. Colouring slightly as he cupped her cheek in his hand. Lips virtually frozen as they pressed to his for a slow-motion peck while the shutters of the palace camera whirred and clicked away.

He forced himself to backpedal. His own annual Christmas, Easter and summer holiday portraits were hardly bursts of spontaneous familial affection. He'd been lucky in that the nannies and boarding schools his parents had chosen for him had been a welcome substitute. He had plenty of friends and mentors from school that he was still in touch with to this day.

Perhaps Lia hadn't had even that. Her parents were divorced. From what he could gather she rarely spoke to her father, and she hadn't so much as mentioned her mother. She'd eagle-eyed a fellow boarding school kid in him, so had clearly done her own stint there, and then, of course, boot camp with the Karolinskan army. That wouldn't have been a touchy-feely thing, even for a princess.

And yet, warrior that she was, the palace still clearly wielded enough power to make her bend to their will to an extent—and that was where the heart of his uncertainty lay.

He jammed his hands in his pockets, and once again his fingertips butted against the small square box. He'd planned to slip the ring on Lia's finger back at the yacht club, suspecting the photographer would be looking for some sort of sparkle befitting a princess, but it hadn't felt right. In the same way staying in England and following his parents' model of living by the rules of tradition hadn't felt right.

A niggle of discomfort wedged between his conscience and his discomfort with Lia over the past hour. He'd left the life he'd been 'born to live' thousands of miles away, just as Lia had. But now that they were going to be parents running away wasn't an option. They had to find a shared strength that would shield their child from repeating the pattern.

'Oliver?'

He turned as Lia waved to get his attention.

'Could you help me with this sail?'

He frowned and apologised. 'Sorry. Away with the fairies.' He looked at the sail. 'Should you be hoisting that? In your condition?'

'I'm not made of bone china. I'm pregnant,' she said, visibly offended.

'I know… I just thought maybe you should take things easy.'

'I'm not going to take to my bed for the next eight

months, if that's what you're thinking.' Her eyes blazed with indignation, then lowered to half-mast as she inspected him, no doubt wondering if marrying him was the last thing she should do.

He wanted to defend himself when suddenly, just like that, he saw her taut, emotionally withdrawn behaviour for what it really was. Frustration with not having a say in her own life. An ache for exactly the same thing he wanted: a normal, happy life.

She must have sensed his empathy because her expression softened. 'Sorry. I'm not really good at being told what to do.'

'I get it,' he said.

'I know. Of all the people in the world who would get it, you are one of them.' She gave a self-effacing laugh and threw him an apologetic look. 'I feel like you see right into my brain sometimes.'

'No.' He shook his head. 'I see right into this.' He pointed at her heart.

She took his hand and laid it on her chest until, sure enough, he felt her heart's rapid cadence through the light fabric of her top.

'I promise I'll be careful. That I'll protect this little one.' She moved their hands to her belly.

They shared a smile that instantly swept his fears away. There she was. Lia the Princess who didn't want to be a princess. The woman who wanted to be a mother…and, hopefully, a wife.

'Here.' He took the line from her and tugged the sail up. 'Think of me as your chief galley man.'

She laughed and said, 'You'd be making lunch if that was the case. How about first mate?'

'Sounds good.' He tied the rope off under her instructions and gave her a salute.

She feigned wiping sweat off her brow and gave him a sheepish smile. 'Sorry if I've been vile. I hate photo shoots.' She shot him a playful smirk. 'And we're going to have to work on your happy-go-lucky look. You looked stiff as board!'

She cackled, then, as if she were a balloon that had unexpectedly popped, suddenly deflated.

'That was awful,' she said. 'You're going to walk away before the month is over, aren't you?'

He shook his head. 'I'll never walk away. You have my word on that.'

She sought his eyes for any hint of wavering. Obviously finding none, she leant in to give him a sweet, soft kiss that filled him with a honeyed warmth.

'I'm sorry I was a pain,' she whispered against his lips. 'I'm not used to someone having my back.'

That admission spoke volumes. Just as he'd built an enormous fortress round his heart after his ex had had her abortion, Lia kept people at arm's length because it was safer than risking the disappointment of being let down.

Brick by brick, she was opening up his fortress.

Millimetre by millimetre, she was letting him in.

He pulled her to him, one hand on the small of her back, one hand cupping her cheek, and kissed her again. More deeply this time. More meaningfully.

I'm here for you, the kisses said. *You are not alone. You'll never be alone again.*

Eventually, they drew apart, the demands of the boat taking precedence over their urge to let the rest of the world melt away.

'Want to teach me how this thing works?' he asked.

They spent a companionable hour or so, working their way through all the boating terminology. And between learning about winches, pushpins, transoms and jammers, he became aware that their bodies organically sought each other's.

The light brush of a hand… Their legs pressing together when they sat side by side… Their eyes catching and heat passing between them as if they were actually sharing energy…

They were far out enough that they also saw a lot of wildlife. Dolphins…some porpoises. Even a turtle or two.

'Ever seen a manatee?' he asked.

She shook her head. 'They're usually in the mangroves, and I tend to stick to the boat rather than the dinghy.'

He looked for and clocked the small RIB attached to the back of the boat. 'Do you ever use it?

She shook her head. 'Not really. I prefer the power of the wind to motorised power.'

'It's definitely more peaceful this way.'

She tipped her head to his shoulder and they stayed like that for a while, her hair occasionally tickling his cheek, their little fingers touching, then linking. They'd be all right, Oliver thought. There would be bumps and troughs along the way, but…they'd be all right.

'Now,' Lia said after they'd brought the boat around to a quieter side of the island, away from the tourist beaches. She turned a knob on the control panel and pointed at the speaker built into the console. 'Are you ready to learn the radio lingo?'

'Absolutely.' Oliver gave her a crisp salute. 'At your service, Captain.'

She grinned, the bridge of her nose wrinkling just enough to give him a glimpse of what she might have looked like as a little girl, before her parents' divorce. Happy, light, carefree. He made a silent vow to provide her with a future where she could honour that little girl.

Give her a second chance to forge a new life for herself and, of course, for their own child.

'Oliver—' Lia's expression changed as she turned up the volume on the radio.

'What?'

'Listen.'

He focused in on the voices on the radio. 'It sounds like a distress call.'

'It is. It's the coastguard. They're on the far side of the island and they…' She paused and leant in to listen. 'It's kayakers. They've got caught in the currents and ended up somewhere around here. In the mangroves, I think. It sounds like one of them needs urgent medical attention.'

'Can we get there?' He looked up at the vast sails, knowing there was no chance they'd get into the thickly forested inlets.

'We can in that.' She pointed at the RIB.

Lia's military training kicked into high gear. She was relieved to note that Oliver worked swiftly and efficiently.

'Two years in a paediatric A&E,' he explained, when she asked if he'd had any emergency training.

'Hopefully you won't need it,' she said grimly as they anchored the boat.

They lowered the sails, tied them off, then quickly got the RIB into the water.

'Do you know the mangroves?' she asked.

He nodded in the affirmative. 'I've taken my kayak in there a lot.'

'You direct, then,' Lia said, taking up a post at the motor.

As they fastidiously made their way through the maze, eyes peeled for the kayakers, they heard shouting.

Nothing prepared them for what they saw.

Two young women—maybe in their late teens—were

in a double kayak. One of the girls was screaming and waving her hands at Lia and Oliver. The second was lying face-down in the small area between the seats, her paddle slipping into the water.

'Barracudas!' screamed the girl. 'We were watching the barracudas jump and then one hit Stephanie!'

Lia's vision clicked into slow-motion frames of information.

The injured girl, Stephanie, had an open wound on her left side, in the gap between the front and back pads of her flotation device. Her lung was visible through her ribs.

After ensuring that the fish were gone, Oliver jumped out of their RIB and began tying the girls' kayak to it. He waded through the waist-deep water and, after pulling on a pair of clean surgical gloves, asked for a moment's silence.

When Lia heard the gurgle indicating a puncture in Stephanie's lung, her first thought was that they were moments away from calling a time of death.

'How long ago did this happen?' she heard Oliver ask.

'Ten minutes ago, maybe?' the frightened girl answered, tears openly pouring down her cheeks.

'What's your name?' Lia asked, her emergency medical training finally clicking into gear, as Oliver's already had.

'Mary.'

'Okay, Mary. Let's get you aboard the RIB.'

Oliver asked Lia for the first aid kit they'd brought along. It was a proper military EMT run bag that she'd used back in her training days, and she'd never been more glad of her precautionary measures to keep it rather than just the customary plasters and paracetamol.

'What's faster?' Lia asked Oliver. 'Getting to shore or sailing back round to the harbour?'

'We can take the RIB in through the mangroves. There's a small docking area not far from here.'

'Can a helicopter land there?'

'Yes. You ring the rescue crew and I'll get Stephanie into the RIB for a needle decompression.'

Lia nodded her agreement. If the injury had happened an hour ago, the girl would have had only a three per cent chance of survival. As things stood, they were at the beginning of the so-called 'golden hour'. They had about fifty minutes to ensure she would survive.

After Oliver had put several large bandages round the open wound, protecting it for the transfer, Lia asked Mary to hold the phone, which was on speaker mode, so she could speak to the coastguard while they gently transferred Stephanie to the RIB.

'She's suffering from a tension pneumothorax,' Lia explained to the woman on the end of the phone.

'What does that mean?' Mary wailed.

As Lia spoke to the emergency services, Oliver explained to Mary that the trauma to Stephanie's lung had trapped air in her pleural cavity—the space between the lungs—and that they had to release it in order to ensure the rest of the body received oxygen.

It was more complicated than that, but Lia appreciated Oliver's attempt to simplify the complicated-sounding situation. The pleural cavity, once filled with air, would cause Stephanie's left lung to collapse, which would then put pressure on her heart, reducing cardiac output, which would make breathing next to impossible and induce tachycardia. Surviving the domino effect of an untreated pneumothorax was impossible.

Half listening to Oliver as she spoke with the coastguard, Lia was impressed with the quick efficiency with which he both worked and talked. He didn't use vocabulary that would alienate Mary. His voice was calm and soothing. He was someone you would trust in an emergency. Someone you would entrust with your child.

'Which hospital?' the woman on the end of the phone asked.

'The Island Clinic,' Lia said.

At the same time Oliver said, 'St Victoria.'

'We have a landing pad—'

Again their voices overlapped.

An ominous sound came from Stephanie's lung. 'You choose,' Oliver said.

There was no doubt that any more time wasted was at this poor girl's peril.

The operator chose for them. 'There's a helicopter already en route to The Island Clinic with a VIP patient in it.'

Time was not their friend. And Lia had no idea what the patient on the helicopter needed. Her hesitation spoke volumes.

The emergency operator said, 'After the drop-off it can come and collect you, but it would be faster to bring her to the hospital. Is that acceptable?'

'Very,' Lia confirmed.

While the facilities at The Island Clinic were well beyond first rate, St Victoria was a great local hospital. It also had an emergency room, and it was closer to the hotel which had its name emblazoned on the girls' kayak. More importantly, this was no time to play 'My Clinic's Better Than Your Hospital'.

'What's a tension pneumonia?' Mary asked, as if absolutely nothing Oliver had said had registered.

She was shivering, the shock of the incident clearly taking root.

'Pneumothorax,' Oliver quietly corrected, handing her an emergency foil blanket, despite the heat of the day.

He began his explanation again in a low voice, so Lia could finish up her phone call with the emergency services.

Lia pocketed the phone after the rendezvous point had been confirmed and they'd settled Stephanie onto her uninjured right side.

'Why aren't we going?' Mary fretted.

'We just need to do this quick release of trapped oxygen and then we'll be off,' Oliver explained.

Lia handed him an eight-millimetre fourteen-gauge needle. His eyes caught hers.

'The military recommends the longer length,' she explained.

Military training had not only toughened her up, it had given her access to learn extensive emergency medical treatment, including the latest methods of pre-hospital pneumothorax treatment. Unfortunately, gunshot wounds and stabbings were part and parcel of active duty—and, more to the point, precisely why the palace had forbidden her from serving in a conflict zone.

'No flash chamber,' Oliver commented as he swept an alcohol disinfectant pad over the spot between Stephanie's second intercostal space and the mid-clavicular line where the catheter needle would release the trapped air.

'No need for this type of injury,' she said. 'It means you don't have to think about it.'

He made a noise, as if he was impressed by the forethought, and then got to work. A swift, accurate needle decompression was the only thing that would save this girl's life.

Within seconds the sound every doctor wanted to hear mixed with the softly cadenced noise of water lapping against the side of the boat: the hiss of released air.

Oliver removed the needle but left the catheter in place. Lia took the needle from him and secured it in a proper disposal box. She handed him some tape and he secured the catheter, so that it would continue to act as a valve for any trapped air. They might have to repeat the process, but for now it seemed to have done the trick. Long enough, at least, for them to get the girl to the air ambulance, where she would be able to get an oxygen mask and other critical assistance.

'Are you ready for me to start the engine?' Lia asked, not wanting to literally rock the boat if he needed it to be still.

'Yes, we're good.' He gave her a nod, his eyes still on Stephanie, two fingers pressed to her pulse point.

She noted a small flush of colour begin to return to the girl's cheeks. They were out of the woods for now.

An hour later, having hitched a ride with the air ambulance crew back to the hospital, Mary, Lia and Oliver were sitting side by side in the waiting room of the St Victoria Hospital, waiting to hear a full report from the emergency team who were in with Stephanie now.

They saw a couple rush in towards the main desk, their faces frantic with worry, and heard them ask after Mary Thewliss and Stephanie Thomas.

'That'll be Mum and Dad, then,' Oliver said, already rising.

Mary ran to them and fell into their arms, crying again, telling them how frightening it had been, and how two people had come to help. She turned and pointed them out.

Lia and Oliver crossed to the couple, who introduced themselves as Stephanie's parents. 'We're ever so grateful you saved her life.'

'Well,' Oliver said humbly, 'we got her to the right place anyhow.'

Alive, Lia thought grimly.

After an incident such as Stephanie had been through,

a patient would always end up here, but if they hadn't been as close as they had…

She shuddered, not wanting to go there.

'Will she live?' Stephanie's mother asked, barely waiting for an answer as she turned on her husband, berating him for letting the girls go out in the kayak.

Just as quickly, she began explaining their life story. They were in St Victoria on holiday, to celebrate the girls' graduation from college. The two of them were best friends—had been since they were young. Couldn't separate them for love nor money. They were even going to the same university. But the girls found everything interesting—*too* interesting—and this was what came of exploring unknown territories. She *knew* they should have stayed in the UK and gone camping. Inland. Where it was safe.

Lia was impressed with the compassion Oliver displayed as he listened and nodded, assuring Stephanie's parents that, pending any unforeseen complications, their daughter would be absolutely fine and have one heck of a story to tell.

Then, after the arrival of the team of doctors who had been cleaning and closing Stephanie's wounds, Oliver and Lia were free to go.

'What do you want to do about the boat?' Oliver asked.

Lia squinted out at the setting sun. Night came early in the tropics and, given how much adrenaline they'd shot in the past couple of hours, she wasn't up for night sailing.

'I can borrow a trailer from the yacht club and pick up the dinghy tomorrow. I'll go out and get the boat after work.'

'I can help,' Oliver volunteered.

She was about to protest, to say she could sort it, but then she reminded herself that this was the man who had put up with her being completely impossible during the photo shoot.

As if Oliver had seen her hesitation—the mix of longing and fear—he gave her arm a squeeze, then took a step back as if to give her room to think, 'You know, I'm actually spending tomorrow at The Island Clinic. I could…if you're happy for me to drive you home…stay there? Maybe try your famed takeaway?'

She was ready to protest again. So far they'd only gone into the clinic grounds under the cover of darkness, and had never appeared as a couple.

She was about to say no when she experienced a lightbulb moment.

Perhaps one of the reasons she found it difficult to make friends was because she'd become too used to protecting her privacy. Too quick to push people away before they could do the same to her. She'd never let previous boyfriends come to her flat, let alone the palace, always finding one excuse or another to keep them at arm's length. Oliver had yet to come to her little cottage on the clinic's grounds.

Her new reality dug its fingers in. If she wanted this marriage to work, she was going to have to find a way to trust Oliver. The palace was clearly on board. Oliver was obviously over the moon about becoming a father. So what else did she need?

Love.

It was what she'd ached for her entire life. Someone to lean on through thick and thin, and not to fear the moment when they stepped away.

She looked at Oliver as he excused himself to sign a couple of papers before they left the hospital. He was kind. Smart. Funny. He definitely fancied her. And he could read her mind. If there was anyone in the world she could fall in love with, he would be a top candidate.

So why wasn't she head over heels right now?

Fear.

Bone-deep terror that he was only marrying her out of duty, for the chance to have an heir for his own family seat, that one day the palace would do to him what it had done to her mother—drive him away, never to return.

Before she could let the ever-increasing mountain of fears consume her, he finished his paperwork, came over and gave her shoulder a squeeze. 'So? What do you think? Shall we head over to your side of the island tonight?'

Crikey. He really could read minds.

She gave a slightly over-enthusiastic nod and said, 'Sounds good.'

'You look thrilled, but you don't *sound* thrilled,' Oliver observed with an easy laugh.

She elbowed him and tried to tease away her nerves with a white lie. 'How will we explain everything in the morning?'

'Well…' He tapped his chin, as if he was giving the matter some serious thought. 'We could tell them I'm actually working for the Karolinskan Secret Service and I'm part of your new Nocturnal Protection Team.'

She laughed. The tight knot of worry in her chest loosened. She could do this. *They* could do this.

The arrival of a brightly coloured shuttle bus caught her eye. It was the free shuttle The Island Clinic provided to bring nurses and doctors and other staff the forty-minute ride between facilities.

As they were without a vehicle, she pointed towards the bus and said, 'Shall we take my horse and carriage? It's got to be home by midnight.'

'With pleasure.'

As if he'd done it a thousand times, he reached for her hand. Her initial instinct was to tug it away. Keep what was happening between them private. But the press release and photos of them as a 'happy couple' would be out the next morning…

So she gave his hand a squeeze and together they boarded the bus.

CHAPTER EIGHT

‘THIS TILAPIA IS AMAZING.’

Lia nodded, her mouth dancing with the myriad of flavours in yet another success from The Island Clinic restaurant. ‘Not a bad place to get takeaway, is it?’

Oliver nodded his agreement, took another bite, then asked, ‘Do you never eat in the restaurant?’

She shook her head. ‘No’.

His eyes widened. ‘Why not? Don’t you like eating with your friends?’

Well, this was awkward. She didn’t really have any.

She tried for a jokey response. ‘You know how it is… trying to fight a reputation for being a picky princess.’

‘What?’ he said with mock shock. ‘You were lying about the peas the other day?’

She quirked her head to the side, not connecting the dots.

‘The other day,’ he said, trying to jog her memory. ‘You made a comment about the peas underneath your mattresses.’

Before she could answer, he put his fork down on the gorgeous wood table situated in the private garden behind her house.

‘Lia,’ he said. ‘I will never know exactly what your childhood was like, but I do know what it’s like to grow up having everyone expect you to act a certain way.’

A welcome surge of connection sent a warmth through her. How did he always know the perfect thing to say?

'It's exhausting, isn't it? Trying to behave one way to counter what you think everyone is saying about you.'

'It's why I moved here,' he admitted cheerfully. 'It's been bliss being plain old Dr Bainbridge.'

She scrunched her nose. 'But you're not plain old Dr Bainbridge, are you?'

'To my patients I am,' he said. 'And to my friends. There really aren't very many people who think of me as the future Duke of Banford—except perhaps my parents and maybe some cousins.' He sat back in his chair and gave her a decidedly wicked smile. 'I hope *you* think of me as something slightly less formal than Dr Bainbridge.'

'Only slightly?' she teased.

'Dramatically,' he conceded, and then, more thoughtfully, 'Seriously, Lia. Apart from the obvious—you, me and the baby—I don't want you to think about me as a duke or even a doctor. I want you to think of me as the man you met at the gala.'

'Gosh,' she sighed. 'All I've *ever* wanted is for people to think of me as a doctor.'

'From what I hear round the clinic, you've got exactly what you wanted.'

The words weren't meant to wound her, but they did.

He was right. Here at the clinic Dr Amelia Trelleburg, neurosurgeon, was the only side of herself she'd ever let people see. Meticulous, serious, solely focused on her work.

She'd been thrilled to be hand-picked by the clinic's founder, Dr Nate Edwards. He'd brought in specialists from around the world and had created an egalitarian environment where no one peacocked or demanded special treatment. They were all here to pour their energies into their shared passion: healing people. And she loved it.

She'd thought that was all that would ever be needed from her—her skills. But three years in she saw that all she'd succeeded in doing was compartmentalising herself. Locking herself away during her non-working hours so that she never had to risk being rejected. Except, of course, for that one night of lust-filled bliss with Oliver.

The truth exploded inside her like a healing tonic. She was the only one standing in the way of receiving the love she so desperately craved.

She looked at Oliver, so kind and generous. Patient. The man was made of patience. And she'd be a fool to test its outer limits.

Right. She could do this. She could be honest. Open. Share private stuff.

She put down her fork and looked him in the eye, forcing herself to think of the 'Amelia trivia' she'd only ever imagined telling her husband.

'Did you know I trained with the military but my family refused to let me serve?'

He nodded.

That wasn't exactly a huge revelation, so she added. 'I was furious at first. So angry I actually considered cutting and dying my hair and going off to battle in disguise.'

He smiled at the thought. 'Did you have the disguise planned?'

'No,' she admitted. 'It was a pretty short-lived rebellion.'

It had been minutes, really. Seconds… She'd given in quite quickly. Too quickly for someone who claimed to want control of her own life.

'What changed?' Oliver asked, steering her away from darker thoughts.

'I found neurosurgery.'

'That hadn't been your chosen field?'

'Not initially. It was combat medicine.'

'That explains your incredible first-aid run bag.' He smiled and gave her a fist-bump.

She giggled with childlike delight. No one fist-bumped princesses. She could see herself getting into this sharing and caring thing. With Oliver, anyway.

And that's the whole point, you numbskull. He's your safe place.

'What is it about neurosurgery that you love?' he asked.

'Giving someone back the power to make their own decisions,' she answered without a moment's hesitation.

Helping people at their most vulnerable—when their crucial decision-making 'machine' was faulty—was an incredible honour. The people who trusted her to perform surgery on them humbled her on a daily basis. If she could build on this…invest the same amount of trust in Oliver as her patients invested in her…they would be invincible.

Their eyes met and locked, and in that moment Lia felt nothing but possibility blossom between the pair of them. Her hand swept to her stomach, and when she looked up she saw his eyes had followed the movement.

'Want to touch?'

He reached across and she put his hand on her belly, resting her hand over his.

They shared the moment in silence and then, naturally, their hands slid apart and they both sat back in their chairs.

'What about you?' she asked. 'Why did you pick paediatrics?'

His expression sobered, then lightened with the thoughtfulness she'd seen in him before. 'A bit like you, I think. I wanted to give children a sense of safety in a place that can be scary. Like boarding school.'

Lia shuddered. '*Bleurgh*. I hated boarding school. Didn't you?'

He shook his head. 'No. Total opposite.'

He gave her a look that said, *I'm going to share something with you that I don't tell most people.*

'It was so much easier for me to be away from my parents than with them. I love them, because they're my parents, but they do not love being parents—and, as a result, they don't really know how to love me.'

Lia sucked in a sharp breath. How awful. It was a different scenario from her own.

Oliver gave her arm a squeeze, as if she was the one who needed consoling and said, 'I don't know why, but I never took it personally. My parents lack...' He looked out into the starlit sky beyond the palms fringing the garden, as if it would provide him with the perfect word. 'They lack the *comfort* that should come from loving someone. Being loved. It's as if they think loving me would make them vulnerable. Weak... So, believe me, I thought boarding school was great. It wasn't just a home away from home. It *was* home. And as I grew older I always saw it as my job to make sure the littler kids felt welcome, too. Not everyone wanted to be away from home as much as I did, but there were a lot of kindred spirits there.'

'I'm so sorry.'

'Don't be. Honestly.' Oliver's expression was genuine. 'I really was better off there.'

Lia had absolutely no idea how he could have emerged from such a cold upbringing as warm and kind as he was. Her parents' marriage had been an unmitigated disaster, but somewhere in there—way back when—she knew it had been founded on love.

When interference from the palace had eventually torn them apart, her father had been drained of any fight he'd once had. And with that loss any love he'd had for Lia had also drained away. She almost literally felt the room turn icy whenever she entered one and saw him there.

A sudden insight into how painful her parents' marital breakdown must have been for her father came to her. Perhaps he hadn't sent Lia to boarding school because he'd hated her. Maybe he'd pushed her away because she'd reminded him of the man he'd used to be.

A rush of affection for her father strained against her heart. Thanks to Oliver's birthright, Lia was going to have a palace-sanctioned chance to have the family her father never could. She wondered if reaching out to him might be the right thing to do, or if her happiness would only make him angrier.

Lia put the idea to Oliver.

He thought for a moment, as she was learning he always did, then said, 'As long as you feel you're strong enough for the possibility that he might not want the same thing you do, I'd say it's worth the risk. And remember you've got me in your corner.'

He did a little boxing move to back the comment up.

'I wish I'd met you years ago,' she blurted.

Something passed through Oliver's eyes that she couldn't identify. A similar wish? Or something brighter that spoke to their shared future.

'That would've been nice,' he said finally.

'I'm sorry your parents didn't make you feel happy at home,' she continued, wanting him to know that she got it. She understood the pain. 'I think it's amazing that you made lemonade out of lemons. I wish I could've done the same. I'd give anything to have a second chance to try and fix it.'

'Hey…' Oliver soothed. 'We all have different sets of clay to work with, and you did what you could with yours. What happened between your parents had nothing to do with you. It's important to look at the positive things in your life. It seems to me you're pretty happy here. You've got your boat. You obviously love your work. You've got me.' He grinned, then turned serious. 'Don't wish away the things you *do* have for things that are out of your control.'

He was right, of course. But common sense was not a fix for a little girl's dreams of a happy childhood.

'I am grateful for everything I have. Truly. I know so many people have it much worse than me. But…there are a couple of things I still wish for,' she said, in a small voice she barely recognised.

'Like what?'

'I wish that we could've got engaged the normal way, for one.' She shot him an apologetic smile.

'What's "normal" these days?' Oliver countered. 'Do you know how many people hunger for exactly what you have? The media at your fingertips… A job at an exclusive clinic… A palace to go home to for the holidays…'

She barked out a laugh, remembering the long list of public appearances that her holidays required. They were more like working holidays than actual breaks. 'If only they knew the reality.'

'Oh, c'mon.' He nudged her toe with his. 'Even though it didn't get a storybook start, life with me isn't going to be that awful. I promise.'

She grinned at him. As far as arranged marriages went… he was right. 'I suppose you're not so bad. Insofar as blokes who live in a treehouse go.'

'Hey! That's our family home you're speaking about,' Oliver protested, his broad smile betraying the pride he felt in his home.

The comment jarred. They hadn't discussed that.

She was about to say she actually preferred the guaranteed privacy of the clinic's grounds, but he looked so contented. So peaceful about the future that had been foisted on him. Which did beg the question…

'If I'd told you I was pregnant and I wasn't a princess… would you still want to marry me?'

'With every fibre of my being,' Oliver replied without hesitation. 'That's our child you're carrying. So I'm in. All the way. And listen, seriously…if you don't like the treehouse we'll live somewhere else. If you've had enough of St Victoria, we'll find another island. If you don't—'

'No! Stop!' Lia protested, giggles forming like champagne bubbles in her throat. 'I think the treehouse is a perfect place to raise a baby.'

He gave her a silly side-eye. 'It's not exactly traditional. The palace might not approve.'

'Oh, they'll hate it,' she said, still smiling.

'In which case…' Oliver got out of his chair, knelt in the grass in front of her and dug into his pocket. He looked down at the small box he held in his hand then said, 'Princess Amelia of Karolinska…?'

'Yes…' she answered warily.

He dipped his eyes, then lifted his gaze so that all she could see was his gorgeous face, open and honest.

'Will you do me the honour of moving in to my not-very-royal residence once we are wed?'

Every fibre of Lia's being was caught in the brilliant flare of Oliver's smile—so much so that she barely noticed the beautiful ring he was slipping on to her finger. When she saw it, her heart melted even more. It was beautiful. An eternity ring. Something that in its colours symbolised her country, their child and, she hoped, the future they would share together. It sang of hope and promise. Joy. Something she'd never equated with marriage.

'Yes,' she said, leaning in for a kiss. 'Yes, please.'

Dinner forgotten, their kisses quickly intensified, leading them to the bedroom, where they discovered a new level of tenderness, a higher plane of ecstasy and a deeper vein of unity.

Later, as they lay in one another's arms, Lia snuggled in close to Oliver's embrace. It was amazing to think this wasn't just a one-off. It was her new reality. She was engaged to Oliver. They were going to have a child. They were going to be a family.

The only thing they had to do was make sure the palace's interference was part of their lives only up until they wed. After that she wanted things to be just as they were now.

Her phone pinged with a text.

The palace.

She threw it into the bedside table drawer. Tonight the palace could wait.

'I see your new fan is back.'

Lia's long-time surgical scrub nurse Grace—a wonderful local woman, with just about the driest sense of humour she'd ever come across—flicked her eyes up to the viewing gallery where, front and centre, Oliver sat mid-way through eating his lunch.

He waved and smiled. Her heart skipped a beat, then recommenced with a newer, happier cadence.

'Fiancé, you mean,' she parried, pleased that she'd managed a vaguely casual tone.

Grace's eyebrows rose.

Fair enough. They hadn't exactly been giggling together by the water cooler over her change in status. Going from a total loner to being engaged to someone she hadn't so much as mentioned deserved the odd *Are you sure about this?* look.

The truth was, she hadn't even put in her vacation form to Nate—which was a bit stupid, since the palace had changed its mind about the wedding taking place in St

Victoria and now wanted it to be in Karolinska, in a 'small private ceremony' in the palace gardens.

She'd protested. Loudly.

Oliver had talked her away from the edge of the cliff by reminding her that choosing their battles would be a wise way to go in advance of her having the baby. They weren't building a track record of conceding to the palace's will… they were building an arsenal—showing willing so that when push came to shove they had ammunition.

She'd had to do the same for him when his parents had revealed their guest list. 'Some of these cousins must've been unearthed from the family mausoleum,' he'd said in disbelief.

'Ammunition,' she'd said to him, and she'd called the palace, green-lighting the Duke of Banford's invitations. 'Ammunition.

Another plus point. She didn't have to worry about planning the wedding or having it invade the lives they lived here.

After ordering some spirit-lifting chocolate cake from the clinic's restaurant, she and Oliver had agreed that they'd fly in, pretend it was the equivalent of a Vegas-style wedding, then fly back home and do something special, just the two of them, to celebrate.

But between the baby, the wedding and the shiny new fiancé, she needed something in her life to stay the same—and that something was work.

'I hope he's not expecting you to do anything fancy today.' Grace clicked her tongue disapprovingly. 'This isn't a bells and whistles number. But it's important.'

'Of course!' Amelia replied, horrified that Grace would think she'd do anything less than her best on any of the surgeries. 'All the surgeries we do here are important.'

It was a straightforward endovascular coiling for an elderly musician's cerebral aneurysm. The minimally invasive technique meant they wouldn't need to make an incision into the skull, and if they were successful the aneurysm would be prevented from rupturing.

Grace clicked again, then continued, clearly unpersuaded, 'We need your full concentration, so I hope you don't plan on blowing him kisses—'

This wasn't like Grace. 'No! *Heavens, no.* I'm scrubbed in, aren't I?'

Her eyes flicked up to Oliver's. He winked and blew her a kiss, clearly having heard the entire thing. A delicious spray of sparkles danced around her tummy. He was so scrummy. And sweet. And kind. And she had never, ever in her life been quite so smitten, quite so quickly.

Pregnancy hormones? Or maybe it was the guy? He wasn't just a wonderful lover. He was an amazing friend. A confidant. Someone she could have an insane morning bed head with, and someone she also wanted to dress up for. He was the real deal and, rather amazingly, he was all hers.

Grace's forehead was a crease of frown lines.

A mischievous thought popped into her head. *Just to wind Grace up*, she justified, and she air-kissed her surgical glove, then blew it up to the viewing deck. Oliver caught it and pressed it to his heart, then took a big, happy bite of his sandwich.

Lia began to hum as she turned her attention to the surgical tray Grace had none too ceremoniously placed in front of her with a loud, aggrieved, sigh.

Was this what it was like to fall in love? To smile at an instrument tray, knowing the person you cared about was there to support you? She hoped so. With every cell in her body she hoped so. Because it felt great. Unlike anything she'd ever experienced.

'Your patient here is a national treasure, I'll have you

know.' Grace was clearly unconvinced that Lia's focus was where it should be.

'Grace,' Lia insisted, 'I'm right here. We're going to do the very best we can.'

Grace harrumphed.

That had Lia's full attention. 'What's going on?' she asked.

Grace swished around the surgical table without saying anything, then stopped and looked Lia in the eye. 'He played at my wedding,' Grace said, a slight catch in her voice. 'That man blessed our marriage with his music and—and I don't want to play any part in seeing those magical skills destroyed.'

'Hey…' Lia soothed. 'We're a dream team. We won't let him come to any harm. I promise.'

It was the first time Lia had ever seen Grace grow emotional over a patient. She thought of the guitarist who'd been playing when Oliver had first taken her in his arms. That music would be with her for ever, she realised, and finally she answered the question that had been playing through her mind for days.

Yes. She was falling in love.

Grace made a decidedly different noise beneath her surgical mask. The crinkles round her eyes suggested she was finally smiling. 'Girl, that man up there has definitely done something to you. Did you know that's the first time you've not gone all "instruction manual" on me?'

Lia snorted, then said, 'What does that mean?'

'Oh, you know… You're not exactly the cuddly, huggy type.'

'I've hugged you—' Lia began, then stopped herself… because maybe she hadn't.

Grace lowered her voice. 'Don't take offence, Doctor. We're used to how you are now.'

'How *am* I?'

'Clinical. You know… Like a training manual. You're all *"Hand me the fluoroscopy aids"* this and *"arterial occlusion"* that. You're… Well, you can't help the way you are. It's not everyone who goes in for emotional folderol, and you're definitely not one of 'em. But it looks like being with Dr Bainbridge up there has made you much nicer. We all like it. I just want to make sure it isn't pulling your focus away from where it should be during working hours.'

She threw a pointed glare up to the viewing room.

'I—' Lia began to protest, her cheeks pinking with the knowledge that Oliver was listening to all of this, and growing properly red when she realised Grace was right.

In her three years here, Lia had made no actual friends—least of all amongst the surgical staff with whom she spent the bulk of her time. She'd always blamed it on her upbringing, but perhaps she'd played a bigger role in her isolation than she'd thought. With that instinctive tendency to keep people at arm's length.

She was like the Princess in *Frozen.* With a warm heart chilled to the marrow because of the burden she bore through an accident of birth.

She looked up to the viewing deck again. Oliver was there, elbows on his knees, all his focus on her.

Her heart gave a hot, skippy beat. They'd had a lovely week. They'd shared meals with other doctors Oliver knew from the clinic and the hospital. Met the locals who Oliver played football with once a week. She'd even exchanged numbers with a teenager who volunteered at the hospital and was considering becoming a surgeon.

Gosh… Grace was right. Oliver Bainbridge was her very own climate change. With his resoluteness of character, his passion for his work and, more to the point, his ability to look past his own cold upbringing and become the warm, caring soul he was… The man exuded possibility. And he was changing her. For the better.

She held her hand above her heart and hoped he knew what it meant. He was melting her heart.

The surgery, happily, went like clockwork.

It was quite an interesting technique and, more importantly for her patient, a lifesaver. It involved inserting a microcatheter with a coil attached through a surgical catheter. Once she'd manoeuvred the microcatheter into the aneurysm, she sent an electrical current through, to separate the coil from the catheter, thereby sealing the opening of the aneurysm.

The patient would need to spend a night or two in the clinic, so they could monitor his progress, but she assured Grace that he would be playing his guitar again as if none of this had happened within a handful of days.'

The rest of the day passed in a blur. After her final surgery and a quick shower she wandered down to the paediatrics department, where she knew she'd find Oliver. It was his regular day at The Island Clinic, and they usually had takeaway from the clinic restaurant.

He was just leaving a patient's room, and he'd spotted her, his smile brightening, when a nurse approached him with a worried expression on her face.

Oliver gave Lia a quick wave of acknowledgement, but listened intently as the nurse, Maddy Orakwee, told him about the call she'd just had from St Victoria Hospital.

His heart crumpled in on itself as he listened. 'Élodie? Really?'

He raked a hand through his hair, as if the gesture would alter the facts.

Maddy nodded, her expression grim.

His young patient had been released a few days ago,

with multiple cautions to call if her fever returned or any of her symptoms worsened. A tough ask for a six-year-old girl who was as full of life as she was.

'She's heading for a case of secondary pneumonia,' Maddy said apologetically.

'They've given her antibiotics?'

Maddy nodded. 'They've put her on oxygen and a drip, but…' She glanced over at Lia, who wasn't doing a very good job of pretending to read a magazine nearby.

'Come on over, Lia,' he said, and then, to Maddy, 'You've met my fiancée, haven't you? Dr Trelleburg? She's the head surgeon over in the neurology department.'

Maddy nodded, and smiled at Lia.

'You were saying about Élodie?' Oliver continued.

'The nurses mentioned she was a favourite of yours, and as it's out of hours, and the emergency room is slammed…'

'Why is the ER so busy? Has there been an accident?' he asked.

Maddy had his and Lia's full attention now.

'Nothing too serious. There were a few stags—you know…' She made a 'muscle man' pose.

'Men having a stag party?' Lia asked.

'Yes. Exactly. Anyway, they were out on jet skis, showing off for a group of girls on a hen do, and—' She threw up her hands, as if that explained everything.

Oliver nodded. She didn't need to spell it out. Wedding season on the island meant one thing: a lot of alcohol-related showing off. Drink, the ocean, and motorised vehicles never made a good combination.

Oliver glanced at his watch. 'Élodie's not alone, though, right?'

'No. There are obviously staff on the ward. But…' The nurse bit the inside of her cheek.

There's no one special there just for her.

The staff at the hospital did their best to make every child feel safe and secure, offering beds in the rooms to parents and loved ones, with nurses and doctors regularly popping in to check on them, but with the hospital slammed, and no spare hands on deck, some children felt the energy of the ward shift away from them and, as such, needed an extra dose of TLC.

Élodie was one of those children. Ultrasensitive to the slightest change of focus.

'What about her aunt and uncle? Is one of them able to go in?'

Maddy's eyes darted between the pair of them, as if she were deciding to confess something, and then she blurted, 'They can't come in for the next three days. They're doing the catering on an island cruise that's not back until the end of the week.'

'What?' *Oh, hell.* 'Where was she meant to stay at night?'

Maddy shrugged. 'Another relative, maybe? I don't know. But in her condition she'll need to stay in hospital for at least the next few nights.'

Oliver stemmed a few curses on the little girl's behalf. Élodie's aunt and uncle worked hard. They each held down two and sometimes three jobs at the local resorts, trying to make ends meet. A private catering job on a yacht meant a lot of extra money.

He knew they would never have made the decision to leave her lightly. They would've put some provision in place for her care. But with their own children to look after, and jobs to complete, staying nights at the hospital was out of the question.

A fortnight ago he would have jumped in his Jeep and headed straight to the hospital. But his reality was different now. He was engaged. He was going to be a father.

He and Lia had agreed that their work wouldn't be sidelined during the lead-up to the wedding, and this week had been a particularly busy one. After a few late nights at work, they had promised each other they'd have dinner tonight. Just the two of them. So that they could regroup, look through the ream of lists the palace had sent for them to go over for the wedding and, most importantly, they write their vows.

While there had been a few lost wars in their skirmishes with the palace over flowers, venue, dresses, even the bows on the chairs, Lia had been adamant about putting their own stamp on the vows, refusing to let the palace have a final say in how they committed their lives to one another.

But Élodie… His eyes drifted to the exit.

'Bring her here,' Lia said, as if reading his mind. 'There are free beds. We can check in on her throughout the night—if you're staying,' she said in a low voice. 'Otherwise take the helicopter back to Williamtown. It'll cut half an hour off your journey.'

'You sure?' He wasn't asking about the timing and she knew it.

'Of course.'

He sought her eyes for any sign of wavering and saw none.

Her smile softened, and she reached out to touch his arm. 'Otherwise you'll spend the entire night wanting to be where you *should* be…'

He gave her a questioning look.

'With your favourite patient,' she finished.

'I don't have favourites,' he protested. Feebly.

Both Maddy and Lia rolled their eyes. So much for being Dr Unpredictable.

He saw her gesture for what it was. Selflessness. Lia had never had anyone in her life who had put her first.

He'd wanted her to know he would be the man to fulfil that role. But…

He took her hand in his. 'You're sure you're sure?'

She squeezed his hand in place of a verbal answer. It was a yes. She was sure.

Oliver felt his reality shift as he continued to wrestle with his decision. He wanted to be the man Lia could rely on—and not just because it was his duty as the father of their child, but because he was falling for her.

'We can sort out her transfer together, yeah?' Lia said, shifting into action mode. 'Then maybe get a snack later, from one of the chefs.'

He grinned. Last week's 'snack' had been a luxurious seafood platter for two. Who knew what the chefs would magic up tonight?

He tucked the happy thought of a midnight snack with Lia away, and focused on the here and now.

A mad half-hour of information-gathering ensued.

One of the 'show-offs' on the jet skis had turned out to be a famous rap star from Miami. He was best man to his producer, who was getting married at a private estate on the island. The rapper, C-Life, had been trying to pull off some wild manoeuvre, and had ended up slicing the cords on a passing kite surfer's rig, before flipping his vehicle and himself into a shallow part of the bay.

The extent of his injuries was still unknown, but his entourage had insisted he be brought to the clinic, where his entire team could be housed in the luxurious hotel there if needed.

The helicopter pilot agreed to do a return journey to St Victoria Hospital, where Élodie was collected and brought back to The Island Clinic.

When the helicopter's arrival was announced Lia gave Oliver a kiss on the cheek, then said, 'I'm going to head over to Intake and see if there's anything I can do to help with the stag party crew. Unless you want me to stay?'

'You go on ahead. We'll catch up in a bit, okay?'

'Okay.' She grinned, her thumb playing at the edge of her engagement ring as if she'd been doing it for ever.

He could get used to this, Oliver thought as he dropped a kiss on the crown of her head before heading off to the helicopter pad. Working together. Playing together. Giving each other enough room to stay true to the person they'd both fought to become.

Lia understood that his work was a calling, more than a job, and more importantly she respected that. He'd got so used to prioritising his work, he'd have to ensure she knew she and the baby were every bit as important to him.

An hour later, after Élodie's oxygen levels had been restored to normal and a fresh antibiotic IV was in place, he gave the little girl a smile.

'Story time?' She looked at him hopefully.

'Story time,' he confirmed.

She scooched over to make room for him on her bed, her lungs making a little wheezing sound as she did so. It took all his power not to gather her up in his arms and promise her he'd look after her always.

Once he was in place, she looked up at him with expectant eyes.

There weren't any books to hand, so he'd have to make a story up tonight. 'What kind of story do you want to hear? Scary?'

She shook her head. 'No.'

'Funny?'

She gave a *Maybe* shrug, then said, 'I want a story about a princess!'

Out of the corner of his eye he caught a glimpse of Lia, in the doorway. She gave him a tiny fingertip wave, then put her index finger to her mouth, indicating that he should go ahead with his story.

'A story about a princess, eh?' he said, thinking for a moment. An interesting challenge, given he was a handful of metres from a real-life one.

'Once upon a time,' he began, 'there was a beautiful princess who lived on an island a lot like this.'

Élodie sighed and let the mountain of pillows she was propped on take her weight, tipping her head onto his arm.

Lia tipped her own head to the doorframe, ankles crossed, clearly settling in to hear the story as well.

'This particular princess,' he continued, 'had never been very good at sleeping.'

'Why?' Élodie asked with a yawn.

'Someone kept putting peas under her mattress.'

'Why would they do that?'

'To see if it made her uncomfortable.'

'Couldn't she just eat the peas?'

He laughed. 'Yes, she could. But the peas were a test.'

'What for?'

Lia's eyebrows rose.

'To find out if she was a real princess.'

'How could a pea know if she was a real princess?'

'It would be proof,' Oliver said, about to explain that it would prove how sensitive she was, because princesses had supernatural sensitivity.

But then, catching Lia's slight flinch as she defensively crossed her arms, he swerved from the original fairy tale. From everything he'd seen, Lia was made of strength, and she was the only one who didn't see it.

'The fact she could feel the pea was not only proof she was a princess—it was proof she was an *extraordinary* princess.'

'How was she extraordinary?' Élodie asked.

'She had a heart as big as the kingdom she'd promised to be loyal to. It was hard, sometimes, having a heart that big. There were days when she felt like hiding away from all those feelings, but then a stranger came into her life.'

'A handsome stranger?'

He smiled. 'Terrifically handsome. But he was also very wise. He admired the Princess for her brains as well as her beauty. And all he wanted to do was to protect her, and her beautiful heart, and all those feelings that came with it that made sleeping on peas so very difficult.'

Lia swept a tear away from her cheek.

'And the handsome Prince could tell all of that from a pea?' Élodie's eyebrows arrowed up into a confused peak.

'Oh, he wasn't a prince.'

Élodie crinkled her nose. 'What was he? A frog?'

Lia stifled a giggle, swiping at another tear.

'Sort of. He was a duke. Not as fancy as a prince, but it did mean he understood the Princess and the world she came from.'

'And he's covered in warts?' Élodie said earnestly.

'Yes. Absolutely. All over.'

'Does he love her?'

Lia uncrossed her ankles and looked away, as if seeking an immediate escape route.

'He's falling in love with her,' Oliver said, his eyes just managing to catch Lia's. 'He thinks she's amazing, and he'll do everything in his power to make sure she knows how special she is.'

Lia's hands flew to her chest. He wondered if the same knot of emotion coiling at the base of his throat was coiling in hers.

'So will he eat the pea?' Élodie asked, clearly much more focused on the fictional Princess's discomfort.

'Yes, he will. He'll eat all the peas he has to in order to

keep her happy. And he'll also go to bed once story time is over.'

After a few more minutes of wrapping up the story, and promising he'd be in first thing in the morning to see her, Oliver gave Élodie's hair a light rub and switched off her bedside light.

When he came out of the room Lia didn't say anything. She didn't have to. Her eyes were still glistening with tears as she took his hand.

'Hungry?' he asked.

She shook her head.

'Shall we go and get some sleep?'

She nodded, her grip on his hand tightening.

But when her eyes met his, lit with a passion he'd not yet seen in them, he knew that sleep was the last thing on her mind. Which suited this particular frog prince perfectly.

CHAPTER NINE

'HERE YOU GO.' Lia handed Oliver a cup of coffee, her body tingling at how pleasurable the everyday gesture was. Maybe because it wasn't everyday to her. It was all deliciously new.

'Mmm…thanks. Smells good.' Oliver gave Lia's cheek a light kiss, took a sip of the coffee, then rearranged himself in the bed.

She liked seeing him in her bed, propped up against the pillows, with the morning light shifting through the curtains when the light breeze blew them inwards. The sexual attraction they shared was still popping and fizzing between them, but there was a new dimension to the energy they shared. Trust.

The most fiercely protected piece of her heart…and Oliver had won it.

She was amazed at how much that shared moment last night with Élodie had made her feel. It had added a new level of intimacy she had never experienced. Made something click in her psyche that she'd not known she was waiting for.

Sure. They'd said they were a team. That they'd 'battle through' the palace's wedding plans together. But who wanted to battle through something that was meant to be joyous?

Once you stripped away the title and the gold monograms and the tiaras, she was just like any other woman. One who sought multiple layers of personal fulfilment. Professional pride. A family of her own. To love and be loved in return.

Her hand swept over her stomach, her thoughts organically shifting to the tiny baby growing inside her. The child she and Oliver would love and cherish, even if its inception had been unexpected and their marriage was sanctioned rather than spontaneous.

A thought occurred to her as she poured herself a cup of herbal tea. Maybe she'd needed the nudge. It wasn't as if she had family or friends she went to when she was tied up in knots, wondering which direction to take her love life. Nor did she have any examples of a healthy, happy marriage. If there hadn't been a crown to answer to, would she have done what she had when things had got too tough in Karolinska? Moved thousands of miles away?

It had been her gut response. And then she'd written a list of facts, in preparation for speaking to the palace. She'd met an amazing man and had accidentally fallen pregnant. She was going to have the baby. She didn't think he felt the same way, so she'd move and save him the trouble of rejecting her.

It was about as Princess Elsa as it got. 'Solving' the problem by removing herself from it.

Fear didn't just make for self-protective behaviour. It also made her myopic. Unable to see what was glaringly obvious. True happiness only came from finding the courage to love, even if that love came with vulnerability.

A wash of guilt churned through her. Was that what her mother had gone through? A loss of control because her father had been raised to believe whatever path he chose was the right one, to the exclusion of his wife's hopes and dreams?

'C'mon over, gorgeous.' Oliver patted the space beside him on the bed, then put on a grand voice. 'Prepare yourself for my great oratory!'

She took a seat in the small eggshell-blue armchair across from the bed. 'I'm ready.'

'What?' he said in mock despair. 'Is my morning breath too horrible to be near?'

'No.' She laughed, her conscience giving her a sharp sting as it pierced through to a deep layer of guilt.

Her 'vows notebook' was still embarrassingly blank. She hadn't been able to nail down what she wanted to say yet. How could she, when everything between them was so fresh and changeable? When she'd not yet been able to tell him she was falling in love with him?

'I've got a better view of you from here.' She gave him her most erudite look. 'Seeing as you've worked so hard on it, I want to…you know…give what you've written room to breathe.'

'That's very generous of you.' He gave her a curious look.

She tried to mimic his lofty, regal tone. 'It's how we at the royal palace like to receive and disseminate information…from a distance.'

She'd meant it humorously, but something dark flickered through Oliver's eyes. Wariness.

'Sorry.' She grimaced, pressing her hands together into a prayer position over her heart. 'I am genuinely interested. More than interested. This is important. I'm just—I haven't written anything yet, and if what you've done is even close to what I want to say, but don't know how to…'

The muscles in Oliver's torso stretched and grew taut, as if he were bracing himself for a blow. His bare chest was distracting. It was all manly and tanned and begging for her to touch it.

She swallowed, and very possibly made a tiny whimpering noise. In a rush, she blurted, 'And if I don't sit over here I'm going to have to rip off your boxers, and you know where that leads, and then we'll both be late for work, and that would be a bad thing. The vows are important. *You're* important.'

They stared at each other. Lia's breath was coming in quick bursts, as if she'd just been running or…slightly more accurately…having athletic sex.

'It would be a very bad thing. Being naked. Together. Before work. Not listening to your vows. Right?' Her tongue swept across her lips.

The atmosphere between them sparked, charged with that delicious shared sexual sizzle. Oliver's shoulders rolled back in a proud, leonine move that gave her a jolt of pride. *She'd* brought that on. Her desire for him had ignited his.

His eyes flicked to the clock. 'We have twenty minutes.' His blue eyes darkened. 'You can do a lot of things in twenty minutes.'

He was right. You could. If you put your mind and your body to the task at hand.

A hot, fast, and utterly sinful session of lovemaking followed. They devoured one another as if it were their first and last time together.

Screaming when she climaxed wasn't an option, because she could hear the clinic's gardeners just beyond her cottage, but the added frisson leant an even sexier edge to their utterly carnal session of hungry kisses and fingernails scraping down the length of each other's back.

A fierce, possessive entry into her most feminine essence forced Lia to stem yet more cries of pleasure by biting down on Oliver's shoulder. Hard. A move which accelerated his powerful thrusts of connection until their bodies united in climax.

As their breathing steadied, Lia ran her fingers through Oliver's hair, still sitting astride him. She revelled in the sensation of feeling both exhausted and exhilarated. Ready to take on the day, but just as excited for nightfall, when once again they would be in one another's arms.

Oliver kissed her shoulder, then shifted her so that she was snuggled up close beside him.

'There,' he said smugly. 'I knew I could get you to sit beside me.' He winked, then grabbed his notebook. 'We have seven minutes left, my beautiful bride-to-be. Now… what do you think of this?'

He put on a comically thoughtful expression, then began sonorously, 'Roses are red—'

She laughed to hide the sting of disappointment. She'd thought he was going to tell her that he loved her the way she loved him.

She supposed she couldn't blame him for his jokey tone. She didn't know how to put what she felt for *him* into words. *I love you* didn't seem a big enough statement to encapsulate everything he'd come to mean to her in such a short period of time. And *You stopped me running for the hills* wasn't exactly the most romantic thing in the world, was it?

'I think it's a very promising start,' she said finally.

He scrubbed his hand through his hair, then turned the paper. It was blank.

Oh. He really hadn't written anything.

He lifted up the printout of suggestions the palace had sent. 'These all seem a little bit dry.'

'As the Sahara!' she agreed, so as not to betray her genuine hurt.

But her response had clearly lurched into the 'too emphatic a response' territory, because Oliver's expression turned serious.

He tucked a finger under her chin and gave her a feather-soft kiss. 'Hey… We'll nail these vows. We'll write something that's personal to us and easily approved by the palace.' He dipped his head so he could catch her eye. 'Trust me?'

She wanted to. More than anything, she wanted to. That was what truly loving him would mean. Trusting him with all her heart.

She sought his eyes for one solitary sign that what they were doing was a bad idea and couldn't find one. Perhaps the pregnancy hormones were also making her paranoid.

A swelling of hope and wistfulness filled her chest as he pulled her close, his warm, citrussy scent surrounding her. 'I wish we were getting married like normal people,' she said.

'We're normal people,' Oliver insisted.

'Not really.' She snuggled in under the comforting weight of his arm. 'I mean…it's not like the gardens in the palace are awful, or anything, but…there's no spontaneity. Not when we have to do everything with a spotlight on us.'

'Like what?'

She shrugged and said the first thing that came to mind. 'What if you want to have a stag do?'

He snorted. 'Get drunk and ride jet skis? No, thank you.'

'I'm pretty sure that's not the only thing men do on their stags. Go on. World's your oyster. What would you do?'

She pulled the sheet around her a bit and twisted her hips so that they were facing one another.

He thought for a moment. 'You know, this probably won't sound very macho, but I'd love to bring some of the kids from the local orphanage down to Turtle Cove to go snorkelling. Have a blow-out picnic. Maybe get some of the other doctors to come down and play some footie. Bring Élodie along. You know…'

She finished his sentence for him. 'Act like the fathers they'll never have?'

The tiny crinkles alongside his eyes deepened as he checked an emotional breath. 'Yeah…'

'Like the father *you* never had?' she guessed.

The crinkles deepened again. This time he just nodded.

Her heart squeezed tight and she silently admonished herself for ever doubting him. So what if he hadn't written his vows? He'd had the same emotionally strangled upbringing she had. One in which you simply didn't express how you felt as it would more often than not be dismissed as 'inappropriate'.

She laced her fingers through his and sat back against the headboard with a sigh. 'I don't have a clue what I'd do if I were having a hen do.'

'No?' His smile was soft and sincere.

'I probably wouldn't have one.' She gave a weak smile. 'Atleast it would please the King and Queen.'

'Go on…' Oliver gave her a nudge. 'What would you like for your fantasy hen do? Tutus? Pin the tail on the paediatrician? Sky's the limit!'

She laughed, flushed a bit, then sheepishly admitted, 'I'd want the equivalent of a twelve-year-old's birthday party.'

He hooted, then clapped his hands, looking both delighted and bewildered. 'What? Why? Didn't you have one?'

'Yes, but it involved more of this…' she did a regal wave '…than this.' She waved her hands in the air as if she were wielding a pair of pom-poms. She glanced at the clock. 'Crikey. We've got to get hopping. I've got surgery soon.'

'Tell me?' he asked, pulling her up out of bed and towards the shower. 'Tell me exactly what twelve-year-old Amelia would have done for her birthday if she'd been in charge?'

And somehow, over the course of him soaping her naked body and helping her dry off, and eventually managing to get each other into their scrubs for a day at the clinic, she did.

Lia finished extracting the surgical camera from the viewing tube. 'Right. Looks like we can close.'

'Hand it over, honey. I don't want you dropping that thing in your excitement.' Grace's quiet cackle made it clear she was teasing.

Lia hadn't seen Oliver for a few days, and even their dinner date today had been provisional. Tourist season had a way of being crazy season in the clinic and the hospital, and this summer was no different.

Grace held out her hand as Lia just stood there. She knew she looked like a numpty, grinning behind her mask at her lovely fiancé. Even so, she couldn't help a slightly miffed, 'I'd never compromise a patient's safety.'

'I know. I'm just saying…'

Grace made one of her *I see everything* noises which, over the three weeks since she'd first met Oliver, had shifted from protective and judgmental to quietly approving. Oliver had noticed the shift too, and had lately taken to bringing Grace small boxes of her favourite coconut sweets, which were only available in Williamstown.

Lia handed over the camera, her smile still hidden behind her surgical mask. To be honest, it had been nice having Grace go all 'Mama Bear' around her. It was the closest she'd come to having a friendship in years. The closest she'd come to experiencing a mother's protectiveness.

'Thank you, Grace,' she said, and then, to the team, 'Another job well done.'

Lia asked her number two to close the small incision they'd needed for the operation and kept her walk as casual and relaxed as she could until she hit the changing rooms, when her pace quadrupled. After a quick shower, she was towelling herself off when Grace came in.

'Lover boy's outside.'

She grinned. 'We're having dinner.'

'I thought you were going to Florida.'

'Oh, *crumbs*!' Her heart sank. 'I completely forgot.'

She had a consultation with a prospective patient who refused to travel to St Victoria without a meeting on her 'home turf' first. She was a grand dame of the Orlando resort scene, if the rumour mill was anything to go by. One with a brain tumour that other doctors had deemed impossible to remove.

Her shoulders drooped. 'Got any good *Whoops, I messed up* lines?'

Grace raised her eyebrows and gave her a mysterious look. 'I'm sure you'll figure something out.'

When Lia came out of the locker room she was surprised to see Oliver with an overnight bag slung over his shoulder and one of her wheelie bags by his foot.

'What's going on?'

'Don't you worry, Your Highness. All your dreams will come true where we're heading.'

She winced. 'Oliver, I can't. I'm going to see a patient.'

'That you are.' He tapped the side of his nose and, with a wink, added, 'And you're going to be escorted to the wilds of Florida by yours truly.'

It was a nice turn of events, but… 'Don't you have work?

'Not for the next forty-eight hours.'

From inside the dressing room she could hear Grace

singing. Also unusual… What was going on? 'Oliver. This is weird. Nice weird, but…' Her eyebrows drew together. 'Why are you coming to Florida with me?'

His smile broadened. 'You'll see.'

'You want me to *what*, now?' Lia threw Oliver an uncertain look as they approached the clinic's private airport.

She held up the wig he'd just handed her, as if she'd just had an *Aha!* moment. The hair was as dark and curly as hers was blonde and straight.

'This isn't some untapped sexual fantasy you want fulfilled before you marry a blonde Scandinavian girl, is it?' She gave her hips a rather too alluring swish.

'No!' Oliver waved his hands in protest. He was seeking discretion, not indiscretion. Although now that she mentioned it…

No.

Playing naughty dress-up was not the point of this trip.

'Oliver? What's going on?' She glanced nervously over her shoulder. 'I don't want the clinic thinking I'm compromising a patient meeting with…you know…our sexy-sexy business.'

He tried and failed to ignore the tug of response. He liked it that they had sexy-sexy business. But she looked worried. Maybe he should just tell her.

No.

The wheels were already in motion, her boss knew exactly what was happening, and now was as good a time as any for her to find out that he was a man who loved setting up surprises. The good kind. It was a big part of who he was, so she might as well know what she was marrying into before he slid the ring on her finger.

An unwelcome chill slipped through him as he thought of his parents' enormous, unwelcoming estate. The one they were still expecting him to move in to once he was married. That would be a surprise, too. One he still hadn't figured out how to handle.

Ignoring the discomfort that came from holding something that important back from her, he held up another wig and popped it on his own head. 'We're both going in disguise.'

'Why? This is a legal flight.' Her expression turned horrified. 'Someone didn't alert the press, did they?'

'No. Absolutely not.' He'd made sure of that.

She scrunched up her face in confusion. 'I'm happy you're coming, but…wigs? I don't understand. This is a simple business trip, Oli.'

'There's someone the hospital's paediatrics team want me to check up on,' he answered smoothly. Too smoothly.

Lia didn't miss it. 'There's something else.' She narrowed her gaze. 'What's going on, Oliver Bainbridge?'

He gave her a mischievous grin, 'You'll find out soon enough.'

'And I need to wear this?' She pulled on the wig, without bothering to tuck her blonde hair beneath the bonnet of dark curls.

He laughed and pulled her to him for a kiss, enjoying the fact that she leaned into him as his lips met hers. It was a sign she was falling for him as much as he was falling for her.

So why not tell her about the UK estate? Tell her how much having this baby with her meant to him? Or, more to the point, why not tell her he loved her?

A knot of discomfort needled at his conscience.

It was a difficult truth to acknowledge but, as much as he cared for Lia, and as happy as he was knowing their future would be a shared one, he was still protecting the part of his heart that had been hurt when his ex had made her decision about her pregnancy.

He was going to have to find a way to lay that to rest. And soon.

Lia looked up at him, sensing his tension. 'Oli?'

Her eyes had gone a deeper shade of blue. Dark with concern. With affection. And very possibly with love. The same slightly guarded love he felt for her. It was a hurdle they simply had to get over before exchanging those vows with one another.

He couldn't marry her with secrets held close to the same heart that beat for her and their child. He'd tell her. About everything. But for now, he hoped the grand gesture she was about to experience would tell her just how much he cared.

He smiled, kissed his index finger, then popped it on her nose. 'All in good time, my darling bride-to-be. All in good time.'

The journey to Orlando was uneventful, if he didn't count Lia playing twenty questions with him for the entire flight.

Luckily, he'd had practice in keeping secrets. He'd given presents to the children at his boarding school whose parents had been too busy to fly them home for the holidays. To draw out the fun, he would hide the gifts and play the whole thing out a bit like an Easter egg hunt.

If his parents hadn't demanded his presence for the annual holiday family photos, he would've happily stayed at school and played board games or read books to the younger children, because leaving those little sad faces behind had seemed ridiculous when he had known the last thing he'd be receiving at home was a warm welcome. He'd made the best of his childhood...but sometimes it had been tough finding the silver linings.

'Hey.' Lia tapped him on the knee as they rode in a limousine to the resort hotel. 'You okay?'

He swept her hand to his lips and gave the back of it a kiss. 'Absolutely. Just taking a little trip down memory lane.'

'Not a very nice one from the looks of it.' She frowned.

He dropped a soft kiss on her cheek, then tipped his forehead to hers. 'Not to worry. All the memories will be good from now on.'

She moved his hand to her stomach. 'We're going to give this one nothing but happy memories, right?'

There was an urgency in her question that he felt in his marrow.

It was their shared fear. That the childhoods they'd had—mired in tradition rather than love—would become their own child's future...for better or for worse. Which was exactly why he'd been struggling with writing his wedding vows to Lia. He wanted them to show her that he had worked so hard to change...to be different. That he wanted more than anything to take a spear to his heart for her. Fight for her.

The easiest way to communicate that was very simple. Three little words that meant the world. Three little words he had yet to say to Lia.

'Hey.' He gave her thigh a rub. 'Did you get your vows written?'

She crinkled her nose. 'Sorry. Still working on them.'

He gave his watch a dramatic tap. 'Only ten more days!'

'Ugh.' Lia dropped her head into her hands. 'Don't remind me!'

'Hey.' He cupped her cheeks in his hands and turned her

face so that he could look into her eyes. If she was having second thoughts about anything, she needed to let him know. 'If you don't want to do this—'

'No.' She put up her hands. 'I mean, yes. I do want to do it. With all my heart. I—'

She stopped herself, and by the way her cheeks coloured Oliver was sure she'd been about to tell him she loved him. He hoped that was true. With every fibre in his being.

He was prepared to sacrifice so much for her and their child. His anonymity. His desire to step away from his 'birthright' duties. His quiet life which, once they were wed, he knew wouldn't be quiet any more. But all that sacrifice would be for a much greater joy. Having a family of his own. To love and to cherish. To honour and protect. He would do all those things and more, but he had to know they were a team.

Which made the fact he wanted to hear it from her a case of the pot calling the kettle black.

'What is it that scares you the most?' he asked her.

She bit down on her lip, then admitted, 'That you'll walk away.'

The confession gripped his heart and then squeezed one painful beat after another out of it until he found his voice again and assured her, 'That will never happen.'

Deep down, he knew he did love her. That he did have the strength to confront his parents…make changes. To trust in Lia the way she was trying to trust in him. He just needed it all to rise through his past, heal it and surface.

She gazed into his eyes for a moment longer and must have found the answer she was looking for, because she leant into a kiss that accepted the spoken and the silent promises.

They could do this, he told himself as the driver announced they were at their destination. They could give themselves, and their child, the happiest of lives.

'Pretty luxurious,' Oliver said as they entered the hotel's penthouse suite.

Lia agreed. 'I don't know what this patient does for a living, but she clearly does well if she can put us up here.'

Together they scanned the place in disbelief. It was even better than he'd imagined when he'd booked it. He presumed Lia was used to luxurious hotel rooms, and he was certainly no stranger to them, but this was on another level.

Floor-to-ceiling windows. Glass. Chrome. A huge rooftop garden with an infinity pool and a waterfall. Towering fruit baskets. A butler who offered a pet hire service in case they were missing their animals from home. A private chef who was on hand to make fresh sushi.

They could have anything they desired—apart from a swim at the lake, which apparently had an alligator in it, but the staff were seeing about offering the gator 'relocation services'.

Lia shot Oliver an embarrassed look. 'Er… I hope you don't get used to this. My princess allowance won't really go this far for our family holidays.'

Oliver laughed and shook his head, as if to say a solid *Don't you worry.* 'I'd be happy with a picnic down at the beach. This is much more my parents' kind of thing than mine.'

As well as the 'old money' his father had inherited, his father's work as a property mogul meant his parents were amongst the wealthiest couples in England. Something they rarely let him forget whenever they tried to pin down his plans for the family fortune once they were gone.

He was happy with his treehouse and a life below the radar, thank you very much. Although a couple of nights splashing out for his future wife in a place like this wasn't strictly a hardship.

He hoped she wouldn't be too cross when she found out there wasn't really a patient.

The phone in the suite rang and the butler answered it, speaking in a low murmur. When he'd finished, he approached Lia. 'Your Highness—'

'Oh, please, no,' she corrected. 'Amelia or Dr Trelleburg will be fine.'

'Dr Trelleburg,' he began again, with a deferential bow. 'That was your hostess. She says you will have to forgive her, but she isn't up to seeing you today and could she please delay your meeting until tomorrow morning?'

Oliver hid his smile as Lia gave him a confused look then said to the butler, 'Please let her know I'm happy to see her whenever it suits.'

He finished the call and turned to leave.

Lia stopped him and gave him a conspiratorial smile. 'Any chance you could let me know who it is?'

The butler stiffened. 'I'm afraid I am not privileged to know that information.'

'Oh. Okay, well…' She gave Oliver a bewildered shrug. 'I guess that means we can have that dinner date after all.' She glanced at the retreating figure of the butler. 'But do you mind if I go over the case notes for twenty minutes or so?'

'Absolutely.'

Oliver knew it was only a matter of time before she figured out that the case notes were from a surgery her mentor had done a year or so back on a cabinet member from the Costa Rican government but he needed to make a couple of quick calls.

After he'd finished, he found Lia thoughtfully eating a peach out in the rooftop garden. He gave her a kiss, enjoying the taste of her lips mingled with peach juice. She pulled back and gave a huge yawn.

'I'm so sorry. It's not you, I promise.'

He gave her hair a stroke and properly looked at her. She looked tired. Full-time work, wedding plans and being newly pregnant were obviously taking their toll. They had also spent quite a few late nights getting to know one another on a more intimate level.

'What do you think about room service and a movie in bed?' he suggested.

She clasped her hands to her chest, practically melting with pleasure at the thought. 'I would love that.'

Within about ten minutes Lia was curled up in bed, her arm wrapped round Oliver's waist as if he was her security blanket and fast asleep. Not quite the night he'd imagined, but every bit as perfect.

The next morning Lia pronounced herself well rested and full of beans.

Just as she was about to start putting on her business suit he asked, 'How do you fancy a little adventure?'

She smiled. 'I'd love to, but I've got to meet my patient.'

His expression turned into one that made it pretty clear there was no patient.

The penny dropped. 'Oliver Bainbridge…what have you done?'

'Nothing bad. Nate knows, so you're all good on the work front.'

'What did you tell him, exactly?'

'That I wanted to surprise my bride-to-be.'

'Will it require the wigs?' She held up the dark wig with a finger.

'Yes.'

One short helicopter ride later, and Amelia let out a scream of disbelief.

'Disney World?' She gave a double-take, and felt her smile reaching from ear to ear. 'I've never been to a theme park!'

Oliver had clearly been panicking that she wouldn't enjoy his surprise, and the look on his face turned to one of relief. He waved his hands. 'Happy Hen Do!'

Tears of joy sprang to Lia's eyes. He'd organised all this for her? Never once in her life had she had a surprise anything, let alone a surprise hen do.

She swept the tears away before they could fall, giggling and hiccoughing, not knowing which way to look. 'How did you know I've always wanted to come here?'

'I didn't.' Oliver was laughing, too. He handed her a tissue, using his thumb to edge away a couple of escapee tears from her cheek. 'I just thought, if I was a twelve-year-old girl...what would I want to do for my birthday? I asked the internet, and then I asked a six-year-old, and between all three of us we came up with this.'

'Élodie?' she asked, instantly thinking of the lovely bond he shared with his recently discharged patient.

'That's the one,' he said.

She wrapped her arms around him and gave him a huge, happy, sloppy kiss. She pulled back, her smile disappearing as she did. 'Hen dos are supposed to be with friends. I don't really have any.'

'Well...you've got me,' Oliver said. 'And a couple of extra people who'd like to think of you as their friend.'

He pointed towards the VIP entrance, where they were headed, and there, holding hands, were Grace and Élodie. They waved enthusiastically. Élodie was already wearing the trademark ears. Grace was too, which instantly made Lia roar with laughter.

'This is great!'

She clapped her hands, finally connecting all the dots.

'And we've got the wigs in case you want to go incognito,' he said.

'I don't want to hide away from the world. You and I are going to be a family. So let's start the way we want to continue.'

It was as close to a declaration of love as she'd let herself come. Her heart was absolutely soaring. Maybe today would be the day she threw caution to the wind and told him she loved him.

He lifted up his wig and gave her a questioning look. Her heart plummeted. Had she misread things so badly? 'Or would you rather people not know we were together?'

'No! God, no. The opposite. I'd shout it from the…' his eyes scanned the area '…the top of that palace if you wanted me to. I just want you to be comfortable. Happy.'

This was love. It had to be. They often communicated things without saying them, and this felt like one of those moments. Perfect synchronicity of their hearts and minds. Love.

'I am happy. Ridiculously happy.' She tucked her hand in the crook of his elbow. 'Thank you. This'll be the best hen party ever.'

'Well, then… It's not your kingdom, but shall we see what sort of magic we can whip up in this one?'

He held out a hand as two 'living' cartoon characters appeared and rolled out an actual red carpet, whilst 'Cinderella' handed out tiaras to all the women and a toy sword to Oliver.

Again, Lia's smile stretched from ear to ear. 'Wild horses couldn't stop me!'

CHAPTER TEN

'THAT WAS THE BEST!'

'The fastest one, for sure! I wish you could've gone on it, Lia.'

Lia smiled. She did, too, but Oliver had gently suggested that being whipped around on a rollercoaster probably wasn't the best of things for a pregnant woman to do. He was right, of course. She must've left her common sense at the gates when she'd entered the theme park!

'I thought the one in the dark was the fastest,' Élodie assured her. It was one they'd all gone on together.

'And the scariest.' Grace shook her head. 'I'm pretty sure when I take these ears off there'll be more grey in my hair than there was at the beginning.'

'What did you think of the Peter Pan ride?' Oliver asked. 'It felt like we were flying along with them.'

'It did, didn't it? I wonder if Tinker Bell ever gets tired.'

Élodie, Grace and Oliver's banter continued unabated as they headed to the next ride while Lia just beamed. A few hours earlier she wouldn't have believed having this much fun was possible. But being with Oliver was like having a special key to entire realms of happiness she'd never imagined, let alone experienced.

She'd put on the wig, in the end. More because Élodie wanted to wear a mermaid wig and Grace was wearing her

Minnie Mouse ears and a tiara, whilst Oliver was wearing a pirate hat, with a plastic sword stuffed in his belt. Rather than be the odd one out, she topped the curly mass of dark curls with a bright red baseball cap with rainbow 'ears'. Not her best look, but it was fun.

And that was what life with Oliver seemed to be all about. Maxing out the good times whilst respectfully acknowledging the tougher ones.

He was simply the best person she'd ever met in her life. Literally swoonworthy. And she was going to marry him in a few days' time. For once, she had the palace to thank for their controlling ways.

He'd chosen her 'hen party' guests perfectly as well. Huge groups weren't really her thing, so this quartet was perfect. None of the eclectic foursome had ever been to this theme park and, as such, they were all equally thrilled with the singing and dancing 'bears', the swirling teacups and even the 'abandoned' treehouse—which, unsurprisingly, Oliver had made them climb up and around twice, as he tried to figure out whether or not he could make a waterwheel out of coconuts for his own tree home.

They had all roared with laughter when Grace, normally so controlled and dignified, had laughed and screamed the loudest when they'd taken a watery rollercoaster ride on huge 'logs'. But it was Élodie who had taken the lead now they'd entered the part of the park which was almost literally awash with princesses. Rather than pity them, as was Lia's gut instinct, Élodie adored them with a passion that was utterly infectious.

'She's in her element, isn't she?' Lia asked Oliver in a low voice, as Grace queued with Élodie to have their photograph taken with a mermaid princess.

'Princess stories are her favourites,' Oliver confirmed.

'Any particular one?' Lia asked.

'I'd love to say it's *The Princess and the Pea*, which is my favourite.' He grinned and slipped his arm round her waist, pulling her in for a light hug. 'But this week she's all about Belle.'

He shook his head and smiled, as if he were going over all the other stories they'd read together and loving it every bit as much as he had the first time round.

More love than she'd thought possible bloomed within her. This was the man who was going to love her child. Love her. If life felt this great now, who knew how happy she could be in a few years' time?

Happier than her parents were, she thought, discreetly crossing her fingers and shooting a *please* look up to the heavens.

'Belle's a big reader,' Oliver said, as if he'd given the matter serious consideration. 'Which is a good thing.' He turned his attention back to her and asked, 'What do *you* think of Belle? A good role model for little girls? Or too much of a dreamer?'

The sting of pain that always came from revisiting her childhood was tamped down by the realisation that Oliver genuinely cared about what sort of role models Élodie chose. Her heart practically swelled to bursting as she thought of him showing the same level of detailed concern for their own child.

She hadn't really read fairy tales when she was growing up. Nor had anyone read them to her. Her parents had made a stab at it, sure, but… They'd been busy with their failing marriage, and her nannies had been much more focused on the palace's long list of rules and restrictions rather than on the actual child they were meant to be caring for.

For her, being raised royal had been basically like being raised in another century. And not a particularly fun one.

'I have to make a confession.' Lia bit her lip and looked up into Oliver's dark blue eyes.

His brow furrowed. 'About…?'

'I'm a bit of a novice when it comes to fairy tale princesses. Which one is Belle?'

'Belle! You know… *Beauty and the Beast. Aaargh!*' He distorted his face and turned his hands into claws, making Lia laugh.

'Which one are you, then?' she asked playfully.

'I thought it would be obvious that you, my dear, are Beauty.'

He popped a kiss on her cheek, then returned his gaze to Élodie as he briefly explained the storyline.

His smile turned thoughtful when he said, 'I think she loves Belle because she isn't scared of the Beast. She's had to face a lot of medical monsters in her time. And, of course, the loss of her parents. She's endured a lot of loss. Too much for a little girl with so much joy to share.'

He gave Lia's hand a squeeze.

'Belle's like you, as well. Smart. Thoughtful. Excellent taste in fiancés,' he added with a cheeky grin, and then, more gently, 'Maybe that's why Élodie enjoys your company so much. You've both borne too heavy a burden of loss, too young, but you're proof that all those hurdles don't have to trip you up. They make you stronger.'

Lia was about to launch into an explanation of how she had been born into her title, whereas Belle had proactively chosen to be a princess, when what Oliver had said gained purchase.

He saw her as strong. As resilient. Someone who had overcome the struggles in her past rather than someone who had been beaten by them. She'd never looked at herself that way.

She nestled into Oliver's hug, hoping he understood how

much his opinion mattered to her. How grateful she was for his positive outlook on life. He was no beast. He was a knight in shining armour. *Her* knight. And she knew in that instant that all her fears that he would change when they were married were unfounded. This was who he was. This was the man she would have the privilege of loving for the rest of her life.

They stood together, looking like all the other happy couples, enjoying the hubbub around them and, of course, Élodie's huge, beaming smile every time she turned round and waved at them, moving closer to the mermaid princess.

Oliver laughed and beamed back, waving like a proud father each time. Kindness radiated from him. His affection for the little girl went beyond that of a doctor and patient, and it dawned on her that he loved her as if she was his own.

Rather than that fact making her feel fearful, or excluded, Lia felt as if she'd been invited into a big love bubble—one that had the capacity to grow into something bigger and better the more their own family grew.

The revelation warmed Lia's heart in a way she'd never experienced. She'd been taught that love was an exclusive thing. A private thing. But it was quite the opposite. Being generous with his love didn't detract from Oliver's love for her, or the child they were going to have. It made it more powerful.

Love, she realised, was Oliver's superpower.

She wanted to give their child that same gift.

She looked at Oliver, enjoying the delight in his features when Élodie made the mermaid princess laugh when as two of them hugged while Grace took their photo. The mermaid wiggled. Élodie wiggled. The rest of the little girls in the queue wiggled. They were all giggling as if this was the very best moment in their lives.

Oliver started wiggling too, and gave her a hip-bump to make her join in.

An ache to be so fun and free wrapped around her heart and squeezed tight. Instinct, or rather training, dictated that princesses did not wiggle.

And then it hit her. Why on earth not? It clearly brought happiness and laughter, neither of which were bad things.

As if the scales had literally dropped from her eyes, Lia saw her future with a new clarity. The way she approached being a princess was up to her. It didn't have to be a horrid duty—a burden she had no choice in bearing…something that came with rules and regulations that strangled like the tightest of corsets. These princesses were all smiles and fun. Okay, sure… They were pretend princesses and they were being paid to smile… But the *joy* they were giving all these children genuinely seemed to be a *shared* joy. Something she definitely wanted to be a part of.

As they made their way around the rest of the magical kingdom Lia had Grace tell her as many princess stories as she could. Snow White's stepmother had sent her into the woods to be killed. Sleeping Beauty had been cursed by an evil fairy. Cinderella had been forced into life as a scullery maid by her stepmother. Rapunzel's mother had given her to a witch as penance for stealing some delicious salad greens she'd craved whilst pregnant.

A few stories in, and Lia was beginning to think she'd not had it quite so bad after all.

When they arrived at the queue for Prince Charming's carousel and Grace paused for breath, Lia asked Élodie, 'Don't any of these stories frighten you?'

Élodie dramatically shook her head, as if the idea was absurd. 'Nope!'

'Why not?' Lia asked, truly interested.

'Because all the princesses win against the scary things,

and the evil people usually shrivel up or disappear in a puff of smoke once they realise good is better than bad.'

'I thought the handsome princes fixed everything,' Grace said, giving Oliver an uncharacteristic wink.

Élodie pursed her lips, as if the idea were ridiculous. 'It's the *princesses* who win. They have the brains and the power. They just need to see things from a different angle and when they do...' She made a swirling motion with the magic wand Oliver had bought her. 'Everything's good again.'

'Girl power. I like it.' Lia grinned. 'Shame about the handsome princes.' She gave Oliver a good-natured elbow in the ribs. 'It's always nice to have a helping hand when the world is coming to an end.'

Élodie looked at her, still as serious as if she were working out a long division problem. 'The princesses and maidens in distress could've totally believed what the evil stepmothers and bad fairies and everyone told them—but they didn't.' She tapped her heart. 'They listened to *this*!'

She leant in to Lia and cupped her hand, as if she wanted to keep a secret from Oliver, but spoke loud enough so that they could all hear.

'A lot of people think the handsome princes do it all, but even though they're really nice, and know a lot about medicine, they are usually cuter than they are smart.'

Oliver clutched his hands to his heart. '*Oof!* What a blow to my ego! And here I was thinking I was going to save you all from peril by the end of the day.'

'Well,' Élodie conceded, 'some of the princes have nice horses, and usually a castle, and sometimes a dog. I think every princess would like a dog with fluffy ears, wouldn't she?'

Oliver choked back a laugh and gave Élodie a *good point* nod.

'Next riders on their mounts!' called the woman in charge of boarding people onto the carousel.

'You've got a great way of looking at the world,' Grace said, guiding Élodie onto a carousel horse while Lia and Oliver mounted the horses just behind them.

Lia grabbed the reins of her horse and pretended to spur it into a gallop as the carousel began its slow whir into action. 'Race you to the finish line!' she challenged Oliver, who immediately 'spurred' his own horse into a gallop.

She felt unbelievably happy. This trip to the theme park was meant to be fun, and it was, but she hadn't expected to learn an important lesson to boot. She was the mistress of her own destiny.

It was all about perspective. If she could tap into the truest part of her heart and realign her perspective…then the rest of her life would pan out to be the happiest.

A few hours later, after they'd dropped Grace and a sleeping Élodie off at their hotel room, they climbed into bed in their sumptuous suite.

'That was the best day.'

'The best?' Oliver let out a low whistle, then pulled her to him. 'I wonder if there's any way we could make it better?'

The atmosphere between them instantly shifted from playful to sensual. As Oliver's bare skin connected with her own, Lia felt electricity pulse through her in a decidedly womanly way. Gone was the little girl princess having innocent fun. In her place was the woman, who was more than happy to show her handsome prince just how much she loved him. So she did.

In the morning, after they'd had some coffee in bed, luxuriating in the rare occurrence of having nothing to do, Lia gave in to a whim and jumped up on the bed and began to bounce. Her hair was flying every which way. She was wearing mismatched pyjamas. There was music playing. It was *fun*! The type of fun she'd never, ever been allowed to have nor, later in life, let herself have.

'What are you doing, you madwoman?' Oliver laughed.

'Things I never did as a kid.' She grinned, beckoning for him to join her. 'It's your fault,' she said. 'You taught me that it was important to be me!'

She bounced until she was high enough to whip herself into a somersault—only to land on her back with an ungainly *thunk*.

She curled into a protective ball. 'Ow!'

Oliver's blood ran cold.

The baby.

He raced to her, all his pent-up fears about losing the chance to become a father surging through him.

'Don't move. Did you hurt your stomach? Anything else? Tell me everything.'

She gave a little groan and pushed herself up. 'I'm fine. Embarrassed at my lack of grace, but fine.' She moved her head around as proof that her neck was all right, too. She swept her hand along her stomach. 'We're both fine.'

Relief was engulfed by something else as he felt the past consume him.

'What were you thinking?' he demanded.

Lia took his face in her hands. 'Hey. I'm okay. It's okay.'

He shook her hands away and bit out in a tone that sounded foreign even to him, 'You've got to be more careful. Don't you *want* our child?'

'Hey!' She held up her hands for him to stop—which, mercifully, he did.

They both stared at one another. Hard. Like boxers squaring off with one another before the referee rang the starting bell.

This was a side of Oliver Lia had seen tiny glimpses of,

but before his concern had always felt protective, a buffer against the rest of the world, not another set of rules and regulations.

Yes, she'd made a bad decision. But enough to warrant accusing her of not wanting her child…? That was a line he shouldn't have crossed.

She reminded herself that this month had been one of extremes. That they were strangers compelled to marry because of an accidental pregnancy and the demands of the palace. Both of them had had to deal with childhoods that hadn't been the happiest. Both of them were facing a future that was very different from whatever either of them had dreamed. But she'd thought they'd found happiness in a new dream. Hadn't they?

Clinging to what remained of her calm she asked, 'Oliver? Is there something going on?'

Everything about him bore an air of gravity and stillness that instantly crushed what remained of her self-confidence. A sharp, icy sensation pierced through to her heart when he said, 'I probably should've told you this back when you found out you were pregnant…'

This was a crossroads and they both knew it. Oliver swept a hand through his hair, wishing he could pull the perfect words out of his brain.

He hadn't meant to keep this from Lia, but the longer he'd kept it to himself, the more it had gained power over him. No matter how many times he'd reminded himself that this wasn't the past, and Lia wasn't his ex, the fear that he might lose this chance at fatherhood had gnawed at his ability to truly open his heart to her.

He tried to force some rational thoughts to the fore.

Lia was her own person. A deeply proud, intelligent, controlled and very private woman who, in the handful of time they'd spent together, he'd seen blossom into a free spirit. And, even though he hated himself for it, there was a part of him that feared the choices she might make without him.

But he loved her, and knew with every second that ticked past that he was pushing her away. She deserved to know where all this was coming from.

'I had a girlfriend once…' he began, his voice ragged with emotion.

Lia nodded for him to continue, but she pulled away from his touch, tucking her knees under her chin and wrapping her arms around them, as if cocooning herself from any harm.

'We met during our internships at Oxford.'

Again, Lia nodded, the wariness in her eyes turning the irises an almost transparent blue.

He forced the words out as neutrally as he could. 'She fell pregnant, but kept the news to herself. And then…then she "sorted it" without even discussing it with me.'

Lia frowned. 'What do you mean, she—?' She stopped herself, her expression making it clear she understood that his girlfriend had terminated the pregnancy. 'I'm so sorry, Oliver. I'm sure she had her reasons, but still… I can't imagine how that would've felt.' She reached out to him, then abruptly pulled back. 'Why would my jumping around remind you of that?'

He was going to have to choose his words carefully. They'd both grown up in strict households with an exacting list of expectations. A regime that hadn't suited either of them. This wasn't an attempt to lay down more rules. But he knew that asking her to be more cautious could come across that way.

He wanted her to know he was here for her. That he wanted to be involved. That he wanted to be a part of this journey with her, every step of the way, supporting her and their child. So when he'd seen her whirl around, then land with a thump, sprawled out on the bed, not moving, his worst fears had taken over.

'I was worried you'd hurt yourself. And the baby.'

Her frown deepened. 'Oliver, women have been doing all sorts of things whilst pregnant—including dancing and working and probably even having pillow fights—and still having healthy, happy babies. It's early days, yet. I'm not even showing. We're still within the three months when most people don't tell anyone.'

'Yes. And the reason they don't tell anyone is because the chances of losing the baby are higher.'

She pressed her lips together, their dusty rose colour whitening from the pressure.

He didn't blame her for being angry. One doctor informing another how the body worked was ultra-patronising. Especially when that doctor was the father of your child.

Lia stared at him. Hard. 'Oliver. You brought me to an amusement park. We were riding on *rollercoasters* yesterday!'

'Yes—and I made sure you didn't go on anything that would harm the baby.'

Lia's blue eyes blazed with indignation. 'Oh, you did, did you? You kept a special eye out for me because you've decided I don't have the maternal instinct to do so myself? I'm not your ex, Oliver. I want this baby every bit as much as you do. I guess the real question I should be asking myself is, do I want you as much as I want the child?'

Oliver felt the impact of her words as if they were a physical blow. What a moment to realise he'd let his past darken his future. He loved her. He did. He wanted to build on the foundation of what they'd been sharing over these last few weeks. But something caught the words in his throat and stemmed them.

Lia swept away angry tears. 'It's pretty clear your priority is our child and not me. Which is a step up from my father's parenting skills, anyway. It's a good trick, though, Oliver. Playing the doting fiancé right up until you get your heir. Well done for keeping me wrapped up in a little princess cocoon. Bewitching me into thinking it was me you cared about.'

He wanted to pound his head against the wall. Turn back time. Anything to fix this.

Tell her you love her.

'Lia, you know I'm not like that.'

'Do I?' she asked, obviously unsatisfied with his response. 'Do I really know anything about you? Up until a few minutes ago I was pretty sure I knew you, and how you felt about me, but now… Now, I'm not so sure.'

Oliver tried to force his brain and his heart to work in tandem. Words clogged up his throat. None of them were the right ones to express how he felt. And his silence fed her anger.

'If you'll remember, *I'm* the one who told you about this child, Oliver. I didn't have to. I'm also the one who told the palace, knowing that they'd force me into this.'

He bridled. 'Force you into marrying me? No one's forcing anyone to do anything. I thought we were having fun. That we—'

She cut him off. 'I don't want to marry someone to be a bit of *fun*.'

He could practically see Lia's emotions withdraw like the tide, and in their place came the ice. So why wasn't he throwing a pickaxe into the wall between them and breaking through the ice to that warm, beautiful heart of hers?

She fixed him with her pale blue eyes. 'I didn't want this. *Any* of this.'

The words hung between them like daggers.

Everything they hadn't discussed about the future hovered above them like an enormous wave, about to drown them with the sheer weight of it all. A wave comprised of one question: did they love one another?

He rattled through a checklist of their lives. The positives? Life on St Victoria was amazing. The past month had been wonderful. They each did their jobs without the impediment of their pasts. The negatives? Lia's life wasn't picture-perfect. Until they'd met she'd been isolated. Lonely. And, when you put a magnifying glass to it, Oliver's life wasn't perfect either. He was caring for everyone but himself. Salving other people's wounds whilst his own remained untended.

Beyond the window he caught a glimpse of the fairy castle. The very turret he'd said he'd climb to tell one and all how he felt about Lia.

But he hadn't.

This conversation, he realised, was what they had to survive before either of them got their happy ending. Their darkest fears had to be confronted.

'What do you want, Lia? What do you really want?' Oliver asked.

'I want to marry someone who wants to marry *me*. Not the palace. Not the baby. Not anything else but me.'

He knew what she was saying. She wanted to marry someone who was in love with her. And of all the people in the world, she deserved nothing less.

He felt the bone-deep ache of knowing he'd approached this from the wrong angle. From the moment he'd found out she was pregnant his focus had been on the baby. He'd been so intent on ensuring he became a father that he hadn't allowed his feelings for Lia the space they deserved.

She'd trusted him.

And, stupidly, he'd broken that precious link.

She spoke before he could. 'I didn't think you had it in you to do something so cruel. But lucky me! Now I know exactly who it is I've agreed to marry, I'm not so certain I think it's a very good idea.'

Washes of hot and cold swept through him so fast he didn't have time to react to either one.

Splitting up when they'd only just begun their journey together was the last thing he wanted, but he wasn't going to insist upon pursuing a marriage she saw as a trap. A cage.

There was only one option.

'All right then.' Oliver looked Lia straight in the eye. 'The wedding's off.'

CHAPTER ELEVEN

OLIVER'S VOICE WAS barely penetrating the roar of blood pounding through her head.

He didn't want to marry her.

She stared at his mouth, trying to parse the words as he spoke.

'Your happiness and the baby's wellbeing are what's important here,' he said.

A complete understanding of the situation cracked open her chest and laid her heart bare. She'd never felt more humiliated. More blind to what had been happening all along. Oliver genuinely didn't want her. He wanted the baby. An heir. A child to replace the one he'd been denied.

Her heart ached for the pain he'd endured, but that was no reason to play such a cruel game with her emotions.

She pulled the ring off her finger, pressed it into Oliver's hand, and fled the room before he could see a single tear fall. She didn't need to listen to the rest of whatever he was going to say before she put his name on the growing list of people who didn't want her.

First her mother, then her father, then a string of so-called friends and boyfriends. They hadn't wanted her. Just something *from* her. Status. Prestige. Their picture in a glossy magazine. Those were the reasons a handful of girls back at school had been friendly towards her. They certainly hadn't actually wanted to be friends.

But wanting her for a baby?

That was a new level of low she couldn't wrap her head around. Nor did it match the man she'd connected with so perfectly that first, undeniably wonderful night. The night they had conceived their child.

She blindly got into the lift, not caring which floor it landed on. What did matter? The one thing she'd thought was a certainty in her life had just been shattered into a million unfixable pieces.

She'd thought the protective shield she'd built around herself was strong enough to endure another assault. A safe haven. But she'd let that shield fall for Oliver. The one man she'd ever let herself truly love. And he only wanted her for the child she was going to bear.

Icy-cold tendrils of darkness swept through her bloodstream and tightened their hold on her heart. She'd thought she'd known loneliness before, but she'd been wrong. *This* was what real loneliness felt like. Bone-crushing loss.

'Lia?'

Lia looked around her. Somehow she'd ended up in front of the hotel.

'What are you doing out here?'

Grace reached out and touched her hand, her eyes dropping to the bare ring finger that was effectively telling the story Lia couldn't yet put a voice to.

Grace's expression sobered—a direct contrast to her theme park tiara and jolly pink and white polka-dotted carry-all. 'You okay?'

No. She was about as far from okay as it got. Not that she could say as much. Especially not to someone she worked with.

Up until a handful of weeks ago, crossing the line between her work and personal lives had been something she'd avoided as if her life depended upon it. Work was the one sanctuary that had never let her down, and merely thinking about letting Grace or anyone else into her private life more than she had terrified her.

'Come, darlin',' Grace said after a moment, her soft island lilt as soothing as her touch. 'Come with me.'

'But...aren't you off to the airport?'

'You can come with us if you want.'

Lia started rummaging round in the tote bag she'd blindly grabbed as she'd left the suite. 'I don't think I have my passport...'

What little self-possession she had began to crumble. There was no way she could go back up there, tail between her legs, and get her passport. Stomping in and out wasn't her style either. Hiding out and reading books and going to work was her style. A desperate longing for her little cottage on St Victoria took hold.

She stiffened when she felt someone else by her side.

'Lia!'

Élodie. Yet another reminder of Oliver.

As Lia did her best to dredge up a smile, the young girl looked up into her face and, with the unerring eye of a child who had known more tragedy than she should have, instantly read the situation.

'Here.' She handed Lia the magic wand Oliver had bought her yesterday. 'I think you might need this more than me.'

Lia made a weird laughing, snuffling, hiccuping noise, then dropped down so that she was at eye level with Élodie. 'Thank you, love, but I don't think even a magic wand can fix things today.'

Élodie looked at her with such disbelief it disarmed her. 'But...' the little girl protested. 'But believing in something hard enough, strong enough, is supposed to make almost every wish come true.'

Lia wanted to refute that. Tell her, no, that wasn't the way the world worked. And then it dawned on her that of all the people in the world Élodie was one of those who knew that every dream didn't come true. No matter how hard she prayed, wished or waved her magic wand, her parents would never come back. Nor would she ever get back one solitary minute of the weeks and weeks of her childhood she'd spent in hospital. She understood what reality was in the deepest possible way, and still she faced the future with hope.

Lia shifted her hand to her belly and forced herself to take a deep breath in and out.

Okay. Things with Oliver might not have gone the way she wanted. In fact, they'd gone completely the opposite way to what she wanted. But she was still pregnant with a little boy or girl who had their entire life in front of them. And she wanted more than anything to make sure that future was a good one.

'I think it's fate we ran into each other,' Grace said gently. 'Please, join us.'

'But…passport…?'

Grace gave her arm a squeeze, then waved her hand. 'I can run up and get that. Not a problem.' She turned to go, then stopped and turned back. 'You know, I'm going to take Élodie to see my daughter and her family when we land. Would you like to come?'

'You have a daughter?'

Grace tried and failed to mask her surprise that Lia didn't know, 'Yes—and a son.'

Lia felt yet another tectonic shift. Not because Grace had children—more because in all of the three years they'd worked together, Lia had never asked her.

Was the cocoon she'd accused Oliver of putting her in actually one she'd made herself? Was the protective shield she'd held up between herself and loneliness actually the reason for it?

'How old is she? Your daughter?'

'Just gone thirty. Given me two lovely grandbabies, she has.'

Lia frowned. How had she not known this?

'My boy is twenty-eight and set to be married next spring… I'm sorry I could go on and on about them,' Grace tacked on in an apologetic tone, 'so I'll stop.'

'No, please. I'm interested.'

Lia felt ashamed. Just because she didn't like people to know about her own life didn't mean she couldn't show an interest in other people's. Grace had been nothing but kind to her through three years, and she hadn't even known she had grown children, let alone grandchildren.

A niggle of discomfort that Oliver might have been right to treat her with kid gloves needled into her conscience. There were a thousand questions she should've been asking him over these past few weeks. About his past, his hopes, his dreams. The same thousand questions he should've been asking her…

'Here's your taxi, ma'am.' A bellhop carrying a couple of wheelie bags splashed with bright tropical flowers bearing The Island Clinic luggage tags gestured to a car a few metres away.

Grace leant in and in a low voice said, 'Élodie's aunt and uncle are still off working on that yacht job, so I thought I'd take her for a playdate and maybe an overnight stay with my daughter's girls, before she heads back to an empty house.'

'Don't the aunt and uncle have children?'

Grace pulled a face. 'They're all teenagers, fresh out of school, and they're working as well,' she explained with a shake of her head. 'I hate thinking of that poor girl spending so much time on her own… Melody won't mind if I bring one more.'

'Melody?' Lia repeated.

'My daughter,' Grace said, as if Lia should know this. She pushed her lips forward, then shifted her weight to her other hip and stared at Lia—*hard.* She blinked once, her expression unreadable, then said, 'Joining us doesn't obligate you to anything.'

Lia wished she could pull their entire interchange from the air and incinerate it. What *was* it with her? She had to stop pushing people away if she was ever going to get that so-called normal life she wanted.

'No!' she insisted. 'Really. That's not it. Not it at all. I just want to— I want—'

She wanted to be with Oliver. Wanted it to be yesterday, when everything had seemed perfect—like a fairy tale. But life wasn't a fairy tale. It was real. Oliver had just called their wedding off. And she had to take some responsibility for that.

Her new life would have to begin with the smallest of steps. Or, in this case, a plane ride. 'Yes, please, Grace. I'd love to come.'

Grace's face brightened into a broad smile and Élodie jumped up and down, shouting, 'Yippee!'

Grace nodded to the taxi and said to Lia, 'You go on ahead and help Élodie get buckled up. I'll go get your passport.'

When Grace reappeared, she wasn't alone.

Oliver was with her, his expression taut with a determination Lia had never seen before. He was as handsome as ever, and his blue eyes glittered with an inner strength that made him appear both powerful and kind. He'd opened his heart to her, told her of his darkest moment, his biggest fear, and she'd made it about herself. Had unleashed her fears on him like weapons.

The fact that he was here made her respect for him soar up a few more notches. He was a man who faced his problems head-on. She needed to prove she could do the same. If it turned out he didn't love her, they'd find some way to deal with it…to move on. To ensure that Oliver was in her child's life.

Would it break her heart? Absolutely. Would she do it for her child. Without reservation.

She stepped towards him. The air around them was electric with the myriad emotions both of them were feeling.

Her list was pretty long: hope, fear, hurt and, yes, love. Still love.

He wasn't saying anything. It was up to her to break the silence.

'Hey…'

She cringed. There was definitely room for improvement in her truce-making skills.

Eyes glued to hers, Oliver said, 'I understand there's cake on offer at Melody's.'

Lia glanced at Grace, who was looking entirely too innocent for someone who had clearly told Oliver his fiancée was trying to run away.

Ex-fiancée.

Her gut churned. She didn't want to be his ex. She wanted to be his someone. For him to be hers. The one person in the world who knew everything about her. The good, the bad, and everything else in between.

A tiny little bloom of hope rose in her chest.

The fact that he was here meant something, right?

Maybe they'd got it all wrong when they'd fought.

Maybe Oliver was as nervous as she was. Just as full of concerns and anxieties about their future.

They should have started talking about more than their favourite colours and dog breeds the day they'd found out she was pregnant. They should still be talking now.

If only he wasn't so utterly kissable!

Not a good enough excuse.

This wasn't the time to think about how much he loved it when she traced her fingers along his collarbone, or kissed him just under the ridge of his jaw, or slid alongside him, spooning their naked bodies together as if they'd been designed for one another.

She looked up and saw that Oliver was examining her, presumably trying to figure out what she was smiling about when he'd just called off their wedding.

A blush crept into her cheeks.

Jumping on him and ripping his clothes off wasn't the solution. Talking was.

Sensing that things weren't going to turn into sunshine and roses and, more to the point, that there wasn't going to be another proposal here in the taxi rank, Grace bustled everyone into the car, where she and Élodie kept up a flow of conversation about the theme park, and how the Room Service fries were curly, not straight, and how they loved the scent of the lotion in the bathroom at the hotel, but how nice it would be to get back home.

Élodie gravely informed them that she'd reached a few conclusions, including the fact that going to theme parks was extra-fun. Especially with adults, because they laughed more than they did in real life. Also, she was going to join the swim team when she was old enough, because mermaids seemed very special indeed, and finally, living like a princess every day did seem to have *some* plus points, but maybe not every day—because princesses probably couldn't have chocolate cake.

Lia managed to share a smile with Oliver at this. The one thing she'd been craving since she fell pregnant was chocolate cake.

Throughout the ride, the flight, and the second taxi ride to Grace's daughter's house, Lia and Oliver were mostly silent. But the angry tension from their fight had softened—largely thanks to Élodie, who could wrap Oliver round her little finger like a soft piece of ribbon. Which, of course, made Lia love him that little bit more.

When they got to the house they both stayed on the porch, saying they needed a minute before coming in.

'I just have to make a quick call,' they said at the same time.

Their nervous laughs twined together.

'I need to call my father,' she said, at the same time as he told her he needed to call his parents.

'To call things off?' she dared to ask.

Grace shooed Élodie inside before Oliver could answer.

'To clear the air,' Oliver said once they were alone.

Which was interesting. Why would he need to clear the air with his parents?

'Should we maybe do that first? Clear the air?' she asked, hoping he wanted to salvage things as much as she did. 'Before we call home?'

He tipped his head to the side, his eyes glued to her as if he was trying to see her from a different angle. She prayed with every fibre in her being that he saw the hope in her heart.

'Good idea,' he said.

And just like that she could breathe again.

As if by spoken agreement they went in and joined

Grace's family, each of them needing just a bit more time to collect their thoughts before they had *that talk*. The one that would decide their future.

Once the little girls had been sorted out with some games, Grace, Lia and Oliver sat on the patio, enjoying the shade over the picnic table as Grace's daughter brought out an enormous chocolate cake.

'Chocolate's supposed to help you fall in love—but I guess you two don't need the extra boost, do you?' Melody smiled at Lia, putting the cake down in front of her.

Lia tried and failed to fight the sting of tears at the back of her throat.

'Oh! Did I say the wrong thing?' Melody's eyes shot to her mother. Grace shook her head.

Oliver cleared his throat and took a long drink of iced tea.

Poor Melody obviously had no idea what was going on, but she innately knew that making a fuss would be a bad idea.

Grace rose and said, 'Melody? I wonder if you wouldn't mind helping me rustle up a few sandwiches for the little ones.'

Lia shot her a grateful smile. She was giving Oliver and Lia some much-needed alone time.

Melody began to head to the kitchen. 'I'm not sure we have any bread…'

'Well, then…' Grace looked positively thrilled by this news. 'I don't think these two will mind if we pop to the store, do you?' She gave Oliver a look. 'If you hear screaming, would you mind looking in on the children?'

Laughing, Melody rolled her eyes. 'We'll take them with us.' She gave her mother a tight, fierce hug. 'I know it's only been forty-eight hours, but it's good to have my best friend back.'

'Your mother, you mean,' Lia corrected, without thinking.

'No…' Melody shook her head. 'She's my mama, but more than that she's my bestie.' She gave her mother a little hip-bump and the two of them shared a complicit cackle, then started rounding up the children.

A deep longing Lia had never acknowledged opened in her chest. A painful, agonising hunger she'd tried to hide for almost her entire life. The hunger for the love and friendship of her mother.

The tears she'd been trying to keep at bay finally began to fall.

Oliver pulled out a fresh handkerchief and handed it to her, then nudged a slice of cake in front of her. 'You know they say a problem shared is a problem halved…'

She let the invitation sit between them, and after a moment's hesitation said, 'Even if we're not getting married any more?'

Oliver drew in a sharp breath, then said, 'Let's not worry about the wedding right now. What's important is that we understand each other.'

'Well… I guess what we need to talk about is the fact you called off the wedding.'

He held up a hand. 'I did that because it seemed like the last thing on earth you wanted. And I don't want it if you don't want it.'

The way he said it opened up a warm ray of sunshine in her heart. 'So…you still want to marry me?'

He took the ring out of his shirt pocket and put it on the table between them. 'Why don't we have a good long talk and see what we come up with.'

So Lia began to talk. And talk and talk and talk. With an openness and candour she'd never allowed herself before.

She told Oliver about her childhood. Her parents' acrimonious divorce. Her mother's exile when the royal council had insisted Lia and her father move back into the palace to 'keep things in order' once the divorce had been finalised. Her father's emotional withdrawal. Boarding school. Her lack of friends. The pleasure she'd found working in medicine. How it had doubled when she'd begun to do it at The Island Clinic in St Victoria.

'And then I met you.'

Their gazes caught and held, the magic of that night returning with a strength she wouldn't have thought possible.

'And you fell pregnant.'

Lia nodded. 'And the palace said we had to get married.'

'And that made you unhappy?' Oliver asked.

It was a loaded question and they both knew it.

'It frightened me.'

'Why?

Again the sting of tears struck, hard and fast. 'I don't want what happened to my parents to happen to us.'

There. She'd said it. And the world hadn't ended. Oliver hadn't fled for the hills. Quite the opposite, in fact. He was leaning in, taking her hands in his, a sweet, gorgeous, earnest expression on his face.

'We won't let it.'

'How do you know?'

'Because we love each other.'

She blinked away a few tears. 'You've never said that.'

He grimaced. 'I know. I should have. I did. I *do*. I just…' He took a steadying breath. 'I let what happened in the past fine-tune my focus on the baby. *Our* baby. It blinded me to the fact that I was falling in love with you. When you left the hotel room today I suddenly realised just how big a part of my life you've become. Obviously I can't wait to meet our baby, but every single moment I think about having is with you. Without you…' He shook his head. 'I don't want a life without you. We're the ones who are giving this child life and I want us to raise it together—as a family. Bring it on trips to Disney World—every year if you want. Or we can lock the rest of the world out and have it be just the three of us, tucked away in the treehouse. Or even living in separate houses—'

'No.' She shook her head, laughing now. 'Not separate houses.' She put her hand on his heart, gratified to feel it pounding as quickly as her own. 'I think I was scared to admit it too. That I loved you. And even now that I know I do, it feels like giving up part of myself. My control.'

He nodded. 'Given your past, I'm not surprised. It seems as if everyone you've let yourself love has disappointed you in some way. I don't want to be one of those people.'

She touched his cheek, speechless. It felt as if they were practically exchanging vows here and now.

She picked the ring up from the table and held it between them. 'What if I were to put this on again and promise never to take it off?'

Relief flooded Oliver's chest. Lia still wanted to marry him. 'You'd be making me a very happy man.'

Lia handed him the ring and, as if they were at the ceremony itself, he slipped it onto her finger.

'Feel good?' he asked.

'It feels perfect.' She looked across at him. 'You know, I've done a lot of pouring my heart out…are there any problems you'd like halved?'

He laughed, his fingers toying with the ring on Lia's finger. 'You don't want the wedding at the palace, do you?'

She shook her head. 'No, I don't. I want it here on St

Victoria. On a date we want, with guests we want and the food we want. Chocolate cake, obviously. On the beach.' Quickly she added, 'If that's what you want?'

'It sounds perfect.' He dropped a kiss onto the back of her hand. 'Especially if we throw in a midnight swim after the guests have gone.'

She grinned, but her smile faded as, once again, reality surfaced. 'I don't quite know how we're going to derail all the palace plans…'

'I have an idea,' Oliver said. 'Rather than make phone calls, why don't we get on planes? To Europe? You and I still have loads to talk about, and by the time we land in England I think we'll have a pretty good game plan.'

'For what?' Lia gave him a sidelong glance.

'For letting our parents know we're our own people now. That we love them, we respect them, but that our futures are precisely that. *Ours.*'

Three days later, Lia felt as if she had literally entered another world. A world preserved in time every bit as much as her own childhood had been.

'Ready?' Oliver asked, giving her hand a squeeze.

'As I'll ever be,' she said, lifting a pair of crossed fingers, which Oliver kissed for extra luck.

Huge stone lions stood atop enormous granite pillars at the top of an avenue of trees that had clearly seen generations of Bainbridges make their way to the family seat.

Summer was in its full glory in England, and the Bainbridges' estate was no different.

'I see Mother's made sure the flowers are all in full bloom for you.'

Lia gave him a funny look, because she hadn't seen anything, and then, as they passed down the final length of the tree-lined avenue she gasped in delight. In front of them was an enormous country house…palace? Whatever it was, it was impressive. A sprawl of windows and climbing roses and balconies and turrets was buttressed by immaculately manicured gardens. There was a huge lake off to one side, along with another smaller but far from small house. And beyond that another.

'The Dowager Duchess's house. Currently empty,' Oliver explained. 'And those are the stables, off to the left. Mostly empty too, I suppose, apart from my parents' horses.'

'And you're sure about your idea? The one you want to put to your parents?' she asked.

'Look at the place,' he said, steering the car with a practised hand into the large circular drive. 'It's enormous. No amount of children we have could ever fill it.'

'Good point.' She laughed, her nerves getting the better of her.

His parents' place—Oliver's birthright—was every bit as grand as the palace she'd grown up in. She leant forward, trying to absorb the splendour of it all, then suddenly, thinking of their lives back in St Victoria, started properly giggling.

'What?'

'You grew up in a stately home and now you live in a treehouse!' She hooted.

Oliver feigned deep hurt. 'I thought you liked my treehouse!'

'I love it more than ever,' she said, meaning it. 'You do realise you grew up in a costume drama, right?'

Oliver laughed. 'It was a drama, all right.' He sighed, his shoulders slumping. 'Cold War more like.'

Amelia turned in her seat to face him. 'Oli… Are you okay? You don't have to do this, you know.'

'I do,' he assured her, giving her a quick smile before

pulling the car up in front of the house. 'Besides, I've got my superpower now.'

'What superpower is that?' Lia asked, thinking of the multitude he already possessed.

'You.'

It took the arrival of a butler to stop the kissing that ensued. Holding hands, red-faced and still giggling, Lia and Oliver went up the grand entrance steps to meet his parents.

An hour later Oliver wondered who had kidnapped his parents and replaced them with the kind, interested couple sitting before him.

Gone were the icy exteriors, the uncomfortable handshakes and awkward chit-chat about the weather. In their place were welcoming greetings, enthusiastic storytelling—mostly embarrassing stories from Oliver's childhood—and a warmth he'd never once experienced in their company.

They were sitting underneath a loggia draped in frothy purple and white wisteria blossoms, eating a rather impressive afternoon tea. The nerves that had been jack-knifing round Oliver's ribcage reached critical mass. It was now or never time.

He felt the weight of his parents' eyes shifting to him. His mother's. His father's. His bewitching bride-to-be's. He drew his strength from her—and her nod of encouragement.

After he'd explained his idea to his parents, he sat back in his chair. 'If you'd like some time to think about it, please do.'

His parents looked at one another, silently exchanging information, and then, as one, gave each other a nod of understanding.

In that instant Oliver understood a thousand things about them that he'd never understood before. They loved one another. Very deeply. They just loved one another in their own way. Now that he was grown, and the stress of parenting had been taken out of their hands, they were able to relax into the lives they had wanted to live all along. Whereas he loved interacting with children, they loved interacting with adults. They loved old—he loved whimsical.

They loved him. They simply hadn't known how to love him as a child.

That revelation cleared the way for an entirely new relationship with them. He swallowed, his heart lodging in his throat. A relationship he might have just compromised with his proposal.

'We love it,' his father said. 'There will be the particulars to organise, of course. One doesn't simply snap one's fingers to change a house like this into an activity centre for underprivileged children, but…yes… I like it.' He turned to Lia. 'The old place has done its time serving the country before, you know.'

'Oh…?'

'During World War I. I hadn't even been born then, but I've seen the pictures. My father, and his father before him, cleared every room in the place and turned it into a hospital for returning soldiers. Wretched business they'd been through, poor chaps.' He stopped and gave his chin a thoughtful rub, turned to Oliver. 'These young ones you're proposing to move in…do you suppose they'd mind a couple of oldies knocking around the place? The estate, I mean?'

'Absolutely not! I didn't mean it needed to become an activity centre straight away. This is your home. You do with it exactly what you want, as long as you want to.'

Oliver gave himself an invisible thump on the head and went on to explain that he'd meant in a few years' time. He and Lia were perfectly happy in St Victoria, and didn't plan on moving back to the UK even when the estate was transformed into an activity centre for underprivileged children. They'd come back, of course. Frequently. But…

'I love you both,' he said. 'But this is how we see ourselves being involved in the estate in the future. I can't do what you did—uphold all those traditions. I'll try my very best to honour them, but we want to live our lives differently. We don't want the wedding in Karolinska. We don't want to live on a huge estate. We're doctors, and in a few months we'll be parents. That's where we want our focus to be.'

'Oliver.'

His mother gave him a look he remembered all too well from his childhood. The *Children should be seen and not heard* look.

He nodded for her to go ahead, grateful for the warmth of Lia's touch as she reached out to take one of his hands in hers. They shared a smile, and any nerves he'd felt slipped away. She loved his idea about the activity centre and had said she'd do everything in her power to support him. Holding his hand in plain view of his mother's stern gaze was all the proof he needed that she meant it.

'Oliver,' his mother repeated. 'Your father and I only live in a few of the rooms here, and we have actually been eyeing up the Dowager's house as alternative accommodation. We needed a bit of a push to get that particular ball rolling and you have now done it. If you would like to turn the estate into this activity place next week, you may…'

She paused and cleared her throat a couple of times, then paused again to clear what Oliver suddenly realised was an unexpected rush of emotion.

She looked at him with her clear blue eyes and said, 'Your father and I would be very pleased…very *proud*…if you were to go ahead with your plans whenever you like.

In fact…' She looked at her husband. 'Why wait? From this very moment it's yours. Consider it an early wedding gift.'

Lia choked on her tea. 'What?'

'Brilliant idea. Wonderful. Yes. The estate is yours.' Oliver's father gave his wife's hand a pat as he spoke, his eyes shifting from Lia to Oliver. 'We didn't give you much of a childhood, son, but we are very, very proud of the man you've become. And if turning this old echoey lump of stone into a house full of children properly enjoying themselves means we'll get to see more of you, the least we can do is start the ball rolling immediately.'

Too choked up to speak, Oliver rose—and for the first time in his life hugged his father.

Lia held her father's hands in her own. Their reunion had been trickier, but no less fruitful. 'And you're absolutely positive you're happy to tell Grandmama and Grandpapa?'

Behind her father, Oliver gave her a double thumbs-up.

She'd done it. She'd told him she didn't want to have the wedding at the palace and that, more than anything, she and Oliver wanted a simple beach wedding, with no press. But, if he was happy to come, she would love him to walk her down the aisle.

'I will tell them tonight.'

Lia winced. 'We're going to be on a plane tonight.'

'I know.'

Her father gave her a wicked grin she hadn't seen for decades—one that spoke of the little boy he'd once been. The one who'd used to learn magic tricks and do puppet shows in the nursery for the palace staff.

'I thought you might like to be a few thousand miles away in case your grandmother screams in protest.'

Lia laughed. 'Should we get you some ear plugs before we go?'

'I think I can handle it,' her father said, his smile fading a bit as their eyes met again. 'Watching this palace empty of young people has taught me something.'

'What's that?'

'That we need to change. *I* need to change. A royal family that no one wants to be in isn't much of an example to the nation, is it?'

The knot of emotion in Lia's chest softened. 'Dad...' she began, her voice less tentative than it had been when she'd told him she didn't want to be married in Karolinska. 'Do you think...do you think Mum could be persuaded to come?'

He shook his head. 'I don't know, love. But if there's anything I can do to help you get her on a plane, I will.'

Lia looked at him and saw that age-old flame he'd held for her mother was still burning bright. She gave him a hug, love pouring through her when she felt his hands close around her back to return the embrace. She would reach out to her mother. If she came, great. If not...perhaps she'd come when the baby was born.

In the car on the way back to the airport she leant back and breathed a sigh of relief.

'Happy?' Oliver asked.

'Mostly,' she said, leaning in to snuggle close to him, her cheek on his shoulder, their hands intertwined.

The reunion hadn't been as horrible as she'd thought it might be. Nor had it been quite as celebratory as Oliver's had. But that was okay, because she knew now, no matter what, that she would have the man she loved by her side from here on out. He was here for her, for her child, and for the family they would become. And that was what mattered most.

CHAPTER TWELVE

ÉLODIE ACCEPTED THE vibrant crown of tropical flowers as a queen might accept a tiara weighted with a nation's finest jewels.

'What do you think?' Lia asked as she turned the little girl around so that she faced the mirror.

Élodie grinned at herself, then up at Lia, who had opted for a solitary white blossom tucked behind her ear. 'I think that you look like a mermaid, and that I look like a princess, and that I'm pretty sure I want to live in a treehouse when I grow up!'

Lia laughed, and then, realising Élodie was speaking of so much more than a roof over her head, pulled her in for a hug, tight enough so that she wouldn't see the tears in her eyes. She felt for the girl and, even though she knew she had their own child growing in her belly, she wondered if Oliver would agree to one last pre-wedding request.

After sending Élodie out to find 'Granny Bainbridge', as Oliver's mother had come to be known, she went to the guest room, where Oliver was getting ready. 'Knock-knock!'

Oliver jumped behind the door so she couldn't see him. 'I thought it was bad luck to see one another before the ceremony.'

Lia laughed, stupidly pleased that Oliver was such a

lovely mix of tradition and quirky uniqueness. She was a lucky woman.

She pressed her hands to the door, imagining his face as she asked her question. 'Oli…?'

'Yes, my love?'

'How would you feel about expanding our family by one more?'

His head popped out from the other side of the door. 'What? You're already pregnant! You can't— Are you—?' Lines fanned out from his beautiful blue eyes as the wheels of his mind whirred to try and make sense of what she'd just asked. 'What's going on? Help a man on his wedding day, my darling bride.'

She grinned at him, unable to resist ruffling his tidy blond hair with her hand. 'What medical school did you go to? It's rare, but you can actually be pregnant with two babies at one time. It's called superfetation.'

His eyes widened. 'It's only been a few weeks. You know already?'

Lia laughed. Their sex life was definitely active enough to have produced another child—but, no. As she'd said, superfetation was an extremely rare occurrence, and that wasn't what she had in mind.

She patted her tummy. 'Just the one baby for now. I was actually thinking of…' She bit down on her lip, her eyes drifting out to the beach, where Élodie was trying to coax Oliver's mother to dip her bare toes into the surf, squealing as the water hit her feet and splashed her shins.

Oliver's eyes snapped back to hers as he finally connected the dots. 'You want to adopt Élodie?'

She raised her eyebrows, sank her teeth deeper into her lip. Until she'd asked it, she hadn't realised just how much she wanted Élodie to be a part of their everyday lives.

Oliver's face broke into a broad smile. Before she could

talk to him about speaking with Élodie's aunt and uncle, and of course the adoption authorities, or say anything practical at all, Oliver had her in his arms and was swinging her round and round, whooping as if she'd just agreed to marry him all over again.

'What's going on up there?' Lia's father called from the beach, where he'd been walking with Oliver's father. 'It sounds as if you're being attacked by a tribe of wild monkeys!'

'Not quite,' Lia called from the balcony. 'We'll be down in a minute. Is everyone ready for the wedding?'

A collective cheer went up from the beach where, in the end, quite a few more friends and family than they'd originally planned to invite had gathered for their small, informal wedding.

Guests had been asked to leave their mobile phones and cameras at home—not out of a strict 'no photos' rule, but out of a desire for them to be present in the moment as Lia and Oliver exchanged their vows. Marriage wasn't just about the two of them. It was about everyone they cared for and everyone who cared for them.

Ten minutes later, her arm tucked into the crook of her father's, Lia was walking down the 'aisle'—a petal path that Élodie was making as she skipped ahead of Lia, fistfuls of flowers floating in her wake. She saw Oliver's parents. Her own parents exchanging surprisingly flirtatious glances. Her cousin. Friends from the clinic. Grace…

The King and Queen of Karolinska had opted out of the wedding, saying something about the tropical heat not suiting their constitutions, but they had invited Oliver and Lia to join them at their summer retreat at the end of the month, for a less formal chance to get to know one another.

Lia's eyes eventually met and locked with Oliver's. This was the man whose smile she knew she would look forward to seeing every day of her life. Today it held an additional secret, of course. The knowledge that they would, once they'd spoken to the appropriate people, invite Élodie to join their small, growing family.

Lia glanced back at the treehouse, easily imagining it filled with the sound of children's laughter, and her heart felt fit to burst.

When their celebrant finished his introductory remarks and began the ceremony, Lia's heart launched into her throat as Oliver's voice grew thick with emotion as he began to recite his vows.

'I seek to know you.' Oliver's eyes briefly met Lia's, his voice catching in his throat as he continued. 'For all the years to come I will take joy in you. I will endeavour to see you as you are and love you for all that is familiar and for all of your mysteries.'

As he spoke, his words so pure in intention, she could hardly believe everything that was happening was real. It was the world's largest *pinch me* moment.

'Amelia? Do you accept Oliver's vows to you?' the celebrant prompted, and their friends and family gave an appreciative laugh. They knew a nervous woman when they saw one.

Lia started. She had been so busy staring into Oliver's eyes, gazing at his mouth, enjoying the sound of his voice, she'd not even noticed he'd stopped speaking.

'Yes!' she cried, and then more gently, as Oliver took her hands in his and her hammering heart calmed itself, 'Yes. I do accept them.' She shifted her dress, the billows of diaphanous blue and green dip-dyed fabric catching in the breeze. 'And with all my heart I will honour them as I hope he will honour mine.'

Oliver said, 'I will!'

Lia laughed along with the crowd. 'You haven't even heard them yet.'

Oliver's face tightened with emotion for the briefest of moments before clearing. His expression told her everything she'd ever wanted to know about him. He loved her and would do anything for her. There might be ups and downs, and he might not get it right the first time, but he'd keep on trying. No matter what, he'd keep on trying until he got it right.

Wiping away a few happy tears, she began, 'Oliver Bainbridge, from the moment I met you I knew in my heart I'd met a kindred spirit. Someone whose word is his passion. Whose passions make his life and the lives of those around him richer, kinder, better. I will respect and honour our friendship, our romantic love, and the path we choose as parents. I will also respect and honour the path you choose as the man who has asked me to walk hand in hand with him throughout this amazing, crazy life we're about to live. It's only just begun, and already I can't wait to grow old with you and love you more with each passing day. I love you. I respect you. And I am truly the proudest woman in the world that you are about to be my husband and the father to our children.'

Before the celebrant could ask Oliver if he would honour and respect Lia's vows to him Oliver was kissing her. It was a fiery, possessive, hungry, happy kiss, and Lia felt every molecule of her body become supercharged when, through it all, she heard the celebrant announce them as husband and wife.

'I would now like to introduce to you Their Royal Highnesses the Doctors Bainbridge!'

As they walked past their friends and family, everyone's faces beaming with shared joy, Oliver and Lia exchanged a secret smile. They knew everyone would be expecting them to head up to the massive buffet, spread out beneath the canopy of tropical trees, but there was just one more thing they wanted to do before they were well and truly married.

Oliver gave Lia's hand a squeeze. 'You sure you're all right with getting your beautiful dress wet?'

'More than.'

And with that they ran into the sea, hand in hand, emerging wet, glistening in the sun and beaming at one another, more certain than they'd ever been that the future would be a much better place because they were together.

* * * * *

REUNITED WITH HIS LONG-LOST NURSE

CHARLOTTE HAWKES

MILLS & BOON

To my beautiful boys.
You may never read my books—trust me,
you may *never* read them…understand?!—
but I love reading your stories about the
time-travelling, space-bending rainbows!
I love you…to infinity.
Xxx

CHAPTER ONE

LIAM MILLER HAD earned his nickname, The Heart Whisperer, because his extraordinary surgical skill could coax even the most damaged patients' hearts back to a perfect, normal sinus rhythm.

It was therefore ironic, he considered, that he'd been battling his own abnormally erratic heartbeat ever since arriving on the stunning island of St Victoria a few hours earlier. Or, more accurately, ever since his seaplane had flown over the stunning three-hundred-square-mile volcanic Caribbean island.

The views were practically spellbinding, from the emerald green of its rainforest canopy to its breath-taking turquoise waters where the light seemed to burst joyously off the coral reefs and sand.

But he would not allow himself to be bewitched.

Even on the short taxi drive from the port to the renowned Island Clinic, Liam had been captivated by the sheer colour and jubilation that pulsed around the island. It was so exuberant, so vibrant.

And it was so *her.*

He tried to push the thought from his head—the way he'd kept memories of her at bay for almost three years—but suddenly, now, he couldn't seem to hold them back. Whether it was the jet-lag, or the fact that he was actually here on her homeland, Liam couldn't be sure; all he knew was that this entire island was everything she'd once described to him. And it epitomised her flawlessly.

Talia.

The woman who had burst into his life a little over three years ago like a spectacular rainbow striking through the dark clouds that he hadn't realised, until that point, had been so very cheerless. She hadn't simply brought colour into his cold life but rather she had pitched it resplendently all over every single wall and surface in his hitherto bleak, grey world.

She had been the very essence of fun and laughter, and she'd breathed life into his very soul. He hadn't realised it immediately, but that black, heavy, icy thing that had squatted so heavily on his chest his whole life had begun, bit by bit, to thaw.

She was the woman who had made him think, against everything his cruel and hateful father had drilled into him his entire life, that far from being to blame, he might actually be as much a victim of his mother's death as his grief-stricken father had been. She was the woman who'd let him believe that perhaps he wasn't as damaged and broken and destructive as he'd always thought. That he might just be worthy of being loved for who he was.

And then, just as abruptly as she'd surged into his life, she'd left. And with her departure every bit of that colour and joy had drained from his life. Only this time it had been even worse because he'd known what he was missing.

With a snort of irritation Liam jerked his head from the huge picture window that made up one wall of the chief of staff's office at The Island Clinic, offering magnificent views. Instead he dropped his gaze to his electronic tablet and the patient file that stared at him from the screen as he waited for Nate Edwards to return.

It galled him that he hadn't yet managed to banish thoughts of Talia Johnson from his head, even all these years later. But, he reminded himself irritably, he wasn't on St Victoria to allow memories he'd tried to bury long ago to be stirred up.

He was simply here for the patients. In particular, Lucy Wells, the fifteen-year-old girl with a congenital heart problem who needed a full aortic arch reconstruction. And he didn't really have to read the notes on his tablet again, if he was honest. He'd been living and breathing this challenging case ever since the phone call the previous week from the clinic's chief of staff, Nate Edwards.

The way he did with every one of his cases—because they all mattered. They would be lying on his OR table, and the very least they deserved was that he knew their case inside out, upside down, and every way in between. Because every one of them could be someone's child, someone's husband, someone's mother—just like his own mother had once been.

The last place she'd ever been and the first place he'd ever been.

The start of his life but the end of hers. The cruellest twist of fate for which his distraught father had never forgiven him.

Never.

Which was why he had spent his entire surgical career doggedly determined that he would save every life he possibly could.

As if saving his patients' lives could somehow make up for his birth having been the reason for his mother losing hers.

As though there was a magic number that—when he achieved it—would suddenly, magically, absolve him. Maybe it would free him of the torment, and instantly lift all that icy numbness. The way he'd once naively imagined Talia had been starting to do.

Enough!

He would only be here for a few weeks, a month at the most, filling in for The Island Clinic's permanent cardiothoracic surgeon following a minor boating accident—not just for the Lucy Wells case, or the several other patients awaiting surgery, but for any emergencies—but then he would be gone.

It might not be a huge island, but it was big enough. He wasn't going to see Talia here. He didn't even know for sure that she'd returned to St Victoria after she'd disappeared, without a word, from his own life. But even if she had, he wasn't about to bump into her.

He could still recall the passion in her voice as she'd described to him her job at the local hospital, across the island towards the more populated area near the capital, Williamtown, but The Island Clinic was isolated. The perfect safe haven for A-listers needing medical treatment in an environment where their privacy could be absolutely assured.

No, he wasn't going to bump into Talia here.

Which was, he assured himself firmly, exactly the way he wanted it.

'Hello, Talia. I can't say I ever expected—or hoped—to see you again.'

A shiver started on the back of Talia's neck and shot over her skin, permeating every inch of her goose-bumped flesh, through to her veins, turning her blood to ice. She couldn't turn around. She could barely even lay the last of the instruments in the metal preparation tray.

Her mind spun.

The voice was Liam's, and yet it wasn't. She recognised the clipped, unerringly professional tone yet there was also an uncharacteristic hint of ice about it that almost made her want to pull her scrubs tighter around herself. Though whether more for warmth or for protection, she couldn't quite be sure.

So he had actually come to St Victoria. Even though she'd known it was happening—even though she was the one who had put Liam's name forward to her chief of staff—she hadn't quite believed it. She'd been almost convinced he would turn down the case just because it was on St Victoria.

The fact that he hadn't only proved one thing…that she was so insignificant to him that she hadn't even factored into his decision-making process. A fact she already knew, of course. She'd discovered that three years ago. To her detriment.

Which was all the more reason why it should make no difference to her whatsoever that he was here, Talia reminded herself desperately.

She hadn't recommended Liam to Nate because she'd wanted to see him again—because she absolutely had *not*—she had simply recommended him because she'd known that Duke Hospital's famous Heart Whisperer would be the best chance for her young, desperate patient.

Her own emotions hadn't factored into the equation at all.

Not at all.

So why was her body trembling as though it didn't believe her?

You're immune to him, she reminded herself desperately, preparing to turn around as she pretended that she didn't feel half as shaky as she did.

Her one consolation was that at least Liam would never know it had been her who had put his name forward. She had asked Nate to keep that part to himself.

'Is this what you intend to do for the next month, then?' His low voice reverberated softly around the room, but she wasn't fool enough to believe that made it no less dangerous to her. 'Pretend you can't even hear me? Only I can't imagine it's going to be the most successful play you could make.'

'Of course not,' she murmured, taking one final, steadying breath before she spun around—a bright, if uncharacteristically tight, smile plastered to her lips. It promptly froze in place the moment she met his expression of cool appraisal.

Pain slammed into her, hard and unyielding.

This was the man who had taught her what it was to ache, need, sear, just with a look. With a *word.* Yet right now he was looking at her as though he didn't know her at all.

Like she was no one more special than a stranger he was meeting for the first time. It hurt more than she could have ever imagined possible.

'Liam,' she choked out, the name seeming to stick in her mouth, as though she was trying to savour it just a fraction longer.

It was enough to make her despair of herself, especially when her eyes locked with his and she was unable to drag them away again. Dark and foreboding.

Yet it wasn't just that expression that was proving her undoing. As Talia found herself struggling for breath, fearing her legs would actually buckle beneath her, she reached behind her and gripped the medical trolley for support.

She'd spent the past three years telling herself that her girlish memories had built Liam up into something far more potent than he could ever truly have been in reality. Yet right now she realised that even her memories hadn't gone far enough.

The man was as glorious as he'd ever been. From the six-two frame outlined with those broad shoulders, down the unmistakably honed chest beneath that immaculate suit shirt—in spite of the eighty-five-degree St Victoria heat, Talia could see that nothing had changed. His square jaw was a study in masculinity, and so sharp that she thought it would cut her even from that distance. His thighs still so impossibly muscled that she practically wanted to lick them.

She swallowed. Hard.

Yep, forget the dulled memory. If anything, he seemed even more chiselled than ever and his face looked as though it had been hewn from pure granite as he glowered at her. She pretended it didn't feel like a tight fist closing around her already fragile heart.

'Is that all you have to say?' His tone was too neutral, his expression giving nothing away. 'My name? You're not even going to explain what I'm doing out here?'

Panic shot through her in an instant, and it was all Talia could do not to show it.

He doesn't know, she reminded herself feverishly. *He can't possibly know.*

She tried to dredge up another smile but it was impossible, she'd have to content herself with a controlled tone. One that didn't betray just how crazily she was shaking inside.

'You're here to take over one of Isak's clinical trial surgeries, I believe,' she managed. 'I'm sure that's what the rumour mill said, anyway.'

His already cold expression changed abruptly, becoming even more closed off than ever. The fist around her heart squeezed tighter. He'd gone from talking to her to shutting her out in an instant. A stark reminder of why she'd made that impossible decision, three years ago, to walk away from the only man she had ever loved.

Three years, two months, two weeks and four days, if she was going to be precise.

Shamefully, she knew it to pretty much the hour, too.

'"That's what the rumour mill said"?' he echoed. 'Is this some game you're now playing?'

The question rasped over her skin, scraping against old wounds she'd told herself were long since healed. Yet now, with a few words from Liam, they felt as raw as they had three years ago.

Leaving Duke's—leaving *him*—had been the most agonising decision of her life. Who, in their right mind, would ever leave a man like Liam Miller? He had earned his nickname around Duke's hospital as the Heart Whisperer for his incredible skill as a cardiothoracic surgeon, but it was equally fitting for the fact that colleagues, patients and relatives alike all fell head over heels for him.

Practically the whole single, female contingent of the place had wanted to be the one woman to catch Liam's eye. The one woman who could reach the distant and seemingly lonely surgeon. The one woman who could heal his apparently damaged soul.

The fact that he'd never dated any of them had only made Liam all the more coveted. It was one of the first things she'd learned from her fellow scrub nurses the moment she'd arrived at Duke's. The last thing she'd expected, then, had been for Liam to apparently break all his own rules when he'd asked her out on a date.

And then another.

She'd felt special. And perhaps she'd let that fact go to her head because she'd fallen in love with him, hard and fast. Moreover, she'd been foolish enough—naïve enough—to let herself believe he actually loved her too. That she had, actually, healed him. That was how much of a fool she'd been.

Which was why, when her father had called her with the dreadful news, that last day at Duke's, she'd known that moving away from North Carolina—away from Liam—was the healthiest move all round.

Yet even though, deep down, she'd understood the logic, it had nonetheless been the most torturous and agonising decision of her life. Especially for a girl who'd once believed in happily-ever-afters, and soulmates, and love conquering all.

But she was no longer that young, naïve kid. Liam had taught her that real life wasn't like that, and the simple truth had been that her love—she herself—hadn't been enough. Not for Liam, anyway.

Tilting her head back and jerking her chin out a fraction, Talia summoned a glare of her own.

'I don't play games. I never did.'

But, Lord, it was hard when he looked more beautiful, more dangerous than ever. So arresting that she was sure her perfidious heart stuttered and stumbled in her chest.

'I used to think that,' he stated flatly. 'Just as I used to think that I knew you.'

Never mind the icy rivers that his dispassionate tone sent coursing through her, it was the way he looked straight through her that sheared off an entire glacier inside her, sending it—and almost her—crashing down to stain the highly polished, ultra-hygienic, stunning marble floor of the painfully opulent, intimidatingly high-tech Island Clinic.

She wanted to rail and argue. But what would be the point?

'It turns out that I never really knew you at all, did I?' Liam added, his acerbic smile so biting she could almost taste the sharp, unpleasant tang of it for herself.

The same bitterness she'd tasted when she'd finally realised that the future she had begun to imagine—one that included Duke's, and Liam—was definitely not the same future he'd envisaged in his own mind. And it never would be.

He might have cared for her, in his odd strange way, but she still hadn't been *enough.*

There was a part of Liam that he had always kept locked away, not just from her but from the world. He'd never truly let her close to him—he'd never let her *in*. If anything, he'd once condemned everything she believed in—love, marriage, family—as whimsical fantasies that had no place in the real world and would never for him.

And, still, the warning signs hadn't been enough to allow her to cut her losses and run. She'd been tied to him. Loving him. Hoping that would be enough to encourage him to open up to her.

Not, of course, that she had expected a man she'd only been dating for a few months to declare undying love and propose marriage and a family. But, equally, she hadn't expected such a man to wreck her in more ways than she'd ever thought possible. Leaving the way she had done had been the only way she'd known to save them both.

And now he was here on her small Caribbean island, and Talia found herself desperately fighting the *maybes*, and the *what-ifs*. As if there was room for such thoughts. But Liam would only be here for a month while he tended to his patient—the kid of one of Hollywood's current brightest stars—and then he would be gone.

She'd be damned if she opened her heart up only to let him wreck her again. She simply couldn't afford to let him see how easily he got under her skin.

How easily he could unravel her.

'I could say the same thing,' she ground out instead. 'But, really, what would be the point of such a conversation?'

'What indeed?'

His dispassion sliced through her all over again. Leaving her with frost that seemed to spread from the inside out, and had nothing to do with the state-of-the-art air-con of The Island Clinic.

People had warned her that she would end up getting hurt. That Liam Miller was a brilliant surgeon but a lone wolf. A good man but a man with walls. She hadn't believed any of them.

She'd been wrong. Terribly, desperately wrong. But hadn't she already shown Liam enough weakness back then? She'd be damned if she gave him a new demonstration now.

'Is that the reason you sought me out, then? To tell me that you never knew me at all? And to tell me that I was the last person you ever expected to see again? Because I can assure you that I didn't expect to see you either.'

For a moment he didn't answer, he merely smiled. An edgy little quirk of his lips that was so sharp it made Talia itch to check that he hadn't actually cut her. And then he took a step towards her.

Just a single step, and Talia felt as though the entire clinic had lifted and tilted. It was a fight just to stay upright, such was the devastating impact Liam Miller had on her.

Had always had on her, from the moment they'd met on her first day at Duke's.

'I've just met your chief here, at this clinic of yours. He's quite inspiring.'

'Nate?' She grasped the apparently safe topic with both hands. 'Yes, he is. He set up The Island Clinic *and* the sister programme with St Vic's Hospital after the hurricane here a few years ago.'

'I'm well aware of the programme.' His smile became all the more sardonic. 'And I know many surgeons who would cut a limb off themselves with their own scalpel for a chance to work at the famous Island Clinic.'

'Right. Of course.'

He'd taken another step towards her and Talia found she was twisting herself up in knots not to react. Not to show any sign of feeling intimidated.

Intimidation? a sly voice asked. *Or attraction?*

'Which made it particularly interesting when the same Nate Edwards contacted me a week ago, asking me if I would like to take a look at a special case.'

Uncertainty coursed through her. His tone was so loaded that she almost thought he knew the truth. But how could he? Nate wouldn't have betrayed her confidence. And now that she'd already pretended not to know what he was doing on the island, she had no choice but to keep feigning innocence.

Still, she flicked a nervous tongue out over suddenly parched lips as she adopted a look of vague interest.

'Oh?'

'Oh?' he echoed, a little too breezily for Talia's liking.

An almost dangerous nonchalance. Which was odd if she thought about it as Liam was renowned for his cool, even temperament. So laid-back that it almost dipped into emotional detachment.

Even with her. Which was the part she'd hated the most.

There had been a few moments over the long summer they'd enjoyed together—the briefest of flashes when she'd thought he was about to let his guard down and talk to her. But then the shutters had slammed down abruptly on her again, and she'd been left out in the cold. All his thoughts and feelings his, and his alone.

'So, to be clear, you knew nothing about my arrival?' he challenged, so close now that she had to tilt her neck up to look into his face.

And suddenly she couldn't pretend any more. The electricity practically crackled in the space between them, leaving her feeling shaky and drained. Like she was coiled so tightly inside that she was at risk of jumping out of her own skin at any moment.

Whatever she'd told herself, it seemed her body was only too willing to undermine it. Even after all this time, it still wanted him. *Ached* for him.

'I knew nothing,' she confirmed, her voice sounding like that of a stranger. 'Obviously, I knew a surgeon was coming in to fill in for Isak on the trial, but I didn't know it was you.'

His eyes bored into her that little bit deeper, causing her entire body to begin to heat. She told herself it was because she hated fibbing. It was why she usually prided herself on never doing so.

'Is that so?' He lifted a hand and, if she hadn't known better, she might have thought he was about to put a stray curl around her ear or caress her cheek.

Obviously, he did neither.

And still Talia didn't answer. She was getting hotter now and somehow the ground had shifted beneath her feet, leaving her scrambling for some kind of purchase. She couldn't explain it.

'Imagine, then,' Liam continued almost conversationally, 'my thoughts when I asked Nate where he'd heard about my work, only for him to inform me that he'd looked into my reputation after one of his scrub nurses had recommended me.'

CHAPTER TWO

'NATE TOLD YOU?' Talia gasped, shock making her forget her little foray into acting—which was probably for the best since she appeared to be terrible at it.

But why would Nate have done that when she'd asked him not to mention her at all to Liam?

'What did you expect, Talia?' Liam asked evenly. 'He's founder and Chief of Staff of a world-renowned facility, not some kids' playground leader. He wanted to be sure that there was no bad blood between us. Presumably that we would be able to work together.'

Her mouth felt parched. Like a scorched area of forest in the dry season.

'What did you tell him?'

'What do you think I told him?' demanded Liam quietly. Too quietly. 'I explained that while there was an intimate history between us, it was long buried. Then I told him that, whatever our past personal connection, you were one of the most professional scrub nurses that I knew, and that I would be more than happy to work with you again.'

'Oh,' she managed tightly. 'And is that…is that how you feel?'

It didn't help that Liam was eyeing her in such a way that it made her skin feel as though it was too tight for her own body.

'Honestly?' His voice was harsh, and she hated the rush of hope that it sent through her. As though the fact that he wasn't entirely at ease might mean something. 'I'd hoped to come here, perform my surgery, and leave. I didn't consider seeing you. I didn't even know you'd come back here.'

'This is my home,' she blurted out, shocked. 'Where else would I have gone when I left Duke's?'

The silence was all too heavy. All too suffocating. It swirled around them, but eventually it was Liam who spoke.

'I neither knew nor cared.'

A wiser woman would have quit now. But Talia feared she'd never been wise where this man had been concerned. And as much as she hated herself for her weakness, and her desperation, she heard herself answering all the same.

'I think you made that obvious at the time.'

'Is that so?'

She didn't know who had inched that fraction nearer. Bringing them so close to each other that she could feel his warm breath brushing over her cheek. And she wanted… *more.* For one crazy moment she almost imagined what it would be like to lean up and press her lips to his.

If it would feel the same.

'I know you came here for the case. I never thought you would come here for me. If you'd wanted to do that, you'd have done it three years ago.'

The words were out before she could swallow them back.

But, boy, did she wish that she could. She didn't even know where it had come from, or that's what she wanted to tell herself. The worst of it was the way his expression changed instantly from that sharp smile to a look of…almost pure contempt.

Yet oddly, whether it was more at her or himself, she couldn't quite be sure.

'Is that what this is all about—some pathetic test?' he

demanded. 'I didn't go racing after you three years ago, but you've finally found a way to get me here now?'

'No,' she cried, horrified. 'Of course not.'

Though it unsteadied her to realise that a tiny part of her wondered if that was exactly what she'd done. She shook her head to dislodge that thought.

'This is exactly why I didn't want Nate to tell you that I'd been the one to recommend you. It isn't about me, or you, it's about a kid who is terrified and has been told by three top surgeons already that her only chance is to get on this trial. And I happened to know that you have performed multiple successful full aortic reconstructions using the RAT approach.'

At least that much was true—he had been successful with several right-anterior thoracotomies—whatever else she might not have realised had been bubbling away in her subconscious.

For several long moments they stood, facing off against each other, and Talia tried to stop herself from visibly shaking.

'I wasn't trying to engineer some ill-fated reunion,' she managed when she couldn't stand the silence any longer. 'Trust me, you're the last person I want to see again, too.'

And it was only as the words came out of her mouth—a touch too melodramatically, if she was being honest with herself—that she realised them for the lie they were.

Ten minutes ago she might have truly believed that she was over Liam but right here, with him standing inches from her, she finally admitted it for the lie that it was.

Liam, however, didn't even blink.

'Funny thing is, I don't believe you.'

'Well, you should. I even asked Nate to take me off surgeries here at the clinic while you were here. In two days

I'm scheduled to start a month-long rotation at St Vic's, across the other side of the island.'

'St Vic's?'

She cranked up her smile once more and told herself that his icy tone didn't hurt. Not at all.

'St Vic's is the local hospital about fifteen miles outside our capital, Williamtown. It isn't a patch on The Island Clinic, of course, but Nate's main aim in setting up the clinic was to enable it to fund new equipment for St Vic's, and for the local community to also have some access to the world-class medical team of the clinic, via an outreach programme.'

'Yes, thank you for the tour-guide spiel but I'm well informed on the history between St Vic's Hospital and The Island Clinic.' His tone was clipped. 'My surprise was more about the fact that you apparently didn't want your chief of staff to know there was any problem between us, yet you asked to be transferred while I was here.'

'Oh.'

She shifted awkwardly and his nostrils flared slightly. Once upon a time it had meant that he wanted her. Now she could only imagine it meant he was resenting the amount of time he was letting her take up.

'I assure you, Liam,' she pressed on hastily, 'if you hadn't arrived here today—two days earlier than planned, I should point out—we wouldn't have seen each other at all.'

Something swept through those green eyes of his and, not for the first time, she wished to God that she could read whatever was going on in this beautiful, enigmatic man's head.

If she'd been able to years ago, surely it would have spared her a mess of heartache? It was almost impossible to remember now how she'd once believed that nothing could ever have made her walk away from someone as incredible as Liam. Or how her love for him had turned, so quickly, to such pain.

'You really didn't expect us to see each other at all whilst I was working on this case?' he demanded curtly, after what felt like an eternity.

Her head was a leaden weight as she bobbed it once in assent. The air pressed in around them, almost suffocating, and she wished it didn't hurt half as much as it did.

'I recommended you when Isak had his boating accident, simply because I knew you were the best chance of a successful procedure for Lucy.' And if there was a little voice in her head calling her out for being a liar, she would be damned if she acknowledged it.

'Why me?'

'Because I know Nate. For him, finding a replacement cardiothoracic surgeon wasn't just about finding one who was at the top of his game—although that's a given, of course—it's also about finding someone who would be the right fit for his team.'

'And you decided that was me? Even meaning we would have to work together?'

'I knew you would fit in. And I was right,' she pressed on, needing to say the words. 'You said you know of Nate Edwards so you must know that The Island Clinic, and its vulnerable patients, are all that ever matters to him.'

'That and the local hospital.' Liam jerked his head in assent. 'I heard that he set the clinic up following a hurricane here, as a way to fund St Vic's Hospital and help the locals.'

It was hell. standing here almost toe to toe with Liam and refusing to let herself back away.

Hell. And heaven.

Only in those late-night dreams, which she'd pretended she didn't really have, had she imagined the two of them ever being this close again.

'Right,' she managed hoarsely. 'But even though The Island Clinic is renowned for its A-list patient base—from the NFL to Hollywood, and from Aruba to the USA—he also ensures locals have full use of the facilities if they need it.'

'I thought the clinic was known as a place for the elite, where they could be assured of utter discretion as they benefited from the absolute gold standard of medical care, with the best medical professionals?'

'It is,' she confirmed. Could he hear her heart thundering on her chest wall? To her, the sound was almost deafening. 'It's a place where A-listers like Violet Silnag-Wells come, whose daughter, Lucy, is your new patient and who needs a full atrial arch reconstruction. But Nate also uses the helicopter pad to fly locals here if St Vic's can't meet their needs. He really cares about patients in both the clinic, and St Vic's Hospital. Every single one of them matters to him and I knew that was something you, of all people, would understand.'

Liam jerked back. She actually saw the minute movement as he moved away from her. As though he hadn't been expecting her to say anything like that. To compliment him.

Instinctively, Talia pressed home whatever advantage she might have.

'It was no wonder Nate practically bit my arm off after I told him about Duke's rising star, Heart Whisperer. But for the record, Liam. I'm not on the trial team. I never was. So this couldn't possibly have been about you and me working together again.

'It only later occurred to me that if you came here, we might end up face to face,' she choked out. At least, that was the story she was sticking to. Even in her own mind. 'Which is why I asked for a month-long transfer. I thought that if I was at the hospital, it would be better all round.'

For one long moment neither of them spoke. And then,

abruptly, Liam took a step backwards. And even though there was no reason on earth for that to make her feel it like a loss, Talia felt bereft.

'Fine,' he ground out, his tone a mixture of irritation, displeasure and something else she couldn't put her finger on. 'That's a solution I can live with.'

Then, before she could even formulate the words for any kind of response, he was gone. His shoes echoed down the corridor, haunting her long after he'd disappeared from view.

What the hell was the matter with him? Liam berated himself furiously as he stalked through the indecently opulent corridors of The Island Clinic. This was his penance for searching her out. Yet what choice had he had? He'd been drawn to seek her out the moment Nate had confirmed that Talia had been the one to recommend him.

Fury, and something else he didn't care to identify, pounded inside him. It thumped along every inch of his skin, bubbling and exploding in his veins, and making him…*feel* things that he had precisely zero interest in feeling. As though he had no control whatsoever of his own body.

He, who prided himself on never letting anything, any*one*, rile him. *Ever.*

Yet if he hadn't walked out of that room at that moment, he feared he wouldn't have been able to stop himself from hauling Talia into his arms and taking that one last truth that existed between them to use it to show her up for the liar that she was.

Because whatever other tales and falsehoods had ever fallen from her mouth—including the lie that she hadn't even realised he was coming to St Victoria—there was one area in which she had never been able to deceive him.

That attraction which had always fizzed and arced between them was no fabrication. It never had been. Perhaps it was the only real thing the two of them had ever shared, but that didn't make it any less effective.

He'd read it in every line of that sensual body of hers. Every shallow breath. Every darkened regard. Whatever else she might want to pretend, she couldn't fake disinterest in him.

And what perturbed Liam the most…was that neither could he.

He could tell himself that he was shocked at seeing Talia again. He could claim that it was seething rage that drummed through his body. But, deep down, he knew it was something far more potent than anger.

It was desire. And it galled him beyond all measure to have to admit it.

He wanted her just as he had always wanted her; from the very first moment he'd laid eyes on her with her bubbling laughter and killer body. Sex—incredible sex—had never been one of their failings. Quite the opposite, in fact. The sex had always been intense. Exceptional.

Then on top of that his attraction to her had swollen tenfold when he'd seen how focussed and skilled she was in the operating room.

The whole package.

But there were some things more intimate than sex even. And if he'd ever stood a chance of opening up to any woman on a more intimate level he'd considered that maybe it would have been with Talia.

Instead, she'd left. Without a word.

Which was all the more reason why he had to stay cool and detached. He had to. Because if he didn't—if he'd stayed in that room with her just now—he was terribly doubtful that he could have controlled that…*thing* from heating up between them all over again. Drawing him in. And he wouldn't have realised until it was too late and the flames were licking around him—like the fable of the boiling frog.

And Liam decided that he had no intention of being like any such member of the amphibian family.

He, who was renowned for his cool head and soothing composure under even the most stressful emergencies.

It wasn't just an art he'd honed as a doctor, and a surgeon; it was a skill he'd been perfecting his entire life. A logical defence mechanism given the way his father had always looked on him as an abomination.

From as early as Liam could remember, his curt old man had pounded into him the need to *be* something, *do* something, prove that his life was worth his mother losing hers. An angry, scornful, grief-stricken man who had never been able to get over the death of the one love of his life; or the fact that it had been his infant son who had caused it.

As a child, he had believed every cruel word of it. By the time he'd grown into an adult it had been too late. His own grief and guilt had permanent squatting rights in his chest, like the kind of dark, ugly, twisted twin gargoyles that had adorned the gothic buildings of his childhood boarding school.

He had realised long ago that nothing he could ever do would ever be enough to satisfy his father, or make up for his mother's death. But the need to try had ended up giving him an incredible career and turning him into the rising star surgeon that he was today. So in some perverse way he was grateful for those ruthless lessons.

And if, on a social level, people thought him cold and detached, what had that mattered? He'd accepted that love was never going to feature heavily in it. He didn't trust it when people said it to him, and he certainly wasn't capable of giving it back.

Until Talia.

Even now, something stirred deep down, even further inside him than the blackness of that hollow pit where he pretended the worst of his guilt and shame did not reside.

Kissing her would have been a miscalculation of gargantuan proportions.

Because the truth was that he had never felt more rattled, his thoughts charging around his head like some trapped wild animal—desperate to break out. But wasn't that the way Talia had always made him feel?

As though his entire life—until her arrival—had been a cage. And she had been the key to unlocking it and finally setting him free.

Now, though, his body felt so tense and coiled that he might as well have gone several rounds in a ring, even though he hadn't boxed since boarding school, and certainly not from the moment he'd realised he'd wanted to become a surgeon.

He felt as though he needed to break out of his own skin.

Having managed to navigate the identical marble corridors back to the indecently opulent consultation room that Nate had just allocated to him, Liam strode inside. Every inch of this place oozed money. A place designed for the celebrity elite. It was such a far cry from the way the rest of the island lived; no wonder Nate had set up the foundation, using the income generated by The Island Clinic to fund an outreach programme to provide better care to the rest of the community.

He reached behind him and closed the door firmly, letting his hand rest there just a little longer. As if satisfying himself that the piece of furniture was closed enough to also shut out the deluge of memories that had threatened to crash over him ever since he'd stood in that doorway and seen Talia inside.

Of course it didn't work—the images swept in all the same. Those vibrant colours were everywhere, and their songs of exuberance, and joy, and vitality were as resonant as ever.

He threw himself down into his ridiculously luxurious chair, his too-long legs stretched out in front of him, disgusted with himself, and angrily schooling his thoughts.

Contempt flooded through him. He was insane, acting like some kind of hormone-ravaged adolescent. He hadn't come here for a woman. He had barely even remembered that Talia had once told him she originally hailed from this glorious island of St Victoria.

Liar, a voice said in his head.

He ignored that, too, instead reminding that snide internal voice that the only reason he was here was because any case at The Island Clinic was a good career opportunity for him. The next step in his bright career. In his future.

Talia Johnson was his past. He'd barely pieced himself back together after she'd left him, Liam thought as he staunchly ignored the pounding that now felt as though it was about to burst its way through his skin.

So the past was exactly where she needed to stay.

CHAPTER THREE

THE KNOCK ON his door came much sooner than he'd anticipated. Though he immediately recognised that he *had* anticipated it.

What he hadn't expected was for the door to open and for Talia to step inside before he could even answer.

'I believe it's customary to wait for the person inside to answer.' He raised his eyebrows, but at least his voice felt more even now. More controlled.

The way it should be.

He just had to remember that coming to The Island Clinic was about a case, a career opportunity—whatever this sorceress of a woman said by way of atonement.

Talia, however, didn't appear in the least bit apologetic. Instead, she kept coming at him boldly.

'I might have waited,' she threw at him, 'if I hadn't thought you'd leave me waiting out there all day.'

It galled that a part of him still admired her characteristic spirit. It was one of the things that had attracted him in the first place—her feistiness, her humour, her intelligence.

And that damned killer body.

Liam despaired of himself as another familiar punch of attraction slammed into him, dragging his gaze across the room and tempting him. The very danger he'd anticipated—and, still, he succumbed. His eyes took in every inch of her—the way he hadn't had a chance to do earlier when he'd been so close to her. When he hadn't been able to resist that magnetic pull between them.

Her eyes were still like the deepest, richest pools of warm chocolate, those dimples still dancing in her cheeks when she talked, the line of her neck as elegant as he remembered. Her hair was tied up in that professional bun she always wore, but he suspected that if he went over and pulled it free, it would be the same glossy black curls that tumbled, wild and magnificent, just past her shoulders. Fierce and charismatic, just like Talia herself.

And then his gaze dropped lower to those generous breasts, which had always spilled so gloriously over his hands; the sweet nip of her waist and then the delectable flare of her hips. He could swear he remembered every indentation and every curve, and his mouth practically watered.

'For someone who has just assured me that we won't be seeing anything of each other at all while I'm at The Island Clinic, I have to say I'm surprised that you followed me.'

She bristled, and he considered it was amazing how he could inject such a note of insouciance into his tone when his chest now felt as though it was so tight that he was struggling to breathe evenly.

Still, she lifted her head.

'I feel I ought to apologise.'

'Is that so?'

Was it so wrong of him to relish the way she blinked then, as if she couldn't quite work him out? Good, let her realise he wasn't the same easy mark he'd been last time they'd met.

'I…shouldn't have fibbed to you about being the one to recommend you to Nate.'

Liam couldn't drag his eyes away. Especially when she

seemed to stiffen slightly as his gaze moved over her, then shifted. A slight movement that made him think, with altogether too much clarity, of the way she'd used to move in his arms. When he'd touched her with his hands and then the way she'd arched when he'd replaced them with his mouth. If he listened closely, Liam was positive he could hear echoes of the way she'd screamed his name as he'd pitched her over the edge and into the brilliant flames.

And he abhorred himself for such weakness. He needed to get a grip. *Now.*

'So why did you?' he demanded. 'Recommend me, that is?'

She wrinkled her nose, as if she was finding the conversation even harder than he was. He didn't care to identify why he found that so gratifying.

'What do you want me to say, Liam? You already know that Nate needed someone who was not only experienced in total atrial arch reconstruction, and in the right anterior mini-thoracotomy, but who would also be an acceptable replacement for Isak to carry on the trial.'

'And you thought of me over anyone else.'

Another nose-wrinkle. He used to know it to mean she was holding something back. Now he wasn't so sure he knew what anything she did really meant.

'I did, Liam, because the trial that Isak was doing is ground-breaking. In precisely the area in which you excel.'

He did not feel flattered. He *would* not feel flattered. He did not feel that unwelcome fist, which pulled tight and rough around his chest. For a man who was renowned for always being self-possessed and confident, no matter what the circumstances, right now he felt about as far from composed as it was possible to be.

Yet as Talia talked he felt some of the heat, the shock of earlier begin to dissipate. He could cope with this professional conversation far more easily than he could handle the personal one. And it was surprising how easily they were falling back into easy conversation now the topic was… safer.

'There have been plenty of studies out there comparing different approaches, including MS, PUH and RAT,' he pointed out. 'They've looked at everything from intubation times to transfusions, surgical revision for bleeding to wound infection, length of ICU stay before in-hospital death, and still the list goes on and on. What makes this one so different?'

She didn't even hesitate.

'Those other studies have compared the three approaches when the right-anterior thoracotamy was a relatively new approach, so surgeons were still on a steep learning curve. It stands to reason that it's taken time to hone the technique, but now experienced surgeons, like you and Isak, have significantly reduced timings such as cross-clamp times, and cardiopulmonary bypass times, resulting in the patient being on the table for up to half an hour less. On top of that…'

'Fine.' He raised his hand to stop her. 'You've made your point.'

She'd always been a great scrub nurse, passionate and knowledgeable, as she'd just proved. Yet she'd claimed not to be on the previous surgeon's team. He couldn't help but wonder why.

'I didn't realise I was making a point, merely answering your question,' she levelled at him. 'Hopefully I've now proved to you that I recommended you to Nate for entirely appropriate reasons and not to…to lure you St Victoria.'

'I didn't say you had.'

'You implied it.' She shrugged.

He didn't bother denying it.

The fact was she had presented a coherent explanation—precisely as he'd challenged her to do. So why didn't he feel entirely satisfied?

Instead, he felt strangely flat, as if a part of him had hoped there *had* been some personal motivation behind it all.

How was it that this one woman always managed to sneak under his skin, when no one else ever had?

It irked. Yet still something had thrummed in his chest. Something he might have thought to be suspiciously like a heart—if he hadn't known it to be impossible. As if he was *glad* she was back in his life.

Liam shoved the thought aside angrily.

For his own sake, he should leave. Get as far away from St Victoria—and Talia Johnson—as possible. Hadn't he learned his lesson with her last time? There was only person in life that anyone could trust—and that was themselves. Everyone else would always let you down in the end.

But this wasn't all about Talia any more. He was committed to The Island Clinic now. To Nate Edwards. There was a patient flying in for his expertise and, no matter the personal cost, he prided himself on his professionalism. He wouldn't let them down.

'I accept your apology,' he rasped out at last.

'My apology?'

'That you shouldn't have lied about being the one to recommend me to your chief.'

'I didn't apologise, I just said—'

'However, I'm satisfied that you recommended me for professional reasons rather than personal.' He knew he sounded stilted, wooden, but he couldn't seem to help himself.

'Oh. Good. That's great.' Her breath came out in a rush,

and if she'd noticed how awkward he'd sounded she wasn't mentioning it.

'Good.'

There was a beat of silence as they remained immobile, eying each other cautiously.

Then another beat.

Furious with himself again, Liam gave himself a mental shake.

'Right, well, if that's it, I have some work to do,' he gritted out.

'Of course.' She spun around quickly, almost stumbling, and he was halfway out of his seat before he realised what he was doing. He was still reacting to her even though she had made it abundantly clear that she was wholly indifferent to him.

He dropped back again and stretched his legs back out so that Talia didn't realise it, too.

But it wasn't enough. He couldn't stop himself, he wanted to affect her the way she affected him. To hurt her, even in some small way.

'I take it your plan is still to work in the other hospital on this island for the duration of my stay?'

She turned haltingly.

'I thought it would be a solution you would prefer.'

'That would suggest I cared one way or another about what you do.' He forced himself to sound detached.

'So...you're happy for me to stay at The Island Clinic?'

Clearly, she loved her job here, just as he'd suspected.

'You misunderstand,' he rasped out. 'I'm not interested in where you work, just as long as you aren't working on my case. Do we have an understanding?'

She flicked her tongue over her lips, suggesting new

nervousness, though he couldn't read the expression on her lovely face. But then he told himself that he didn't want to.

'Yes, okay.' She dipped her head once. 'We have an understanding.'

And then she turned again, closed her fingers around the door handle and began yanking it open as if she couldn't wait to get out of there.

Which suited him just fine.

Talia was halfway to stalking out of the room and into the corridor before her newfound meekness began to disappear, eroded by the temper that people rarely saw but never forgot.

Liam had never seen that temper. But, then, she'd never seen this side of him either, so she supposed that made them even.

She'd always known he was authoritative. A strong, confident surgeon who ran his operating room precisely how he liked to. But *this* Liam—the one who seemed just a little less self-restrained, as if something was bubbling terribly close to the surface—was a different entity entirely. As if their unscheduled reunion had unsettled him just as much as it had her.

And Talia found she rather liked it—the idea that she was seeing another side to this fascinating, infuriating man.

What appealed to her far less, however, was the way he had just dismissed her; waving her away like some kind of irritating mosquito.

Swinging around before she could second-guess herself, Talia marched back across the room to stand in front of his desk, her arms outstretched as she leaned on the table.

'You know, for a man who never wanted to see me again, and whose career trajectory these past few years has pretty much only been matched by that of a space rocket, you seem to be surprisingly bothered by my presence.'

She realised her mistake too late. Her moment of bravado, striding up to his desk, had brought her altogether too close to Liam.

As he jerked up to his feet, the movement brought him forward until there was barely a few inches between them.

Again.

Close enough to touch him.

Her heart kicked hard. She clutched harder at the edge of the table in an effort to keep her hands in check. *Lord help her but if she leaned forward, she could kiss him.* She might have resisted insane impulses once, but she wasn't sure she had the strength to do it again.

'I have to say, Talia, I always knew you had passion—I admired it, in fact—but I don't recall you being this vehement.'

'Perhaps I wasn't quite as much myself with you as I always thought I was.' The words spilled out of her mouth before she'd even thought them in her head.

Liam frowned, clearly not liking that. She didn't know whether that was a good thing or a bad one.

'Which means what? Precisely?'

Talia didn't answer. Was this really the conversation she'd wanted to have?

'Please, don't stop now.' He arched an eyebrow. 'A moment ago you clearly had something you wanted to say.'

He was goading her, and that stab of ire flashed though her again.

'All right,' she bit out. 'I think perhaps these past few years have given me a little more clarity, and I've realised a few things.'

'Indeed?'

'Yes.' She pursed her lips. 'I wonder if I was ever entirely myself around you, Liam.'

'And by that you mean?' He clearly didn't like what she was saying.

His expression told her as much.

'I mean that, as much as I've hated to admit it, I think I was a little in awe of everything back in North Carolina. A new hospital, a new country, a new way of life. And then, on top of all that, *you*.'

'Me, on top of all that?' he drawled. 'I'm piqued.'

'That isn't what I meant.' She flushed, instantly trying to shut down the memory, but she was too slow.

Heat spread through her, intense and decalescent, as she recalled just how Liam had made her come apart with the faintest touch of his hand—or his tongue. She wondered if he was thinking the same. How he had made her plead, and sob, and scream until she'd been drained and exhausted, sprawled in his arms and still wanting more.

Always wanting more. Little wonder that she'd believed herself to have been in love.

Now she wondered if she'd allowed herself to be swept up in the sheer Cinderella nature of their relationship, without ever admitting that she'd been slightly intimidated by him.

'Your body tells me different,' he ground out, and she felt a wallop of something entirely inappropriate as he leaned over the other side of the desk.

She was powerless to drag her gaze from his physique, once more on display.

What was the matter with her?

Tick.

She could actually hear the clock on the wall above her head, and still neither of them moved. Or spoke.

Tock.

His brows knitted together tightly in a way that was so agonisingly familiar that Talia—despairing of herself—had to clutch the desk white-knuckle-tight in an effort not to reach out and smooth it out.

Tick.

Desperation lent her another burst of daring—or maybe it was foolhardiness. Who knew?

'And what if it did?' she demanded hotly. 'You made it clear you weren't interested in me.'

'I didn't say anything of the sort.'

His voice grazed through her, like a blade that scraped at her and made her raw. Only somehow it was more stimulating than agonising.

She tried to speak but the words stuck in her throat. 'You said—'

'I said that I hadn't ever expected—or hoped—to see you again,' he rasped. 'Not that I wasn't interested.'

Talia was aware that he was advancing on her but she couldn't seem to make herself move. She shook her head wordlessly, unsure if it was the uncharacteristic, dangerous edge to his tone or his sheer, dizzying proximity that was sending her head into a spin. More likely it was the three years' worth of feelings she'd thought long dealt with but which, it was now turning out, had only barely been repressed.

'You still want me?' she managed at last.

Whole lifetimes might have passed, or maybe it was instantaneous, but suddenly his hands were deliciously on her shoulders, as big and strong as she remembered, and his face right next to hers. Eyes that were simultaneously black with desire and hot shimmered in front of her, making her feel...*everything.*

'Against everything my head is telling me,' he growled.

'I came here for my patient, not for you. Yet here you are, haunting me like some kind of spectre.'

Abruptly, like some flip of a switch, he seemed to stop fighting and his mouth came down on hers, as if staking his claim after too many years apart—possessing her. Like leaping headlong into a volcano just as it was erupting.

He kissed her long, and thoroughly, and expertly, as only Liam had ever done to her. A kiss that was simultaneously a punishment and a gift.

His hands held her head just as he wanted it, taking the kiss deeper and deeper. Lazy, drugging kisses that were more and more perfect with every delicious stroke of his tongue, leaving her feeling high and as though she was bouncing off the walls.

'So what is this?' she muttered almost feverishly, when they finally came up for air, barely able to tear her mouth from his for fear that he wouldn't let her back again afterwards. 'Some grand reunion between two old lovers?'

'No reunion,' he rumbled ruthlessly, his voice all silk and menace as the words rasped against her lips and reverberated straight down to between her legs. 'Try more like a long-overdue exorcism.'

CHAPTER FOUR

THE WORDS SHOULD have pulled her up sharply, but Talia was already too far gone to react.

She was heat and need and fire. Scorched through. It felt as though she was about to burn alive, caught in a blaze that was as thorough as it was devastating. And she revelled in every single second of it.

It was as if this, Liam, now, was all that existed, and none of the other stuff even mattered. As if they could stay like this all day. All week.

For ever.

But they can't, yelled a faint voice. It was muffled, indistinct, as though buried under thousands of tons of glowing magma, but it was there all the same. Prodding her with all the things she wanted to forget, especially right at this moment. Reminding her that a world existed outside this dangerously temporary, recklessly seductive little bubble.

She lifted her hands to his chest, telling herself that she needed to push him away. But somehow her arms couldn't quite summon the strength. Instead, she found herself defiantly gripping his lapels and obstinately pulling him closer. And Liam seemed only too willing to comply.

His kisses changed. Less volcanic now, taking on an almost lazy rhythm as his tongue dipped in and out of her mouth, sampling, teasing, and leaving her aching for more.

She could hear the soft little greedy sounds coming from her own throat, but she was helpless to stop herself. This was so much like before, in North Carolina…only not. He took his time, indulging and demanding. His tongue teased hers, slick and hot, before his teeth grazed her lips, making her crave more. Over and over, like they had all the time in the world.

And Talia didn't know whether it was the separation, or that she was older, or a change of perspective, but however intense and glorious it had ever been with Liam three years ago, it felt like a pale imitation of whatever seared between them now.

It was as though time had heightened all those sensations, magnified all those emotions, instead of diminishing them, like it was supposed to have done.

His hands felt molten hot and a slick lava flow eased magnificently over every inch of her body, making her long to tear away the fabric barrier between them. Liam's eyes held hers so darkly, fixedly. As though he could read those wanton thoughts. As though nothing else mattered. As though she was the only thing in this world for him at this moment.

He moulded her to him and once again every inch of them pressed against each other, and she shivered as she felt her softness press against the hardest part of him. When all the words and emotions were stripped out, it all came down to this, didn't it? Man's most primitive, licentious desire.

And the physical side of their relationship had never been a concern, had it? She'd lost count of the number of blissful times they had merged so closely—so carnally—that they hadn't known where one of them had ended and the other begun.

It was only the emotional side of things that had been all barriers and barbs.

She didn't know how she found the strength to lift her head and bring her eyes back to his. But when she did, the air left her lungs with a whoosh. His eyes were dark, wanton, the message in them clear and unmistakable, and calling right down to the depths of her very soul. And he was still staring at her as though she was the most precious thing in the entire world.

But you aren't, screamed that same faint voice, and even though she wanted to pretend otherwise, Talia knew what was happening was sheer madness. Nothing had changed between them and deep down a part of her knew that. And still she couldn't tear herself away, she couldn't stop this inexorable pull to him. More to the point, she didn't want to.

His tongue slid rapturously against hers as he kissed her over and over. He cupped her cheeks, angling her head for a better fit.

She was caught in the devastating flow that was rolling over them both, a slow swell of memories that melded the past and the present, making the moment all the more delicious. And even though she knew she shouldn't—even though she knew the sanest thing would be to stop this madness and walk away—she couldn't. She wanted more. So much more.

Before she could second-guess herself, Talia ran her hands over his chest, forcing herself to slow down and savour the moment. It was impossible to stop herself from trembling. His sculpted abs were unmistakable under the thin fabric, their feel so painfully familiar.

How many times had they danced this tango? Toppling through the door of his apartment, often not even able to make it to bedroom before his hands were on her. His mouth. His tongue. And she'd welcomed him—more than welcomed him—she'd ached for him. Coming apart over and over, before pressing him down to the bed and straddling him, while he'd let her take control.

Had she ever been foolish enough to think that the power had really been hers, though? Liam had always been the one to wield it, hadn't he?

She had always lost her head where Liam was concerned, turning her back on everything else, even her own family. Her old life. Staying in North Carolina in the vain hope that he would begin to feel about her even a fraction of the emotions that she felt—*had* felt—for him.

But they weren't in North Carolina now, were they? They were *here.* In St Victoria. *Her* home. And they'd already agreed that whatever happened over the next month meant nothing. It was about the physical, not the emotional. This magic that had always existed between them and which, no matter what else had gone so inevitably wrong in their relationship, had always been so very perfect in and of itself.

And the truth was that she'd lost something infinitely more precious than her head. She'd lost her heart. So really, she thought dizzily, was it any wonder that when he gathered her in his arms and moved them both around until her bottom was perched on the edge of his desk, she didn't resist. Or when her wrists were encircled by one of his hands, pinning them up against his chest.

If she'd wanted to pull herself free, she could have. It was therefore telling that she did exactly as Liam silently commanded.

And then he began to trace his way down her body, taking in every dip and every curve, as if relearning them, for the first time in three years.

Talia couldn't have said exactly what it was that rolled through her at that moment. A kind of bitter-sweet regret, perhaps, which stole the breath from her lungs. She only knew she wanted this moment to go on for ever, even as she despaired of herself for her weakness.

The way she melted as he slid his hands up and down her sides, inching their way until they were cupping her too-heavy breasts and then, after what felt like an eternity, raking his thumb pads over her achingly sensitive nipples.

Even through her scrubs, the effect was electric, evidenced by the involuntary, raw sound that was wrenched from her throat.

'All in good time,' Liam muttered immediately.

Gratifyingly, his voice was nowhere near as composed as she thought he might have liked. There was comfort to be taken from that, at least.

But then she couldn't think any more because he was trailing his hands lower. Down her sides, and around to the small hollow at the base of her spine. Caressing and re-educating himself like she was a new, fascinating subject in which he wished to school himself.

And then he was sliding his fingers under the hem of her top. Inching under so that they skimmed her bare waist, making her entire body contract with desire. Dear God, if he made her this edgy from mere caresses, what might happen if he did more?

She couldn't manage more than a whisper, though she could hear her deep breaths loud and clear.

'Liam…'

She ought to remind him where they were…if only her mind wasn't a dim fug of nothing.

'Like I said, all in good time,' he repeated, his voice scratchy.

And then, as her hooded eyes caught his, she felt his hand dip beneath her waistband, down, lower still, until her throat was too choked to speak, and her body too aroused to object.

He teased her. Taunted her, even. Letting his fingers creep lower as they traced exquisite whorls wherever they went. *Everywhere* they went. Except for where she needed him most.

'I know,' he muttered, as some desperate squeak escaped her. 'Trust me, I understand.'

But if he did, then he wasn't giving in to it. Not quite yet. He wanted to keep her dangling, like a fish on a hook as the fishermen did out there in the deep blue sea.

'Liam,' she managed again.

'Why the rush?' he growled.

'No rush.' Talia had no idea how she managed to answer, though she sounded embarrassingly out of breath. 'I just...'

'You just...?' he echoed mercilessly. 'Just this, perhaps?'

But before she could reply, he dipped his fingers lower, dragging through her hair and sending devilish shivers right through her body.

'Or this?'

With another twist of his wrist, he let his fingers abrade her. Right where she was hottest, slickest—where she needed him most.

'Like that, then?' he confirmed, a certain triumph in his tone.

Clearly, he didn't need her to answer. Her body's reactions did all the talking for her.

As he stroked her, flicking his fingers over her, tearing low cries from her with every pass, sensations pummelled her from every direction. So much more than every fantasy she'd had over the last three years. Because there had been no one else for Talia in all that time.

What would have been the point? No one could ever

have matched Liam. She wondered if he knew that. If he knew that he was the only person who had ever, *ever* gone where he was now.

'Is this what you want?' he demanded, his tone thicker now.

Talia couldn't answer, it was taking all she had not to cry out. He was stroking her fast now, one hand in her panties, the other cupping her cheek. When had he released her hands? She didn't even know, but now they lay almost flimsily against that granite chest.

He angled his head to kiss her again, his fingers still playing that irresistible rhythm on her body, and she was helpless to resist. Between his mouth and his hand, she was adrift. Floating off on a sea of bliss with every skilful stroke.

He built the tempo quickly—or maybe it was just that she couldn't stop herself. That wild, wanton pace that dragged such low, primal sounds from deep inside her, and made her entire body begin to quiver, pushing herself against his hand as though it could somehow hasten those glorious final moments.

And then, as the edge of that chasm raced ever closer, and her body began to shake and come apart, Talia felt his lips on that sensitive hollow of her throat, and she couldn't fight it any longer.

It was like being hurled into the air. Flying and hurtling, all at once. Not even caring that she was out of control, as long as she kept coming apart, over and over again. She thought he would stop, but he didn't. He just kept going, sending her off in this direction and then that one. Propelling her wherever he wanted her to go.

And she simply gave in to it. As if there was nothing else she could do. As if there was nothing else she *wanted* to be doing.

Finally, she began to fall. Twisting and spinning as she gained more and more momentum. The ground was racing towards her too fast. Dimly, Talia realised, the best that she could hope for was that Liam would be there, at the bottom, to cushion her fall.

Liam felt her pull away from him, a startled sound on her lips.

Doing something like this in his new place of work should have been the most indecorous thing he'd ever done. Yet watching Talia—his Talia—crack and splinter beneath his touch was too raunchy for him to care about what was proper and what wasn't.

It felt as though he'd been waiting a lifetime for this moment again. And now it was here, he didn't want to let it go.

Talia, however, clearly had different plans.

He stood motionless as she put some distance between them, then adjusted her scrubs with shaky hands. When she stood up again, her eyes blazed at him.

'What the hell was that about?'

'Do I really need to explain it?' he questioned dryly. 'You're a medical professional after all.'

She actually gritted her teeth at him, and it was all he could do not to smile at how adorable she looked.

'I mean, was that your way of proving a point?'

'A point?'

'You thought I recommended you to my chief of staff to get you here, to St Victoria. Is this your way of proving that was true?'

'I wasn't actually setting out to prove anything,' he replied evenly, though the dangerous fact remained that he hadn't been able to think of anything at all. 'All the same, it's a little late to be acting so prudish, don't you think?'

She glowered at him even harder.

'No, I don't think it's too late at all.'

'Really?' he challenged. 'When I only have to do this to taste you?'

And then, to ram the point home, he lifted his hand to his mouth and sucked on his fingers.

She made a half-gurgling sound, and her eyes widened all the more. Liam was grateful for her indignation. At least it meant she was too preoccupied to see how affected he was by what was happening between them. How badly he wanted to taste her on his tongue properly.

He really needed to get out of the office and take a moment to regroup.

'I think it was,' she whispered, at last.

Too quietly, for Liam's peace of mind. Too controlled. He wanted to find safe ground before he lost what was left of his fragile self-control with Talia but the left and the right side of her brain didn't appear to be on the same page.

'Was what?'

'A test,' she said. 'You wanted to get your revenge.'

'Revenge for what?' he bit out instantly.

'You more or less accused me of leaving Duke's—*you*—in the way that I did because I wanted to goad you into racing here to St Victoria, after me.' Her voice shook, though he thought it was more out of shame than anger. 'I think this is your way of getting revenge.'

'I'm insulted that you would think so little of me,' he ground out. 'I might think any number of things about what happened three years ago, but what just happened was about primal lust. Revenge didn't come into it for a second.'

However, he had no intention whatsoever of revealing what emotions *had* entered into his decision to blow up every career rule he'd ever had, and do that with Talia. Here. Now.

He could barely even think straight. He might have given

Talia her release, but he had denied himself his own. Now his body was making it clear to him exactly how badly it wanted to claim her the way he knew they both wanted. However much they were each trying to deny it.

But these were base desires, and he refused to give in to them. He tried to focus on her words.

'You still want me, but you don't love me,' Talia was hurling at him. 'You told me that you never could.'

'That isn't who I am,' he said curtly.

'Why not, though?' she cried. 'Because your mother died and your father is a bit cold?'

'You're venturing onto thin ice, Talia. I suggest that you think carefully about voicing next whatever is in your head.'

'That's always the problem, though, isn't it?' she challenged. 'Any time things get too personal, you back away.'

'I have never backed away from anything.' He narrowed his eyes, but it hadn't escaped her that he'd hesitated for a split second.

Sucking in a deep breath, she pressed on.

'That's exactly what you do, Liam. Any time we ever veered towards the personal, you found a way to change the conversation.'

'I beg to differ.' His tone was easy, almost scornfully amused. 'You told me all about your parents and your two younger brothers; even how close you are to your grandmother. And, equally, I told you about mine,' he countered before he'd even thought about it.

He only realised he'd said something out of keeping when Talia froze, blinking at him.

'Your grandmother?' she asked. He didn't elaborate, so she pressed on. 'You never once even mentioned her, let alone told me anything about her.'

Had he not? He was sure he had. He'd thought about it, from time to time, anyway. The only other person to have ever shown him affection, aside from Talia. In some respects, his fiery St Victorian woman had resembled his spirited grandmother. Gloria by name, and by character. The only person who had ever stood up to his father and stood up for Liam himself against her only son's hatred of his own child.

But that had been before she, too, had died. Abandoning him once again to a lonely life with the old man.

'I told you about her when I showed you that box I had.'

She tilted her head to one side.

'You showed me a box which you told me contained photos of your mother that you never looked at. But you never once mentioned your grandmother, Liam.'

Had he really never mentioned her to Talia? Even once? He didn't realise that he'd said the words aloud, until Talia responded.

'No. You didn't. You never really told me anything. Did you never ask yourself why I left, Liam? Did you never wonder about anything?'

'I wondered,' he stated simply. 'But if you'd wanted to tell me, you would have.'

'I *did* want to tell you. I didn't feel I could. You actively avoided conversation about your own family. I know because I tried—several times. You shut me out, Liam. You always shut me out.'

'I barely knew you,' he countered. 'Was I to tell you my entire life story?'

He might have known she wouldn't be so easily put off.

'Have you ever told it to anyone? Any part of it?'

Liam didn't answer. He wasn't entirely sure what had happened in the last few moments. His head was swimming and he didn't even know where to start with untangling the knot of conflicting thoughts.

How had this unwanted conversation even begun? If he

could go back and stop it, he would. As it was, he needed to find a way to change it. Now.

'This is a pointless conversation.' He barely recognised his own clipped tone. 'It isn't going to get us anywhere.'

'No, you just won't allow it happen.' There was a sadness in her voice that clawed at him.

He thrust it aside.

'I came here for my patient, and for the trial,' he managed coldly.

For a moment he thought she was going to argue something more, but then she lifted her shoulders in the briefest of shrugs.

'Fine. I know how important it is to Nate and his team to have you on this case. I can assure you that I'll be at the hospital from tomorrow onwards, and there will be no need for our paths to cross again.'

She stopped abruptly and the bleak look in her eyes did little to dissipate the churning sensation low in his gut.

He lost sense of time, unsure how long they remained where they stood across the room from each other, neither of them saying a word. The silence seemed to grow heavier with each passing moment, pressing on them like the heat that wrapped itself around the inhabitants of St Vic just before the storms she had once told him so much about.

Hotter, and tighter, the closer the turbulence drew, and he couldn't help hoping that if he just stayed still, it would pass over them both.

Finally, he felt as though he'd regained some sense of equilibrium and he just about offered a curt dip of his head.

'I'd appreciate that,' he bit out.

And before Talia could answer, he was gone. The door closed softly on its dampeners behind him, doing nothing to diminish the disdain that swirled around him in the wake of his words.

CHAPTER FIVE

IT COULDN'T REALLY have gone much worse with Liam, Talia decided miserably the next day as she counted the instruments ready for the next surgery.

Ten sponges.

The confrontation yesterday had been so unsettling. She should have known he would want to arrive early to give himself a chance to familiarise himself with the clinic and his patient. Typical Liam pragmatism. She was a fool to have taken it personally, letting even a tiny part of herself think that he had come down specifically looking for her.

Six needle-holders.

Still, she and Liam now had four days working in the same clinic where they were bound to run into each other. Perhaps starting over would be a good move?

Two curved forceps.

Not even that morning's procedure—a Nissen fundoplication to help a patient suffering from gastroesophageal reflux disease—had been enough to stop her from thinking about Liam. She suspected she was going to replay the same doomed conversation—and impossibly hot encounter—over and over in her head for the next month.

Certainly until he left St Victoria.

'Ready, Talia?'

Talia blinked as two of her colleagues entered the sterile

area, prepped for surgery. She glanced around the OR and gave a satisfied nod. At least, even with her head filled with thoughts of Liam, she'd completed the pre-surgery routine quickly and systematically.

'Ready,' she confirmed.

But now she had to get her brain straight. Her high level of training meant that while she might be able to get away with a degree of being on autopilot for the prepping, and while this morning she'd been the circulation nurse, this afternoon she was the scrub nurse. Blood clots, bleeding, infection and problems with anaesthesia were all risks associated with the procedure, and as her patient's best advocate in the OR for the next few hours, she could not afford to be distracted by thoughts of her personal life.

Besides, she loved her job, and prided herself on the skills she brought to her role.

Olivia, the surgeon, stepped through the door and Talia concentrated on helping her gown up, and then for the next few hours Talia sank into her role of assisting.

It was lunchtime by the time she was finished and yet the moment she stepped back outside, it was Liam who was on her mind once again.

The last thing she expected was for him to be waiting for her in the corridor.

'Talia, can I have a moment?'

Her heart thumped hard against her chest wall, but she restrained herself to a mere nod of her head as she wordlessly followed him down the corridor and back to his temporary office. It was useless trying to block out the events of the previous day but she tried all the same.

'Yesterday should never have happened,' he began curtly—his version of an apology. 'Call it jet-lag, or shock at seeing you again, or sheer lack of control, but I shouldn't have let it get that far.'

She twisted her mouth ruefully. They were all plausible excuses for his behaviour, but what about her? She couldn't really claim shock, she'd had been preparing herself for the possibility of seeing him again—however much she'd tried to pretend that transferring to St Vic's would negate that—for weeks. She certainly couldn't blame jet-lag. That only left sheer lack of control. And what did that say about her?

Or either of them, for that matter?

'No,' she agreed. 'I shouldn't have either.'

'I would rather that it didn't happen again.'

As though it was some insignificant thing, and not the fact that she'd broken apart in his hands.

'Of course.' She drew in a steadying breath, wishing it didn't hurt so much. 'Like I said, we have four more days to get through where our paths may well cross and then, after that, I'll be on the other side of Williamtown.'

'So you mentioned.' He dipped his head but she couldn't make out his tone. It was too even, too neutral. 'However, I wanted to talk to you about that.'

'Oh?'

She couldn't have said why her pulse kicked up the way that it did. And there was no reason at all for her skin to prickle or for that strange sensation, which couldn't possibly be excitement, to ripple down her spine.

'I understand Lucy Wells was originally your patient, which is how you knew the case well enough in the first instance?'

'She was.' Talia lifted her shoulders. 'But once she was accepted for this trial she became part of the clinical trial team's caseload.'

And she knew he would have been poring over all their notes, ensuring he knew the case inside out. He always liked to be as thorough as he possibly could be, whether the surgery was an emergency, or an elective. It was part of what made him so good at what he did.

'But you aren't on that clinical team?' He frowned. 'Why not? You've been an OR nurse in these types of procedures before back at Duke's. With me.'

Talia's mind spun, a thousand replies all cramming her brain at once. But what would be the point in any of them? She'd already said more than she'd ever intended. In the end, she settled for the practical.

'The previous cardiothoracic surgeon had his preferred team from before I even arrived at The Island Clinic, and I wasn't part of it.'

Liam frowned at her again, but this time it felt different.

There was a beat of quiet.

'Did you want to be on the team?'

She blinked, taking a moment to process the question.

'Sure, it's a fascinating surgery and Lucy's a good kid.'

'As far as I'm concerned, you're one of the best scrub nurses I've had in my OR,' he said candidly. 'Isak would be a fool not to want you on the team.'

Gratitude and something else she didn't care to identify shot through Talia. In spite of all they'd just said to one another, he still didn't think twice about telling her that she was a good nurse.

'Thank you.' She pulled her lips together. 'But I also don't know much about the procedure.'

He frowned.

'You've been part of atrial repairs before back at Duke's. With me even.'

'None of the surgeries I was ever on with you were total atrial arch reconstructions.' She shook her head. 'I've worked on a handful of traditional two-stage elephant trunk procedures, but you're skilled in the single-stage approach.'

'I didn't realise,' he mused, and a heavy weight of regret plummeted through her.

After what had happened in his office less than twenty-four hours ago, it might have been good to have something less...intimate between them. Maybe even get them back to an easier, more neutral footing with each other.

But now he was going to rescind his offer to put her on his team, and she felt a stab of regret. He opened his mouth to speak and she steeled herself for the inevitable.

'Well, you're going to have to learn at some time. I'd still like you on my team.' Liam shrugged, as though it was no big deal. 'So if you want on, I'll talk to Nate in the morning.'

She could almost feel the silence in the room, swirling around her.

'Why? Why are you doing this for me?' He didn't answer, and she was forced to carry on. 'Is this about last night?'

'I don't make decisions about my OR for personal reasons.' He looked distinctly unimpressed, and she knew what he must be thinking. She knew that was true better than anyone else. 'My patients deserve the best team they can get. I've no doubt Isak's team is brilliant but I haven't worked with them all before. I have, however, worked with you and I rate your skills highly. So, as the surgeon running this operation, you are a logical choice.'

Talia couldn't contain her smile, though she cursed her heart for the way it leapt in her chest. He was still prepared to give her a chance, and it struck her as so typically Liam that no matter how badly the two of them were communicating on a personal level, when it came to surgeries, he was the most approachable surgeon she could ever hope to work with.

Professional, and generous with his time and knowledge. Not every surgeon could boast those same qualities. A pang of emotion shot through her, and she could only put it down to some kind of wistful nostalgia.

'And regarding what happened yesterday…?'

She'd never been known for her poker face, but if only she could display even a fraction of the reserve that Liam had.

He was paying her a professional compliment, not a personal one, though that didn't seem to matter to her weak-willed organs. And it was typical Liam to put his patient before everything else. It certainly didn't mean he wanted her around for his own purposes, she wasn't going to be foolish enough to let herself think otherwise. No matter how much that traitorous part of her might want to.

'We both said things I think we'd rather take back, but we can't. Therefore I propose we put it behind us and move on.'

By 'it', she presumed he meant the kiss…and more. Was she being perverse, wanting to remind him once again that this was exactly the problem? The way he moved past personal issues but never actually tackled the source?

Maybe, maybe not. She shrugged inwardly. But the last thing she wanted was another row. Shoving her personal feelings down, she offered a tentative nod.

'You're right, we're different people now. Whatever went wrong between us back then, it's long since buried.'

'Agreed,' he answered, too easily for her peace of mind.

She forced herself to smile.

'It doesn't matter anymore.'

'Precisely,' Liam approved, and she hated his matter-of-fact tone, without even a trace of fondness. Especially when she couldn't fight back those unwelcome waves of nostalgia. 'So shall we grab a coffee and you can tell me what you know?'

'Sure.' Talia drew in a steadying breath. This was her moment to prove herself and she wasn't about to blow it. Of all the surgeons to learn from, Liam was certainly one of the best.

It felt odd, walking with him down the hospital corridors. As if everyone was looking and could read what had already happened between them when logically she knew they couldn't know.

Clearing her throat, she fought to sound purely professional. 'I understand this technique allows you to combine the traditional two-stage surgical and endovascular procedures for complex aortic lesions into a single surgery.'

'Shall we wait until we sit down?' he suggested dryly.

'No.' She shook her head, and took another breath. The sooner she put things onto a professional footing, the better.

Were they walking too close to each other? Should she move out to the side more, or would that look too obvious?

'This trial is to see how recent advances in the right anterior mini-thoracotomy approach mean reduced post-op pain and faster patient recovery, among other benefits, right?'

'Right,' he concurred as they reached the cafeteria. 'Do you want to find a table while I get the coffees?'

She could feel even more eyes on them. Scrutinising them. No doubt she'd be subjected to any number of interrogations from colleagues after this, ranging from curious to downright jealous. Like at Duke's, it was clear that Liam had attracted plenty of attention.

Not that she cared, Talia reminded herself hastily, they were just friends. Whatever had happened yesterday.

'Your coffee, you still take it milk, no sugar?'

'That's fine, *Dr* Miller.' She hastily took the drink, and ignored the odd look he cast her way. 'So, anyway, there are a couple of different kinds of prostheses, too, aren't there?'

He only hesitated a fraction of a moment but it was

enough to make her feel foolish. What was she doing, letting other people dictate how she reacted, especially when she thought about Liam's father? The irony of it didn't escape her. She forged on regardless.

'I've been reading the notes from previous operations for this trial and I noticed that with an open prosthesis a one-thirty-millimetre stented graft…'

'Talia, this is ridiculous.'

'…is used with the supra-aortic vessels implanted as….'

'Talia,' he repeated, 'what's going on?'

'I…' heat suffused her cheeks.

'Is this going to be a problem for you? Working with me on this case?'

Panic shot through her. His expression was closed, giving nothing away as usual, yet there was an edge in his tone that she didn't recognise. If she had to guess, she might have thought it was disapproval.

'I'm sorry,' she blurted out hastily. 'I'm just…aware that people are watching us.'

'I'm the stand-in surgeon for the great Isak Nilsson.' Liam shrugged. 'People are going to be interested.'

'Do you think they know?' she muttered into the coffee cup. 'Do you think they can tell?'

Whatever she'd been expecting, it hadn't been Liam's forthright reply.

'That we were intimate yesterday? I don't think they can tell that, no. Though they might guess if you look any more furtive.'

She couldn't answer, though she could feel the heat racing over her skin.

'Talia, we're here legitimately discussing a mutual patient. If you don't want people to gossip then stop looking edgy and don't give them a reason to.'

All at once, her sense of discomfort and guilt morphed

into old feelings of frustration and hurt and she swallowed down the urge to scream. The simple truth was that she didn't want to be here with Liam in the clinic cafeteria, discussing a patient.

She would far, far rather have been back in the privacy of his office or, better still, in the suite he'd been allocated in the clinic's luxury hotel, which was well equipped to deal with entire Hollywood entourages, let alone a single surgeon.

And she would far rather have been engaged in more diverting activities than discussing a patient—as much as she wanted the best for Lucy Wells.

But such a fantasy was pointless. Liam had already been more than explicit that yesterday's intimacy had been a mistake not to be repeated. He didn't want her.

But she, to her shame, still wanted him.

'Did you know Nate has provided me with a chauffeur-driven car to give me a tour around the island?' Liam asked her, without warning. 'Apparently, your chief thinks it's important for me to get to know more about the island.'

And, in spite of everything, Talia laughed. The idea of Liam exploring an island when he could be working on a new, challenging operation was almost laughable. But how typical of Nate to encourage it, all the same.

'He's proud of the island.' She grinned suddenly. 'We all are. And you have a reputation for burying yourself in your work, so I imagine he's trying to ensure you take some time out, too. Then again, he could be hoping you might take a swing by St Vic's Hospital. They're always in need of medical staff to offer their time for free.'

'And do you?' asked Nate. 'Offer your time free.'

'Whenever I can,' she confirmed with another grin.

She liked it that it seemed to catch him off guard for a

moment. But she wasn't ready when he turned around and did the same.

'Fancy showing me around?' he asked abruptly.

Her entire body felt as though she'd slammed into a wall. She didn't want to consider why that might be.

'Me?' she asked tentatively. 'Why?'

'Maybe we can find some common ground, make it easier to work together.'

He even offered her a bright, airy smile, his voice even and unaffected, but she hadn't missed that pause for a fraction of a second first.

'You always promised me a guided tour,' he pushed when she didn't answer. Though she wanted to. So very badly.

'Over three years ago,' she managed instead.

'And now here we are. So, how about we meet outside The Island Clinic entrance, any morning this week at eight? I seem to remember we were both always early risers.'

She flicked her tongue over her lips and pretended she couldn't understand Liam well enough to know that he'd felt a punch of victory. His words had been designed to hit their mark. To remind her of the number of mornings they'd woken before their alarm and spent the last possible moment in bed, making love.

'Liam—'

'I seem to remember a St Victoria native once recommending that a good place to start would be the Beics.'

'I didn't think you ever listened to me,' she said shortly.

'I listened,' he said with another smile.

'Well,' she scraped around for another excuse. Anything. 'I didn't think you'd have any free time. You're usually buried in work.'

'Aren't you the one who always told me the pace of life was different, here on St Victoria?' he challenged her. 'And according to your chief, his focus is on quality over quantity.'

Yes, she could well imagined Nate having given Liam plenty of challenging cases, but also a fair amount of downtime.

'So let me know which morning suits you,' Liam continued. 'And I'll see you then.'

Talia met his steady gaze right then, and didn't know if what she saw in them was a promise or something far, far, greater. But, then, it didn't matter. She stared at him for another long moment before finally pushing herself to her feet and picking up her still half-full coffee cup.

'I'll think about it,' she bit out, wishing her heart wasn't leaping around in such delight.

'I'll take that as better than a flat-out *no.*'

'It isn't a *yes*, either,' she pointed out. Though she suspected they both new how tempted she was.

On all counts.

CHAPTER SIX

'THE SURGEON SAID something about whirlpool signs? I just don't understand exactly what he wants to do to Obi.'

Obi's mother's voice pitched upwards in panic and Talia fought to smother the irritation that swelled inside her at thought of the departing paediatric surgeon.

The guy was evidently in far too much of a hurry to get back on the helicopter that would take him out of the community hospital and back to the unmistakable luxury of The Island Clinic. Clearly, he was far too keen to return to fawning over all his A-list clientele, to take the time to simplify a complex procedure for a concerned mother.

He was a brilliant surgeon but not a very pleasant man who had never been a fan of The Island Clinic-St Vic's outreach programme, which would bring eight-year-old Obi to The Island Clinic for her surgery.

It was why he wasn't going to last long with Nate as Chief of Staff. Whereas Liam…

An image of Liam popped, uninvited, into Talia's brain and she found it was impossible not to compare one man with the other. If this had been a cardiothoracic case, and young Obi had been one of his patients, Liam would never have left a panicked mother with a bunch of unanswered questions.

She heard that only the previous night, Liam had spent

a good couple of hours with Lucy Wells, and her mother, Violet. Explaining things in detail and answering all their questions. He was so skilled at pitching things just right. Simplifying things just enough for a lay person, without becoming condescending.

Talia could never imagine the mother of one if his patients being so confused.

But Obi wasn't Liam's case, and letting her mind wander to him served no purpose other than to distract herself. Hastily she turned her attention back to Obi's mother.

'That's why I'm here,' Talia soothed quickly, reaching out to take the young woman's hands in her own. 'I'm your liaison between here and The Island Clinic, and I'm here to explain anything I can.'

Obi was a local girl who had been diagnosed at birth with congenital intestinal malrotation, but whose condition hadn't previously been serious enough to warrant surgical intervention before now.

The girl had recently begun presenting with abdominal pain of a chronic and diffuse nature, and the team at St Vic's had conducted a series of medical images to determine the position of the duodenum and the proximal small bowel, as well as looking for the 'whirlpool' sign typical of volvulus.

'Sonography has revealed that a part of Obi's gut has now twisted around on itself completely—that's the whirlpool sign the surgeon mentioned—which has changed her medical status from asymptomatic to acute, and which now necessitates surgery. She will be flown to The Island Clinic tonight—we have family accommodation for you to stay, so don't worry—and a nasogastric tube will be inserted through Obi's nose into her stomach and placed on low intermittent suction; we will ensure any fluid or electrolyte deficits are corrected and she will be placed on broad-spectrum antibiotics before surgery.'

'Because she has appendicitis, too?' the mother asked anxiously.

'No.' Talia shook her head gently. 'Actually, it's the contrary. During the procedure, the intestine will be straightened out to reduce that so-called whirlpool effect, and the small intestine will be folded into the right side of the abdomen while the large bowel—or colon—will go on the left-hand side. Now, usually the appendix would be found on the right side of the abdomen, but where there is intestinal malrotation it has often moved to the left.'

'So it would be in the way.'

'Although it is rare, there is always a possibility that the artery to the appendix could be damaged in the course of the surgery,' Talia conceded. 'But the other reason is because, should Obi ever develop appendicitis in the future, the atypical location of it could complicate diagnosis and treatment.'

For a further half-hour Talia continued to answer questions, feeling a sense of deep satisfaction as she managed to calm the understandably frightened mother and prepare her for the short flight to The Island Clinic with her young daughter.

Finally, the two of them emerged from the quiet consultation room, and Talia headed back to the nurses' station to go through other patient notes before she, too, left St Vic's Hospital.

'Talia, girl, haven't seen you for too long. How've you been doin' up at that posh Island Clinic of yours?'

Talia snapped her head up from her notes as she was greeted by one of St Vic's longest-serving staff. She was an older woman who was both fun and friendly to work with, and an experienced nurse.

'Nyla.' She let the woman embrace her in a crushing hug. 'It's been good up there, though I've been here in the community clinic from time to time, but we've kept crossing shifts. Don't tell me we'll finally be working together?'

'No,' Nyla said mournfully. 'I've been on night shift. I'm heading off in half an hour.'

'Oh, no,' commiserated Talia, genuinely sorry. It would have been good to have a shift with Nyla. Perhaps it would have helped to take her mind off anything *Liam*-related. 'Who's going to give me all the up-to-date gossip?'

'Well, we've got half an hour to make the most of it.' The older woman's eyes gleamed and Talia realised, too late, that the gossip was going to be about her. 'So I understand the new clinic surgeon is your old beau.'

'Don't know what you mean.' Talia shook her head, wishing that she was a better liar.

Or at least that Nyla wasn't so damned shrewd.

'Oh, girl, don't even try to feed me that line.' Nyla shot her an empathetic look. 'I can read you too well, child. But if it makes you feel any better, no one else up there has any idea, they're all too busy trying to snag him for theyselves.'

'Then how did you know?' She was genuinely curious.

Nyla tapped her nose and laughed. *'Boonoonoonoos!'*

'He's not my special friend, Nyla.' Talia wrinkled her nose.

'Sure he is. You know me, I've always had a sense for this stuff. The moment I saw your pinched little face from across that corridor, it all fell into place. The new doc from North Carolina, the fact that you suddenly got you'self transferred here for a rotation, the way you look as though you're about to jump out of you' own skin any minute.'

'I do not.' Talia frowned defensively, then shook her head at her own blunder. 'Okay, maybe a little.'

'So he is the one who hurt you.' Nyla raised her eyebrows knowingly.

A week ago, Talia wouldn't have thought twice about confirming it. Now, though, his words rang in her head.

'Yeah.' She nodded slowly, then pulled a face. 'Though if you'd heard him speak the other day, you'd have thought I was the one at fault.'

As usual, the words were out before she could stop them but instead of looking surprised Nyla gave a half-shout of delight.

'We knew it.'

'Sorry?'

'Your mama and I, we always knew it.' Nyla reached a plump arm out and squeezed Talia's shoulders. 'We al'ays said he be a fool to hurt you; maybe he is hurting a little himself, no?'

'You and Mama said that?'

'Sho' we did.' Nyla nodded triumphantly. 'It took him all his time to come after you, but we al'ays thought he would.'

Whatever foolish glimmer had made her heart thump like a dog's tail feebly wagging for a scrap was snuffed out in an instant.

'No.' She shook her head, trying to sound resolute rather than miserable. Not that she wouldn't have trusted Nyla to see a little of the torment she was putting herself through, but if she let it in, even just a little, what if she couldn't shut it off again.

'He didn't come here for me.' Talia forced a smile. 'He came here for a case. Nate picked him.'

'Yet he knew this is where you were?'

'Not exactly.' Talia frowned, remembering Liam's words. 'He didn't know where I'd gone.'

Nyla let out an incredulous bark of laughter.

'You believe that, girl? 'Course he knew. This is your home, where else would you be? And after all, he's here now, isn't he?'

'He isn't here for me,' Talia reiterated, though perhaps more for herself than for Nyla.

What was the point in false hope? She would only get hurt again.

'I see.' The older woman nodded sagely. 'He said that, did he?'

'Yes. We had an argument and he was painfully clear.'

'Aye.'

There wasn't explicit encouragement in Nyla's tone, yet Talia heard it all the same. And she couldn't help herself from admitting more.

'Then we apologised…' She bit her lip. 'He offered me a place on the operating team.'

Nyla didn't say anything. She didn't have to. Eyeing her triumphant expression, Talia felt that tiny flame of hope flicker back into life.

'He asked me if I'd show him around the island. I said that I'd think about it because it can't be a wise idea, can it?'

Another sage glance from Nyla had a grin spreading, uncontained, over Talia's face. She felt the corners of her lips being pulled up, an almost lightness invading her body, swiftly followed by a veritable kaleidoscope of butterflies.

'You think I should go, don't you?' she asked Nyla, who threw up her hands in true dramatic fashion.

'Don't ask me, child, I'm just here to listen. If *you* think you should go, that's what matters.'

It was hardly the instruction Talia had been looking for, but that didn't seem to matter. She was shuffling her notes and moving as though spurred into some—any—kind of action.

'I'll go and see if my patient and her family have arrived,' Talia declared.

'And shall I get the number of the hotel room where the new doc is staying?' demanded Nyla dryly. 'You can pop up there after your shift.'

'No need,' Talia sang out, already making her way along the corridor to the waiting area. 'I have their number on my phone anyway. I can just call and leave him a message. It doesn't have to be a bigger deal that that.'

Because it *wasn't* a bigger deal that that, Talia decided firmly. It was two old friends setting aside personal differences and being professional. He was handing her an olive branch by offering her a place on his operating team, there was no reason why she shouldn't do the same by showing him around the island.

Her island.

It was no more, no less than that.

'So these are the Beics,' Talia told him, two days later, as she pointed across the breath-taking, aquamarine waters of the bay. 'Three volcanic peaks, or plugs, are linked by the Bec Ridge. The smallest one is around two thousand, two hundred feet high, while the tallest is just shy of three thousand feet.'

'And they're called the Beics because they look like bird beaks?' Liam guessed, trying to pretend his body wasn't reacting to her all-too-familiar shampoo scent of coconut and hibiscus.

The way he'd been fighting against doing that all morning.

'Exactly.' She laughed that soft laugh of hers. 'You have Petit Bec and Grand Bec, which I guess speak for themselves, and then the jagged middle-sized one is known as Bec Dentelé.'

That laugh did things to him that he felt it had no business doing. He tried to push it out of his head, but it was proving impossible. His senses were already on overload and he couldn't seem to shut them down.

St Victoria was stunning, and loud, and vibrant. It oozed life and fun out of every bright, laughter-filled street, every evocative steel band, and every incredible view. And every bit of it reminded him of how Talia had seemed to blow into Duke's, four years ago, filling his world with sound and splashing vibrant colour all over the dull walls of his previously black and white life. How he'd felt like he was being brought to life—when he hadn't even realised he'd needed to be.

It had felt...*right.*

For possibly the first time in his life, he'd felt...if not love then certainly care. Tenderness. And although it had felt strange at first, he'd found himself quickly growing accustomed to it, liking it, even beginning to return it.

But then, without warning, she'd disappeared as abruptly as she'd arrived, and everything had faded to monochrome again in an instant. Only this time Liam had known what he was missing, which had only made it seem all the bleaker. All the emptier.

He'd be damned if he was going to let that happen again. He'd come here to take this new case, not to seek out old demons, but if he was going to have to face them here, he had no intention of letting them get the better of him a second time.

'I seem to recall you once telling me that you can climb the Bec Range?'

'Yeah, you can hike them easily enough, especially Petit Bec and Grand Bec, and the ridge isn't too bad to cross.'

'And lots of tourists visit for the hot springs.'

Too late, he tried to swallow back the statement. It felt too personal, too intimate somehow. A hark back to the conversations they'd once shared as a couple, when she used to talk about her home, and when they both imagined him one day coming to see it with her.

As though they'd really believed in that future.

'Right.' She swallowed hard, as if she was trying to shake the same memories. 'But you have to be careful of the fumaroles.'

His mind latched onto the safer topic as he searched for something less personal to say.

'So you get a few burns at the hospital, especially in tourist season?'

Her mouth crinkled up and he pretended that he didn't notice.

'You always have your surgeon's head on, don't you? Yes, we do get cases at the hospital. But there are some great guided tours available, you don't have to risk life and limb to visit them.'

'I'll bear that in mind,' he offered sardonically, wishing he didn't overthink every statement she made.

Was that why she'd left him? Because he was always focussed on his patients and his career? And if that was true, why did he even care what she thought?

Why did he want to spin her around and ask her why she'd really put his name forward to her chief of staff? Had it really been about her patient? Or had there been a part of her that had wanted to see him again?

Because, however much it galled him to admit it, there was certainly a part of him that wondered. And he hated it that she haunted him in this way.

'Of course, there are plenty of other places to visit if you're nervous.'

Her wry voice cut through the air and he blinked, the cogs in his mind trying to recall the last part of their conversation.

'Nervous?' he rasped out.

'If you don't trust me not to lead us into any dangerous fumaroles?'

'Ah, I see.' He could think of being places with Talia that were a damned sight more dangerous than mere fumaroles.

And even though he knew she was teasing him—even though he knew it wasn't a wise idea to respond—he couldn't help himself.

'I'm game if you are. Besides, you also promised to take me scuba diving on the reefs, and ziplining from the rainforest canopy.'

Her gaze turned to him, seeming to almost burn into him, but he could work out what she was thinking. Her dark eyes, the colour of the richest cacao, had often been an enigma to him.

For several long moments they simply watched each other. Liam wasn't even sure if he stopped breathing. And then, at last, she broke the silence, her voice perhaps a little too unnaturally breezy.

'What did you think of Lucy Wells? I heard you finally had chance to meet her in person.'

He cast her a thoughtful glance.

'She's clearly a bright kid. And mature for fifteen. But then, given her medical condition, that's understandable.'

'True,' Talia nodded. 'And Violet?'

He knew what she was doing, trying to get the conversation onto a professional footing. But it wasn't territory in which he was comfortable. He wasn't the only surgeon who liked to meet his patients and get some understanding of who they were yet didn't generally like to consider their personal circumstances too deeply.

If surgeries didn't quite go to plan, it could sometimes make it hard to make the difficult decisions.

'Violet is clearly a mother who fiercely loves her daughter, but I was surprised at how pragmatic she is, too.'

Talia nodded.

'Not the overbearing Hollywood type you were expecting? Throwing her money or power around?'

'I try not to pre-judge,' he grimaced. 'But I suppose that's true enough.'

He was grateful when Talia didn't press the matter. Another gentle silence swirled around them, until she spoke again.

'So, the island really is a place of two halves. Approximately eight hundred square kilometres from the wild yet quiet mini-jungle at one end, and the noisy, bustling city of the historic centre nearer the other.'

'Impressive,' he acknowledged. 'Anything else?'

They both knew he wasn't referring to the sightseeing tour, though he didn't know why he was trying to make things more personal. Shouldn't he be relieved that Talia had been working so hard to keep things on a neutral footing?

'No more facts about the flora?' He heard his quiet challenge. 'The fauna?'

What was wrong with him?

Talia's eyes locked with his, a flicker of uncertainty under all that smoky heat. She licked her lips even as her eyebrow arched up.

'I could tell you that around three hundred plant species have been identified on the Beics, ten of them rare, as well as some thirty-odd bird species.'

He didn't miss the slight hitch in her voice, however, and he suppressed a smile. At least he wasn't the only one finding the entire day awkward.

Like a date that they'd never actually had.

Don't even go there, he warned himself hastily.

'So you're happy back here?' he asked abruptly.

Hardly an improvement. He wasn't surprised when Talia snapped her head around to him.

'Sorry?'

He didn't repeat the question, there seemed little point.

'I like it back here,' she hazarded after a moment. 'It… isn't as bad as I once thought.'

He assumed she was referring to all the times she'd told him that she hadn't been able to stand living on St Victoria. That moving to the States, to somewhere like North Carolina, had been like a dream to her.

'You once said that you would never come back here. That it was too small, too insular.'

'I was wrong,' she bit back. 'About a lot of things.'

He frowned. It sounded as though she was having a go at him, but he couldn't imagine for what.

'You're referring to me? You were wrong about me?'

She shrugged, but didn't answer.

'I thought I was about the only thing that remained consistent throughout,' he pressed, not liking the inference but unable to put his finger on quite why it rankled the way it did.

'Is that what you think?' she demanded suddenly.

'I told you who I was, what I believed, from the outset. I never wavered on that.'

She glared at him for another long moment.

'No.' She blew out a breath at last. Long and heartfelt. 'I don't suppose you did.'

But it sounded less appreciative than Liam might have

expected. And then she threw herself back in the seat and turned her head to stare out of the window, the conversation clearly over.

So much for trying to establish some kind of working connection.

Because, of course, this was what today had been about, that sly voice insinuated in his head.

He found he didn't care for it much. He cared even less for the fact that it was right. Accepting the medical case had been as much about coming to Talia's home island as it had been about the challenging surgery. And that, in itself, was an issue.

Yet, like every other reservation he'd had in the past couple of weeks, Liam thrust it aside and turned back to the creature he couldn't seem to shake from his head, no matter how he tried.

'Okay, where now?'

'Now?' She didn't exactly squeak it, but her voice sounded a fraction higher than normal.

She cleared her throat again and checked her watch. Liam suspected it was more for something to do than because she actually needed to. Still, a faintly relieved expression skittered over her lovely features as she realised the time, tapping on the panel to the driver and issuing some polite instruction before sitting back in her seat next to him.

'Now we go and get lunch.'

CHAPTER SEVEN

BEING WITH LIAM was even harder than she'd anticipated, Talia admitted to herself an hour later as they threaded their way through the colourful, loud Williamtown streets. And she hadn't expected it to be easy to start with.

She'd tried to be a good guide, showing him the St Victoria that she would have been proud to show to any other visiting surgeon. But, then, Liam wasn't any other surgeon, was he? He was Liam Miller, the man who had always been able to twist her inside out.

It seemed that nothing had changed.

It didn't help that the tour itself felt altogether too much like a date. At least, it did to her. So much for having told herself that it was just two old friends offering an olive branch to each other, no more and no less. Who had she been kidding, anyway? They'd laughed their way around the island—*her* island—and it had felt good.

And odd.

And conflicting.

Seeing St Victoria through his eyes had been something of a revelation. Almost a chance to see the island afresh. And, in line with everything she'd been feeling more and more this past year, she began to wonder why she'd ever been so desperate to leave in the first place. Or why, when she'd felt those pangs of homesickness in North Carolina, she'd stuffed them down and instructed herself that they hadn't existed.

She pretended that she didn't know that the answer to the latter was walking right beside her. So close she could actually feel the heat bouncing off his body into hers. Seeping right through to her very bones and making her wonder if—as mad as it sounded—should he suddenly turn around over lunch and ask her to return to Duke's with him she wouldn't agree.

Could she really sacrifice the island that held her soul for the man who held her heart? Because, whatever she'd pretended to herself, the truth was that he did still hold it. She could claim she was over him as much as she liked, but it didn't make it true.

Some tour guide you are, she berated herself, trying to drag her focus back to the task in hand.

They were going for lunch.

Nothing more intimate that that.

And yet it didn't feel that easy. Everywhere they turned, people were laughing, smiling, welcoming them. She hoped Liam didn't have enough patois to understand what was being aimed their way, people clearly seeing them as some kind of couple.

Even now, a handful of street vendors was trying to tempt them with local cuisine cooked right in front of them as they addressed them as the *happy newlyweds.* Talia squeezed her eyes shut. Tightly.

It terrified her how utterly seduced she was by that simple notion. Even now—all these years on.

She shook her head in frustration.

'Talia?' His hand curved around her elbow, strong and steadying. 'Everything okay?'

The last thing she needed...and the very thing she

wanted. Sensations charged around her body like volts of electricity.

She sucked in a deep breath and somehow—she would never know how—spun quickly so that it wrenched at the contact without looking as though that was what she'd intended at all.

'I'm fine.' She smiled brightly and convinced herself that she looked serene and happy—not like some demented grinning gecko.

Liam cast her a sceptical glance.

'What's happened? A moment ago we were getting on well, now suddenly you seem…edgy.'

'Nonsense.' Even she didn't find her sing-song voice believable.

'Do you want to try that again, only this time with more feeling?'

She didn't want to laugh, she didn't even want to smile. It was too painful to realise how easily he could still read her.

'Go on,' he encouraged, clearly sensing her weakening. 'I'll feed you the line again. Talia, everything okay?'

'Idiot.' She batted his arm lightly with her hand, the corners of her mouth twitching upwards all the same.

'Better,' he approved, and warmth flowed through her.

She told herself that she hated how something so simple from him could affect her. Perversely, it made her want to say something to get under his skin, too. Just to prove to herself that she wasn't the only one on edge today, despite how well it had seemed to have been going.

'If you must know…' she craned her neck up to look at him '…they were calling us *newlyweds*.'

To his credit, Liam didn't back away the way she'd expected him to. That didn't mean to say she couldn't feel that momentary tension from his body.

'I see.'

'They think we look loved up.'

Her heart felt as though it was climbing up her chest and into her throat, but Talia stuffed it back down. Memories of the other day still flooded her body every night, it was hardly surprising that they'd flood her mind right now, too.

'I suppose we might look like a couple,' he conceded at last, to her surprise.

She twisted her neck all the more.

'It doesn't bother you more?'

'Should it?'

'The last time I even voiced anything to do with marriage, you told me that it was an outdated institution that wasn't for you.'

He actually looked shocked and, for a moment, she thought she must have imagined that entire nightmare conversation of three years ago. Then, at last, his expression cleared.

'And that made you think I wouldn't want to hear someone calling us *newlyweds*?'

She lifted her shoulders, no longer quite as certain.

'It crossed my mind. We seem to have been getting on so well that I didn't want anything to…spoil it. Besides, I know how you pride yourself on your reputation for professionalism.'

'You're giving me a guided tour—we're hardly walking down the street, giving people a public show,' he answered, but his voice was tighter than before and Talia knew the conversation was getting to him.

She wanted to stop it, but it was like opening the lid on an ant farm—impossible to get everything back in.

'No, but still…' She splayed her hands out when words failed her.

There was so much more she wanted to ask—to know—

but this was hardly the time or place. Perhaps nowhere ever would be now. It was too far in the past.

But, still, as she watched him, a hundred thoughts swirling around her head, she got the feeling he was trying to pull himself back to the present.

It was shameful how fervently she wished she knew what he'd been thinking.

'I think—'

'Perhaps it would be better to abandon this conversation.' He cut her off with forced joviality. 'Get back to where we were a few minutes ago.'

It was more of an instruction than a question and Talia wondered what he would say if she pressed the point.

But the truth was that she didn't want to. Today had been so nice, so comfortable, with Liam that she didn't want to ruin it now. She wanted to hold onto it, for as long as they could.

'Right.' It was all she could do to match his level of conviviality. To motivate her body back into action and keep them moving through the market. 'Good idea.'

As if her heart wasn't breaking inside all over again.

It shouldn't surprise her that he was pushing her away again, she told herself. And it really shouldn't dismay her at all.

Heat shimmered in the already searing air as mouthwatering scents floated tantalisingly towards Liam. One vendor offered some sort of stunning salt-fish dish, another had a glorious soup that appeared to be made from a plant Talia teased him about not even properly recognising.

Yet he felt as though he was moving through a fug.

He'd felt like this all day, all week. Ever since that kiss in his office, if he was being honest. And this latest conversation hadn't helped. Reminding him that, in spite of every bad thing he knew about marriage, and family, and despite every promise he'd made to himself never to go down such a destructive route, three years ago he'd actually entertained the notion of asking Talia to spend the rest of her life with him.

When she'd left, he'd convinced himself it was if not a good thing then at least for the best. But now that he was here in St Victoria, with Talia, it was becoming harder and harder to remember that.

And though Liam didn't care to examine why, he could feel this thing that had begun to hum inside him and he couldn't—didn't *want to*—switch it off. A cadence, a rhythm he hadn't heard in such a long time, like the way the air seemed to pulse with the beat of the fantastic steel drums being played in the park across the way. The marketplace bustling with life and colour, as though the hurricane of several years ago was nothing more than a distant memory, though he remembered it from the news and from the little Talia had told him.

He didn't like to press her on it. She was clearly trying to lighten the mood from a moment ago, and doing a better job of it than he was.

'The fried plantains are good. As is the breadfruit when it's mashed with coconut milk and baked in banana leaves like that.' Talia's voice broke through his thoughts, causing a fresh kick inside his chest before he reined it back under control.

It seemed the day together had made him forget to keep his guard up. Perhaps, for both their sakes, he ought to remedy that but he couldn't seem to bring himself to do it.

'I recall you telling me once before.' He smiled.

She blinked at him in surprise.

'I did?'

'You did,' he confirmed. 'Back at Hal's Diner, round the corner from Duke's—you remember? We were having breakfast one morning and you looked at your pancakes and pondered what you wouldn't give to have a forkful of coconut milk breadfruit for once.'

'Oh.'

'You suggested that, should we ever visit your family, you'd introduce me to some typical St Victoria culinary delights.'

The air shimmered between them, only this time it had nothing to do with the food being prepared.

He recognised only too well the way that she pulled her mouth a fraction to one side. He just didn't know what it meant.

Had his stirring up of old memories somehow spoiled what had otherwise been a pleasant—more than pleasant—day? Ruining things between them?

Just like you did last time.

The smug voice came out of nowhere, its almost triumphant tone echoing around his head. A voice which, Liam considered abruptly, sounded remarkably like his father's voice.

He stared around the square, almost as though he expected the old man to materialise at any time. But this wasn't Duke's, or even North Carolina, where Donald Miller seemed to haunt his every move, even though he'd learned long ago that he had to cut all ties to such a toxic old man.

No, this wasn't back there—a place he didn't even think of as *home.* This was St Victoria, a Caribbean island so far from home that it felt like a whole other life. And maybe here, Liam realised with a jolt, he could be someone different. Someone other than the man whose every decision in life had to make up for the way his mother had lost hers.

Just for a while.

He turned to Talia, but whatever he might have been

about to say next froze on his lips as he caught sight of a kid racing straight towards Talia. The language was partly patois, but Liam caught enough to know that a man had been hit by a car in a nearby street and a neighbour, having seen Talia at the market earlier, had sent the boy to find her.

Neither of them waited to hear any more. Almost in unison, they both instructed the boy to lead the way, hurrying behind the kid without a word needing to be spoken. Slipping back into that old working harmony they'd once shared, as if it was an old friend.

By the time they arrived, an ambulance—one of the four new highly equipped donations from The Island Clinic—was already on scene, and it took Liam and Talia little time to ascertain that the man had indeed been involved in a car-versus-pedestrian collision, with the man having been anaesthetised before for transport. However, before he had been able to be loaded onto the ambulance, he'd gone into cardiac arrest and the team had pushed fluids into him via a drip, as well as beginning CPR, with no response.

Watching another round of CPR being carried out, Liam was all too aware that time was running out for the patient, and although it was a great effort by the team already on scene, if they were unable to get his heart restarted there would be little point in loading him into the ambulance for St Vic's.

'What are you going to do?' Talia placed her hand on his arm as he stepped forward through the crowd.

He dropped back, lowering his head so no one could overhear. No use in panicking anyone else around.

'If they can't resuscitate him this time then there's only one other option I can think of...'

'You're going to open him up here? On the street?' Talia nodded. 'Massage his heart to try to get it to beat again?'

'It's a bit of a Hail Mary, and the chances of success

aren't good,' he admitted, 'but we have to at least try to manage any internal injuries and get his heart restarted.'

Biting her lip, she offered another short nod then stepped after him, pulling aside one of the senior paramedics to introduce Liam as The Island Clinic's cardiothoracic surgeon. He would have had to have done it without her, if she hadn't been around, but there was no doubt that Talia's established relationship with the existing team helped them to accept his solution quicker. And, for this patient, every second counted.

As hastily as he could, Liam sterilised himself and the patient while Talia worked with the paramedic to pull together as much kit as possible, and then he opened up the man's chest and went to work.

Later, much later, he knew he would reflect on how easily and naturally he and Talia had worked together, managing to stem the significant internal bleeding and massaging the man's heart back into rhythm within a matter of mere minutes.

But for the moment all Liam could concentrate on was the patient in front of him, the familiarity of the procedure, despite the circumstances, seeming familiar and oddly soothing.

This part of the heart—the actual physical manifestation of the muscular organ in the human body—was what he could deal with. It was what he understood best.

A world apart from the other, less tangible role of the heart—the emotions and connotations it raised. And those thoughts that had churned through his head earlier—the idea of trying to be someone different from the man he was back in North Carolina—were stronger now.

Life was so short, and so very precious, something he should know more than most. He'd thought he was living his best life being a successful surgeon. Emotions were a weakness, and meant for other people. The effect Talia's leaving had had on him, three years ago, had proved that.

Only now…he wasn't sure it had proved anything of the sort. Now, suddenly, he knew he wanted something else. Something…*more.*

He just didn't know what he was supposed to do with that knowledge.

CHAPTER EIGHT

'SMALL YOURSELF UP, Talia.' Nyla squeezed past her at the desk and reached for a bag that had been stuffed underneath. 'Now we finally have a full shift together, I'll show you what my eldest granddaughter brought home the other day, thinking that she was going to wear it.'

Squeezing in to let her colleague pass, Talia welcomed the distraction. Once again, she felt the need to get out of her own head. To get some distance from the questions that were chasing around her brain. Like her island tour with Liam a few days previously.

Was she imagining things to think that he had been more open and more honest with her during those few hours than he'd been during their entire relationship?

It had felt as though they were finally getting closer… right up until the accident had wrenched them away. After that, there had been no time to stop, with Liam even accompanying the man to the hospital to operate on him. Volunteering his time, just as Nate Edwards had always hoped his staff would do.

Talia clenched her jaw tightly, unsure how she felt about the notion. The more time she spent in his company, the harder it was becoming to keep that lid on all the emotions she'd stuffed down for the past three years.

Liam was every inch as raw and magnetic as he'd been back then. Only now there was that added factor. Something that hadn't been there last time. It made her think that maybe, just maybe, he finally wanted to lower those barriers that had always come between them.

Or perhaps she was just being as foolish as ever and seeing what she wanted to see.

She needed some space to think. A chance to get her head straight.

So for the next few minutes Talia welcomed the distraction of Nyla entertaining her with a pile of clothes, recognisable as coming from the local markets. A veritable wardrobe of garments so tiny that the entire collection could have been kept in little more than a shoebox. Everything that a sixteen-year-old girl might need to look on trend but which a grandmother and parent would consider indecent.

'I mean, look at this skirt.' Nyla held up a flimsy bit of fabric that wasn't much bigger than the head caps they wore in Theatre. 'And what about the bikini?'

'It looks like a handkerchief tied with dental floss.' Talia laughed, wondering how Nyla's granddaughter had even hoped to get away with it.

'It will send all the boys mad.' Nyla threw her hands up.

'It's sort of pretty, though.'

'On a woman like you, perhaps,' scoffed Nyla. 'But not on a kid.'

'I assume you're taking them back to the market stall?' Talia smiled as Nyla put the box away and sat down in front of the computer.

'I am. Maybe between all the items, we can buy her something that she likes but won't be giving me, or her parents, apoplexy.'

'Good luck with that.' She didn't like their chances. 'So, any changes since yesterday?' Talia asked.

'A couple of discharges, several more admitted.' Nyla replied.

'Oh, and Augustin had a pericardiocentesis.' One of the other nurses, Mia, appeared behind her as Talia snapped up from her own notes.

'Augustin? The eleven-year-old who was admitted for pneumonia last week?'

'Yep.' The nurse nodded. 'He deteriorated rapidly last night. Thanks be that Doc Bashy was here to save him.'

'That's enough, Mia,' Nyla cut in quickly.

Perhaps a little too quickly. Talia's stomach began to tense, the way it always did when it was ready to flip-flop.

'Doc Bashy?' she repeated carefully.

Bashy was local slang for hot, or good looking, and while there was no reason for her to suspect Mia meant Liam, her gut was making its feelings loud and clear.

'You haven't met him yet?' Mia let out a long, low whistle. 'Girl, you haven't lived! He's the new surgeon taken over from Isak at The Island Clinic. Apparently, they call him the Heart Whisperer, but we decided he was Doc Bashy...because, he is F-I-N-E *fine.*'

'Okay, that really is enough, Mia,' Nyla repeated. 'Can you go and check on Mrs Frances in bed five, please.'

'Now?' Mia looked surprised, but Nyla was firm.

'Yes, please.'

Talia held herself straight, unmoving, as the younger nurse hurried away, but her mind was already racing. Liam was still here at St Vic's Hospital? Surely he ought to have returned to The Island Clinic by now? Slowly she turned to Nyla.

'I knew he performed a one-off surgery here the other night,' she hazarded. 'Now he's volunteering for full shifts?'

'First one last night,' confirmed Nyla. 'Think he prefers being here to being up there. And now practically every single nurse in this hospital is clamouring to be on his next shift. But none of them know he's your Dr Miller.'

'He isn't my Dr *Anyone*,' Talia managed, her tongue feeling altogether too thick for her mouth. 'Is he still here?'

'Just going off shift,' Nyla replied, though Talia had to strain to hear her. Incredible how hard it was to hear anything over the thundering of her own heart. 'Wait, Talia, is this really what you want to do? Confront him here?'

Talia didn't answer. She was already racing to the changing area doors just as Liam stepped out.

'What happened with Augustin?' she demanded instantly.

Liam paused, and eyed her curiously.

'Good morning to you, too. Is he your patient?'

'Well…' She hesitated, momentarily thrown. 'I was the one who admitted him a few days ago and diagnosed pneumonia.'

'You're a scrub nurse. You're the one who admitted him?'

'The community clinic is a hands-on, all-in affair. Besides, it's good to keep other skills going.'

'I see.'

Without warning, she bristled defensively.

'The symptoms he presented with were consistent with pneumonia.'

'Did I criticise in any way?' Liam asked evenly.

It did little to assuage Talia's tenseness.

'No, but—'

'There is no *but*,' he cut in smoothly. 'It was a logical assessment, and the past few days offered no further clues from what I can tell, although there was no improvement. However, overnight his condition deteriorated acutely and he developed more intense chest pains, shortness of breath and diaphoresis. It was fortuitous that I was on the floor, and that the nurse on shift thought to get me.'

A hundred questions jostled on the tip of her tongue, ranging from her patient to why Liam had even been volunteering after claiming he wouldn't.

In the end, it was her concern for Augustin that won out. 'And?'

'The patient was afebrile, with a respiratory rate of thirty-six, he had a heart rate of one-twenty, and blood pressure of one-eighteen over seventy. He hadn't undergone an EKG—'

'Because it presented as pneumonia.'

'Again, I wasn't criticising,' Liam replied simply. 'But since I was there, I performed a bedside ultrasound, in the first instance as a lung ultrasound and, as I suspected, the lungs were obscured by a large anechoic structure.'

Talia sucked in a deep breath. An anechoic structure was often an indication of cysts, fluid or gallbladder ascites. Should she have seen that herself, earlier?

'You carried out a cardiac ultrasound,' she pressed Liam urgently.

'I did.' He nodded. 'It revealed a large circumferential pericardial effusion, right diastolic ventricular collapse and the inferior vena cava was dilated without respiratory variation.'

'So you carried out a pericardiocentesis? What did you yield?'

'About one thousand and fifty millilitres of serosanguinous fluid that have been sent off for further diagnostic evaluation.'

Meaning cultures and cytology, Talia thought, her head spinning. Hadn't she read somewhere that around sixty-five percent of pericardial effusions were sanguinous? And that around twenty-five percent of these were, in turn, caused by malignancy?

Desperation sliced through her, but it was the sharp edge of guilt that lacerated her most.

What if she'd missed something? What if it recurred? Augustin was just a kid; only eleven years old. But cardiac tamponade meant extreme pressure on his heart, preventing it from functioning properly, and next time, if his heart couldn't pump enough blood to the rest of his body, it could result in Augustin going into organ failure, and dying.

'You couldn't have seen it. And let's wait for the results before we assume the worst, shall we?' Liam's voice cut into her thoughts, as though he was reading her mind.

'How long will that take?' She didn't meant to snap at him.

But even though he hadn't levelled any criticism at her, she felt responsible that she had missed something that Liam had so easily picked up on.

In typical Liam manner, however, he didn't seem perturbed and was as cool and controlled as ever.

'Long enough for them to see whether the fluid we yielded grows mycobacteria or reveals malignant cells.'

It wasn't the answer she wanted to hear. Then again, she wasn't sure what she did want to hear. She felt itchy, somehow, and unsettled. Like her own skin was too small for her.

'You can't heal everyone with a wave of a magic wand, Talia.'

'I never thought that I could,' she scoffed, but she heard the tremor in her voice, and she knew that Liam heard it, too.

His gaze narrowed, too sharp, too astute.

'What is it?'

'Nothing,' she lied unconvincingly. Frustration bubbled through her. 'I don't know, maybe it's because Augustin is one of my kid brother's friends. They're in the same class. And his mother and mine used to be such good friends.'

'Used to be?' His forehead knitted together. 'Has Augustin lost his mother recently?'

If she could have snatched the words back and thrown them over the harbour wall and into the ocean beyond, she would have. But she'd had to open her big mouth, hadn't she? And now Liam had her pinned down with that all-seeing gaze of his.

She hated it.

Hated.

'Forget it, it isn't like that.' It took everything she had to force her legs into something resembling a forward motion. Faster, and faster, as she began to hurry down the corridor and away from the man who seemed to crawl under her skin no matter how tightly she'd thought she'd stitched it back up.

'Talia…?'

'I have work to do, and your shift must be over,' she ground out. 'I'm glad you were there for Augustin. I have to go.'

'Talia, wait,' he called her back and, to her eternal shame, she obeyed.

As if compelled to do exactly as he commanded.

At least she could take some comfort from the fact that he strode up the corridor towards her, meeting her halfway. But that no doubt held more significance to her than to him.

'What is it?' She forced a professional smile. At least, she hoped it was professional.

Yet when he took her arm and steered her into an empty side room, she was powerless to stop the blood from racing through her. The door closed and she looked up at him expectantly.

She certainly wasn't prepared for the unreadable expression in his eyes.

'I was sorry to hear about your mama,' he told her quietly. Sincerely.

Talia froze, all the same.

'How did you find out about that?' she managed to ask.

'It's a hospital, you know how people talk,' he replied with a half-smile. Not exactly an apology, but closer than not.

'What did you hear?' She didn't really want to know the answer, but she felt compelled to ask all the same.

'Just that she died a couple of years ago.'

And she could have left it there. She could have breathed a sigh of relief that he didn't know anything more than that.

'Three years ago, actually,' Talia burst out before she could stop herself, as if she wanted him to finally know.

She didn't care to examine *why.*

'Three years?' He frowned, his gaze sharpening on her. 'After you'd left… Duke's?'

'*When* I left,' she stated flatly.

He stared at her, almost icily, for far too long. It was all she could do not to shift uncomfortably.

'But that isn't why you left?' he asked at last. 'Because your mother…mama had died?'

'No, but…it was a short illness.'

'You used to talk to your family every Sunday.' His frown deepened. 'You never once mentioned she wasn't well.'

She didn't realise she'd bitten her lip, hard enough to draw blood, until she tasted the faint metallic taste.

'I didn't know. She made them keep it from me because she didn't want to ruin my move to North Carolina.'

A hard ball lodged itself in her throat and she couldn't continue.

'So, what happened? They called you that last day to tell you and you jumped straight on a flight?'

'Pretty much,' she mumbled.

Even now, three years on, it still pained her to think of that day. The realisation that her mama was so ill, and the guilt. That overwhelming sense of remorse.

'I guess I'd known something was wrong for a while,' Talia heard herself confessing. 'She hadn't looked quite... *right.* And she was always so tired. I just didn't want to see it so I think I told myself it was nothing.'

His eyes glittered, a tautness shifting around his face, and something twisted inside her. She told herself that she didn't care what that *something* was, but deep down she knew that wasn't entirely true.

'Why didn't you tell me?' he demanded eventually.

'You were at work.'

Censure moved over his features. And something else that she didn't care to identify.

'I would have been there for you.'

'Would you?' The words slipped out unchecked. More of an accusation than a question. 'You were always about work. It came first, second and third to you. And you'd already told me about the surgeries you had that day.'

It was only later that she'd really analysed just how many of their conversations had revolved around work, patients, procedures.

Work and sex. That was all they'd had. There had certainly been no opening up to each other about themselves as individuals.

'Besides, I rarely even talked to you about my family because I was always conscious that you never talked about yours.'

'I told you about mine.' He shrugged. 'My mother died when I was younger, my father and I aren't close, and I don't have any siblings.'

'And that's it.' She threw her arms up. 'That's all I ever knew about you.'

'Because that's all there is to know.' He sounded so casual that anyone else might have believed him.

But she knew better.

'I don't believe that, Liam.' Talia shook her head. 'In all the time we were together you never shared any childhood memories. Not one. You never had any stories.'

'I'm a surgeon, Talia, not a storyteller.' His tone was as even and controlled as ever.

She gritted her teeth, deciding she'd never hated it more.

'And that's another thing you always did,' she told him. 'Whenever I tried to get to know you, you always shut me out.'

'This conversation is going nowhere,' he stated flatly.

'Of course it isn't, because you would never let that happen. But there has to be more to you than surgeries and your career, Liam.'

'Talia—'

'It's too much, Liam. No wonder I couldn't bear it that you never shared anything with me. *Never.*'

'Because I don't throw open my life for the whole world to see everything about me?'

'I'm not talking about throwing anything open, and I'm not *the whole world*,' she cried. 'I just wanted to feel like I was a part of your life, not merely a convenient warm body.'

'You were never *merely a convenient body*,' he exploded suddenly, and what did it say about her that she felt some tiny victory that she'd finally pushed his resolve enough for him to lose that famed control? 'I'm insulted that you can even accuse me of that.'

'Well, you hardly wanted to share your life with me—which was all that I ever wanted with you.'

'So much so that you didn't even contact me when you

found out your mama was ill. You didn't even leave a note. You just left.'

'Don't tell me you're offended that I didn't share details of my life?' The irony of it pulled at her mouth until she felt something of a bitter smile. '*You?* Of all people?'

'So that's why you left,' Liam said scornfully. 'Because I didn't tell you all the ins and outs of my life? My past?'

'You're oversimplifying it.' She blew out a breath of frustration, as Liam looked as more distant and forbidding than ever.

'Whilst you're overdramatising it.'

She didn't miss the way he had pulled himself harshly back under control. Or was on his way to doing so, anyway. That flash of emotion had been locked away somewhere deep inside him, as he always did.

She began to remark on it but then the words stuck in her throat as a great swell of sadness washed over her. What was the point of them arguing? What did she even think that might achieve opening up old wounds?

'What is it?' He frowned.

'Never mind.'

He eyed her disparagingly.

'You've said plenty already, why stop now?'

'Because I don't want to go down this route any more,' she confessed. 'Do you?'

He looked a little taken aback but he recovered quickly.

'No,' he answered frankly. 'I do not.'

Talia nodded.

'So…where do we go from here?'

He didn't move, but she got the impression he was regrouping. Steadying himself again. And then he smiled. A reserved but genuine expression that seemed to pull at her heart.

'Your island tour the other day was something of a blast of fresh air.'

'It was,' she agreed.

It had been more than that, though. She'd felt more alive than she'd done in a while. The fact that it had been with Liam couldn't just be a coincidence.

'So why not enjoy each other's company for the remainder of my stay? What harm could it do?'

'I'd like that,' she answered softly.

The strangest thing about it was that, having finally confessed to him about the catalyst for her leaving North Carolina, it was as though some weight had lifted.

She missed her mama, she always would, but a part of her felt as though she'd been grieving for the past three years. Not just after losing a precious parent but having it come so closely on the heels of losing Liam, too. Or, more accurately, losing the relationship she'd imagined they might have.

But now things felt different. She felt renewed somehow, spending time with Liam and talking to him. They were almost, *almost* back to the good times that she remembered. Without the sex, of course.

And who needed sex? She swallowed hard.

The point was that this time was different. This time she was in no danger of losing her heart. They were friends, nothing more, and in another few weeks he would be gone from her island.

Why not enjoy this unexpected friendship for what it was? And for the short time it would last? But she needed something different. Something thrilling, that Liam had never tried before.

Tossing her head back, she flashed him her brightest smile.

'New plan, let's go bodyboarding.'

'Bodyboarding?'

He arched his eyebrows.

'I seem to remember taking you skiing, back in North Carolina. Your balance was shocking, or don't you remember falling off that T-bar lift and taking out the next five couples like a bowling ball knocking down pins?'

'Until some lad caught me by my hair. She winced. 'The shameful memory is imprinted into my brain for ever. I must have looked such a state.'

Liam grimaced.

'Not so much of a state that he didn't start chatting you up. I wanted to punch him to get him to take his hands off you.'

'I don't remember that.' She looked at him in surprise, trying to work out whether she was more startled by the idea of Liam sounding almost jealous or the idea of him punching anybody.

He hadn't given her the slightest indication of either at the time. She decided she couldn't even imagine the latter. The ego boost was nice, all the same.

'Well, bodyboarding is nothing like skiing,' she declared emphatically. 'I've been teaching my brothers. If you want a lesson, Liam, meet me on the beach this afternoon.'

'I don't have anything to swim in. Or a board, for that matter.'

'We can hire boards at the beach as well as surf tops for upper body protection.'

She was warming to the idea more and more. And judging by Liam's grin, he was equally taken with the idea. But, then, he had always loved his sports—it was one of the areas where they'd bonded the most.

'Okay,' he agreed. 'Which beach?'

She gave him the directions, watching him leave and trying not to feel so pleased with herself.

It was only afterwards that she considered that she didn't have her swim gear with her—unless she was planning on bodyboarding in her scrubs.

She could head home as soon as her shift finished but it was in the opposite direction from the beach, and it would be better if she could head straight there if they were going to maximise their time. There was nothing else for it, she was going to have to head to the local market on the way over.

Unless she borrowed something.

The thought walloped into her hard, as her mind conjured up an image of the bikini Nyla had shown her.

Was that why the beach and surfing had been in her mind?

Admittedly, the bikini was less of a swim *piece* and more of a swim *bit.*

Did she really dare?

She tried to imagine Liam's reaction, and then caught herself. What was she doing, imagining eliciting some reaction from an old boyfriend?

Except that Liam wasn't simply some old boyfriend. He was the only man she'd ever loved. And she was giving him a bodyboarding lesson because they were friends, and to help them in working well as colleagues. It wasn't about anything else.

As many times as she seemed to remind herself of that fact, her brain seemed determined to ignore it. How many times did she need to learn the same lessons?

Talia blew out a long breath. If she wasn't careful, she was afraid that she was more at risk of falling for Liam than ever.

CHAPTER NINE

HE DID *NOT* like her bikini, Liam growled to himself a few hours later. Or, more accurately, he liked it rather too much.

A gloriously vibrant yellow thing with bright green floral detailing, which appeared to be little more than four triangles of fabric connected with other narrow strips of the same energising green material as the flowers.

It made that feral beast inside him roar with approval.

Mine.

He hadn't been able to keep his hands off Talia the other day when she'd been fully clothed. How the hell was he supposed to concentrate on his damned lesson with her looking like *that*?

So much for just trying to be friends. Apparently, it didn't matter what his brain—or logic—dictated, his body seemed hell-bent on proving otherwise. His teeth actually itched—as if they were resisting some carnal urge to rip the flimsy swim-set off, right there and then.

He watched her manoeuvre the board. So graceful, so supple. Doing little to help him clear his head of the unwanted, unhelpful images. The way they had been together. That heat. That fire. Like nobody else.

Because that was the truth of it, wasn't it?

There had never been anybody like Talia. Not before, and definitely not since. From the moment they'd met, that flame had burned within him. Hotter and brighter than anything he'd ever dreamed could exist. He'd lost himself in her more times than he'd been able to count, and the worst of it was that, deep down, he'd believed it was always going to be that way.

It was almost a relief when she stopped at the edge of the ocean and pulled on the surf top, covering a swathe of mouth-watering skin. *Almost.*

She looked up at him and flashed her trademark grin.

'Okay, put your top on, it will help protect your body, though I don't imagine you'll be riding any serious waves to result in a real wipe-out.'

Was it his imagination or was her smile even brighter—wider—than he remembered it from three years ago? Pulling on his top and heading towards her, Liam mulled the idea over.

She'd always claimed that she couldn't wait to get away from St Victoria and see the rest of the world. Yet it seemed to him that she was more relaxed here than he'd ever seen her. Happier, somehow. As though this place fitted her better than she'd claimed it had.

'Good.' Talia dragged him from his internal ponderings. 'Now, take your board and tie the leash around your upper arm. Great, now let's practise. Lie down on the board with your stomach on the back end of the board and your hands on the nose.'

'It might be more effective to get into the water first,' he suggested dryly, but Talia only shot him a dark look.

'It's easier to practise on dry land than to try it for the first time in water. Look, I'll show you.'

She dropped the board and moved agilely into position, showcasing her athletic build and, though he tried not to stare, her peachy round backside. It occurred to him that dropping down to lie on the board might not be the worst idea in the world.

'So, when we paddle out, you'll need to move yourself further up to the centre of the board and propel it with your arms like this...'

Dutifully, Liam obeyed, fervently hoping that by concentrating he could take his mind off Talia's body and that undeniable chemistry that was once again arcing between them.

For several moments she showed him what they were going to do, and then she leapt up and grabbed her board.

'Cool, okay, let's go.'

They waded out until they were about knee-deep before she instructed him to lay his board down and try getting on it to paddle, and he couldn't help but think she was enjoying herself a little too much. As if she thought he had decided it was all too easy. But he wasn't that naïve.

Carefully, he followed her instruction, noting how she didn't take them out too far but looked for waves that were coming in as square on to the beach as possible, and he strove to do the same, only to get flipped straight over.

'Nice attempt.' Talia grinned as he resurfaced. 'Next time, try adjusting the angle of your weight on the board.'

Another attempt, another flip. But on his third go he managed to control the board all the way.

'Impressive,' she conceded, only half grudgingly, he thought. 'I knew you'd be athletic enough to pick this up quickly.'

'I'll take that as a compliment,' he shot back, privately admiring the way she managed to steer her board left and right with the surf, back arched and head high, while he barely kept in whichever line the wave carried him.

Time after time, he practised the moves, listening to her instructions and modifying his approach until he felt he'd really got the hang of it. It was certainly even more fun than he'd anticipated, though whether that was the sport, the heat or the company, he wasn't entirely sure.

'You want to try going out a little further?' she asked after about an hour. 'There are some bigger waves out there.'

'No, I think I'll go back to the beach and catch my breath.' He laughed.

He'd thought himself fit from all the swimming, skiing and running he did, but this was something else entirely. His heart was hammering with the effort of controlling the board and his body, and the sand had never looked so appealing.

Plus, he needed a moment to sort out the jumble of… *things* in his head.

'You stay out if you want,' he added, as he caught her eyeing up the bigger waves slightly wistfully.

'You're sure?'

'Absolutely.'

Picking up his board, Liam headed for the beach, only too grateful to reach the shore and detach the leash before crashing on the still-warm sand, his chest heaving slightly with the exertion.

Back out in the ocean, Talia was already duck-diving beyond the smaller waves to catch the bigger breakers, and spinning three-sixties on her board, both horizontally and vertically, all while still riding the wave. More than impressive.

He felt that familiar pull of desire and tried to shove it back down again. But he'd noticed that the more time they spend together, the more difficult it was to ignore. And he wasn't the only one apparently admiring her. He'd spotted a couple of other bodyboarders making their way over to talk to her earlier as well as some surfer, and he'd had to remind himself that who she flirted with, or even dated, was none of his business.

It hadn't been for the last three years. But that knowledge didn't seem to make him feel any less…agitated.

Flopping back onto the beach, he forced himself not to watch. Not to give in to this ugly, clawing thing inside him that he knew couldn't possibly be jealousy. A pointless, distasteful emotion that he'd always sworn would never have a role in his life. Especially seeing how it had played out in his father.

Seeing the grief at losing his wife, warring with his jealousy that their infant son—he himself—still had his life.

Liam was so wrapped up in his thoughts that he was caught completely off guard when a stream of cold water dropped mercilessly onto his stomach.

Leaping up with a low curse, he reached out and snagged a giggling Talia as she tried to dart away.

'I thought you were going to play in the big waves,' he growled.

'I was,' she sounded breathless. 'But it wasn't as much fun without you.'

He didn't answer, instead choosing to haul her closer. It was only when he felt the electric contact of skin to skin that he realised it was her surf top that she'd removed and wrung out over him.

Now she was clad only in that flimsy bit of bikini. And it was the only thing between his skin and hers as she was pressed against him.

Liam commanded himself to release her, but his body had chosen that moment to refuse to take orders. And when he looked at her, her eyes seemed to shimmer up at him as her lush body brushed gently against him. But he didn't think she was any more in control of the moment than he was.

'This can't happen,' he managed, his voice unmistakeably hoarse. 'The other night…we already agreed.'

She made a low sound at the back of her throat that could have been either an agreement or a rebuttal, with neither of them daring to move. Echoes of the way she'd come apart in his arms, only days ago, seemed to swirl on the light breeze around them.

He could still remember her intoxicating taste, and the heady way her eyes had widened, and darkened, when he'd lifted his fingers to his mouth.

All he could think of now was crushing his mouth to hers, and then pulling aside each of those scrappy triangles in turn to take each of those dark, pert nipples that the bright green and yellow dye did nothing to disguise, and lick them and suck on them until she was moving against him, crying out his name.

Just like she'd done countless times in the past.

'It makes no sense to muddy things between us.'

His mouth was millimetres from hers, her hot, sweet breath skating over his lips. Seducing him.

'None,' she murmured.

And still they stood there—perfectly still. Yet whole currents of attraction arced between them, neither of them daring to speak again.

Liam wasn't even certain that he hadn't stopped breathing.

Faintly, so very faintly, the sound of voices finally began to penetrate his consciousness, and he slowly remembered they weren't alone. Against the objections of every fibre of his being, he leisurely peeled his hand from the perfection of the small of Talia's back and took a small step away from her.

The slight downturn of her mouth was nothing in comparison to the howling going on inside his body.

He made himself take another step, though he had no idea how he managed it.

'I think your surf mates were getting ready to close up their cabin,' he managed to bite out. 'We should take the gear back to them.'

'Right.' She sounded as dazed as he felt, though he wasn't sure if that was a comfort. 'I'll take the boards back now. Do you want to gather up our other stuff?'

He bobbed his head, suddenly aware that he was in no position to go anywhere. His body was still hard, ready. For Talia. Torpedoing every lie he was trying to tell himself about their relationship. Proving that the chemistry was as dangerous as ever.

He headed for the water before he broadcast to Talia just what power she still had over him. This non-date had already stirred too much in him. He couldn't tell whether it was the holiday-style destination or the reunion with Talia, but this didn't feel like just a medical trip any more.

Perhaps it never had. Either way, something seemed to have shifted inside him. And he couldn't afford that.

He needed to get back to his hotel room and regroup before he lost control as he had done back in his office. Perhaps spending time with the woman he'd once cared so deeply for wasn't the best option after all. It seemed it was making him lose his mind.

Why else would he have to keep reminding himself how she had walked out on him without a word? Without even the slightest indication. Just like everyone else in his life had done.

But that time—with Talia—it had more than hurt. The pain had turned him inside out. Until he'd barely been able to tell who he was any longer.

It had taken him a shamefully long time to resurface. To stop feeling as though everything he did was a battle through some dense, suffocating fug. To feel vaguely human again. Or perhaps it was more that he'd managed to stop himself *feeling* at all.

He'd even tried dating. Doomed, painful occasions that he could count on one hand—not that his dates had given any indication that they'd found it equally as laboured. They'd even hinted at second dates, which he'd been compelled to studiously avoid, without causing offence.

Because what was the point? None of them had quite been…*her*. None of them had even come close to getting under his skin the way that Talia had.

And even though he'd told himself that was *exactly* what he wanted—someone who was nothing like *her*—none of those other, perfectly lovely, women had been enough to arrest him the way that Talia had.

'What is this? A final swim?'

He swung around as he heard her splashing through the waves behind him; graceful strokes that once again put her elegant body on display. Precisely the opposite of what he was trying to achieve right now.

'Something like that,' he answered, launching himself into the waves and setting off on a freestyle across the section from one rocky breakwater to the next.

A punishing pace designed to occupy his body *and* mind.

Everything had changed since he'd come to St Victoria—Talia's home island. Her presence was threatening to turn everything upside down again and he couldn't seem to stop her because, despite everything, God help him, it seemed he wanted her as much as ever.

In the physical sense, anyway. This unfinished business was about the hunger that still gnawed at them both. It had been in their kiss on that first day, and he'd seen it in her eyes back in the marketplace. It was in the way her breath caught, matching the hitch of his chest as if they were in perfect harmony.

She wanted him just as badly as he wanted her. That *thing* between them had always been so primitive, so feral that it had always seemed to have a life of its own.

It had wound its way through them, binding them together. Hadn't he learned in basic chemistry—back in that boarding school that had seemed like bliss compared to any semblance of *home life* his father could have offered—that heat, oxygen and fuel were all the necessary ingredients for a perfect fire triangle?

Take away any one of them and the fire died.

The problem with he and Talia had been that the flame had never had a chance to die out by itself—naturally—the way it surely would have done in time. They'd parted way too early, and that was surely what made this attraction all the more compelling now. They hadn't given it long enough for the passion to exhaust itself and fade away by itself.

So was this Fate giving him another chance? Not just bringing him to The Island Clinic to run a highly coveted medical case, but also a last opportunity for him to indulge in Talia until they were both—finally—well and truly sated.

Until there was nothing left between them?

Until he finally got his *closure*?

This wasn't about renewing anything with Talia, or picking up their life together where they'd left off—they'd both agreed that wouldn't work. This was about the physical connection. Pure and simple. It was about glutting themselves until there was nothing left. Only then could they finally each go their separate ways without that weighted tether of unfinished business.

As if to emphasise the rightness of his decision, the ocean chose that moment to lift up another huge wave and slam Talia back into him. And if he took the opportunity to manoeuvre himself just a little more directly into its path, to catch her against him, surely that was of no interest to anybody else?

Before she had chance to pull away again he wrapped her legs around his waist and hauled her to him. Not close enough to touch. Not quite. But close enough to feel her heat. And close enough for all that delicious *need* to pool between them.

She braced her hands on his shoulders but neither pushed him away nor pulled him closer, as if she was engaging in an internal battle as fierce as his own had been moments earlier. And when she finally spoke, her voice caught in her throat; breathier, hoarser than he knew she would have preferred.

A lick of triumph ran through him. Almost visceral.

'What are you doing, Liam?'

'Such a redundant question,' he murmured, letting his words skim her silky, wet shoulders while taking care to hold himself still and not to move against her, even as every fibre of his being ached to do that.

Giving her chance to… He didn't know what.

'You made it abundantly clear to me that you didn't want this.'

Her voice sounded thick, choked. He found he rather liked it.

'I think we both know we want this,' he murmured. 'We just don't *want* to want it. But maybe I'm tired of fighting. Maybe I just want to give in to it for once.'

'Maybe I want that, too,' she breathed.

And, still, she didn't move. If anything, Liam fancied that she held herself impressively still, as if to avoid breaking the perceived fragility of the moment.

For several long moments neither of them spoke. The

only sounds were those of the birds flying overhead and the water *shushing* onto the shore behind them.

And still he resisted the waves' movements as they rocked Talia's luscious body against his. Her breasts, as full and perfect as he remembered, brushed tantalising over his chest, but he refused to allow contact any lower. Not yet. Though it was nearly killing him not to do so.

'I want to hear the words, Talia,' he growled eventually. 'After the other night, I find I need to hear you *say* that you want it.'

'Is that so?' she muttered.

He felt frayed. His self-control shredded. Reaching out, he wound a coil of deep black hair around his finger and tugged gently. A tiny gesture he didn't like to admit he'd missed over the past three years. Her sigh was involuntary and instantaneous.

Liam reached for another glorious curl, taking his time. Playing with her. Toying, one might say. She was getting as tightly wound as his hair around her finger, he could feel it in every roll of her body.

With a careful movement, he allowed one hand to sweep over her. Down that uncommonly toned, impossibly soft, expanse of back that he could picture as though even through his very fingertips.

'Liam…' she sighed.

'The words, Talia.'

Trailing lower, he grazed over the delectable curve of her backside, skirting the flimsy fabric as though his fingers might just, possibly, inch beneath. He didn't know who he was tormenting more, Talia or himself.

Lord, how much had he had missed the way her eyes darkened as they locked with his; and the faint parting of her lips as her breath escaped, ragged and torn?

Even now she flicked her tongue out over her lips, as effective as a lick over the hardest part of his body.

'If we don't get out of the ocean soon, I think we might end up giving people a show,' she whispered.

'The words, Talia.' His voice scraped through him, and as much as he hated that he was revealing so much, he was helpless to prevent it.

'You're impossible,' she managed at last, and he revelled in the undiluted surrender in her tone. 'Fine, I want this. *You.* Are you happy now?'

'Ecstatic,' he growled, pulling her right up against him and slamming his mouth into hers.

Because whatever else he told himself, he'd been dreaming of her—intimately—ever since that first day in his office. Every fantasy hotter than the last—yet not a single one of them matching up to how she truly felt in reality.

The way her lips parted for him, her head angling for a deeper fit.

He ran his hands over her again, glorying in the way she moulded herself to his touch. Matching him as naturally as ever. Somehow, still—even he wasn't even sure how he kept his resolve—maintaining that tiny pocket between them where her heat would otherwise have met his need.

As if it had only been yesterday, and not three years ago, that she'd left his presence for good. As if all that torment had been little more than some dreadful phantasm. As if she'd never broken him at all.

Enough.

Abruptly, he released her, dropping her lightly into the ocean and letting the water swirl all that heat, all those memories away. They didn't belong in this new scenario and he had no intention of letting them hop along for the ride.

'Let's go.'

Her breathing was shallow and fast, and the beast in him revelled in that fact.

'Where?'

'My hotel room,' he barked out. 'Any objections?'

'Not exactly.' And there it was…that hint of mischief he loved so much. 'In fact, I thought you'd never ask.'

CHAPTER TEN

IT HAD TO be the longest walk from the beach to find a taxi, with neither of them wanting to speak or to break the spell that seemed to entwine them. Not an awkward silence but more a laden one, heavy with anticipation.

Then they slid into the taxi, Liam's leg pressed tightly against hers, searing her where she sat, yet both of them fighting every primitive urge to touch anywhere else lest they found themselves unable to keep their hands off each other.

The back of a taxi was certainly not the ideal setting, the audience even less so.

The journey seemed to take an eternity. With every second that delicious fraught, charged need between them cranked up another notch. Then another.

But finally they arrived, the stunning Island Clinic's hotel, a more than welcome sight. It was all Talia could do not to tumble out of the taxi, but she was gratified when Liam, having shoved more than enough money at their driver with a hasty word of thanks, grabbed her hand and hurried them both through the lobby and into the elevator.

His arm was snaking around her waist even as the doors pinged closed, hauling her to him and claiming her mouth with his own as if he couldn't wait a moment longer.

She knew she couldn't.

Looping her hands around his neck, Talia pulled her body as close to him as possible, moulding herself to him so that there wasn't a spare millimetre of space between them. But it still wasn't close enough.

He plundered her mouth with his tongue, thrilling and daring, and it felt like both a promise and warning of what was to come. He kissed her until the roaring in her ears felt almost deafening, and then he blazed a trail all the way across her jaw and down the line of her neck, stopping only to offer extra special consideration to that sensitive hollow by her collarbone.

How had she forgotten quite what that talented mouth could do to her? Even in the fantasies she'd like to pretend she didn't have, the memories she'd replayed like old, X-rated movies, she had somehow downplayed the incredible effect he had on her.

It was a wrench when he tore his mouth from hers as the elevator finally slowed, and Talia felt almost ridiculously grateful when he took her hand once again, striding down the corridor and sliding his key card against the room lock.

And then, *at last*, they were inside. The door closed tightly. Alone.

'Next time,' Liam managed gruffly, sweeping her against him again, 'we don't go so far from the hotel.'

'Less talking, more kissing,' she muttered, pressing her lips to his and pouring herself back into the moment.

Because she wanted him more than she could ever remember wanting—*needing*—anything. And what was the point of thinking any further outside that simple truth? As soon as Liam's case at the clinic was complete he would be gone, and she would still be with her family where she was most needed. So she had nothing to lose.

Right?

Dragging her mouth from his, she began languidly unhooking the first button of his shirt, the second, the third, deliberately taking her time and giving it her full attention, until the two sides fell away in front of her. It was worth the wait, exposing all those mouth-wateringly hard ridges that made her hands ache to touch and her lips yearn to kiss.

She bent her head as if to do just that but Liam, it seemed, had other plans. Hooking her legs around his waist, just as he had done in the sea what seemed like a lifetime ago, he manoeuvred them both until her back was pressed against the wall, his hardness pressed into her heat.

He breathed in sharply, and she heard a low carnal groan of pleasure that took her a moment to realise was her. Three years of missing him—and pretending that she wasn't—and suddenly here they were. She didn't want to wait any longer.

Rolling her hips, she pressed herself against him again, revelling in the way he inhaled again. Even sharper this time. He afforded her another intense look, his green eyes almost black, but he didn't move.

'Forgotten what to do?' she teased, her own voice sounding gravelly in her ear.

'Oh, trust me, I haven't forgotten a thing,' he gritted out, and it rasped over her skin, leaving a trail of goose-bumps in its wake. 'Just giving you chance to change your mind.'

Desire fired anew along her veins. She shook her mind, her voice almost deserting her for a moment.

'I have no intention of changing my mind. I want this, Liam.'

She just about managed to slam her mouth shut before she added, *I want you.*

'Good,' he replied, and for a fraction of a moment she wondered what he was replying to.

Then, without another word, he swung her—legs still wrapped around his hips—around and carried her across the threshold to the huge bed that dominated the other room. And then she was sprawled on the bed as he concerned himself with stripping her very efficiently and very thoroughly until the only thing that remained between them was a tiny triangle of emerald-green lace.

Her heart thudded loudly in her ears. Like the down-draught from the celebrity helicopters that landed so frequently on the helipad at The Island Clinic—only ten times louder. And harder.

She felt wild. Incredible. The best she'd felt in three years. Or longer. Because he'd never quite looked at her the way he was looking at her now—as if that invisible cage that he pretended didn't confine him back at Duke's no longer existed.

Abruptly, she realised that he'd been looking more and more relaxed with each passing day here on St Vic and she opened her mouth to tell him, before abruptly snapping it shut again.

Now definitely wasn't the best time to tell him.

'Some other clever quip you thought better of?' he demanded, a smiled twisting one side of his mouth.

Talia forced a smile of her own.

'Something like that.'

'Then allow me to disabuse you of any more of them,' he growled, before sinking to his knees, sliding his hands under her backside and using those powerful shoulders of his to part her legs a little further.

And then, in a sublime flash of colour and heat, he buried his face between her legs and Talia forgot anything else.

The flimsy fabric was gone in a second and, *Lord*, if she didn't taste even more incredible than he remembered. Caramel and cream, hot and perfect on his tongue. Liam drank her in deeply. *His* Talia. A woman wholly unlike any other.

Three years had done nothing to diminish the compulsion he'd felt for her. The other day had been little more than an appetiser and he'd been on tenterhooks ever since. Now he had her back again—if only temporarily—he intended to indulge in every last second.

He licked around her, his tongue and fingers in harmony as he played with her, teased her. She was so very slick, and hot, and he revelled in the way she gasped and writhed beneath his touch. The way she arched her body that moved those perfect breasts tipped with obsidian, and the way she rolled her hips towards him as if she couldn't stop herself from trying to get closer to his mouth.

Those feral sounds she was making at the back of her throat did little to ease his arousal, so hard that it was almost painful. But Liam ignored it. This moment was about Talia's need, not his. Not yet. After all, they had all night.

He licked deeper, letting his voice rumble and vibrate against the very centre of her need as he let her know just how remarkable she was. He basked in the sensation of her hands reaching for him, her fingers biting into his shoulders.

Her moans were becoming louder now, more insistent. Each one jolted through him like flashes of spectacular lightning.

How he'd missed this. *Her.* Her sound, her scent, her taste. It made him ache again and, this time, he couldn't take any more. Moving his mouth that final millimetre, to the very centre of her core, he found what he was looking for and sucked. Hard.

Talia screamed. A low, glorious sound that seemed to echo all around him. Her grip tightened on his shoulders as she bucked wildly at his mouth, but he held her backside and licked all the more. Again and again, she shattered beneath him and it occurred to him that surely he had never seen her as beautiful as she was now.

The woman he'd thought he'd lost—and perhaps he had—but he had her back now. If only for a single month. He might not be able to offer her the marriage or the family that she wanted, but since she hadn't yet found it with someone more worthy then he could offer her one final, perfect month.

'Aren't you overdressed?' Talia panted when she finally came back to herself, as if it had suddenly occurred to her that she was the only one fully undressed.

He liked the fact that it had taken her quite a time. And he also liked the slight flush of colour he could detect in her cheeks. Exertion? Embarrassment at her abandon? Or both?

'If you want me undressed, you only have to ask,' he remarked dryly.

She narrowed her eyes at him, flipping herself into a sitting position before he realised what she was doing. That suppleness, litheness that he'd always admired. Reaching out with her hand, she caught him by the waist of his cargo shorts, and pulled him closer, her eyes locking with his.

'Who said anything about asking?'

The husky tone threaded its way around the room, and right through Liam. It coiled low in his abdomen.

And lower again.

He couldn't pull his gaze away for a second, her rich brown eyes captivating him as she stared at him; a gleam telling that she knew precisely what she was doing with every slow pull of the zipper. Right over where he was hardest for her.

The sight of her mouth, right there, so close to him, was almost too hard to handle. And then she flicked her tongue over her lips as if she knew exactly what he was thinking. *Dear God*, if she did that, he feared he might embarrass himself right there and then.

'Not yet,' he growled out, pulling away from her.

'Why not?' It was more of a challenge than a question. His Talia had never been a shrinking violet, either in bed or out of it. It was one of the things that he admired most about her.

She was stunning. Incredible. She had haunted his dreams but he hadn't expected to ever see her again in the flesh. Then he'd received that call; discovered that she was the one who had put his name forward. And now they were here, and she was real; and he'd be damned if he'd let things go off like that. With him in her mouth.

Stripping off the rest of his clothes, he pushed her gently back on the bed and nudged her legs apart again with his knee.

'Stop asking questions and just kiss me,' he ordered instead, nonetheless with a thread of surprise when she sighed softly, looped her arms over his neck and simply complied.

He had no idea how long they kissed, lost in the glory of each other. He relearned every inch of her delectable body from the long, elegant line of her neck to the exquisite swell of her chest.

He took one nipple in his mouth, lavishing such care and attention on it that he thought he might burst from his own need, then he turned his focus to the other. He traced the dip at the side of her waist and drew whorls with his fingers and his tongue, all the way to her belly button, and the ring that he remembered nestling in there.

'This all feels rather…one-sided,' she breathed at one point.

He could barely make his voice work long enough to assure her that it wasn't. It wasn't at all.

And it wasn't just about rediscovering her body, the hazy realisation crept through Liam's mind at one point. It also felt as though he had found where Talia had been hiding all this time. He just had no idea what he was supposed to be doing with such a discovery.

She shifted abruptly, and he wasn't ready for it. All of a sudden he found himself nestled at her entrance. His blunt head against all that wet heat, and he couldn't run any more. Even if he'd thought to, Talia suddenly slid her hands down his back, raised her hips, and drew him straight inside her.

He groaned as she swivelled her hips, drawing him as deep as she could. So deep that as he scooped her to him and began to move, he couldn't be sure where one of them ended and the other began.

She clung to him, her hips moving to his rhythm and meeting him stroke for stroke. With his free hand, he allowed himself to roam her body, caressing her velvety skin, his mouth pressed against that hollow that he knew sent her wild.

Her gasps and moans were like a song, swelling in his chest. He slid out of her, then back in, and the song grew louder. He moved again, then again, and again, the pace becoming more and more devastating each time. A wildfire that was growing too much to contain.

He ran his hand down the front of her body, feeling the way her body rippled beneath him, until he reached between them right to where her body knew its desire, driving her to the edge. Closer and closer, until he could barely hold his own control any longer.

And this time when she went catapulting upwards, soaring into some blissful oblivion and sobbing his name, Liam finally let himself follow her.

CHAPTER ELEVEN

It had definitely been about revenge, Talia decided several days later as she ushered her patient gently out of one of the St Vic's Hospital's dressings rooms and began cleaning it down before she could call the next patient through.

She'd been aching for him ever since their night together. Practically climbing out of her own skin every time she replayed it, but helpless to do anything. He'd reached for her again and again during that perfect night, but when she'd finally woken the next day—sated and deliciously sore in places she'd forgotten even existed—he'd been gone. Called back to surgeries, the way he always had been.

They hadn't talked. Or, at least, about nothing of any consequence. It had been more than apparent that it had been about a physical union, but not an emotional one. She shouldn't have been surprised. But even so, since then she'd spent every moment snapping her head around every time someone walked around a corner, just to see if it was him.

It never was.

Now that he had what he wanted, was that supposed to be it? Hardly the Liam she'd known...but, then, they both knew where that had got them.

Talia sprayed down the plastic chair, almost angrily, and began to vigorously swipe at it. The problem wasn't what that night *was*, she decided crossly, as much as what it *wasn't.* She'd wanted the sex, yes, but she'd also been foolish enough to want more. Naïve enough to think that emotions might follow. Even though they never had before.

She wanted *more.*

Maybe she shouldn't have given in to the temptation that was Liam Miller. That bikini might not have been her best idea, though she hardly doubted that what she wore had anything to do with how much he desired her. It was gratifying to know that he'd wanted her just as badly that first day dressed in her scrubs.

And so what if he wasn't offering anything more than a month-long booty call? She could handle it. She wasn't the naïve girl she'd been three years ago, and she wasn't in a position to look for a relationship any longer.

Not that she *wanted* a relationship, she reminded herself hastily. There was still too much to resolve here with her brothers and her father before she could start thinking about herself.

Nonetheless, every night she played her own private home movie of their time together. If she'd thought it had been bad over the last few years, it was nothing compared to the wealth of sensation he'd unleashed in her since the day in the ocean.

The worst of it was that she could now recall every single intimate moment with Liam in brilliant, graphic detail. Every kiss, every taste and every last damn carnal sound.

So the fact that Liam had her constantly on the precipice of thrilled, nervous excitement, while he hadn't made contact even once during the past few days, was nothing short of *revenge.*

Hurling the wipe in the bin with unnecessary force, Talia eyed her dressings room with satisfaction. Time to stop thinking about Liam, she concluded firmly as she headed to the main desk to collect her next patient's notes.

'This is looking so much better, May.' Talia smiled approvingly as she carefully peeled back the dressing on a patient she'd been getting to know over the past few days.

'So no more honey?' the older lady asked.

'You still need the honey gauze.' Talia shook her head. 'It acts as both a cleaner and a feeder and is great for the kind of burn you have. But I think we can leave it a little longer between changes this time. What about three days this time?'

Her patient didn't look impressed, and Talia could understand it. The woman had to catch two buses to get the hospital every other day. It couldn't be easy for her. But meticulous debridement of the wound would prevent any infections from taking hold, and the honey dressing with its anti-inflammatory, anti-bacterial, antioxidant properties seemed to be working especially well.

'As long as we keep it clean and cleared out, it should only be for a little longer,' Talia encouraged. 'But if any infection got in there...'

'I know, I know.' The older woman waved her hands to cut her off. 'Three days, okay?'

'Good.'

Flashing her the kind of smile a satisfied teacher might bestow on a petulant child, Talia busied herself with cleaning the wound before cutting a small, fresh rectangle of gauze, then folding it up to place inside the wide but shallow wound.

Five minutes later and she had another satisfied—relatively—patient. Even so, as she opened the door to let the lady leave, Talia flashed her a bright, almost breezy smile.

'Don't worry about forgetting to go to the appointment desk. I'll book the appointment for you from here.'

'There's no need for that—' the older lady began, but Talia wasn't fooled.

'I know, but I'm sure you don't want me turning up at your house again.'

The only response was a grunt, and Talia smiled to herself. It was odd, the way working back here, back *home*, made her feel these days. So different from the way she'd felt three years ago.

Perhaps, if she hadn't been so blind, so pig-headed…but, no, it was pointless hanging off the *what-ifs*.

'Do you make house visits to all your patients, then?'

Talia swung around, but it was too late. Her body was already reacting, sparking, just from the sound of his voice.

She fought to rein it in and sound composed, was impressed when she even heard a bit of sass in her own voice.

'Only when they're an eighty-year-old woman who doesn't book an appointment when I tell them to.'

'I didn't realise you were so dedicated.'

She glowered at him without realising it, and was gratified when he looked instantly remorseful.

'I take that back. Of course I've always known you were dedicated, I remember several times how you rang up to check on patients who you didn't think were taking proper care of themselves. I just meant I didn't realise that you actually turned up at people's homes.'

'I couldn't in North Carolina, I would probably have been arrested for harassment, or stalking, or something. But this is St Vic, we look after each other.'

Yet another reason why this place wasn't as bad as she'd once felt it to be. And another nail of shame for her coffin of guilt.

'What is it?'

Talia didn't realise that Liam had closed the gap between them until she felt his hand on her shoulder. Worse was that look of concern on his face that made her want to break down and tell him everything. About her mother, her father, the lot.

She considered herself fortunate that pride reasserted itself just in time. Flashing him a beam so bright that it made her face literally ache, she forced out a light laugh.

'It's absolutely nothing. What are you doing here, anyway?'

He eyed her closely, but then he abruptly filed away whatever else he might have been going to say and suddenly she knew what he was going to say.

Her entire body started to fizz in anticipation—like she was some kind of teenager on a first date again.

'I'm taking you out for a meal. You can choose the restaurant.'

'I'm working,' she told him primly, perhaps as some kind of payback for making her stew, alone, for so many days.

'Your shift ended forty-five minutes ago,' he replied evenly. 'I know, because I've been waiting outside for the last hour.'

Oh.

'Oh.'

She tried not to grin, but it was an effort. Especially when he told her he'd leave her to change but that he'd be waiting at what passed for Reception, and that he hadn't eaten since breakfast.

She didn't know why that should make her feel so special. Like he'd spent the entire day waiting for this moment. Like she wasn't just an afterthought. It was all she could do to take her time heading to the locker room, showering and changing.

Throwing on her clothes and skipping through the hospital would only make her look too eager.

But soon enough they were walking out of the doors, her arm linked through his in a way they'd never done at

Duke's, so that all their colleagues could see they were together and Talia revelled, for the first time ever, in how that felt.

'So, where are we heading?'

'A little restaurant called Auntie Zinia's. It's homely but it's good. I think you'll like it.'

At least, she hoped he would.

'This place reminds me of The Coals House, back in North Carolina,' Liam told her, as he finished up the last mouthful of his Auntie's Curry, with its island spices, coconut milk, almonds and cashew nuts. 'Only the food is even better.'

'Yeah, I always used to feel a little bit of home whenever we ate there.' She smiled warmly. 'And you remember those orange and blue cocktails? Dream Fusions, were they called? Either way, they were lethal.'

'You missed St Victoria.' He shook his head, as if ignoring her attempt to distract him. 'You used to tell me how much you'd always wanted to get away, and I took it at face value. I don't know why I never considered you might still miss it.'

She shrugged, looking around at the old but loved décor, and the happy patrons who were more like family than customers.

'I think it maybe took being away for me to realise how much I really loved this place.'

'And your mama?'

'I think she knew how I would end up feeling. I like to think that's why she encouraged me to go. They say if you love something then you should let it go free. If it comes back to you…'

She tailed off, unable to finish.

She'd returned to St Victoria, her mama, almost too late. But, in the process she'd felt as though she'd lost Liam.

It had taken her years to accept that, like the old saying, he'd never come back to her so he'd never really been hers to begin with. But now he was here and in an odd way it was to reverse all the steps she'd made these past few years. She loved this place, and coming home had been the best decision. Yet if Liam asked her to return to North Carolina with him…would she?

She shook her head, irked by her own thoughts. This wasn't a real date. They were only enjoying each other's company for the time that he was on the island but he was never going to ask her to return with him. He was only here for one case, and after that he would be returning to Duke's alone.

So why spoil a pleasant evening with thoughts of what could never be? Shaking everything from her mind, she tilted her head to one side.

'What is it you want to know?' he asked, almost amused.

'Who says I want to know anything?'

'You always do that with your head.' He demonstrated. 'And you twirl your thumbs around each other, faster and faster the more agitated you are.'

She didn't need to glance down to check, although surreptitiously she tried to stop circling them.

'So, go on, what did you want to ask?'

She pulled a rueful face.

'I just wondered why it took so long to ask me on this date,' she asked eventually. 'Especially after what happened the other night.'

He'd spent the evening—the last few days—trying not to think about what had happened in the ocean the other day. And afterwards, of course. Not that he'd succeeded. The memory of their bodies entwined, him buried so deep inside her that he'd had no idea where she'd ended and he'd begun, had been too much to push aside.

'Why?' He schooled himself to stay calm. 'Did you think I'd forgotten?'

'No, but I began to wonder if you were drawing it out deliberately. Or think maybe it was some kind of ploy.'

'Is that right?' He let out a low, incredulous laugh, trying not to let his gaze linger too long on her body as she shifted in her seat. 'It's hardly flattering, how little you think of me, Talia. But, no, for the record, it wasn't a ploy.'

'Then why?'

'Sometimes I forget how tenacious you were. *Are.*'

'That's funny, because I never forget how quick you can be to divert conversations, particularly if they veer near the personal.'

Dragging his eyes up, he forced himself to accept the criticism, as much as he might have wanted to deny it.

'Fine,' he conceded after a moment. 'You really want to know why I waited until tonight?'

'I do.'

'I wanted it to be…right. Not rushed. Not just another night of sex—although I have to confess I'm more than open to that possibility too. But I knew you had a day off tomorrow, as do I, and I thought it would be nice to take the evening to have a meal, and talk, without either one of us having to rush off for work the next day.'

'Ah.' She looked vaguely sheepish before another expression clouded her eyes. A decidedly naughtier expression that he remembered from three years ago. 'Just to have a meal and talk?'

'Talia…' This conversation was hardly helping him keep his libido in check.

Talia had always found it far too easy to affect him like this. He wondered if she'd ever realised it.

'Only I understood this was about giving in to that attraction between us. No romance, no dating. And what you're describing sounds lovely and all, but it also sounds an awful lot like the latter.'

'What would you have preferred, Talia?' he asked, struggling to keep his tone light. 'A text instructing you to come straight to my hotel after your shift finished for a quick booty call?'

'Isn't that what the other night was about?'

'Whatever I say here, I'm damned, aren't I?' he acknowledged wryly. 'I wanted to take you out on a date. But what can I say, Talia? If you just wanted the sex, what do you think I'd have said? At the end of the day you're a stunning woman and I'm still a red-blooded male.'

She eyed him for a moment before dropping her head back and letting out a clear, slightly wicked laugh that licked up his sex as surely as if she'd been using her tongue.

'Good to know…' She lifted one smooth, bare shoulder, then dropped it. 'So why are we sitting here discussing dessert when there are far more tempting choices on the menu?'

Her eyes gleamed mischievously, and Liam found himself struggling to clear his suddenly parched throat.

'You want to leave?'

An impish smile tugged at the corners of her mouth as she made a show of smoothing down her sundress.

'I thought you'd never ask.'

He should have resisted. He wanted to. At least a part of him wanted to—the logical, rational part of his brain.

Sadly, right now he realised that his brain wasn't the bit of his anatomy that appeared to be in control. Not when a woman like Talia was casting him such decidedly wicked glances.

Forget the *woman like.* Only Talia could unbalance him like this.

He paid the bill as quickly as he could without his haste

appearing unseemly, and then he slid his hand to the small hollow of her back—a gesture which she'd always loved—and guided her outside.

The joyful sounds of a street party slammed into them both, as did a swell of undulating bodies.

'Down this way.' Talia laughed, grabbing his hand and pulling him down a narrow street.

'A shortcut?'

'Geographically, it's the long way round…' she laughed again '…but tonight, yes, it's a shortcut.'

'The parade would be that difficult to navigate?'

She looked suddenly sheepish.

'That, and the fact that my brothers are in there somewhere. Fate means they would inevitably spot me with you.'

'And that's a problem because…?'

She only hesitated for a fraction of a moment, but he didn't miss it.

'Because they've only just forgiven me for not being there earlier for Mama. If they see you and me together, knowing you're from Duke's too, they might start…jumping to conclusions.'

Did she mean they blamed him for Talia not being in St Victoria?

Why wasn't he surprised? His father was right, he seemed to ruin everyone who got close to him. Except for his patients, and surgery of course. That was the only thing he had ever really had.

But he thrust that aside for now. *Just for tonight*, he told himself as they moved quickly down the cobbled alleys, ducking washing and dodging kids playing football. Even getting an odd look from an elderly woman sewing and overseeing her grandchildren from her chair in a nearby doorway.

'Didn't you say that your grandmother used to get you to read to her? And that she taught you to cook?'

He didn't even know where the question had come from—possibly from talk of her family—and by the look on Talia's face, she hadn't expected him to remember either.

Even so, her expression of surprise quickly gave way to fondness.

'She still teaches me to cook.' Talia smiled. 'She says that no one can make that kitchen sing the way that she can. And she's right.'

'I seem to recall you cooked some incredible food when we were together,' he couldn't help himself saying.

'Well, if you meet Gramma, don't tell her that.' Talia chuckled. 'She'll probably try to beat you with the soft end of a sweeping brush. Actually, one look at you and she probably wouldn't. Anyway, she used to let me sit on a stool and try the batter. Though she always said that a good gramma lets her grandchild lick the beaters, but a great gramma turns them off first.'

'My grandmother taught me how to bake too.' The detail slipped out without warning, and Talia almost tripped over the cobbles in her shock.

He caught her, wondering what the hell he was doing.

'Did she?' Talia asked, and he knew she was trying to sound casual.

Another time it might have made him smile but he was too busy trying to silence his uncharacteristic thoughts. They were still moving along the narrow streets but their pace had slowed considerably.

'Her favourite was walnut cake.'

'You made me that once,' Talia gasped.

'Did I?' He shrugged as though he didn't recall it but the memory was shamefully clear.

It had been near the end of their relationship, about a week before she'd walked out without a word.

'You just never mentioned who taught you how to bake it.'

He could see that she didn't mean to push him. She looked almost thrilled and terrified all at once and he could understand why.

Three years ago there was no way he would have ever confided anything so personal to her. To anyone. He'd barely been able to show her the box that contained painful photos of his mother. Certainly nothing else it kept so secure inside it.

He didn't know why he was opening up now. It was as though he couldn't shut himself up.

He could only put it down to the odd spell this enchanting island had been weaving around him ever since that first, stunning view from his plane.

They popped out of the warren of streets just by a taxi office, the taxi itself fortuitously parked outside.

'What else do you remember about her?' Talia pressed gently as they slid into the battered back seat.

'I don't remember her that well,' Liam heard himself say, though he couldn't have identified where the memories ever came from.

They were always little more than fuzzy images swimming in the recesses of his brain. Or a sparse jigsaw box of partial pictures. Snippets of conversation.

'Her name was Gloria, but people called her Glory.' Something new swam past his consciousness and he grasped at it. 'I think I called her… Glammy?'

He fought to focus but it was like dredging a memory up from a muddy, silty riverbed. It might have had form, but he couldn't quite be sure. He thought back to Talia and her grandmother, and something else clicked awkwardly into place.

'I think… I think I remember her giving me the beaters when she'd mixed something.'

'So she was kind?' Talia asked cautiously.

A flash of a silver-grey bob laughing over him, perhaps? Gnarled hands smoothing hair from his forehead? Fleeting, and hazy. Maybe not even real at all.

And yet…he'd always felt as though they were. And now he found that he wanted to say that he thought she had loved him. But how could he know that?

'I think so. I used to think she loved me. But then…she went away.'

He didn't say die. He didn't think that was what had happened. He seemed to recall arguments on the phone with his father when he'd used her name. It had always made him believe that she was his maternal grandmother rather than his paternal one. And it was what had left him with a bitter taste in his mouth that she, too, had ultimately abandoned him.

If she had once loved him, it hadn't been enough.

Not that it deterred Talia. He knew why. She'd had such a happy childhood, despite the lack of money, that she hadn't been able to understand the relationship between himself and his father. She wanted him to have what she'd had.

'Is it possible you suppressed the memory?' she mused, oblivious to his internal ramblings. 'Maybe it hurt too much. Do you remember what happened to her?'

He opened his mouth to tell her that not everybody's families could be like hers, then closed it again. Why destroy her moment of hope? Hadn't he already damaged her enough?

'Not for certain.' He probed his brain to remember whatever tiny fragments were there.

And it was odd, but now he knew something was there those tiny shards were coming back to him, the tiniest sliver at a time.

'I think we might have gone to her funeral.'

Although not when she'd initially disappeared from his life. But perhaps a few years later. Was that the image he always remembered? He'd always assumed that snapshot he had of his mother's funeral had been something he'd created in his mind based on his father's description of his mother's funeral. Perhaps a photograph?

But perhaps it was actually a real memory, his own memory. Not of his mother's funeral, of course, but from his grandmother's funeral that he had actually attended?

Somewhere in the back of his mind he'd always thought he could hear a voice. A woman's voice, telling him how much his mother had loved being pregnant. How much she'd wanted to be a mom. He'd always wondered if that had been her—his grandmother.

But he couldn't be sure. And what was the point in guessing?

'If she did, I can't even remember it. I certainly don't feel it,' he ground out at last, shoving aside the uninvited feelings that were currently, suddenly, threatening everything he'd ever believed to be true.

All because of Talia. He thought it was that, perhaps, that angered him the most. This was why he should never have let things get so far—so intimate—between them.

The taxi pulled up outside The Island Clinic's luxury hotel, though he'd barely even registered the journey. He should put Talia back in the cab and send her home. But then she slid her hand into his and he forgot to do anything but walk with her.

'Liam—'

'The point is that you can now see why I really am not

capable of loving you the way you want to be love,' he gritted out.

They were still moving in the direction of his suite and even though his brain was roaring that this was no longer the time, his body seemed quite content to go along with it.

'That's what you said the other day,' she pointed out evenly.

'And, dammit, Talia, it's no less true now. Why do you insist on thinking better of me than I really am?'

'And why do you insist on thinking worse?' she asked softly. 'You keep saying that you aren't capable of love but I think you're more than capable.'

'Then you're a fool,' he told her, but it lacked any real heat.

And Talia just smiled at him, gentle and encouraging.

How the hell had they got to his hotel suite?

'I think you repressed that memory, though I don't pretend to know why. It has always been there, buried, just waiting for the moment when you would start to dig it out.'

'You're wrong.'

He had been wrong to let her get so close.

'I'm not.' She smiled at him, a too-bright smile that seemed to pierce through every defence he tried to erect between them. 'But enough of that now. I didn't bring you this way to make you walk down paths you aren't ready for. I just wanted a quick way to the hotel room.'

'Talia...'

As quickly as he was trying to put up the blocks, she was tearing them down. Coming up to him and looping her arms around his neck as she wielded her body like a weapon against him.

The most effective weapon he'd ever known.

And when she pressed her soft breasts, with the taut

nipples, against his chest, letting her lips brush against his, Liam let her.

After all, he was only a man, and not always a good one, at that. And then he saw the shimmering in her eyes and automatically he held his arms out for her to go to him; drawing her into his embrace as if he was a different man.

Scooping her into his arms, he carried her across the room, laying her down almost reverently on the bed, before he began stripping her. Taking his time and turning the whole thing into some elaborate show that seemed to have Talia as transfixed as he felt.

Her shoes came off first, followed by her flirty skirt, then her cropped tee, and the removal of each garment was punctuated by long, hot kisses as he reacquainted himself with every swell and every hollow.

As if the more tenderness he showed, the better he could protect her from whatever demons were loose inside himself.

CHAPTER TWELVE

TALIA HELD HER breath as Liam gowned up, ready to operate on little Lucy Wells. And once he made his first incision—a four-centimetre incision in the midclavicular line—the procedure would finally be underway.

The past few days had been more like a dream than anything else. Pure bliss. The workplace had been harmonious, even sharing a few cases both in The Island Clinic, as well as at St Vic hospital. And when they'd been alone again, she'd lost count of the number of times he'd reached for her, and still that feeling of being sated had only lasted a short time before she'd found herself craving him again.

Like an itch she couldn't quite scratch, she thought, grinning to herself as she imagined his aghast reaction if she ever dared to use that expression with him.

Perhaps she should, just for fun.

It was as though that moment in the alley when he had finally, shockingly, let her into a tiny part of his past had brought them closer. As she'd always hoped it might.

Was it too much to hope that his barriers were at last beginning to, if not crumble, at least soften? And she didn't know if it was the years that had passed, or the fact that they weren't the same people they had been back then, or simply the enchanting location of St Victoria, but it felt so tantalisingly close to the life she had once begun to imagine for her and Liam.

And now they were working together again, just like old times, and little Lucy was at last ready for her procedure. Talia couldn't shake the feeling that it was a portentous day.

Even as she finished gowning Liam, he was speaking with the anaesthetist, confirming the wholly intravenous anaesthesia, and trans-oesophageal echocardiography that would allow Liam to monitor the heart and valve function without the lungs or ribs getting in the way.

The next time Talia had time to think, the operation was well underway.

A pillow had been positioned under the little girl's right shoulder, a soft tissue retractor helping to open up her chest wall, over the right ventricle, and Talia watched as Liam pulled three deep stay sutures towards him to ensure optimal surgical exposure as she passed him the necessary equipment.

He worked quickly and efficiently, his experience and skill more than evident. And still he talked through what he was doing, allowing her to learn as he went. As if he understood how nervous she was feeling given that that the rest of the surgical team had experience of this procedure with the previous cardiothoracic surgeon.

There was no doubt that Lucy was in the best possible hands, and Talia felt a lance of pride as Liam worked.

So far so good.

'So now I'm placing these pursestring sutures to avoid any haematoma of the ascending aorta wall,' he showed her, as she peered over the little girl's body.

'Yes, I see,' Talia confirmed, studying the way he placed the venous pursestring around the left atrial appendage—a small ear-shaped sac in the muscle wall of the left atrium—and reinforced it using suture pledgets.

If she remembered everything correctly, he would first place a venous cannula, using the inside of the left ventricle. Then an antegrade flow cannula would be inserted in the ascending aorta.

But still, watching him work was mesmerising. It made her feel privileged to be a part of something truly special, and Talia realised that was something she'd been missing ever since leaving Dukes.

Leaving Liam.

If she had been more a part of Isak's team, it might have helped. But she suspected that was only part of it.

'Once we've initiated perfusion, we'll stop the heart and remove the aortic valve,' he glanced up at her as though reading her thoughts.

This was the part of the operation she didn't know at all. Even though Liam had used this approach back at Duke's she'd never actually been on one of those procedures with him. She tried to remember what she'd read about him suturing the non-stented graft to the left subclavian artery, but as she watched the surgery unfold, it was easier just to watch and absorb than to try to over think it.

Time passed so quickly in the OR, especially watching someone like Liam work, that Talia was almost shocked when Liam concluded his closing.

The operation was over.

And had been successful.

'So how was your first right-anterior thoracotomy?' he asked, almost twenty-four hours later as he was emerging from his hotel suite's shower. 'With a side of frozen-elephant-trunk technique?'

He'd spent most of the past day and night in his office at The Island Clinic, attending to other cases but mostly ensuring that little Lucy Wells didn't suffer any post-surgery complications.

Something she knew he would have loved to have been able to do for every other patient he'd ever operated on.

But a few hours ago, he'd finally allowed himself some downtime. He was all hers…and Talia was definitely enjoying the view. Even the towel, slung low over his hips, offered her a mouth-watering sight as she reclined, naked and sated, in his bed.

'Try saying that after a mouthful of those Dream Fusions.' She laughed, propping herself up on her elbows. 'The surgery was incredible, just don't let it go to your head.'

'I'm just relieved there weren't any complications,' he stated evenly. As humble as she remembered him.

'I imagine Nate and Isak feel the same. I take it you've spoken to them?'

'I briefed Nate, although I know he was hovering about the gallery, watching, a couple of times.'

'You never let it show.' She drew in a breath, knowing that her chief's primary concerns would have been Lucy Wells, and Liam, but hoping that she had acquitted herself well, all the same.

'Why would I?' He didn't exactly shrug, but his voice did it for him. 'I'm bringing my A-game whether my chief is there or not. He isn't going to change that.'

'That's such a *Liam* thing to say.' She grinned, dropping a kiss onto his bare, muscled chest and loving the way he slid his hand instinctively around the back of her neck as he bowed his head to kiss her properly.

How was it so easy, so *right* between them?

She should have known it couldn't last.

'Nate also mentioned something else,' he began, and she couldn't have said why her stomach flip-flopped. 'Isak has pretty much recovered now, and since Lucy Wells's surgery is now complete...'

'You'll be leaving St Victoria.' Her breath came out in a rush.

'Nate's secretary is looking into flights for me,' he confirmed.

Talia froze, saying nothing though she wanted to ask him why he'd waited until this moment to tell her.

But if he wanted her to go—and something ached deep within her chest at the notion—then he was going to have to say it. She wasn't just going to leave. Not this time. She'd spent three years dreaming of this moment—of being back with Liam—and it was pointless lying about that to herself any longer.

Or lying to him.

'You've fitted in so well that I'm surprised he didn't offer you a permanent role here.' She plastered a bright smile on her face, although she wasn't sure he bought it, especially when he didn't answer, and she could feel the corners of her mouth tugging downwards. 'He did, didn't he?'

'Not in as many words,' Liam hazarded.

She should have taken that as the end of conversation, but something egged her on.

'Which words, then? Precisely?'

For a moment she thought Liam wasn't going to reply. But then he spoke.

'He mentioned that I seemed a good fit and that the team could always use an extra surgeon like me.'

A job offer by any other standards.

'You could always take it,' she heard herself saying. Boldly—if she was being honest. 'You said yourself that any number of surgeons would cut off their own limbs with a scalpel just to get to work here. So what's stopping you? You could easily stay.'

He only hesitated for a beat.

'Why would I do that?'

She wanted to say *her*. But that sounded too arrogant.

'Because I would want you to.' She wrinkled her nose. 'And I thought you might want that as well.'

The silence swirled around them, just like the grey mist that crept in over the jungle part of the island and usually heralded the start of the hurricane season. She could imagine that this storm would be no less brutal.

'I don't.' He spoke at last.

And what did it say about her that she didn't believe him?

'Liam—'

'You don't love me.' He cut her off, his voice abrading her. Almost from the inside out. 'And you don't want me to stay.'

Carefully, she sat up in the bed, pulling the sheet around her, unsure whether to go or to stay. But far from sounding as though he was trying to convince her, it seemed as though he was trying to convince himself.

The thought lent her courage.

'I know what I want, Liam.' She thought she even sounded a touch snippy.

'Really?' he challenged instantly. 'So you want your family to hate you?'

He was warming to the topic now, she could tell by the way he threw the words at her with that hatefully impassive green-eyed stare.

'That's what you're saying you want, is it, Talia?' he pushed her when she didn't answer.

'What? No, of course not, but—'

'Only that's what would happen,' he continued ruthlessly. He was disengaging, she could read it in the set of his jaw and the turn of his body, and she thought it might kill her to see him like this.

'You told me yourself,' he pointed out, and a wiser woman would surely have heeded that tone to his voice. Too controlled and even to be anything other than wholly dangerous.

But she couldn't seem to stop herself.

'No…' she cried. 'Liam, you've got it all wrong.'

'I don't believe I have anything wrong,' he countered quietly.

And whatever emotions she had felt coursing through him these last couple of days had clearly been stuffed firmly back down. Now he was pulling on that armour of detachment that he always wore.

And Talia hated it. *Hated it.* Even though, more and more, she was beginning to think it had never suited him at all.

'That night after going to Auntie Zinia's, you avoided the parade and you told me that you didn't want your brothers to see you with me. You said that they had only just forgiven you for being with me three years when you should have been home with your family. With your mother.'

'But—'

'You said that to me, did you not?'

'Yes, but…' she faltered, flustered. 'They're still teenagers, they haven't met someone they love yet. They don't understand.'

'What about your father, Talia? Is he a teenager?'

'Of course not.'

'But I'm guessing he blames me, too.'

She didn't answer. What could she say?'

'And if he feels that way about me,' Liam forged on, 'how would he feel if you left St Victoria again? With me?'

'They would come round,' she said hesitantly.

The worst of it was that she wasn't even sure they would.

'I won't accept that,' Liam ground out. 'I won't have you

lose them. You don't know what it's like not to have anyone, Talia. But I do. And I wouldn't wish that on anyone.'

'We would have each other,' she ventured.

'No. I can't be that someone for you, Talia. I don't know how to love. And I certainly can't take the place of your father, your brothers or your beloved grandmother. Even all the people you know here on this island. People who love you. People like Nyla.'

'You could try,' she whispered.

'I wouldn't want to,' he told her flatly, his cloak of indifference now firmly back in place.

She wanted to reach and tear it off him, or at the very least press her palm against his cheek and make him see all the good in himself that she saw. She could wrap her arms around him and pour herself into all the ways she loved him—had once loved him. But she didn't dare. It might lead to physical proximity but it wouldn't close that emotional divide between them. Not even an inch.

And she thought that was what destroyed her most of all.

Liam hated himself.

Talia's pain was so utterly evident. And knowing he had been the one to cause it made that black thing inside him—the one that might have been a heart in anyone else—splinter and cleave, but he told himself he couldn't weaken. For Talia's sake.

He couldn't bear to see her give up everything she cared for, everyone she loved, for him. A man who was so damaged and irreparable that he couldn't possibly be good for her.

Yet there was something about her willingness and her ferocity that lodged in his chest. Right *there.* A tiny ball so hot and bright as the magnificent St Victorian sun that he thought it might, for the rest of his life, light his way and keep him warm in those cold, lonely moments when he returned to North Carolina.

There would never be anyone else for him but Talia—he now knew that for a fact. But she deserved better than him. More than he could ever offer. More than this man who had just broken her.

But he should have known that his feisty, strong, powerful Talia wouldn't be stay that way for long. He watched transfixed as she appeared to straighten her back and elongate her limbs, still filling his bed in the most tempting way.

She craned her neck to look up at him. Her voice was quiet but true.

'Will you answer me something?'

He ought to refuse.

'Anything,' he bit out instead.

Foolishly.

She flicked her tongue out over her lips, and even though he knew there was nothing sexual in it, it did nothing to stop that spiral of desire from curving its way down his spine.

'What happened between you and your father?'

Desperation might as well have been a hand reaching into her chest and squeezing. This was not a conversation he cared to have. It wasn't one he ever *had* had with anyone. Ever.

Yet he was filled with a surprising need to accommodate her in any way he could.

'My mother died in childbirth.' Liam stilled as the atmosphere in the room seemed to change in an instant.

It went from urgent and cold to raw and jagged in what felt like a heartbeat. A shimmering menace skirting around the edges of the clean walls and tasteful décor. But Talia didn't seem to have noticed, which meant it was all in his head.

'I'm so sorry.' She was shaking her head, obviously getting over the shock of his announcement faster than he was. 'I know you told me she died when you were younger, but I didn't realise.'

'How could you have?' he clipped out. 'I've not mentioned it before.'

'It must have been so hard for you, growing up without her.'

'Harder for my father. She was the love of my father's life. He has never cared for anyone the way he cared for her.'

'Except for you.' She nodded, thinking she understood.

And he could have left it at that, with Talia thinking he'd opened up and that she knew more now. He didn't *have* to say anything more.

'No, he's never cared for anyone else, especially not me.'

Confusion lapped in her eyes like the soft waves on the shore behind them. For a brief moment he wondered what it must be like to have a family care so much for you that you couldn't quite grasp the idea of a father not loving his child. Then he shut it down because, frankly, what was the point of even thinking that way?

'Especially not you?' she prompted gently, when he didn't say anything else.

He told himself to stop talking, but the words kept coming.

'My father has never forgiven me.'

'Forgiven you?' Her brow knitted in confusion. 'I don't understand.'

He waited, suppressing the urge to ball his hands into fists to fight off the gamut of...*feelings* that were crowding around the periphery of his mind.

Her face cleared abruptly, then assumed an expression of abhorrence.

'He *blamed* you?'

'She died in childbirth, and I was the baby.' It took all

Liam had to keep his tone even. 'As far as my father was concerned, the cause and effect were undeniable.'

Was he really trying to explain his complicated relationship with the old man to Talia? He had never felt the need to explain himself to anyone, ever. More than that, he could never have allowed himself to be so vulnerable in front of anyone before—even Talia. Yet now there was something inside him making him say things he told himself he didn't want to say.

'That's nonsense,' she snorted delicately.

'My father feels otherwise.'

'He really blamed you?' Talia asked tentatively, her voice shaking as if she couldn't quite believe it.

'He was grieving.' Liam shrugged. Because what else was there to say?

Talia, it seemed, was having none of it. Her expression was growing tighter and angrier by the minute. *For* him. Another ball of warmth and light to file away for later.

'And you're making excuses for him? What about your grief?'

'I didn't know her.' The words came naturally. An echo of a thousand times his father had ever spoken to him, and he'd grown to believe it in time. More than that, he'd evolved to feel that way. 'You can't lose what you never had to begin with.'

'You can't really believe that!' Talia exclaimed. 'She was your *mother*, and you never even got the opportunity to meet her. Of course you can grieve. How can you think you don't have that right?'

'Because I don't,' he answered simply.

Because his father had told him, over and over, from the moment he was born. And because, no matter what logic as an adult might dictate, the bald statement was so deep inside him—so ingrained—that Liam had never felt any different.

He didn't know how to.

'So why are you telling me any of this?' she asked softly, with a tinge of sadness that shot right to his core.

'I want you to understand.'

'Understand what, exactly?' Again, that gentle voice that threatened to creep under his skin.

He fought against it.

'That this is who I am. This is why I can't be the man you want me to be. I was never him.'

'I don't believe that,' she disagreed, shaking her curls furiously. 'You're more than just an extension of someone else, here to make amends for an event that happened at your birth, and over which you had absolutely no control. You deserve more than that, Liam. You always have.'

And Liam couldn't say what it was about her reaction that made him feel less...broken. As though he wasn't as culpable as he'd somehow believed.

'He blamed me for a reason, Talia.'

'No, he took his grief out on you,' she countered. 'A baby. And it was the cruellest, saddest thing he could have done. But that doesn't make you all those horrible things he's always told you that you are. And you're not the only one with regrets, Liam.'

'The only regret you should have is ever meeting me,' he told her vehemently.

'I don't believe that. And if you really believe it then it's a problem we're going to have to work on. Together.'

She sounded so positive, so hopeful it scraped at him. He braced himself against the unwelcome sentiment. That wasn't the point of this conversation.

What was the point of it, then? a snide voice echoed in his mind, but he shoved it aside.

Talia needed to believe there was more to him than there was. She wanted to understand why he didn't love her the way he suspected she had once loved him. She didn't understand why he wasn't capable of doing so, and he'd never been able to tell her.

But perhaps now he could.

Maybe this was his chance to finally show himself to her for who he really was. Prove to her, once and for all, that he wasn't worth her attention or kindness. This could be his final gift to her before he left the island.

'No, you're not listening to me,' he bit out. 'There is no *we*.'

His voice was harsher than he'd intended but that couldn't be helped. He felt more broken now, opening up to Talia, than he ever had before.

And yet, somehow, something inside him felt more… *whole* than it had in a long time. Perhaps ever.

'Was there no one else?' Her voice cut across his thoughts, shocking him.

There was no hurt in her tone, it was simply brimming with compassion. He hated that he didn't deserve it.

'Tell me more about your grandmother.'

'I told you, I don't remember much.' He tried to dismiss the question but that felt too much like dismissing Talia, and suddenly he found he couldn't bring himself to do that.

'I have a few vague memories of her. She made life more…bearable. I think I remember her arguing with my father, and then she was never around again. Whether she'd cared for me or not, the long and short of it was that it wasn't enough to stick around. *I* wasn't enough to stick around for.'

'You don't know that, Liam.' Talia shook her head vehemently. 'You've never told me about your father before, but he seems…awful. I'm sorry, but it's true. Maybe your grandmother had no choice.'

'Maybe,' was all he replied.

Because he'd told himself that same thing for years to make himself feel better. But when it came down to it, it didn't matter if it was true or a lie, it still meant she'd walked away and he'd been left alone with a man who resented his very existence.

'And there was no one else at all?' she hedged, after a few moments.

'I don't need anyone else.'

It occurred to him that his choice of tense was all too telling.

'We all need someone, Liam. Someone to fight for us. To be on our side.'

'You aren't listening to me,' he growled, but far from backing off she looked all the more caring.

'On the contrary, I've heard everything you said.'

He glowered at her for a long, long moment, but she didn't budge. She didn't even blink. It finally became clear to him that she wasn't going to relent. And, to his shock, he found himself capitulating instead.

'There's been no one.' His tone tried to show her how little that mattered to him.

'Then that's truly sad,' she told him simply, her eyes conveying so much more than he thought he could bear. 'I can't imagine how difficult that must be. I always had my parents, and if I hadn't had them then I could at least go to my gramma.'

'So now do you understand why I can't allow you to lose all of that for me? A man who they hate?'

'They would come to accept it once they saw that I was happy,' she argued fiercely. 'I would make them.'

And it didn't help that what she wanted was the same

thing he wanted too. Deep down—where he'd tried to bury it. But even if he couldn't give her that, he could give her something better. He could give Talia her freedom.

'But I'm not the one to make you happy, Talia,' he ground out. 'So even if you brought them round, it would change nothing. Nothing at all.'

It felt like an eternity passed as they remained face to face, with her on the bed and him in his towel. And his stone-of-a-heart was more leaden than he'd ever known it.

His case load was clear, and his main-case, little Lucy Wells would soon be able to be discharged. It had yet to be decided whether he would fly to Los Angeles—where Lucy and Violet lived—or whether Isak would take over the post-op follow-ups now that the man was back, but either way Liam would be leaving St Victoria in a few days. And he wouldn't return.

He would be alone. Just like always.

Just as he preferred.

CHAPTER THIRTEEN

TALIA FELT AS though she was in mourning.

Liam had said that he couldn't lose what he'd never had to begin with, but she didn't agree. She'd never had Liam, not really; and yet that was exactly how she felt—as though she was losing him.

It was as though the freer, less-constrained Liam she'd been getting to know over the course of the past couple of weeks was at war with the man loaded down with assumed responsibilities and unrealistic expectations she'd known back in North Carolina.

Only now she understood him better. This clever, funny but detached man who had evidently been told how little he was worth his entire life, right from the cradle. Hated by the very person who should have loved his infant son the most, the person who should have protected his baby boy the most fiercely. But he hadn't. He'd blame an innocent baby for a tragedy that Liam could have no more understood back then than prevented.

But all that had turned Liam into the driven, focussed man he was now. So what was she supposed to do about it? She couldn't change who he was or what he believed, and she'd already tried being there for him and showing that she loved him.

Hadn't she?

'You accused me of leaving three years ago without even a note, and I never explained myself. The truth is that I didn't leave because of something you said, or did, I left because of what you *couldn't* say.'

'And you were right to,' Liam said. It was more of a statement than a question, and without a hint of censure in his tone. As though there was nothing left to say.

Talia couldn't breathe. Desperation wound through her, lending sudden urgency. It felt like she'd only just found Liam after all these years. He'd finally let her in yet now she was about to lose this last precious opportunity.

'You aren't the only one with scars, Liam,' she choked out.

It was like a band tightening around her; the truth, squatting on her chest with a weight that she didn't think she could stand any longer. She wanted to tell him. To show him her own wounds. She pushed gently back from him and when she spoke, her voice was little more than a whisper.

'I knew.'

Liam didn't answer. In some ways she was grateful for that.

'I knew something was wrong long before that final call from my father.'

It was almost unbearable—hanging in the air, almost acrid. At least to her.

Liam waited.

'All the signs had been there for months…if only I'd chosen to read them. The way her face had been getting more and more pinched. The heaviness around her eyes.'

'There could have been any number of explanations for that.' He knew where she was heading and he wished he could spare her the guilt. 'You can't torture yourself like that.'

'I didn't even take the time to ask her, though. I didn't even spot it.'

'Because of me,' he stated flatly, hearing the accusation that was there, even if she hadn't voiced it. 'I've ended up causing pain to anyone who might dare to care for me, Talia. Can't you see that?'

Yet more proof of how he brought darkness and anguish to those around him. His mother, his accursed father, and now even his extraordinary Talia.

'That's nonsense,' she refuted. 'I didn't spot it by my own choice. Because I didn't want to see it, I guess. Maybe because that would have meant I'd have to do something about it, and I was too selfish to return home.'

'You weren't selfish,' he countered immediately. 'You just didn't notice it because you trusted your family to tell you something like that, but they kept it from you. And before you get defensive, I'm not criticising them, they only kept it from you because they didn't want you to worry. They wanted you to enjoy the new life you'd found for yourself in North Carolina.'

'Is it any wonder, after I'd complained at them so many times that I wanted more for my life than growing up on a small island?'

'You can't beat yourself up for that, Talia, it was perfectly natural for you to have wanted to spread your wings.'

She didn't point out that Liam hadn't spread his wings, that he'd allowed himself to be fettered by the guilt of causing his mother's death. She couldn't have even if she'd wanted to, she was too caught up in her own grief.

'I made them feel like they weren't enough. Like she wasn't enough,' Talia choked.

'I would say that you made her feel like she'd raised a bold, confident woman who wanted to see more of the world. But in the end you realised that home was the place you wanted to be. Wasn't that precisely what you said when you talked about setting something you love free?'

She didn't answer, she simply drew her knees up to her chest and dropped her chin on them.

'So why didn't you simply tell me this, Talia?'

'I don't know,' she lied.

'I think you do.'

And despite all her cautions to herself, Talia could feel things beginning to shift inside her. He'd revealed so much to her tonight. Well, perhaps not *so* much but definitely more than she had ever imagined he would. She couldn't help but wonder if she'd finally found a way to bypass that ancient armour of his.

So how could she expect him to trust her more if she couldn't equally trust him?

'I didn't tell you because… Oh, there wasn't just one reason.' She shook her head uncertainly. 'I don't know if I thought I'd be back or not. I think a part of me thought I would. I had no idea how bad it was with Mama so I could never have imagined that she would…that I would lose her.'

'I was sorry to hear that, you know,' he told her quietly, and the gently sincerity in his voice was unmistakable.

'You've said that once already.' She jerked her head in a semblance of a nod but she didn't add that knowing he could never confide in her, open up to her had been the proverbial final straw.

That every day that he'd kept himself from her had hurt that little more and, despite it all, nothing less than her mama's illness could have torn her away from him. Even though she'd known it wasn't the healthiest relationship, she'd been too addicted to him.

Was still addicted, if she was honest. Because it felt as though his admission about his father had been opening the door a crack, and she was already there, metaphorically trying to jam her foot in the minuscule gap before he could slam it shut again.

She couldn't accept that in a matter of days he would be leaving St Victoria. It seemed too cruel.

As if on cue, the bedside phone rang and Talia didn't need him to answer to know what it was about. It seemed even fate was conspiring against them.

She remained immobile, wrapped in her sheet on his bed as Liam crossed the room, the white towel still clinging lovingly to his form.

The parallels weren't ideal.

As he answered the call, she listened to his monosyllabic words of acknowledgement. His gruff thanks and the click as he replaced the receiver.

'Arrangements for your flight?' she asked at last into the silence.

'Yes,' Liam answered.

And then, when she couldn't bear the stillness any longer, 'When?'

'Tomorrow morning.'

A whoosh of breath escaped her.

'So soon,' she managed.

He didn't reply. But, then, she supposed, what was there to say? And that truth twisted inside her even as she could feel the inferno building from the pit of her belly, hot and needy, and enough to burn her from the inside out. He was leaving and all she could think was that she wanted him one last time. And that a perverse part of her almost welcomed the pain of closure.

So why not put it all on the line?

He needed to move. At the very least, he needed to step back away from the bed, away from the temptation of Talia.

He did neither. He simply stayed where he was, and he had no idea how long he stared at her, watching a host of emotions chase through her lovely, expressive eyes. He was only aware of the furore raging inside him. Devouring him from the inside, then threatening to burst out of him at any moment, wild and unrestrained.

He still hadn't fully processed the fact that he'd talked to her about his father. Telling her things he had never dreamed he would tell anyone. It ought to have alarmed him enough to send him out that hotel door instantly.

Had he forgotten how Talia had left him three years ago? Or how long it had taken to piece himself back together?

Another person abandoning him. Discarding him.

Breaking all his rules could only be deleterious; it only proved that he really was as damaged as he'd ever feared. Worse—as much as his father had always told him.

But the worst of it was that even through everything he said to her, and the fact that he was trying to push her away, the only thing he really wanted to do was to pull her closer than ever.

He wasn't aware of moving or approaching the bed, but suddenly there he was. He reached out and moved a stray curl off her damp cheek.

But, Lord, he wanted to do so much more.

Haltingly, she pulled her head back, her lips parted and her breathing shallow, betraying the fact that she felt the same way.

'We agreed no more.' His voice cracked.

'*You* said no more.' She eyed him steadfastly. 'I didn't. I asked you to stay. So it's up to you, Liam. I'm not the one waging some kind of internal war.'

'You just told me how you regret what happened with your mother. You lost sight of yourself because of me.'

'I regret that I didn't pay more attention,' she concurred.

'And that I was self-absorbed. But I didn't lose sight of myself because of you. And, even if I had, I know who I am now. Just as I know what I want. Even so, if you want to finish this once and for all, I'll go now.'

And even though he knew he should, he found he couldn't. He didn't have the mental strength to do it again, not knowing that in twenty-four hours he would be gone. That he would never see her again. Or touch her. Or taste her.

He'd pushed her away too many times. This time was different. And as he reached for her, admiring her grace as she knelt up on the bed before he hauled her back into his arms, Liam thought that she'd never looked so soft or at peace.

She was right, she was no longer that girl he'd known in North Carolina—and he was no longer that man.

But he still wasn't enough for her. *That hasn't changed*, Liam reminded himself.

But he wasn't listening.

He wanted her too much. *His Talia*—a woman who knew her own mind. He found that more tempting than anything and he couldn't resist her. More to the point, he didn't want to.

'I can't offer you more than this,' he muttered.

'I know.' Talia ran her hand down his chest slowly and deliberately. 'Maybe in a different life. Or a different time.'

Or if he had been a different man. But he didn't voice that one.

'You're sure?' he ground out.

'That I want you?' She sounded breathless and incredulous all at once. 'Liam, I'm sure.'

Liam couldn't hold back a low growl. It was a pale echo of the howling that he felt inside but audible all the same.

He sank back down on the bed, discarding his towel and her bedsheet in one efficient movement.

And then he flipped on his back, lifted his Talia into the air and settled her on top of him.

She looked magnificent. More vibrant and full of life than he'd ever seen her before, and he stilled, drinking her in. If this was one of the last images he was ever going to have with her then he wanted to remember it in every last, stunning detail.

Something shifted inside him. A jolt and a start, as if his long-dead heart had just kicked back into life. But he pretended he didn't care about that. He wasn't going to overthink it any more. She was offering him tonight and he would move heaven and earth to take her up on it. Even if it was all he could give her.

By this time tomorrow he would be gone. He could deal with the fallout then.

If she was going to give herself to him one more time, Talia told herself ferociously as Liam settled her over him and stared at her as though she was the most precious thing in the world, she was going to make it count.

Really count.

She basked in the way he gazed at her—as if she was infinitely precious to him—and then revelled in the way he let his hands wander over her, smoothing his way and setting every inch of her skin alight in the process. She decided he knew just how badly he was driving her crazy when he trailed his tongue over her bare flesh and straight past her aching, straining nipples.

He skimmed his fingers down the sides of her torso, snaking over her belly and splaying his hands across her skin as he tested her and teased her. But none of that was anything compared to the way he gazed at her.

Three years ago, she'd loved the way he'd studied her, his eyes so green as they'd glittered with undisguised hunger. Even greed. He'd always made her feel so very beautiful and desired. But now…?

Now there was a different edge to his gaze. Desire, yes; but also something else. Something deeper. Something that made her feel not just wanted but needed. Adored. He made her feel precious.

He made her think she could see a future.

This is just about living in the moment, she thought in a panic, shaking such dangerous notions from her head and forcing herself back to the present. And it was almost a blessing when he lowered his head to take one nipple, lace bra included, into his mouth, as all other distractions fell away.

He lavished attention on one breast, his hand cupping her gently while his tongue drew whorls and patterns over her nipple. Abrading her skin and heightening her sensitivity. Once he was satisfied with one side, Liam shifted to the other, until she was shivering with pleasure, her breathing harsh and fast as she begged him for more.

Instead, he walked his hand down her body, over the swell of her stomach and beyond until he was circling around her sex, making it thrum with longing. Instinctively, Talia raised her hips, wanting more contact, more friction.

'Patience,' he murmured, still tracing his lazy shapes around her but never touching where she needed him most. 'All in good time.'

She groaned, resisting the urge to roll her hips again, knowing he would only punish her by prolonging the wait. That deliciously wicked streak that she'd always loved. Reaching her hands out, she slid them through his hair instead, as if that might somehow ground her when he finally ended this exquisite torture.

'Better,' he muttered, letting his knuckles graze over her.

If he continued like this then she feared she was going to come apart with him barely even touching her.

And then, finally, he twisted his wrist around and cupped her, her molten heat spilling out over his palm.

'So beautiful.' Dipping his head, he kissed her again. 'So perfect.'

Then before she could move, or even register what he was doing, he was sliding his fingers into her slick centre. Talia groaned, rolling her hips again and needing more contact as he played with her, almost sending her mindless with need.

She could feel that fire building already, racing her to the edge far faster than she was prepared for, but she couldn't do anything about it. Liam was all she'd dreamed of this past week, replaying their weekend together over and over again, thinking that was all she would ever have. And now they were back here, and she didn't think she could hold on much longer.

It was too fast. Too...rushed.

'Relax,' Liam murmured, dropping a final kiss on her abdomen before choosing the moment to flip them both around. He moved to the end of the bed while she pushed herself up onto her elbows to watch, a savage hunger joining that fire inside.

He was magnificent. He was always magnificent. His athletic physique a symphony of rock-solid ridges and corded muscles. And this time, when he lowered himself onto the bed on top of her, Talia gripped his shoulders and turned him over as she moved astride him.

'That's how you want to play it?' he rasped. A rich, throaty sound.

'That's exactly how I want to play it.' She moved her hands reverently over that incredible body, committing every last millimetre of him to memory, though she couldn't have said why.

She tasted him and teased him, grazed his skin gently with her teeth then followed with her tongue. Her hands, her mouth slid over that hewn chest, the rippling stomach muscles and that perfect V-shape where his lower abs moved against his obliques like tectonic plates shifting beneath the earth's crust to create the Bec Range that they had admired together a lifetime ago.

And he was every bit as awe-inspiring.

It was only as she moved lower that Liam caught her hips and moved her back up his body, and she couldn't help but think that she'd always loved how his hands were so large and powerful that it always made her feel all the more feminine and dainty.

Then he shifted position so that her heat was pressed against the hardest part of him, and she didn't think any more. She just felt. Letting him lift her slightly as his blunt tip edged into her, taking it slowly as she braced against his shoulders, her breath catching in her throat.

It took Talia a moment to realise that he was letting her control the pace. Letting her rock against him, her body thrumming and clamouring for him, as it always had. Leaning forward, she laid her body over his, every inch of them touching as she let him cup her cheeks with his palms and trace her jaw with his fingers.

Then, very languidly, very deliberately she reached down between them and took hold of him, wrapping her fingers around his long, thick length and testing his heavy, glorious weight in her hand. He groaned, and she exulted in the sheer freeness of the sound. Wishing it was a sound she could hear for ever.

There was something about being here, on St Victoria,

that made her feel unburdened and lighter, in a way that she'd never felt back in North Carolina.

Or perhaps it was she who was different. Or Liam.

A stab of sadness shot through her, swiftly followed by a shot of urgency. He couldn't stay here any more than she could return to Duke's. So if this was all they were going to have, she wasn't about waste it on melancholy and *what–ifs*. Guiding him back to her softness, she began to move again, rocking against him as she moved back up to a seated position and then taking him inside her heat.

'So tight.' Liam groaned again, and a tremble rolled through her.

She inched down again to the same response, and again, until he was as deep as he could be. Then she lifted off him and did it all again in a private tango all their own. A bliss like no other as they built up the rhythm, lazy and indulgent at first, picking up pace and urgency in time, that edge heading towards her, faster and faster.

And then, suddenly, he reached down between them to press down where she ached most, and she felt herself catapulting over that abyss. Tumbling and falling with no safety net as he surged inside her, and as they plummeted back to earth together she couldn't help calling out his name.

Or the fact that she loved him.

But she didn't realise that she'd actually voiced it aloud until he froze against her, his length still inside her but no longer holding her as he had been a moment ago. The bliss around them shattered, with no way to piece it back together.

Well, she'd told herself to put it all the line for him, and this was undoubtedly a spectacular way of doing precisely that.

CHAPTER FOURTEEN

THE DECLARATION HUNG in the air between them and, for what felt like an eternity Liam was too stunned to answer. And then, suddenly, he lifted her off him and flipped from the bed, grabbing a pair of cargo shorts in the process and hauling them on.

How could such beautiful, simple words actually sound so damned ugly? Or perhaps it was more that they made him *feel* ugly, because they reminded him of the truth he'd spent the past weeks pretending didn't exist.

Or maybe it was because a wretched part of him bellowed to echo it back to her—and that was a terrifying thought because he was already fighting the urge to acquiesce to her early suggestion of staying on St Victoria.

'No, you don't,' he bit out eventually, stalking the room.

His voice was too controlled and yet razor-sharp, as if he could silence her. As if he could reverse the last thirty seconds by sheer force of will alone.

Because even if he did say it back, and even if he thought he might mean it—somehow—he knew it would be duplicitous since he didn't understand the concept of love. Not really. However much he wanted to.

And that meant, in the end, he would end up letting her down. Hurting her.

'I love you,' she repeated, quiet but firm, wrapping herself up in the pure white bedsheet that somehow only served to enhance her appearance of fragility. And made him feel even worse, as impossible as that was.

'You're wrong.' He gritted his teeth. 'Mistaken. Whatever you're feeling right now, it isn't…*that*.'

He'd silenced the rage inside him for all these years—because *love* wasn't something that had ever been crafted for him. Yet right here, right now, the rage was nothing compared to that part of him that ached to be able to say those three simple words back to her. That wished he wasn't so damaged.

It didn't help that Talia somehow looked both stunned and defiant at her unexpected confession.

'First you tell me that I don't know what I mean when I ask you to stay,' she retorted, an echo of their earlier conversation. But, just like then, he heard the tremor in her voice. 'Now you're saying I know what I feel.'

'That's exactly what I'm saying.'

'Well, I dare say I know better than you do, given that these are *my* emotions. And given that you can't even bring yourself to utter the word.'

'Emotions aren't real. And at best, *love*…' He paused for a fraction of a second, that one word—four simple letters—taking an age to fall off his tongue. Then he regrouped. 'It's like temporary inebriation after the brain has had a cocktail shot of norepinephrine, dopamine, phenylethylamine.'

He stopped, terribly afraid it wasn't the sound of the word he hated as much as his inability to really understand all it stood for. If their earlier conversation had thrown him, he didn't want to think how this one might go.

Which was all the more reason to end it. Now. He told Talia as much.

'Liam, do you know what you sound like?' she asked gently, almost pityingly.

And he thought that was what he hated most of all. That, and the growing suspicion that she might be right.

Yet he forged on anyway.

'At worst, it's a weapon that the cruellest of humans use to wield against the people they claim to care for the most.'

Too late, he realised he was giving away too much. Exposing his own vulnerabilities by revealing how his father, his grandmother, even Talia herself had managed to hurt him.

'I'm sorry.' She shook her head, leaving him in no doubt that she was sorrier for *him* than actually sorry for what she'd said. 'I know you don't believe in it, and believe me that I never meant to say it.'

'So you're taking it back?' he demanded.

It struck him suddenly that he didn't even know whether he wanted her to take it back or not. But, worse, he knew he would accept it if she did. Take it at face value, and continue where they'd left off barely a few minutes before.

The way he had after their last conversation. So what did it mean that he would readily pretend she'd never uttered the words?

Instead, Talia seemed to sit up straighter on the bed, proud and strong. And looking almost ethereal.

'I don't take it back, Liam.' She shrugged her shoulders. 'I didn't mean to say it, granted, but it's true all the same. I love you. That's why I suggested you stay on St Victoria before. Why I still want you to stay now.'

Something sat on his chest, squashing the air out of him. He fought to surface.

'I don't accept that.'

'Because you fear it.' She held her hands up as if to soothe him.

As if he was some wounded wild animal who couldn't

understand anything else. The worst of it was that was partly how he felt.

'I don't fear it,' he denied angrily. 'I just don't *believe* in it.'

'After everything your father put you through as a child, that's understandable. As is your desire never to have children, for fear of putting them through the same. But can't you see that will never happen?'

He heard the plea in her voice and, for a moment, he almost went to her. Because the truth of it was that he wanted nothing more than to believe her. But he'd had this dream before, three years ago, when she had told him the same thing. A few days later she'd left him.

He'd thought he'd been setting her free by letting her leave and not chasing her down and now, despite everything that had happened between them this past month, he knew that if he still wanted her to be free, this time he was going to have to be the one to walk away.

Because he only ever wrecked things.

'You're letting your dreadful father win again, can't you see that?' Talia begged softly.

'I told you that,' he faltered, not wanting to examine why he *had* told her that, 'by way of explanation. Not as ammunition for you to now use against me.'

'You would think that opening up to a person automatically means they're using it as ammunition.'

He blew out scornfully, but she forged on.

'I don't know what your father did to make your grandmother leave, but I have to believe that she left to protect you somehow. It's clear that she loved you a great deal because even through your fuzzy memories I see the kind, patient man you are today and I know that had to have come from someone. From her.'

'You see what you want to see, Talia.'

'And if I did, is that such a great flaw? That I should want to see that goodness and kindness and love in you?'

'It isn't love,' he gritted out, but it was becoming harder and harder to sound convincing.

And the more he tried to distance himself, the more she seemed to level observations at him that he wished, oh, so fervently were true. If only he was a man as promising as the one she was describing.

If only he was worthy of her. But he wasn't.

And maybe she was right about him letting his old man win, but what choice was there? Even if everything he'd been learning about himself this past week were true, even if he was finally beginning to have his eyes opened, it didn't change the man he'd been for most of his life.

Maybe he hadn't set out as the bleak, corrupted kid that his father had told him he was, but he'd certainly become that person over the years. Not least when first his grandmother and then Talia had proved that to be true.

Pain rained down on him, like tiny shards of ice. He grasped at them as if they were somehow going to save him, even though a part of him recognised, on some level, that it was only because it was easier to be angry than it was to face his greatest fears.

He'd opened up to her in their last conversation, and look where that had got him. He sure as hell wasn't about to make that mistake again.

Instead, he focussed on telling himself that it was almost incomprehensible that *this* woman, of all people, would dare to talk of love to him.

Talia had waited, her breath caught in her throat, unable to inhale or exhale. Silently, she'd willed him to trust her. To come back to her. And for one long, heart-stopping moment she'd thought he was going to.

But then he took another step back and folded his arms across his chest, distancing himself—the way he had always done in the past—his cargo shorts riding so low on his hips that she could see that perfect V where his obliques met his abdomen.

And it struck her that it somehow seemed so intimate a view in the face of such a hostile conversation. As though his mind might be trying to shut her out but his body certainly wasn't.

That begged the question—was he more furious at her for telling him she loved him or himself for wanting to believe it?

Maybe she was reading too much into things and giving herself false hope, but she was inclined to believe it was the latter.

'I love you and I think you love me too.'

'You've got the wrong man, Talia. That isn't me.'

His face hardened and something cracked in her chest and broke.

'I wish you could see yourself as others do,' she murmured sadly. 'As I do. And look at the stories you've started to tell me about your grandmother. They aren't the memories of a kid who never believed in love, which is all the more reason for you to realise how powerful that emotion can be. How the love of just that one person carried you through those years in spite of everything else.'

'I told you that in confidence,' he bit back. 'Not for you to analyse me. Certainly not for you to use it against me.'

'I wasn't—'

'You were,' he cut in harshly. 'You thought you could level a few so-called *home truths* at me and I'd fall at your feet in gratitude. I can tell you that isn't going to happen, Talia. But allow me to do the same for you.'

And she didn't like that clipped voice or those cold eyes. Not one bit.

'Liam—'

'You talk of my father and my grandmother. You speak of love, and how it's a powerful emotion. Shall I tell you what I know of *love*?' He practically spat the word out, as if the very taste of it was toxic in his mouth. 'I know that people use it to excuse their behaviour. My father used his *love* of my mother to excuse the way he treated me.'

'You father doesn't know what love is.'

'My grandmother told me she loved me,' he continued, as though Talia hadn't even spoken. 'She promised that she'd always be there to protect me from my father, and then she simply abandoned me to him. And then there's you.'

'No… Liam…'

Talia knew exactly where she was going before he said any more. Her heart punched into her chest, almost winding her. But there was nothing she could do to stop it.

'You were the one who spoke of *love*,' he said harshly. 'But love is about more than words. It's about actions. And you proved to me, beyond all question, three years ago that you don't know anything more about love than I do.'

A kind of desolation began to fill her. She wanted to argue but found she couldn't.

'You claim to love me, Talia, but you were the one who walked out back then without even a word.'

Just like his grandmother had, she realised. Liam didn't actually say the words but they hung there in the air, strangling and weighty, all the same.

'You know that was because I'd just had the call from my mother.'

'I understand why you had to leave,' he countered grimly. 'I'm pointing out that the way you left isn't *love*. You could have told me. You should have.'

'Yes, well, hindsight is twenty-twenty, isn't it?' There was a bitter hint to her own tone that she hadn't been expecting.

'Tell me one thing, Talia. If the circumstances were the same, would you change things or would you make the same decision over again?'

She wanted to answer. She wanted to tell him there was so much that she would change if she could. But as much as the thoughts swirled and crammed in her head, nothing came out of her mouth.

How could she change any of it? Maybe if her mother hadn't been ill, and she hadn't had to return home. Perhaps if her father hadn't fallen into depression and her brothers hadn't needed her help. Or conceivably if Liam had been able to tell her once, just *once*, that he loved her.

But a do-over changed none of those factors. So how could she choose any other path but the one she had chosen before?

'Just as I thought,' he answered for her, when it was clear she couldn't—wouldn't—answer for herself. And she thought it was that wholly dispassionate tone that hurt the most. 'Which is why you aren't what I want.'

Misery swelled inside her but she forced it back. His words were intended to cause maximum effect, hurting her the way she'd hurt him three years ago. He wanted to push her away and a few weeks ago, when he'd first arrived on the island, it might have worked. She might have believed him.

But they'd spent so much time together since then that the words no longer fitted. He cared for her more than he wanted to admit to her. Possibly more than he wanted to admit to himself.

'Do you even know what you do want, though?' she asked gently.

He offered a scornful laugh, but it sounded too hollow for her to believe.

'I'm a surgeon, Talia, I save lives every day. How could I want anything more than that?'

Her heart might well have broken at the loneliness of that image. He was the most intelligent, skilled, handsome man she'd ever known. The most incredible surgeon she'd ever watched perform any operation.

But somewhere deep inside him there were still traces of that broken kid he'd once been, and he thought it was too late to fix that. He thought he was too damaged. And she was partly to blame for that.

She owed to him—and to herself—to fight for him this time.

'You're also a man, Liam. A human being.' She was almost pleading with him. 'We aren't designed to be completely alone. There's a reason they say that everybody needs someone.'

'And there are always exceptions to every rule.'

'Even if that's true, you aren't that exception. You think you're too damaged to ever love or be loved. But that isn't true.'

'Believe me when I tell you that you are wrong.' And it was the bleakness in his gaze that cut her deepest. 'I am more damaged that you can ever imagine.'

'You're not,' she whispered. 'You're good, and kind, and self-sacrificing.'

For a moment she thought he was wavering. Taking a moment to let her words sink in. And maybe that was true—for that moment. But then his jaw pulled so tight that she could see a tic flicking irritably. As though he was angry at himself for even entertaining what she was saying.

'This isn't making your case for you, Talia,' he ground out. 'Allow me to prove it. I don't want you. I want a woman

I can trust. Whose word I can believe. I don't want someone who says one thing but then acts a different way.'

'Where is this coming from?' she gasped.

But she was afraid she already knew.

He'd opened up to her—finally—when he'd told her about his father. The first time he'd ever really talked in any significant detail about his past. And then he'd received the confirmation of his flight and now he was regretting his moment of perceived weakness.

It wouldn't matter how much she told him that confiding in her was the ultimate strength, he wouldn't believe her.

He didn't trust her. That much was true.

'I'm leaving tomorrow, Talia, to go back to North Carolina. And Duke's.'

Not *home*, she noted joylessly, his words scraping her raw inside. That meant that St Victoria could be his home as well as anywhere else. She opened her mouth to speak but let it close again, resignation pouring through her.

Liam had said that love was about actions, not words. So there was nothing she could say that would ever change his mind about her.

For the first time she felt defeated.

'I should go,' she murmured, silently praying for him to ask her to stay.

His expression remained as closed off as ever.

'I think that would be best.'

Talia jerked her head in a semblance of acknowledgement. She'd lost him, it was impossible to pretend otherwise.

Whatever these last few weeks had been about, it hadn't been about picking up where they'd left off. They'd already agreed that at the beginning of his brief trip out here to St Victoria.

The simple fact remained: she'd lost him three years ago.

CHAPTER FIFTEEN

'I ASKED NOT to be disturbed,' Liam growled without lifting his head as a heavy rap sounded at his office door.

He returned to glowering at his latest set of patient notes—the words swimming before his eyes for the third time in the past post-midnight hour—before the door swung open. He lifted his head furiously.

'I repeat—'

'I heard what you said.' Her voice—the last one he'd ever expected to hear again—cut him off breezily. Almost amused. And his words tailed off.

He wasn't even sure if he kept breathing.

'Talia.'

It was a less of a greeting and more of a prayer. At least, that was how it sounded in Liam's head. The woman he was trying to keep from haunting every last corner of his brain was now standing, in the very real flesh, in his office.

All at once he was aware of a good many things, not least being his uncharacteristically unkempt appearance and his office's uncommon messy state.

What the hell was she doing in North Carolina?

What the hell was she doing in his office?

He didn't realise he'd actually voiced the questions aloud—bitten out, if he was honest—until he heard Talia begin to answer them.

'I came to see you.' Her voice even managed to convey a light shrug. As if the answer should be obvious. 'I figured flying up here was the easiest option, especially since you didn't seem to be picking up your phone.'

'I've been busy.'

His tone was more defensive than he might have intended, and he cursed himself for his weakness. So much for never allowing himself to be vulnerable again. But, then, he hadn't expected her to be standing in this office again. Her very presence was like a filter pouring colour into every inch of his drab, grey world.

Just like she always had.

It made something scrape inside him—as though this was somehow further proof of just how wrong he was for her. Surely she could see that as clearly as he could?

Yet she seemed oblivious. Instead, in typical Talia fashion, she almost seemed to shimmer across the room as she swept his notes neatly and efficiently from the only other chair and into their appropriate files in the tall cabinet, before sitting gracefully on the incommodious scratchy wool-upholstered chair.

'I've heard how busy you've been,' she said, almost conversationally, though he knew he wasn't wrong in detecting a note of censure in there. And something else. Concern. 'Taking on case after case, researching, studying; practically living here in your office or in that operating room.'

'It's called work.'

She shook her head.

'It's called avoidance, Liam. You and I both know it. Days filled with back-to-back surgeries, nights filled with working on new cases, and only the minimum amount of sleep you need to stay on top of your game. You're throwing yourself into work to avoid thinking about what happened between us—and you're driving yourself to exhaustion in the process.'

He hated the way she could read him so easily. He, who was meant to be inscrutable. Composed. One tug from this woman and he would unravel right there and then. Right into that deep, pitch-black abyss, on the brink of which he was teetering.

But he wouldn't look down. He couldn't. Because if he did, he was afraid he might topple. The chief had just imposed three days of forced holiday on him, and he had no damn idea how he was going to fill his days, just to keep his mind off the woman now standing right in front of him.

'I don't have time for this, Talia,' he snarled. 'What are you doing here?'

She looked less than impressed. She certainly didn't look intimidated.

'I'm here to be with you.'

Her response was so succinct, so unexpected that for a moment Liam thought his heart had actually stopped beating. For one long, long moment there was silence and then he became aware of a slow whistling sound in his head, building and building until it became a long shout.

An unending roar.

He had no idea how he managed to speak over it.

'I don't want you here.'

She eyed him curiously. Unblinking yet, apparently, unhurt.

Had he wanted to hurt her, then? He must have. A stab of remorse jabbed at him.

'You shouldn't be here, Talia. Your home is on St Victoria, and it's evident that you love it there.'

'My home is with you,' she replied easily.

And it was the simplicity of her words that made his

heart slam so hard against the wall of his chest. Hard enough to cause damage.

'Walking away from you last time…' she paused, shaking her head '…not trusting you with my truth was the worst decision I ever made. And, still, for three years I've been pretending to myself that it was the right one. I was still lying to myself when I pretended that the only reason I gave Nate your name was for that patient.'

'Stop, Talia.' The words might as well have been ripped from his throat. 'This can't help either of us.'

'No.' She shook her head, a tremor in her voice even as she held her hand up. 'I flew for nine hours and on two planes just to tell you this. So hear me out, Liam. Please.'

Their gazes collided. Nothing else felt sure. Or safe. Like the rocks at the edges of that precipice had just crumbled and were slipping away beneath his feet. He had no idea how long they didn't speak and then, at length, he nodded stiffly. A tacit assent that she accepted nonetheless.

'I love you,' she breathed out on a shaky breath. 'But you already know that. I think I've loved you from the first moment I met you. And that long summer we had together were the most incredible months I've ever known. Right up until I got that call from Papa.'

'When he told you your mama wasn't well,' he confirmed.

She let her eyes drop to the floor for a moment then seemed to steel herself and lift them to his gaze right away.

'Like I told you that last time we were together, the worst part of it is that I knew Mama wasn't well. And that's what's left me racked with guilt all this time.' Her voice sounded so stilted and awkward that he couldn't bear her discomfort.

He might not have known exactly how it felt—after all, how could you mourn the loss of something you never remembered having to begin with?—but he knew how it felt *not* to have a mother.

'You don't have to do this. You don't owe me any more explanations,' he ground out.

'I *do* owe you more explanations.' Her expression was so earnest, so fierce it was impossible not to feel himself getting swept up in her words. 'Even though you didn't tell me...how bad your father was, I knew you'd grown up without a mother and with a father who didn't show much love. To be fair, it was easy enough to read between the lines and realise you'd had a something of a lonely childhood without much love.'

'It was fine.' Liam stiffened defensively. He tried not to but it was too ingrained. 'Other kids have it worse. I've seen that all too often in the hospital.'

'And yet other kids, like me, enjoy wonderful childhoods with loving families.' She lifted her shoulders delicately. 'I just didn't appreciate that fully until these last few years.'

'I'm glad that returning to St Vic...*home*,' he corrected, 'was so rewarding for you.'

And he truly meant it. If it came down to a choice between having her with him and seeing her happy among people who knew her well and loved her, there was really no contest.

'Yet here I am, having spent the best part of a day travelling, to come and say these few things, which should tell you all you really need to know. Back on St Victoria you asked me why I didn't tell you I was leaving three years ago, and I didn't answer. And then you accused me of playing games, trying to get you to run after me.'

'You don't have to say anything, Talia. It was wrong of me to accuse you of anything. I can only imagine how frightened and confused you must have felt,' he assured her, but she cut him off with a gentle shake of her head.

'The things is...' She drew in a breath. 'I don't know that you were entirely wrong after all. I did feel guilty about my mother, it's true, and my head was a mess when my father called. But now, with the benefit of three years on, and everything you said to me those last weeks, I wonder if there was maybe an element of truth to what you said.'

'What kind of element of truth?' he rasped.

He wanted to say more but no words came. What *could* he say?

'I...' She faltered, then picked herself up again, and he thought it was that strength that he admired most in her. 'I knew I loved you, even three years ago. But I also knew that as much as you cared for me, you didn't necessarily feel *love.* I certainly didn't intend it as a test, but I think that maybe there was some tiny part of me that wondered—hoped, really—if my leaving would cause you to realise it.'

'You wanted me to chase after you to St Victoria?' he demanded, but the strange thing was that the idea didn't rile him the way it had before.

In fact, he couldn't really work out why he hadn't done precisely that. Why, when he'd returned to his empty apartment and seen the gap in his closet, in his bathroom, in his life, he hadn't chased straight after her.

Why he wouldn't let himself feel that love—even now, when he so desperately wanted to—let alone act on it.

She was right, he had always pushed her away. Keeping her at arm's length before she could get too close to him and hurt him. But the sad thing was that he didn't know how to do anything else.

'I didn't envisage you racing to the island after me.' She splayed out her hands stiffly. 'I think I just wanted you to... I don't know...realise that I mattered to you. Enough to do something about it. Call me. Tell me. Anything.'

'I couldn't,' he stated flatly. 'I can't. That isn't who I am. I don't know how to.'

'I know that now.' He didn't realise that Talia had slid off her chair until she was suddenly in front of him, crouched down, his face cupped in her soft—so soft—palms.

'I am my father's own son, incapable of loving. Only I'm worse, because at least he once loved my mother.'

'No, Liam.' Her eyes glistened and he braced against a sudden wave of emotion. 'You aren't worse. You never got to see what love was because he never showed you. Your father lost his wife and it's tragic, I understand that. But when she died, *you* were born. A pure, innocent baby, who didn't even get the chance to know your mother. You needed your father's love more than ever. But, instead, he was too wrapped up in his grief.'

'You have no right to judge,' he gritted out, even as he felt the heavy weight in his chest rock and shift. It was still there, but for the first time he began to realise that it could be moved. He wasn't sure he liked that. He'd grown perversely accustomed to it over the years.

'I think I have every right,' she argued. 'Because it tears me up to see what pain his selfishness has caused you all these years. How his actions have made it so you don't even know how to love or be loved, let alone want it.'

'That isn't true.'

Except that it wasn't untrue either, was it?

He stared at her as though it could somehow explain to her what was going on in his head. But he knew it couldn't. He couldn't even explain it to himself. It was as though the very air was shifting around them. Pressing in on him. Making him…wonder.

'Three years ago, we didn't trust each other enough to be honest. But I'm changing that because I'm not that naïve girl any more, and because I can. This time I'm here, choosing you. Choosing to be with you. I need you to know that, out of everything that I love in the world—my family, my home on St Victoria, my job at The Island Clinic—there is one thing that I love above all else. And that's you, Liam.'

'So, that means what?' he demanded gruffly, because he couldn't help himself.

'That means I've already spoken to the chief about coming back to my old job at Duke's.'

'You're leaving St Victoria?'

'If you want me here.'

'You can't do that,' he managed gruffly. 'You love it back there.'

'I do love it,' she agreed. 'But without you, there's no point. So here I am. Yours. This time I'm choosing *you.* This is what love is, Liam. Your father may never have shown you love but I know your grandmother, Glory, did. And I want to pick up where *she* left off. You just have to let me.'

'No. You can't do that.' He had no idea how he spoke with the lump l that seemed to be blocking his throat. 'You can't give up everything you love.'

A thousand emotions poured through him. They seemed to sweep from his head right down to his toes. A terrifying deluge. Too hard, and too heavy for him to process.

'I'm not giving up everything I love. I'm simply choosing the one I love most, *you*, over the other things.' She smiled. Shaky, but irrepressible.

Her hands shook slightly beneath his and Liam blinked in shock. When had he raised his hands to cover hers? Had he meant to hold them or wrench them away?

He didn't know.

'I won't accept it,' he began, louder now. Horrified.

Or was it actually something else entirely?

Yet, rather than cowing, his beloved Talia stared at him

all the more steadfastly. Her smile chipping away his armour. Making him start to believe.

'Love is—' he began again anyway.

'Real, Liam,' she finished for him. 'It's not just some brain tipsy on a neurochemical triple shot. And I get how that scares you, and that you don't know how to deal with it, but I'm here to teach you how. And we'll take as long as you need.'

'You're asking too much, Talia.' His voice cracked but he pretended not to notice.

'I can only hope that isn't true,' she answered, an echoing hitch in her voice as she scribbled on his pad of paper. 'You told me that words weren't enough. That it was easy to claim to love someone but much harder to actually prove it. So here I am, following you to North Carolina to prove it in the only way I know how to.'

'Talia—'

'This is the hotel where I'm staying if you want to contact me. But I'm not holding you to ransom, Liam. If you decide this isn't what you want—that *I'm* not what you want—I will understand. I'll go back to St Victoria.'

'Talia...' he began as her voice trembled, but she pressed on.

'I've said what I came to say. It's on you now, Liam,' she managed.

And then, before his brain could even begin to process all that she'd said, she left. Walking out of his office with her back straight and her head high.

Making him respect her show of naked vulnerability all the more.

Work was impossible after that. He sat at his desk and glowered at the open files on his screen, but he didn't read a single one of them. The words simply swam in front of his eyes.

Eventually, when he could stand it no longer, he launched himself out of the chair, out of his office, and out of the hospital.

Liam had no idea for how long he pounded the streets. This city where he'd been born, and that he knew like the back of his hand but had never, not once, thought of as home.

He walked for hours—not that he would have known had it not been for the way the moon moved in the sky above him. Or the changing light levels as the sun finally began to make its way to the horizon. But all of a sudden he found himself in the cemetery.

The place where he never came because it held no memories for him. It gave him no connection to his mother. She was simply a woman he'd never known.

And yet now, today, it was as though seeing that headstone with her name engraved on it might somehow answer all of those last questions that had burned inside his entire life.

Liam rounded the corner of the building, a vague idea of where the grave was, and then stopped abruptly. He might have known his father would be there. The man had always visited the grave daily when Liam had been a child. It had been his pre-dawn ritual. Why would it be any different now?

He was just about to turn and leave when something made him take another look. A closer one this time. And all at once Liam was seized by the incongruity of the scene. The man that he'd built up to be such a heartless titan all these years was now gone, and in its place stood a hunched, wizened, sad creature.

But it was the profile that drew Liam's gaze. Such an angry set to a jaw that matched Liam's own bone structure, an unpleasant grimace to the mouth, and even the nose threw off baleful vibes.

This was the man who had once told him—bawled at him—that he hoped his son would never get to be happy. That Liam didn't deserve to find joy, or comfort. That he certainly didn't deserve to find love.

How had he allowed this man and his spiteful words to colour his life all this time? Liam wondered abruptly. How had he allowed himself to miss out on so much? To lose so much? To lose Talia?

You haven't lost her. Yet.

The voice was quiet yet urgent. And all of a sudden Liam could see the colour and vibrancy all over again. As if Talia's very presence in this city had already begun to infuse it with new life.

He'd already pushed her away once, was he really going to stay silent, too afraid to open his heart even for a chance at love, and risk pushing her away again?

She was right. He wasn't his father. He never had been.

Spinning around, Liam hurried back to the hospital and got to his car. This wasn't the place for him. It was too full of death and sad memories.

Talia was the one who signified life for him, she always had. And surely it was time for him to grab that life by the proverbial horns?

He practically threw himself into his car, pulling the door closed and revelling in the low, powerful thrum of the engine, as if it approved of his intentions.

Fanciful, perhaps. But after the decades of sombre solemnity this moment of whimsy seemed somehow fitting.

Executing an efficient turn, Liam wasn't sure how he controlled his speed as he drove up the hill and back to the main road. And then at last he opened her up and let her fly, racing towards Talia's hotel and his new life.

A life he should have claimed long before now.

And every junction, every set of lights, every turning

seemed complicit in the plan as they each emptied or turned to green on his approach. The entire universe seemed to be coming together to ensure he didn't change his mind at the last moment.

But he wasn't going to. Because now, after all these years, he understood what love was. And he didn't know whether to be more annoyed or regretful that it had taken him all this time to realise that true love didn't resemble anything like his father's display.

Pulling the car to a halt in the car park of the hotel, Liam covered the potholed tarmac in a matter of a few short strides and headed across the clean—if a little tired-looking—lobby and to the reception desk. Then another lifetime as he waited for the receptionist to call through to Talia's room and then send him up.

But then, at long last, he was there. Standing in the corridor as she held open her door.

'Are you coming in?' she asked, a nervous smile lifting those lovely lips. 'Only I don't think I want the entire floor hearing our conversation.'

He wasn't sure how he made his wooden limbs move as she opened the door wider to let him in, turning slowly as the almost paper-thin door closed and she stood, eyeing him with an expression that couldn't decide whether it was more nervous or excited.

A dilemma with which he could fully empathise.

And at that instant he fully believed everything she had said to him.

His incredible, soulful Talia.

Because when she looked to him like that, and smiled at him in a way that poured sunlight and warmth into every last corner of his blackened soul, he didn't know how he could ever have thought otherwise.

Or why he had ever been so afraid of it.

CHAPTER SIXTEEN

'I DON'T HAVE a conversation in mind,' he bit out.

She tried, and failed, to rein her heart in.

'Then…?'

'I simply came to tell you that I love you,' he muttered slowly. As if testing the words out, taking them for a spin—those words that she had longed to hear for over three years.

She tried to respond but all she could do was nod her head, some sound caught in her throat but unable to come out. It was like magic sprinkling around them and making the moment all the more beautiful.

He cupped her face, his thumbs skimming over her silken skin almost in wonder.

'I *love* you, Talia,' he affirmed, more boldly this time.

'I know,' she choked out, not sure it was entirely the best response. But Liam didn't seem to mind. He offered a half-rueful smile.

'I always thought it was a cliché, but I think you know me better than I know myself.'

'No, I just gave you more credit than you gave yourself,' she answered. 'Hardly surprising, given how your father treated you.'

'Enough about him,' Liam managed gruffly, taking her by surprise. 'I've spent too long being the man he wanted me to be. Playing the lonely, damaged surgeon and believing that I didn't deserve happiness in my life. In trying to ensure I never turned out like him, I ended up being exactly like him. But I won't be that person any more. That isn't who I want to be.'

'And who do you want to be, Liam?' she asked breathlessly, unable to control the wild fluttering of her heart in her chest.

'I want to be the man *you* see when you look at me. The man who deserves a woman as extraordinary and unique as you. You light up every dark corner of my world and you fill it with colour when I didn't even think it could be reached. You have this incredible way of making everyone around you feel cherished, and special, and I want to bask in that warmth for the rest of my life.'

'You make me sound like some kind of saint.' She reached her hands up to cover his as they cupped her face. Revelling in the feel of them. 'But I'm not. I'm just the woman who loves you.'

'Which is more than I ever thought I deserved. You've saved me, Talia, when I didn't even want to acknowledge how lost I was.'

The raw quality of his words reached inside her, making her feel happy. So happy. It was almost perfect.

'I think we saved each other,' she told him solemnly. 'We fit, Liam. We each need the other, which is why I couldn't stay on the island without you.'

'And that's the one thing I can't accept.'

She froze as his words sank in. The grave expression on his face chased out that happiness she'd felt a moment ago.

He loved her but he didn't want her to stay?

'Liam—'

'I can't accept you giving up your life, your family for me,' he cut in, stopping her. 'St Vic isn't just a place where you work, or live, it's where you belong. It's the very essence of who you are. Vibrant, and exciting, and vivacious. I always knew it. But seeing you here, and seeing you back home, there's no comparison. St Vic amplifies everything that's so wonderful about you.'

'I can't leave you.' She shook her head, not understanding how he could claim to love her one minute and say he wanted her to go back home the next. 'I won't—'

'That's not what I'm saying.' His voice cracked, the mere idea of it almost too much to bear. Something he'd never thought he'd feel. 'I'm saying that I want to return with you.'

'Wait, you want to…what?'

'We'll go back to the island together. Nate already made it clear that he'd liked me as a surgeon. Even if there's no opening at The Island Clinic team for the moment, I can work for St Vic's hospital.'

'You're right.' His hands moved to grip her shoulders. Not painfully, more like enough to give her heart a thrill of excitement. The hint of a promise. 'I want a new start, Talia. A kick-start to a new life. *Our* new life.'

'And that's back on St Vic?'

'Back home,' he said gently. 'Because being there is the closest I've ever felt to having a home.'

'But your work? Your career?'

'I love my job, and what I do. But you were right, I've been living my life in the shadow of my mother's death. Every move that I've ever made has been part of a quest for acceptance from a man who will never accept me. I can't make up for my mother's life. She was unique, and precious. But her death was as much my loss as his. He has spent my whole life denying me that, while I've been twisting myself in knots, trying to make amends for something that was never my fault. You finally helped me to see that, and I will always be grateful.'

Her hand went to his cheek again as Liam smiled at her, shaking off any sadness.

'You would do that?' She could hardly believe what he was suggesting. 'But your career? You're a rising star here at Duke's.'

'All the more reason for Nate not to waste this opportunity of securing me for The Island Clinic team, then.' He laughed, but his voice was thick with emotion and Talia found she liked this honest, exposed side of him all the more.

Because it was only for her to see.

'I know Nate would snap you up,' she managed. 'He said as much last week when he asked me if I thought you might take on another case.'

'And what did you say?'

'I didn't believe you would.' Talia shook her head incredulously. It had been a mere few days ago yet it felt like a lifetime. 'I didn't think you'd ever set foot on the island again.'

'I wouldn't have,' he agreed, 'without you. Nothing is worth it if I don't have you.'

'Is that really how you feel?'

It was odd, the way that even though she knew he'd told her already, and even though she knew he'd never say it if he didn't truly believe it, she found she needed to hear it again. And again. Almost as if it was too perfect to be true and she hadn't yet taken it all in.

And so she certainly wasn't prepared when he sank to his knees, right there in the hotel room, and took her hands in his.

'It's not nearly how I feel,' he bit out suddenly. 'I'm a surgeon, Talia. I'm good with my brain and my hands, but words…well, they were never my thing. All I can tell you is that I love you more than I ever thought it was possible to love. And I want to share the rest of my life with you.

Every single, glorious moment of it. Because as long as I have you, I know that's what it will be.'

'For someone who isn't very good at words,' she choked out with a wobbly smile, 'you just did a pretty good job.'

'Good,' he managed gruffly, 'because there's more. You've saved me, and you've started to make me whole again, when I never thought that was possible. You make me want to be the kind of man who deserves you, Talia. A better version of myself.'

'You were already a good man, Liam. I just want you to also be a happy one.'

'And I will be—with you. So marry me, Talia, and I vow to you that I'll spend the rest of time doing everything in my power to make you happy. The way you make me happy.'

'I know you will,' she whispered, her hands still gripping his tightly.

And then, before either of them could say any more, he stood up, lowered his head to hers and claimed her lips with his own. As if that, somehow, could articulate all the other emotions that were careening joyously around the room.

Emotions that they would work though in time. They just weren't needed right at this instant.

EPILOGUE

THEY WERE MARRIED twelve months later.

A quiet but perfect ceremony back with Talia's family and what felt like half the island's population in attendance. The sound of the waves lapping on the shore, the birds overhead, and the steel band at the far end providing a backdrop better than anything they could have planned.

It had all fallen into place so flawlessly that Talia might have been forgiven for thinking it was all Fate's design. The moment they'd called Nate he'd confirmed that not only was Talia's job hers to take back if she wanted it, but that there was also a Liam-shaped gap at both The Island Clinic and St Vic should he choose to fill them.

And then, a month later, as they'd been packing up the last of Liam's items and preparing to fly home, he'd gone down on one knee again and produced a ring box.

'It was my grandmother's,' he'd told her quietly, as Talia had stared at the diamond ring inside.

A vintage pear-cut with split shoulders, it was exquisite. And she'd told him so.

'However did you get it?' she'd asked in awe.

'It was in that box I once showed you.'

'The one you never opened?' Talia had asked incredulously. 'The one with all the photos of your mother?'

'She'd put her ring in it, too.' He'd nodded. 'Along with a note about giving it to the one I loved.'

Talia shook her head incredulously.

'You never said,' she'd murmured.

'I never thought there would be anyone like that for me. And then you burst into my life. Again.' He'd grinned suddenly.

A relaxed, open smile that Talia had known she would never tire of seeing.

'Thank you, Gloria,' she'd whispered softly, loving the expression on Liam's face.

It had been everything she might have dreamed about, had she ever dared to dream this big.

And when, the following year again after the wedding, she stared into the puckered face of her hours-old daughter, she realised that she still hadn't woken up from that dream.

'What do you want to call her?' Liam whispered, awe laced through his voice as he gazed, mesmerised by his brand-new daughter.

He reeled off the three names at the top of her list. Beautiful names that Talia had loved from the moment she'd heard them. But as she stroked the tiny, flawless fingers of her baby she realised they didn't suit her. They weren't perfect enough.

'None of them,' she whispered, still wholly unable to drag her eyes from her daughter.

'None?' She could hear the frown in Liam's voice and a gurgle of happiness bubbled inside her.

'Her name is Gloria.'

Talia felt him tense beside her.

'You're sure?'

'We'll call her Glory for short.' Talia smiled at the tiny

bundle in her arms, who almost seemed to sigh with approval. 'I think it suits her wonderfully, don't you?'

'Wonderfully,' he echoed, as if slightly stunned.

And then he wrapped his arms around them, both her and their perfect new baby, and held them tightly, as if he would never let them go.

'I love you, Liam,' she breathed softly.

'I love you, too.' Emotion rang through every syllable and she knew without him saying anything that he was finally free. The very last seed of doubt planted by his vicious father had finally died, the moment Liam had laid eyes on his daughter.

'I love you both,' he repeated contentedly. 'And I always will.'

* * * * *

COMING SOON!

We really hope you enjoyed reading this book. If you're looking for more romance, be sure to head to the shops when new books are available on

Thursday 19th August

To see which titles are coming soon, please visit

millsandboon.co.uk/nextmonth

MILLS & BOON

Coming next month

SECOND CHANCE WITH HER GUARDED GP
Kate Hardy

'In London, I never really got to see the sky properly,' he said. 'Out here, it's magical.' He turned her to face him. 'You make me feel magical, too, Gemma,' he said softly. 'And, right now, I really want to kiss you.'

'I want to kiss you, too,' she said.

He dipped his head and brushed his mouth against hers, and her lips tingled at the touch.

'Sweet, sweet Gemma,' he said softly, and kissed her again.

It felt as if fireworks were going off in her head. She'd never experienced anything like this before, and she wasn't sure if it made her feel more amazed or terrified.

When Oliver broke the kiss and pulled away slightly, she held his gaze. His pupils were huge, making his eyes seem almost black in the twilight.

She reached up to touch his mouth, and ran her forefinger along his bottom lip,

He nipped gently at her finger.

Suddenly, Gemma found breathing difficult.

'Gemma,' he said, his voice husky. 'I wasn't expecting this to happen.'

'Me neither,' she whispered. And this was crazy. She knew he was only here temporarily, and he'd probably go back to his life in London once his locum job here had finished and his twin had recovered from the transplant. Was she dating him purely because being a temporary colleague made him safe – she wouldn't be reckless enough to lose her heart to someone who wouldn't stick around? Or would it be like the misery of all those years ago when her parents had moved and left her behind?

'We ought to be heading back,' she said. Even though both of them knew there was no reason why they couldn't stand on the cliffs all evening, just kissing, the unexpected intensity of her feelings scared her.

Continue reading
SECOND CHANCE WITH HER GUARDED GP
Kate Hardy

Available next month
www.millsandboon.co.uk